Please return / renew by date shown.
You can renew at:
norlink.norfolk.gov.uk
or by telephone: 0844 800 8006
Please have your library card & PIN ready.

1 3 DEC 2007

15 | 11 | 13

NORFOLK LIBRARY
AND INFORMATION SERVICE

DEAD MEN TALKING

Stories from East Anglia

Chosen by
Peter Tolhurst

Foreword by
D J Taylor

Black Dog Books

First published in England 2007
Black Dog Books
104 Trinity Street, Norwich, Norfolk, NR2 2BJ.
www.blackdogbooks.co.uk

Foreword © D J Taylor 2007.
Stories © Individual Authors/Authors' estates.

A CIP record of this book is available from the British Library.

ISBN 978-0-9549286-2-9

Typeset in 11 point Berkely Book.

Printed in Great Britain
by Biddles Ltd., King's Lynn, Norfolk.

Contents

Foreword by D J Taylor

Watermarks

Headlands

Tidelines

Acknowledgements

I would like to thank the following for permission to reproduce copyright material:

For *Christmas Sheep* by Tessa Newcomb, the artist; for 'The Man Who Loved A Double Bass' from *Burning Your Boats* (1995) by Angela Carter, published by Chatto & Windus, Rogers, Coleridge & White; for 'Dual Balls' from *Love Your Enemies* (1993) by Nicola Barker, Faber & Faber; for 'Tricky's Mother And The Widow' from *Tales From The Fens* (1963) and for 'How They Buried Grandfather' from *More Tales From The Fens* (1964), both by W H Barrett, Taylor & Francis Books UK; for 'Poison' and 'A Stranger With A Bag', the title story from the 1966 collection by Sylvia Townsend Warner, published by Chatto & Windus, the Random House Group; for 'In The Hours of Darkness' from *Mrs Reinhardt and Other Stories* (1978) by Edna O'Brien, published by Weidenfeld & Nicolson, Orion Publishing; for 'Down By The Sea', Elspeth Barker; for 'A Simple Melody' from *The Complete Shorter Fiction of Virginia Woolf* (1985), published by the Hogarth Press, the Random House Group; for 'In The Net' from *The Bedroom of Mister's Wife* (1999) by Philip Hensher, published by Chatto & Windus, the Random House Group; for 'The Shadows of The Living' and 'Everything a Man Needs' from *The Stories of Ronald Blythe* (1985), published by Chatto & Windus, Ronald Blythe; for 'The Coin' from *Acky* (1973) by George Ewart Evans, published by Faber & Faber, Mathew Evans on behalf of the author's estate; for 'Cranked Up Really High', D J Taylor; for 'Look At All Those Roses' from *Collected Stories* (1980) by Elizabeth Bowen, published by Jonathan Cape, Curtis Brown Group on behalf of the author's estate; for 'Overlooked' by Nicci French, Nicci Gerrard and Sean French; for 'Bed Bugs', the title story from the 1982 collection by Clive Sinclair, published by Allison & Busby, the author; for 'Peerless' from *The Darkness of Wallis Simpson* (2005) by Rose Tremain, published by Chatto & Windus, Sheil Land Assocs.; for 'The New Puritans' from *Exhibitionism* (2002) by Toby Litt, published by Hamish Hamilton, Penguin Books Ltd.; for 'A Bit of Singing and Dancing' from *Farthing House and Other Stories* (2006) by Susan Hill, published by Long Barn Books, Sheil Land Assocs.

Peter Tolhurst
Black Dog Books
2007

Foreword
D J TAYLOR

Not long back I found myself sitting in on a debate convened by the organisers of the King's Lynn Fiction Festival on the subject of 'regionalism and the novel'. The principal debaters were Robert Edric, who had previously read from a short story set on the East Coast, and Maggie Makepeace, recent author of a novel set in the Somersetshire 'Levels'. What one had presumed would be a united front swiftly declared itself as a polar opposition. Edric, who has written an entire crime trilogy set in Hull, began by denying that the genre he was supposed to ornament even existed. If there had been such a thing, he argued, then it had perished sixty or even seventy years before. Nowadays, in a centralising culture, with a Tesco at the end of every street and local accents disappearing beneath an Estuarine tide, all the novelist could do was to offer variations on a theme. A novel set in North Yorkshire was merely a novel set in North Yorkshire, and the hills and dales in which its action took place were incidental scenery.

The argument about regionalism burns on endlessly through discussions of modern English literature. Romantic novelists who have thought that it might be nice to set one of their books in picturesque Southwold have been unwittingly drawn into it. Safe within the strait-jacket of the M25 corridor, gnarled exponents of the Hampstead adultery novel disdain it from afar. What might be called the Edric thesis is one of its most dominant notes. We live, this theory goes, in a monoculture where the once highly significant affiliations of place have ceased to matter. You and I watch the same television programmes, read the same newspapers and are subject to the same consumer pressures, and if we choose to write a novel the neuroses lurking beneath its surface will be the same whether we live in Blackpool or Budleigh Salterton. The cultural assumptions on which modern life is predicated grow ever more homogenous, and the fact that novelist X and novelist Y write for the *Guardian* or teach Creative Writing at the University of North Staffordshire is far more important than the fact that the view from their respective desk-tops takes in the Lincolnshire Wolds or the Cumbrian cliff-tops.

Perhaps one ought to start with first principles and ask: just exactly what is an example of regional writing? Well, *Jude the Obscure* certainly is, and so is *Sons and Lovers*, along with *Cider With Rosie* and even such a recent and criminally under-rated work as Peter Benson's *The Levels*, set in the Maggie Makepeace territory mentioned above. Their defining characteristic, broadly set out, is that they could not, in terms of the human situations offered up to the reader, be set anywhere else, that the landscapes, mindsets and attitudes on display – what now gets known as 'psycho-geography' – are, on the one hand, unusually distinctive and, on the other, integral to their conception. To put it another way, a novel like Graham Swift's *Waterland* could never be set in a Surrey suburb. Regardless of whether you believe that this kind of book can still exist in the early twenty-first century, the argument has been complicated by the fact that, from the angle of the literary marketplace, the last decade and a half has been characterised by a wholesale flight to the regions and a determination – exhibited by dozens of novelists and short story writers – to prove that it is possible to maintain quite a decent literary career two or even three hundred miles away from the fleshpots of the metropolis.

There are several reasons for this diaspora. The most obvious is financial. London, a magnet for the aspiring writer since the days of Fielding and Smollett, has grown too expensive for most twenty-five year-olds with literary ambitions to live in for very long. Telecommunications have lessened the need for writers to be permanently present on the doorsteps of the newspapers and magazines for whom they write. Then again, the past twenty years have seen the rise of regional publishing firms such as Tindal Street in Birmingham and Flambard in Northumberland: to be published these days, and to be published successfully, it is no longer necessary to have an editorial sponsor who sits in a ziggurat in the Fulham Palace Road or St Martin's Lane. Finally, there is the inexorable march of provincial university creative writing courses, which, whatever you may think of the merits of creative writing courses, need people to teach them and generally find these recruits in novelists lured out of London by the promise of lower housing costs and a study that doesn't look out over the thump and judder of the South Circular. The result of these individual pressures is that most English cities now boast a collection of writers, some but not all engaged in university teaching, whose gaze is not automatically set on London and who, for the most part, are quite happy where they are. Kingsley Amis's *Lucky Jim* (1954) famously ends with its absconding history lecturer hero standing on the station platform with a series of metropolitan place names running seductively through his head. Jim's modern equivalent, Professor of Creative Writing, let us say, at the University of Stoke Poges, would probably opt to stay where he is.

On the other hand, none of this means that Professor X of the University of Stoke Poges, when he isn't writing job references or planning the latest round of guest lectures, will be engaged on a 'regional novel'. Can such a thing still be written? A glance around the ranks of contemporary novelists and short story writers suggests that it can. The point, for example, about the Cumbrian novelist John Murray (b. 1950) is that he lives six or seven miles outside Carlisle. Cumbria, in a novel like *Samarkand* (1985), a portrait of the fading north-western industrial belt of Murray's childhood, or the semi-autobiographical *Kin* (1986), is not simply a matter of steeply-rising fells and lake-water but an abiding cultural presence, without which Murray's imagination could not function in quite the same way. This tendency runs through nearly all his books and be can be seen most conspicuusly in *Reiver Blues* (1994), which takes the local obsession with borders and the debatable lands of the Anglo-Scottish frontier and converts it into an edgy metaphor for the realignments then going on in Eastern Europe.

Even now, in a rural world changed out of all recognition by the rise of the agri-business, the destruction of the hedgerows and the flight from the land – as Ronald Blythe has pointed out, the distinguishing feature of countryside these days is its silence and lack of movement – the same is true of East Anglia. The ominous self-containment of the Fens manifested itself in fiction long before *Waterland* (see here the stories by Chafer Legge and Sylvia Townsend Warner) and goes on to dominate Nicola Barker's 'Dual Balls', set in the long shadow of Ely cathedral. And then, everywhere from the Suffolk back-lanes to the Norfolk flats, there is the unignorable influence of the landscape. The infinitely sinister quality of M.R. James's East Anglian ghost stories has quite as much to do with the flat, undeviating countryside – brooding heaths, murky sea-shores, low, desolate hills – as the antiquarian horrors that lurk beneath. Philip Hensher's 'In the Net', in which a middle-aged city dweller relocates to a Suffolk cottage, neatly conveys this sense of constriction, of hidden boundaries and buried angst. 'He went for a long walk the next day. The wind was up, blowing against his face, and quickly the sense of pointlessness of walking in Suffolk settled on him. Without hills, in a place where the walker cannot see where he is going, nor where he has been, but is just walking in the empty unmarked landscape; he could see little point to it.'

In some ways, though, these surface attractions pale before the varieties of local idiosyncrasy, quiddity and rootedness – all still going strong despite the influx of second-homers and the noise of Wellington boots bought in Chelsea grinding up the gravel of the Holkham beach. As someone who left Norfolk at the age of nineteen and came back to it at forty, I can confirm that the natives have a sense of irony unlike that of any British ethnic group. When, as a boy, I used to ask my brother to run an errand for me, he would offer the time-honoured reply: 'Reckon I will.' This, a close reading insists, does not, in the manner of most ironising, mean its exact opposite. It implies a relationship. What 'Reckon I will' means, approximately, is 'Our intimacy is such that you know already that I will not do what you have suggested. Therefore, by suggesting it, you have given me the opportunity of making a joke at my expense – as it discloses my own incapacity – but also at your expense, because it indicates the futility of your asking me to do anything which I do not want to do.' A power struggle, in other words, and of much more interest to the average novelist, it seems to me, than adultery or what happens around Mr Gordon Brown's cabinet table.

Here to support this thesis, are two dozen of East Anglia's finest. They range from M.R. James and Ronald Blythe to the incomparable Victorian-era Norfolk farmer's wife Mary Mann, more recent fabulists such as Angela Carter and Clive Sinclair and comparative newcomers like Toby Litt (a notably creepy piece about pornographers on the Suffolk coast.) Taken together, they are a demonstration of what, even now, is East Anglia's 'otherness' – a separation from the mass cultural dustbin which, in the age of Cambridgeshire's Silicon Valley, the despoiling of the Shotley peninsula and the dualled motorways coursing on through the Norfolk heaths, it seems vitally important to preserve.

Watermarks

Angela Carter (1941-92): By turn a journalist, formidable academic who taught latterly at UEA, critic and one of the most original novelists of her generation, who became a notable exponent of Magic Realism in novels such as *The Magic Toyshop* (1967), *Nights at the Circus* (1984) and *Wise Children* (1991). Her several volumes of short stores include the collection of feminist fairy tales, *The Bloody Chamber* (1979) but 'The Man Who Loved a Double Bass', her earliest story, only appeared after her death in *Burning Your Boats* (1995), her collected short stories.

The Man Who Loved A Double Bass
ANGELA CARTER

All artists, they say, are a little mad. This madness is, to a certain extent, a self-created myth designed to keep the generality away from the phenomenally close-knit creative community. Yet, in the world of the artists, the consciously eccentric are always respectful and admiring of those who have the courage to be genuinely a little mad.

That was how Johnny Jameson, the bass player, came to be treated – with respect and admiration; for there could be no doubt that Jameson was as mad as a hatter.

And the musicians looked after him. He was never without work, or a bed, or a packet of cigarettes, or a beer if he wanted one. There was always someone taking care of the things he could never get around to doing himself. It must also be admitted that he was a very fine bass player.

In this, in fact, lay the seed of his trouble. For his bass, his great, gleaming, voluptuous bass, was mother, father, wife, child and mistress to him and he loved it with a deep and steadfast passion.

Jameson was a small, quiet man with rapidly receding hair and a huge pair of heavy spectacles hiding mild, short-sighted eyes. He hardly went anywhere without his bass, which he carried effortlessly, slung on his back, as Red Indian women carry their babies. But it was a big baby for one so frail-looking as he to carry.

They called the bass Lola. Lola was the most beautiful bass in the whole world. Her shape was that of a full-breasted, full-tripped woman, recalling certain primitive effigies of the Mother Goddess so gloriously, essentially feminine was she, stripped of irrelevancies of head and limbs.

Jameson spent hours polishing her red wood, already a warm, chestnut colour, to an ever deeper, ever richer glow. On tour, he sat placidly in the bus while the other musicians drank, argued and gambled around him, and he would take Lola from her black case, and unwrap the rags that

3

padded her, with a trembling emotion. Then he would take out a special, soft silk handkerchief and set to work on his polishing, smiling gently at nothing and blinking his short-sighted eyes like a happy cat.

The bass was always treated like a lady. The band started to buy her coffee and tea in cafés for a joke. Later it ceased to be a joke and became a habit. The extra drink was always ordered and placed before her and they ignored it when they went away and it was still on the table, cold and untouched.

Jameson always took Lola into cafés but never into public bars because, after all, she was a lady. Whoever drank with Jameson did so in the saloon and bought Lola a pineapple juice, although sometimes she could be prevailed upon to take a glass of sherry at festive occasions like Christmas or a birthday or when someone's wife had a child.

But Jameson was jealous if she got too much attention and would look daggers at a man who took too many liberties with her, like slapping her case or making facetious remarks.

Jameson had only ever been known to strike a man once when he had broken the nose of a drunken, insensitive pianist who made a coarse jest about Lola in Jameson's presence. So nobody ever joked about Lola when Jameson was there.

But innocent young musicians were hideously embarrassed if ever it fell out that they had to share a room with Jameson while on tour. So Jameson and Lola usually had a room to themselves. Away from Jameson, the trumpeter, Geoff Clarke, would say that Jameson was truly wedded to his art and perhaps they ought to book the bridal suite for the pair at some hotel, sometime.

But Clarke gave Jameson a good job in his trad group that was called the West End Syncopators. Ignoring the august echoes of the name, they dressed themselves up in grey toppers and tail coats when performing and their souped-up version of 'West End Blues' (plus new vocal) had penetrated to the lower reaches of the top twenty.

They all looked grotesque in grey toppers and none more grotesque than Jameson; but the band still made money.

Making money, however, meant day after day spent in a converted Green Line bus travelling up and down the country from one one-night-stand to the next. It meant dates at corn exchanges, town halls, grimy back rooms in pubs. It meant constant bone-weariness and constant cash and credit and the band all loved it. They all shared a crazy jubilation.

'The trad boom ain't going to last for ever, so let's enjoy it!' said Len Nelson, the clarinettist.

The Man Who Loved A Double Bass

He was an incorrigible fornicator, whose idea of profiting from the trad boom was to lure star-struck young girls from the provincial clubs and concerts up into his hotel bedroom and there copulate with them. He loved success. And, to a lesser extent, they all exulted.

Except, of course, Jameson, who did not even notice that trad was booming. He played just whatever he was told to play. He never really cared what it was as long as the quality of the sound he produced did not offend Lola.

One night in November, they were engaged to play at a small town in the Fenland wastes of East Anglia. Darkness came with the afternoon, dragging mist with it to fill the dykes and shroud the pollard willows. The band bus followed a straight road with never a turn or dip and when they reached the pub where the jazz club at which they were to perform was held, and climbed from the bus, the darkness fell around their shoulders like a rain-soaked blanket.

'Are they expecting us?' asked Dave Jennings, the drummer, anxiously. Not a light shone in the pub.

A frayed poster pinned to the closed main door announced their coming. But the chronic Fenland rain had so softened the paper that the slogan: 'Friday night is rave night – with the raving, rioting, hit parade happy West End Syncopators' was almost indecipherable.

'Well, it's not opening time, yet,' comforted Len Nelson.

'More's the pity,' grunted Jennings.

'Of course they're expecting us,' said Geoff firmly. 'The club booked us up months ago, before the record even. That's why we accepted a date in this God-forsaken hole, isn't it, Simeon?'

The manager was a peripatetic Jew named Simeon Price, a failed tenor sax man who travelled with them out of nostalgia for his swinging days. Simeon was staring at the pub with bright, frightened eyes.

'I don't like it here,' he said and shivered. 'There's something in the air.'

'Bloody lot of wet in the air,' grumbled Nelson. 'Bet the dollies round here all got webbed feet.'

'Don't come the mysterious East,' Geoff urged Simeon.

Simeon shook his head agitatedly and shivered in spite of the great, turned-up collar of his enormous cashmere coat. He always dressed like a stage Jew. His race was his gimmick and he always affected a strong Yiddish accent although his family had been respected members of the Manchester bourgeoisie for nearly 150 years.

But then the landlord appeared and then the two sixth form grammar

5

school boys who ran the club and there was beer and chat and warmth and laughter. Jameson was very worried in case the damp should hurt Lola, warp her, rot her strings. He allowed one of the grammar school boys, they called him the Boy David at once, to buy her a rum and orange, for her health's sake. Nelson and Jennings had to take the wondering Boy David off into the Gents and explain about Lola, quietly.

But Simeon's slender, delicately pointed nose was almost aquiver with sensibility, smelling something wrong, trouble in the wet air. The East Anglian air was bad for his weak lungs. The Boy David was talking about his club.

'Bit old world, the membership, really, though we get people in for the club from quite a way away – art students, even, and a few sharp youngsters, and leather jackets who come from miles on their motorbikes. But the local teds, well, they still even have sideboards and velvet collars to their jackets!'

There was a chorus of incredulous mirth and the boy at once became embarrassed and bought more drinks to cover his confusion. The band were to stay the night at the pub, which hid a number of bedrooms behind its unimposing facade. Simeon crept away from the bar to feel the sheets on his bed. They were damp. His throat immediately set up a sympathetic tickling.

Jameson, humping Lola, also crept away, to the back room where music and dancing were permitted. He unwrapped his instrument and sat huddled over it in the cold, caressing with his silken rag. The room around him waited for the club to open, the shabby lines of quiet chairs waited, the little platform for the musicians waited.

But there was a potent unease in the night. The musicians sensed it and their laughter became defiant as they tried to frighten the uneasiness away with their merriment. And they failed. Their young hosts caught the silent, depressed infection until they were all just sitting around, drinking for want of something else to do. But Jameson was happy; he was the only one happy, sitting away from them all, with Lola between his knees.

As the band assembled on the cramped platform, the first customers arrived and stood around with their first half pints of bitter. Music began; the customers waited passively for the first extrovert couple who would start to dance.

They were an easily recognisable type, these early ones. The boys wore pale, loose sweaters with paisley silk scarves tucked casually into the vee necks and the girls were tricked out in pseudo beat style, black or heavy

6

mesh stockings, loose dresses heavily fringed. They were the children of local doctors, clergymen, teachers, retired soldiers, probably students in their last school year. They wore duffel coats and drove battered old cars and had a tendency to collect those little china ashtrays with veteran cars on them.

Just before the first break, a black-legged girl in a short little pleated skirt and a youth in cavalry twill trousers ventured, giggling, on to the floor to dance; they did so in a peculiarly self-conscious way that made the musicians wink and grin at one another. Gradually the room began to fill. Art students from a nearby town, sniggering at the bourgeois who aped them; a party of crop-haired modernists, who had also travelled some distance. The modernists had sharp, pointed noses and Italian suits. Their girls dressed with studied formality, faces stylised, pale cheeks and lips, vividly painted eyes, hair immaculate, stiff with lacquer.

The modernists chaffed Simeon, who lingered by the pay desk because the boys in charge were so young that he worried for them. The modernists joked about the grey top hats and the striped trousers and were patronising about 'West End Blues' and, in fact, the whole trad set-up altogether; they were here, they implied, just because there happened to be nothing else doing that night. Simeon smiled with professional warmth and wondered whether he dare slip away to spray his throat.

But his eyes slitted with suspicion when he saw a group of youths were parking motorcycles outside the pub; he could see them through the open door. They took off their crash helmets and left them under their cycles, where they gleamed whitely, like mushrooms or new laid eggs. Then the boys approached, plastic jackets creaking. Simeon personally tore off their jackets for them and watched them anxiously as they fought for brown ales at the bar.

'Now, those chaps are really far less potential trouble than those modernist friends of yours,' admonished the Boy David. Simeon sighed.

'You wouldn't have, by any chance, such a thing as an aspirin – and perhaps, might it be possible, could I get a glass of hot milk?'

Inside the club room, a thick smoke haze dimmed the already low lighting and the room was in semi-darkness. Arms and legs flailed, beer slopped. The music was so loud it seemed almost a tangible, brazen wall. The West End Syncopators were half-way through another successful date.

But the leatherjackets kept apart from the main, happy crowd. They had taken over one particular corner for themselves and were not dancing but standing up to their beer, laughing and grinning.

The boys in the band played and sweated and gulped restorative bitter

7

between choruses. They undid their silk waistcoats and their black ties and mopped the red indentations made on their foreheads by their top hats. It was just like any other date.

Just like any other date until one of the leatherjackets spilled his beer all over the olive green buttocks of a thin girl in a sheath dress who jived backwards into him. She turned, angry. He apologised with profuse irony and that made her more angry still. The girl complained to her sharp, short-jacketed escort and the leatherjackets stood all round and leered.

'And aren't you going to say sorry to this young lady, then, mate?' the girl's dancing partner shouted above the music.

The leatherjackets closed ranks like a snapped clasp-knife. Their indistinguishable, pallid, slack-jawed faces all grinned at once.

'And what if I ain't particularly sorry? Wasted all my beer, I have.'

A group of Italian youths deserted their girls to gather behind the olive-sheathed girl's defender. And that was how it started. The quarrel boiled up into a fine ragout of cries, shouts, blows and the dim interior whirled with thrusting limbs and crashing bottles as the eager youths met in fight. A bottle smashed the single, red-painted electric bulb and there was a horror of darkness. In the chaos, a pair of leatherjackets launched an attack on the musicians who were moaning and terrified and striking little matches to see something of the battle.

'That such a thing should happen when we're in the top twenty!' gasped Simeon.

The Young Conservatives came scurrying past shepherding frightened Susans, Brendas, and Jennifers. But the art students clustered safely at the door to giggle. The tight-skirted teddy girls dropped their impassivity; like valkyries they rode the battle, cheering the fighters on. Their exalted faces flickered in and out of the light that trickled through from the public bar.

Now the musicians cast aside their top hats, their instruments and their neutrality. Simeon saw Len Nelson – as jerky and uncertain in the intermittent light as a man in an early film – leap from the dais and seize an Italian youth by his narrow and immaculate lapels and shake, shake, shake him until the boy's mouth gaped open, howling.

'Nothing like it ever happened before!' the Boy David kept exclaiming in an apologetic frenzy. There were crashes and splinterings and the landlord appeared, trembling. Simeon took him into the private bar to soothe him with his own Scotch.

'Quite like the old days, before we got famous,' panted Nelson, defending the microphone.

But it was all over very quickly, when someone shouted something about the police and the room emptied like a bath when the plug is pulled out. The musicians' heavy breathing and little exclamations of triumph and sighs were the only sounds in the room.

'Would I be such a fool as to call the police?' demanded Simeon rhetorically. So they all laughed and went for a drink.

'Here,' said someone later, 'has anyone seen Jameson?'

'Not since the lights went out.'

'Well, what does it matter? I'm going to bed,' said Simeon. 'I've a dreadful cold coming, I feel it. Not that going to bed will do me much good; wringing wet, the sheets are . . . '

Then they all of them forgot about Jameson until very much later, when all but Geoff and Nelson had finally followed Simeon up the stairs to bed. Geoff and Nelson, decently happy, decided to go and have a look at the damage in the club room. They took a light bulb from the bar and plugged it into the socket where the red light had once been. And into focus leapt all the shattered glass and broken chairs and brown beer puddles soaking into the floor.

Sobered at once, Geoff climbed on to the stage and poked anxiously among the instruments remaining. Miraculously, the drum and its accessories had survived and – he sighed – there seemed not a casualty on the dais. Then he found a terrible thing. Where Jameson had sat with Lola, there remained nothing on the floor but a heap of chestnut-coloured firewood.

'Oh, Christ,' he said. Nelson looked up, startled at the tone of the other's voice. 'Jameson, how are we going to tell Jameson, Len? His bass . . . '

They stood together and gazed at Lola's pathetic fragmented corpse. Both were touched with a cold finger of awe and dread and a superstitious sorrow; the lady who did not go into public bars was suddenly no more than a few graceless splinters.

'Do you know if he knows?' whispered Nelson. It did not seem right to talk in a loud voice.

'I haven't seen him since the trouble began.'

'Even if he does know, well, he ought to have a bit of company, at a time like this, a few friends around him . . .'

'Maybe he's up in his room.'

They found out from the landlord that Jameson had been lodged in an attic room high at the top of the old rabbit-warren of a place. Fenland mist had crept into the pub and it blurred their vision as Geoff and Nelson climbed flight after flight of stairs. It was very late, now, and cold, with a bone-chilling, wet, cold. Then, without warning, every light went out. Stricken, Nelson clutched at Geoff.

'Len, it's all right, don't take on. It must be a fuse, or something, perhaps the wiring – rotten old wiring they have in houses as old as this.'

But he himself was badly scared. They both felt an alien, almost tangible something in the darkness, felt it in the damp kiss of the mist-soaked air on their cheeks.

'A light, Geoff, now.'

Geoff clicked his cigarette lighter. The tiny flame only intensified the darkness around them. They reached the topmost landing.

'Here we are.'

The door swung open. Geoff held his lighter high. They saw first a chair, overturned on the floor. Then they saw the open, empty case of a double bass on the cheap taffeta bedspread. The case was shaped for all the world like a coffin. But Lola would not lie in it, although it was her own.

And in the still circle of light, swung a pair of feet, gently, backwards and forwards, forwards and backwards . . . Geoff raised his lighter above his head until they could see all of Jameson, hanging from a disused gas bracket, his gentle face black and twisted. Bedded deep in his neck was a brilliant silken rag, the rag he had used for so long to polish his bass. Something glinted on the floor beneath him – his glasses, dropped, broken.

A sodden wind came in through the open window and swallowed the lighter flame at once. Then there was engulfing darkness and in the darkness no noise but the slow creak, creak, creak. And the two men grabbed at each other's hands like frightened children.

In a room beneath them, the same little wind trickled through an ill-fitting window frame and tickled Simeon Price's throat so that he coughed and stirred a little, uneasily, in his sleep.

* * * * *

Nicola Barker: Born in Ely and educated at King's College, Cambridge. Her novels include *Reversed Forecast* (1994), *Wider Open* (1998), *Clear* (2004) and most recently *Darkmans* (2007). In 2003 she was one of Granta's 20 Best Young British Novelists. 'Dual Balls' in which she returns to the Fens, is from *Love Your Enemies* (1993), the first of several acclaimed collections of darkly comic and surreal short stories, which won the The David Higham Prize for Fiction.

Dual Balls
NICOLA BARKER

Selina Mitchell had never been particularly free-thinking. Since she was fifteen she had been completely under the sway of her dominant and rather single-minded husband Tom and her dominant and rather light-headed friend Joanna. She had always lived in Grunty Fen. If you grow up somewhere with a name like Grunty Fen you never really see the humour in the name, and Selina was no exception to this rule. She never thought it was a particularly amusing place to live. In fact she hated it most of the time. It was physically small, socially small and intellectually small. It wasn't even close enough to Cambridge to bask in any of the reflected glory; but if ever Selina had cause to write a letter to London or Manchester or Edinburgh for any reason she invariably wrote her address as *Grunty Fen, Combridgeshire*. She hoped that this created a good impression.

The only scandal that had ever caused real consternation, discussion and debate in Grunty Fen was when Harry Fletcher had started to wear Wellington boots to school (in summer) and the school had been forced to alter their uniform rules in order to acknowledge that Wellingtons were a legitimate item of clothing for school wear. The teachers had seen this new allowance as a victory for the environment over the purity of education, a muddying of the intellectual pursuit. The kids all wore wellies to school for a while and then switched back to mucky trainers after their initial *joie de vivre* had worn off.

Selina had been a quick-witted student – by Grunty Fen standards – and had been one of the few children at the village school bright and determined enough to go to teacher training college. At seventeen she had packed her suitcase and had gone to Reading to learn how to be a teacher; to spread discipline and information.

At seventeen she had thought that she would never return to Grunty

Fen again, but inevitably she went home during her vacations to visit her parents and wrote long, emotional letters to her boyfriend Tom, who had tried to stop her going to college in the first place by asking her to marry him.

After three years at college Selina had returned to Grunty Fen, 'Just until I decide where I really want to go.' Eventually she had married Tom and had started teaching at the village primary school.

She disliked children and didn't want any of her own. Tom liked children – probably because he wasn't forced into a classroom with thirty of them every day – but he realized that if he wanted to hang on to Selina (she was one of the intellectual élite) then he would have to bow to her better judgement.

Time rolled by. Selina's life was as flat as the fens and just about as interesting. Nothing much happened at all.

Joanna, Selina's best friend, had lived a very similar sort of life except that she had enjoyed little success at school and had never attended teacher training college. She had got married at sixteen to John Burger whose family owned a large farm to the north of Grunty Fen, and had borne him two children before she reached twenty. She had always been wild and mischievous, but in a quiet way, a way that pretended that nothing serious was ever going on, or at least nothing seriously bad. Joanna was the bale of hay in Selina's field. She made Selina's landscape moderately more entertaining.

Joanna didn't really know the meaning of hard work. Most country women throw in their lot with their husbands and work like automatons on the farm. But Joanna had more sense than that. She preferred to stay at home 'creating a friendly home environment' and cultivating her good looks.

At the age of thirty-nine she aspired to the Dallas lifestyle. She spent many hours growing and painting her nails, making silk-feel shirts and dresses on her automatic sewing machine and throwing or attending Tupperware parties.

Joanna was Grunty Fen's only hedonist, but hedonism wasn't just her way of life, it was her religion, and she tried to spread it like a spoonful of honey on buttery toast.

They were in a café in Ely, a stone's throw from the cathedral, eating a couple of cream eclairs with coffee. Selina was making fun of Joanna but Joanna didn't seem to mind. She pulled the chocolate away from the choux pastry with her cake fork as Selina said laughingly, 'I still cant think of that birthday without smiling. My fortieth, and I thought it would be some sort of great landmark. I was so depressed. I opened Tom's present and it was a home first aid kit. Of course I said how lovely it was. Then, trying to hide my disappointment, I opened your present, firmly believing that it would contain something frivolous and feminine. But inside the parcel there were only ten odd pieces of foam, all neatly and pointlessly sewn up around the edges. Neither of us knew what the hell they were. I thought they might be miniature cushions without covers. Tom thought they were for protecting your knees during cricket games, a sort of knee guard, I even thought they might be a pair of falsies.'

Joanna smiled. 'This must be one of the only places in the world where a woman of forty doesn't understand the basics of sophisticated dressing. I thought you could sew the shoulder pads into all your good shirts and dresses. It's a fashionable look, Selina, honestly.'

Selina shrugged her non-padded shoulders. 'I will sew them in eventually, I promise.'

Joanna grinned to herself. She looked rather cheery. Usually before, during and after consumption of a cream cake Joanna panicked about its calory content and moaned about its probable effect on her midriff.

As Selina waited for the inevitable outburst she said, 'If we didn't come to Ely every few weeks for a chat and a break I'm sure I'd go mad. Ely. Imagine! This small, insignificant town has come to symbolize freedom and independence to me. It's rather sad; it's like the Americans symbolizing freedom with a sparrow instead of a bald eagle.'

She looked into Joanna's face. Joanna was smiling. It was as if she was listening to a song that no one else could hear. Selina stared at her silence for a minute or so and then said, 'What is it, Joanna? I'm sure you're up to something.'

Joanna's eyes were vaguely glassy. Selina frowned. 'You've not been taking those tranquillizers again, have you?'

Joanna laughed. It was a sort of throaty, gutsy laugh. 'Oh Selina, if only you knew. If only! What's Tom like in bed at the moment? Has it improved since our last little chat?'

Selina shrugged and her cheeks reddened. 'Nothing much has happened in that department. Are you enjoying that cake?'

She had finished hers several minutes before, but Joanna was still (uncharacteristically) pushing her cake around her plate. Selina added quickly – to distract Joanna from intimate territory – 'School's been awful.

Felicity has been sitting in on classes, It's to do with the new assessment rules from the education authority. The classroom is no longer my kingdom. It's been taken over by men in little grey suits. Of course Felicity loves it all. She even had the cheek to offer me a few tips on my teaching technique the other day. I'm surprised she was capable of taking any of the lesson in. Most of it she spent fiddling with her hearing aid. Anyway, everyone knows that Heads are incapable of controlling classes and that's why they become Heads in the first place. Maybe I'm just bitter, but the thought of that old crone deigning to tell me how to handle a class! She said something like, "Be freer, Selina, be more adventurous, take risks!" I tried to tell her that the syllabus had destroyed all elements of spontaneity in the classroom. If the kids want to cope with the workload nowadays it's all blackboard, chalk and copying.'

As Selina finished speaking Joanna shuddered slightly. Selina smiled. 'Ghost walk over your grave?'

Joanna shook her head and then giggled furtively. 'Look Selina, it's not that I'm not interested in what you are saying about school – God knows, my two did well enough under your tuition and they thought you were a great teacher – it isn't that I'm not interested, but I just must change the subject for a moment.'

As Joanna spoke, she leaned towards Selina conspiratorially and her voice dropped to a whisper, 'Selina, I'm wearing Dual Balls.'

Selina frowned. 'What do you mean? Is it a girdle of some kind, or some sort of skin ointment?'

Joanna never ceased to amaze her with her violent enthusiasms and frivolity. She pushed a slightly greying brown curl behind her ear and thought abstractedly. 'I must have my hair cut, it's almost touching my shoulders now.'

Joanna's chair scraped along the floor as she pulled it up closer to Selina. Selina could smell her perfume – something heady like Opium – which flushed through the air like bleach through water. Joanna whispered again, 'I've got Dual Balls, Selina. I've had them in since I left the house. It's been incredible.'

Selina shrugged, 'You're going to have to explain this to me, Joanna. I don't know what Dual Balls are.'

Joanna bit her lip and stared at Selina through her heavily mascaraed lashes for a moment, then she said, 'I got them from an underwear catalogue. I ordered them and they came in the post. John doesn't know anything about them.'

14

Selina cleared her throat nervously, 'Are they something rude, Joanna?' Joanna winked saucily. 'I should say so. They're like two small round vibrating grapes. Battery operated.'

Selina took a sip of her coffee to try and deflate the tension, then said, 'Have you got them in your bag?'

Joanna snorted loudly and several people at other tables turned and stared at them both for a moment. Selina felt slightly embarrassed. Joanna soon recovered from her fit of hilarity and whispered, 'They're not in my bag, stupid. I've got them in my fanny.'

Selina was not initially so much shocked by the idea of Joanna's little vibrating grapes as by her casual use of the word 'fanny'. It was an old-fashioned word. She had once had a great aunt called Fanny, a gregarious, light-hearted aunt who had always seemed very old to her as a child; old, frail but charming.

She didn't really know how to reply to Joanna, how to disguise her intense unease and embarrassment. Luckily Joanna had other things on her mind. After a few seconds silence she squeezed Selina's arm and said, 'I'm going to nip into the toilets and take them out, then you can have a proper look at them.

Selina's expression was querulous. Joanna noticed as she stood up, and grinned. 'Don't worry, Selina, I'll give them a good wash before you have to have any contact with them.'

Selina sighed. 'Joanna, please be discreet. This is only Ely after all, not San Francisco.'

Joanna didn't reply.

Once she'd gone Selina relaxed and drank a large mouthful of her coffee. She stared out of the window at the cathedral. She thought, 'God, I feel old. Maybe it's teaching. It just beats all the enthusiasm out of you. I'm sure I never used to feel this way. The kids are no better or no worse than they were twenty years ago. It must be me that's changed.' She sighed and waited for Joanna's return.

After about five minutes Joanna emerged from the toilets looking furtive but self-satisfied, like a large tom cat on the prowl, about to spray an unsuspecting territory with his rank odour. Selina thought, 'This room belongs to Joanna. She doesn't give a damn about anything.'

Joanna sat down next to her again and Selina said straight away, 'I don't know where you get these ideas from – or your nerve for that matter – look at you, as bold as brass!'

Joanna smiled and patted her chestnut perm with one of her bright-pink-fingernailed hands, 'Don't look at this hand, look at the other one under the table.'

Selina moved backwards slightly and stared down at Joanna's other hand which held the Dual Balls like a couple of freshly laid eggs. Selina said, 'They're bigger than I thought they'd be and attached to each other. I imagined that they'd be a sort of flesh colour, not that strange off-white.'

Joanna raised her eyebrows. 'Flesh is off-white, Selina. Are Tom's balls a very different colour to these?'

She smiled provocatively. Selina shook her head disapprovingly. 'Tom's . . .' she couldn't use the word – 'Tom's aren't anything unusual, Joanna, and I certainly don't make a habit of trying to use them like you've just used those. Also, his don't use batteries and they aren't attached by a small piece of cord.'

Joanna smirked. 'You wish Tom's balls were like these. They're very effective, and so discreet. I think the thrill of using them is trebled by the fact of wearing them out. It's so arousing.'

Selina grimaced. 'Walking can't be easy with them in. Why don't they just drop out?'

As Selina spoke Joanna switched the balls on, She waited for Selina to finish talking and then said, 'Why don't you try them and see?' The balls vibrated vigorously in her hand. They sounded like a quieter version of an electric razor. Selina was sure that everyone could hear. She whispered frantically. 'For God's sake Joanna, switch them off.' Joanna frowned. 'I worry about you, Selina. You're becoming very old-maidish, very schoolmarmish. You don't have any spirit of adventure any more.'

Selina didn't rise to the bait. 'I've never had any spirit of adventure and you know it.'

Joanna nodded. 'I suppose that's true. No backbone, no spontaneity. No interest in what's state of the art . . .'

Selina raised an eyebrow – 'Where did you come across that little phrase? Something on television, something American I suppose?'

'You wouldn't have the nerve to wear these out, no way,' Joanna interrupted.

Selina smiled. 'I'd have enough nerve, Joanna, just too much sense, I don't need something like those. I think they're horrible. Now switch them off.'

Joanna turned and stared out of the window at people passing by. An old lady staggered past pulling her shopping trolley. Joanna pointed at the woman, 'I bet she'd wear them out. I bet she's got more spunk in her little finger than you've got in your entire body.'

Selina almost smiled at this but then stopped herself. 'Possibly. Look, the waitress is coming over with the bill. Please turn them off.'

Joanna didn't turn them off, but started instead to lift up the hand containing the vibrating balls until they were almost at a level with the surface of the table. Selina was excruciatingly embarrassed. 'Joanna, switch them off and put them away. You're embarrassing me.'

Joanna was staring at the Dual Balls rather thoughtfully. After a moment she said, 'I dare you to wear these when you're teaching one of your classes. Just for one lesson. I dare you!'

Joanna loved dares. This was principally because she always thought of them and didn't therefore usually do them herself. 'Go on Selina, I dare you!'

Selina laughed. 'You've got to be kidding. Those horrible little things are having no contact with my intimate body whatsoever.'

Joanna lifted the balls slightly higher than the table and said, 'If you don't accept the dare I swear I'm going to put these into your coffee cup when the waitress comes to clear the table. That should be in about twenty seconds.'

Selina saw a couple of people at the nearest table to them discussing something and laughing. She was sure that they had noticed. She said, 'Joanna, put them down, please.'

Joanna held them even higher. The waitress started to walk towards them. When she was about five steps from the table Selina said, 'OK, I promise to wear them, I promise, all right?'

Joanna switched the balls off immediately. It seemed very quiet without their buzzing.

On her way home Joanna passed John in the tractor. He stopped so that she could overtake him then waved his arm so that she would pause for a moment. She wound down her window. 'Yes?'

He shouted from his high seat, not bothering to switch off the tractor's roaring engine, 'Did she take them?'

Joanna nodded emphatically. 'Yes. It worked like a dream. She was really shocked when she thought that I was wearing them. It was a real effort not to laugh.'

He smiled. 'You must be a great actress then.'

She shrugged. 'I did all right.'

She crossed her fingers down by the steering wheel. He frowned – although he couldn't see her hands – 'Joanna, you were just acting?' Joanna guffawed. 'Don't be ridiculous. I'd probably have crashed the car if I'd worn them driving . . . Of course I wouldn't dream of wearing them anyway, why should I?'

She winked. He smiled. He obviously believed her. She uncrossed her fingers, waved at him and then drove on.

She negotiated the turn into their driveway with special care; she'd almost driven off the road there on the trip out.

One of the favourite pastimes in Grunty Fen is Chinese Whispers. People whisper gossip like it's going out of season. They also discuss what's happened in all of the major soaps and mini-series on television. Mostly though they prefer to gossip because it's a tiny place and everyone knows everyone else's business.

John got pissed in the local pub on Saturday night and told several of his cronies about Joanna's dare. The men all laughed loudly at the notion of someone as staid and strait-laced as Selina experimenting with sexual gadgets. They knew she wouldn't do it, but they enjoyed thinking about it just the same. A couple of them went home in their cups and told their wives. The women were shocked, interested and surprised on the whole; a small proportion were slightly jealous.

After Sunday lunch Selina was doing the washing up in the kitchen and Tom was sitting at the dining table in the next room doing the *Sunday Telegraph* crossword. Occasionally he read out loud to Selina any of the clues that had completely eluded him.

Selina washed the soapsuds from the final plate and placed it with the others on the drying rack. Tom seemed busy and preoccupied so she took this opportunity to clean out the sink and refill it with very hot water and a squirt of bleach. She went and found her handbag and took out the Dual Balls which she had placed inside, wrapped up in a tissue. She opened the tissue and removed the Dual Balls then placed them in the hot water and bleach, still wearing her rubber gloves. As she rubbed the balls with her hands she felt like a fetishist.

At the sound of Tom's voice from the next room she jumped guiltily and her heart lurched; then in a split second she had grabbed the washing-up cloth and had dropped it over the balls, covering them completely. Tom was saying, 'Thirty-one across. Vulgar Cockney squeezes ends of these into tube. Six letters. I think it's an anagram.

18

Any ideas, Selina?'

At this exact moment, a mile or so away, Joanna and John were still eating their lunch of beef and roast potatoes. John had a slight hang-over. Joanna had prepared a meal for four but neither of the children had bothered hanging around for it. This made John even more ill-tempered and grouchy. He kept saying, 'It's such a waste of good food. Those two don't know what it's like to do without. You spoil them.'

Joanna ignored him. She was thinking about Selina and the Dual Balls. She wondered whether she would use them or not. Selina rarely broke her word, if ever.

She cut into a potato and watched the steam rise from its hot centre. She speared a bit of it on to her fork and prepared to put it into her mouth. Before she had done so, however, John said, '1 told a couple of the fellas about your joke with Selina last night.'

Joanna stared at him, dumbstruck. 'You did what?'

Her voice was sharp and strident. He shrugged. 'I know I promised not to but it sort of slipped out.'

She put down her fork. 'I don't know why I tell you anything. You're totally unreliable. I'm sick of you spreading my business about and sticking your nose into everything. This was none of your affair in the first place.'

He frowned. 'Well, why did you tell me about it then?'

She pushed her chair back from the table and stood up. 'I didn't tell you about it, you opened my bloody mail. You have no right to open letters and parcels that are addressed to me.'

He shook his head, confused. 'You don't have anything to hide from me, Joanna. What's the problem all of a sudden? This isn't like you.'

Joanna slammed her hand down on the table, rattling the plates and glasses and cutlery. '1 am a woman, John, women have secrets. That's one of the few good things about being a woman as far as I can see. Now that you've told everyone about this thing with Selina she'll be a laughing stock. She's my friend, for God's sake.'

John stood up and moved around the table towards Joanna. His head ached with every twitch of his body. 'Everyone knows that Selina won't use those things, She's not like that. It was a silly idea in the first place really.'

Joanna felt tearful. She shouted, 'Well, it seemed like a good excuse at the time!'

19

Then, grabbing her plate, she marched off into the kitchen, where she threw her lunch into the bin.

John sat down at the table again. He felt somewhat confused.

Felicity Barrow received a telephone call from her friend Janet Street on Sunday afternoon. Janet was extremely excited because she had a bit of amusing gossip to impart about one of the teachers at Felicity's school. Felicity liked to call it 'my school', even though she was only the headmistress.

Janet had a rather puffy, breathy, light voice, and the scandal in her news almost extinguished it altogether. She gasped down the phone, 'Jim told me that Selina Mitchell has been wearing some sort of sexual device to school and using it while she's teaching classes.' Felicity interrupted, putting on her best head-teacherish voice. 'What on earth are you saying, Janet? And do speak clearly, I haven't adjusted my hearing aid yet.' On concluding this sentence she sipped her tea and took a large bite out of a mint-flavoured Viscount biscuit.

Janet gulped. This noise travelled all the way down the telephone line and into Felicity's ear. Then she whispered, 'Well, Jim said that it is a sort of vibrating machine which is shaped like the female sexual organs, but convex. It is attached by elastic to the two thighs, I think the elastic goes around the buttocks at the back . . . anyway Jim says it's very discreet. What happens is that it is battery-operated and it presses into the vagina while methodically rubbing at the clitoris. Apparently after several minutes this stimulates a sexual climax.'

Felicity tried to suppress the impulse to laugh, but finally gave into a throaty chuckle. 'Janet, I think what you're saying is untrue. We both know Selina Mitchell, we've both known her for years. I was headmistress at Grunty Fen Primary when she was a pupil at the school herself. There has never been anyone in the school whose dignity, discretion and professionalism I have held in higher regard. Just the other day I sat in on her class and assessed her performance. My only advice to her was that I thought her techniques too staid, perhaps a jot unimaginative . . .'

Janet interrupted. 'That's all well and good, Felicity, but you know what they say, there's no smoke without fire. She did go away at the end of the sixties, after all. Who knows what sort of habits she picked up then. . . .'

Felicity's initial amused indulgence at Janet's news suddenly evaporated. She snapped, 'Stop talking such absolute rubbish, Janet. I'd certainly have expected that you of all people would be the last to surrender your credulity to the clutches of vicious and totally unfounded gossip. I don't want to hear anything more about this subject, and if I do hear anything from a different source I will be forced to presume that it originated with you. Do I make myself clear?' Janet answered breathlessly in the affirmative and the conversation ended abruptly shortly afterwards.

Felicity had been headmistress at Grunty Fen Primary for almost thirty years. The time had come and gone for her to retire but she had ignored suggestions from various departments – chiefly from her husband Donald, who was several years into retirement himself – and had carried on giving her all to the young children of the district.

She took her vocation very seriously. Her main problem was that she couldn't be convinced that anyone else she knew would be suitable for her job. The ideal candidate would be a woman – she thought that women made the best Heads because they were much more frightening than men – and preferably they would originate from Grunty Fen or the surrounding area. She believed that Fen children had to be taught by people who were familiar with the various interests, problems and subtleties of their character. She knew that Selina Mitchell was keen for promotion. She had been coolly vetted for a favourable reference from Selina herself on several occasions, but nothing had come of it.

Felicity put her feet up on to her foot-stool, took out her hearing aid, leaned back in her chair and took another bite out of her biscuit. She had resented Janet's news because she felt that anything bad said about her staff reflected badly on the school and ultimately on herself. She was rather proud and vain but disliked these qualities in other people. Selina, she believed, was far too proud and vain for her own good. She was too closed, not sufficiently free-thinking. Felicity found her distant and arrogant. Selina found Felicity interfering and arrogant. Neither side would bow down to the other. They weren't destined to be good friends, but Felicity often regretted that they had never even managed to become formal friends.

She took another sip of tea and decided to call Selina into her office for a serious chat first thing in the morning. She picked up a copy of the *People's Friend* and ran her finger down the list of contents, muttering. 'No smoke without fire, indeed!'

Selina didn't dare carry the Dual Balls to school in her teaching bag in case any of the children poked around in it looking for a pencil or a book and came across them. Instead she wore a smart blue blazer with a deep inside pocket in which she carefully placed the Dual Balls before breakfast.

On arriving at school she went straight into her classroom to enjoy five minutes of quiet contemplation before the start of the day. She was keen to avoid Felicity and other members of staff, who on a Monday morning always seemed to try extra hard to be sociable and community spirited. Selina hated all that 'bonding' business. It wasn't her style. She rarely went out for drinks on a Friday night with her colleagues; even so, she always saw them over the weekend because Grunty Fen and the surrounding areas were so sparsely populated that a trip to the shops usually meant a trip to meet everyone from your past, your present and your future that you were keen to avoid.

She sat at her desk and put her hand into her inside pocket to feel the Dual Balls. They felt cold and smooth; highly unerotic. She looked around the classroom and thought, 'I'm so bloody sick of this routine. I'm sick of teaching. I just wish that it was heading somewhere or that something would come of it, but nothing will. I've vegetated, stultified.'

The room smelled clean but of chalk and paper and dust. Her mind turned to Joanna and their conversation at the weekend. This raised a smile. She thought, 'Of course she's right. I don't have any real spirit of adventure,'

The bell rang and the day began.

Felicity had popped into the staff room at the beginning of the day to ask Selina into her office for a chat. Unfortunately Selina didn't materialize so Felicity had to content herself with the idea of meeting her during lunchtime. She checked the wall chart in the staff room to make sure that Selina wasn't on play or dinner duty.

It was a hot day. After several hours Selina became uncomfortable in her blazer and took it off so that she could cool down, hanging it carefully over the top of her chair and keeping a firm eye on it. The morning droned on and eventually it was time for lunch.

All morning she'd had half of her mind on the Dual Balls. A part of her really wanted to fulfil her dare and show Joanna that she was a woman of her word. Another part of her baulked at the idea of using the balls in principle. They were crude and revolting. Secretly she was rather interested to know how they would feel, but only in a silly, inquisitive way that took no account of what was right or for the best.

As the last child left her classroom Selina made a firm decision. She resolved to go and 'try on' the Dual Balls and to try them out for several minutes in the privacy of her classroom at the beginning of her lunch hour. Then, if Joanna asked, she could say in all honesty that she had in fact worn the balls at school in the classroom.

The day was very still and warm. She opened the top button on her shirt to let the air circulate more freely around her throat then strolled to her chair and put on her blue blazer. It felt heavy and made her skin feel sticky. She felt ridiculously tense and strung-out. Luckily the toilets were close to her classroom. She worried about walking with the Dual Balls in; Joanna hadn't cleared up that little chestnut during their coffee and eclairs.

The toilets were empty. She chose one of the two cubicles and locked herself in. She was glad that she had opted to wear a skirt and sheer stockings for easier access.

Inserting the Dual Balls gave her a feeling of youthful mischievousness, as though she were one of the children in school doing something secretive and wrong like puffing on a cigarette.

The Dual Balls felt cold, bulky and stupid. She pulled the string that switched them on. In her hyper-sensitive state the buzzing of the Balls seemed like the violent crashing of cymbals. Although the toilets were empty apart from herself, she coughed loudly with embarrassment to try and hide the initial shock of the sound.

After a few moments of acclimatization Selina rearranged her clothing and stepped out of the cubicle. The balls felt like an inordinately large blue-bottle whizzing around, lost inside her knickers. She took a few experimental steps around by the sinks – where she fastidiously washed her hands – and the Dual Balls stayed firmly in place. She breathed a sigh of relief, then steeled her resolve and nerve as she headed for the door.

Once out in the corridor, surrounded by screaming, sweaty, excitable, break-enjoying children, Selina was able to relax. She felt less furtive and guilty out in the public sphere. She reached her classroom without misadventure; though her variation on a John Wayne swagger may easily have aroused interest in any but a child's mind. She pushed open her classroom door and went in.

Her heart sank. Sitting in the front row of desks, dead centre, was Felicity Barrow.

Smiling broadly, Felicity said, 'Oh good, Selina, I was just about to give up my search and return to the staff room.'

Selina's entire body felt stiff and immobile; only the Dual Balls continued on moving naturally inside her. She tried to negotiate the walk

23

to her desk as freely and casually as possible. To distract Felicity's attention she said, 'Lovely day isn't it?', and pointed towards the window. Felicity turned towards the window and stared out through it at the blue sky. 'Yes, it is lovely.'

She was pleased that Selina was trying to be friendly. Selina took these few seconds' leeway to trot over to her desk and plop herself down on to her hard wooden chair. She noisily cleared her throat so that Felicity's silent contemplation of the day's glory wouldn't emphasize the jubilant buzzing of the Dual Balls. Felicity's gaze returned to Selina's face. 'You're looking very well, Selina, if I may say so, very bright.' Selina smiled. 'I think I'm actually just a bit warm. Perhaps I should take my blazer off.'

She performed this simple action with as much 'involved noise' as possible, concluding with the scraping up of her chair closer to the table. Her hands were shaking slightly, so she took hold of a pencil and tapped out a tiny, slight rhythm with it on the table top.

Felicity watched these adjustments very closely, then said, 'You seem unusually tense today, Selina, any particular reason?'

Selina shrugged. Inside she was boiling with embarrassment and unease but she endeavoured not to let this show. 'I don't know, Felicity. I feel all right really, just a bit, I don't know, a bit frustrated, rudderless . . .'

She didn't really know what she was saying, but after she had said it she felt as though she was talking about sex, as though she was an actress in a dirty blue film. She pinched herself and blinked her eyes, then looked over at Felicity.

Felicity was still smiling at her. 'Maybe you're upset about all that ridiculous gossip that was circulating this weekend?'

Selina was still recovering from the tingling pain of her self-inflicted pinch. The pain seemed rather arousing, and the discomfort too. She asked automatically, 'What gossip?'

Felicity's cheeks reddened slightly. She had hoped that Selina would have been willing to make this conversation easy and unembarrassing. She cleared her throat and to hide her discomfort adjusted the position of her hearing aid in her ear. 'Apparently someone has been spreading a rumour about . . . about your purported use of sexual stimulants during school time.'

Selina's face flushed violently and her jaw went slack, 'I . . . I don't know what to say Felicity. What can I say?'

At that moment in time she felt as though her head was clouding over, clouding up, as though she were in a plane that was going through turbulent clouds. She felt quite willing to admit to everything.

Whatever doubts had clouded Felicity's mind evaporated immediately when she saw the strength of Selina's reaction. She had expected Selina to keep her cool and to utter a cold, cynical, stinging reply. Instead her reply was so unguarded and natural, so loose and out of character, almost intimate, that Felicity could not stop herself from smiling warmly at her. 'Of course I knew it was untrue. I just thought you should be aware of the kind of things that a couple of nasty people are saying.'

Selina couldn't meet Felicity's gaze. She looked down at her desk and tried to call on an inner reserve of strength. Unfortunately this moment of introspection only re-emphasized in her mind the furtive activities of the Dual Balls. She was so tense that her body had become extremely dynamic and excitable. The hard wooden chair wasn't helping matters either. She shuddered, and suddenly her brain felt like sherbet.

The strength of Selina's reaction made Felicity's heart twist in sympathy. She bit her lip for a moment and said nervously, 'Selina, I'm sorry. I didn't think that this would affect you so badly.'

Selina felt as though she was on a roller-coaster ride. She said, 'I feel as though I'm on a roller-coaster ride, Felicity. I don't know what to say.'

She was all gaspy and uncontrolled, her insides churning with a sort of ecstatic violence. In the silence of the room she heard herself breathing heavily. Felicity sat quietly, saying nothing.

After a minute or so Selina began to gasp. She was totally out of control. She threw her head down on the table and shuddered until the shudders turned into enormous, violent, gasping, wracking howls.

Felicity froze. She had never seen such a forthright display of uninhibited emotion before and from, of all people, Selina Mitchell. She felt a terrible sense of guilt that she should have provoked such a display, but also a sense of pride that Selina should have chosen to share this wild moment of release and abandon with her, Felicity. She stood up and went over to Selina's side and placed a gentle hand on her back which she moved up and down, up and down, as though comforting a small child or burping a baby.

Selina felt Felicity's hand massaging her back but felt far too gone to respond coherently. She just said. 'Oh God, oh no, oh my!'

Felicity moved her hand from Selina's back and grasped hold of one of her hands. She said, 'Selina, listen to me. This isn't as bad as it seems to you. It doesn't effect the respect and regard that I have for your teaching abilities. You are one of my best members of staff, in fact you are my very best member of staff.'

Selina heard Felicity's words but their sounds washed over her and made very little sense. She was at the edge of a precipice and in the next moment she was falling, flailing, floating. Her ears tingled as the wind rushed by. She steeled herself for a crash landing, but instead her landing was cushioned by a million feather eiderdowns, each as soft as a poodle's belly. Everything solidified again.

Felicity was pleased to note that after a minute or so her piece of encouragement had appeared to get through to Selina. She was calming down. After a while her breathing returned to normal and she raised her head slightly from the desk. Several seconds later she said quietly, 'Felicity, I feel terrible about this, but it was just out of my control. I feel so embarrassed.'

Felicity clucked her tongue and shook her head, 'Dont be silly, Selina. I know how these things build up. I'm just glad that you were able to let go of all that anguish and to share it with me.'

Selina felt as though she was floating in the Red Sea, lifted above the water by the sodium chloride, the sea like a big marshmallow. She blinked several times and sat up straight. She noticed that Felicity was holding her hand. She smiled at Felicity and said, 'Things have been building up inside me for a long time. I feel so much better now, so buoyant.'

Felicity gave Selina's hand one final squeeze and then let go. She said, 'I know that you are a very controlled person, Selina. I've known you for most of my life and you've never let your emotions rule your head. I think you very much deserved this opportunity to vent your feelings.'

Selina was now fully recovered. She felt stupid but also surprisingly smug. She said. 'I hope you don't think this silly outburst will have any bearing on my discipline and dignity before my classes.' Felicity shook her head. 'I know that I can always rely on you, Selina. I'm certainly quite positive that you are an indispensible asset to this school.'

Inside Fellicity's head an idea was turning. It was as though a light had been switched on or the last piece of a jigsaw puzzle snapped into place. She said, 'Trust me, Selina, you have a great future ahead of you at this school. I'm going to see to that.'

Selina began to smile. She said, 'Felicity, you've been very kind and very understanding. Thank you.'

Felicity shrugged, 'It was nothing. Now clear up your face. Here's a tissue. A bit of spit and polish should do the job.'

Selina took the proffered tissue and applied it to her running mascara.

Felicity walked towards the door. 'This has been an invaluable chat, Selina.'

Selina nodded and pushed her hair behind her ears, 'It has, Felicity, and thanks again.'

Felicity smiled and opened the door. Before she closed it behind her, however, she turned and said somewhat distractedly, 'I'm sorry to rush off like this, Selina, but my hearing aid is playing me up. I think it's dust or the batteries. It's been driving me mad with its buzzing for the last fifteen minutes or so.'

Selina smiled. 'That's all right.'

As the door closed, she stuffed Felicity's tissue into her mouth and bit down hard.

* * * * *

Chafer Legge: A remarkable collection of stories, *Tales From The Fens*, appeared in the 1960s, edited by Enid Porter, Curator of the Cambridgeshire Folk Museum. Many came from the area around Brandon Creek and were told to W H Barrett as a boy c.1900 by Chafer Legge, fen tiger and one of the last great story tellers. The macabre tales of cruelty, witchcraft and drunkenness laced with gallows humour are what survive from a rich oral tradition that once thrived in isolated riverside pubs such as the Ship Inn.

Tricky's Mother And The Widow
CHAFER LEGGE

I don't suppose any of you remember Tricky Porter for it's a good many years ago that, after swallowing several pints of Hall's Ely Ales, he said he wasn't going to waste time walking three miles to cross the river by the bridge, he was going to show he could cross it anywhere he liked. And that was the last that was seen of him till he turned up, a fortnight later, floating on his back as he waited to go through Denver Sluice as soon as the gates were opened.

Tricky had a little more oil in his lamp than most of the Fenmen had and he was always welcome at a wedding or a funeral or any other frolic where a good tale could be told. He never left for home sober, but I will say this, he may have been a poor hand at walking on water but he took a lot of beating when it came to telling a good Fen story. He used to say this was because part of his life had been spent in Cambridge, where he was a B.A. He got that handle to his name when he was very young as his mother gave it to him when she was skivvy at one of the colleges. She hadn't told anybody there would be another freshman in the college soon, so when the doctor came, there wasn't anything for him to do as it was a case of Born before Arrival.

There weren't any relieving officers in those days so his mother was sent away from the college and put in gaol, where she had to feed herself and young Tricky on prison gruel. Having plenty of time on her hands she spent most of it counting up on her fingers to find out who was the one who'd got her where she was and reckoning her chances of getting even with him.

When she was turned out of gaol she found lodgings with a widow woman whose husband had been in the prison till he'd been hanged. The two women got on well together and Tricky was very little trouble. Besides his milk he was allowed a dollop of gin every day and the only time he ever howled was when they left the bottle standing where he could see it. The widow said she was pleased to have the baby and his mother with her as they'd be company for her; she didn't want any money from them as she was well off for the time being. Before her husband had been caught he'd given her a tidy bit of cash; and before he was strung up he'd told her where he had banked the rest of the money he'd found in a farmhouse in the Fen, after he'd put the old farmer's lights out.

After a few months of good grub Tricky's mother soon had the roses back in her cheeks and, with the widow's help, she dressed herself up in silks and satins and spent a good deal of time looking at herself in the shop windows in Sidney Street, where the college lads pushed up against each other trying to catch her eye. But she'd pretend not to be interested in them and would walk off with her nose stuck up in the air. One day the widow said she was running a bit short of money and would have to visit the bank and draw a bit out; if her friend cared to come with her she'd be glad for her to do so, but it was a two-day trip there and back. So early next morning, they were on the bank of the Cam and when a string of barges came along they shouted to the man in the first barge to ask where they were going. The man said they were heading for Lynn and pulled into the bank. The widow asked how much he wanted to let them ride on the barge down to the Lark, but the man, looking them well over, said it would be nothing for the women and a tanner for the baby.

It was a good trip to Ely where the barge pulled in; the man said he had to pick up a bit of cargo there but the barge behind his would take them the rest of the way. An old man was in charge of this boat and he wanted a bob apiece for the women and a tanner for the baby. The widow said that wasn't fair as the other man had brought them from Cambridge for nothing.

'He may have done,' said the man, 'but he's younger than me. Besides, my wife's asleep in the cabin and when she's aboard I daren't carry such good-lookers as you are on a free pass.'

So they paid the fare and when they got to the Lark they were put ashore. The two women walked along the bank till they came to the Dog and Duck on the other side of Prickwillow. Going into the pub they surprised the landlady who wasn't used to seeing such well-dressed women in that part of the Fen, but she told them she could put them up for the night if they didn't mind sleeping on oat-flight mattresses and making their supper off salted herring and baked potatoes.

After supper they put Tricky to bed and told the landlord they were going for a short stroll in the moonlight along the river bank. The landlord said he'd better go with them in case they slipped up in the greasy gault, but his wife said he wasn't to in case he slipped up too. About half a mile from the pub there was a fence and a stile across the bank and when the widow reached it she followed the rails down to the water's edge and, after fumbling about in the reeds, found a line staked to the bank. Pulling in the line she landed a leather bag which she unfastened and, putting in her hand, pulled out a handful of golden sovereigns. She did this four or five times, putting the money into another bag she had brought with her, then, making sure the first bag was fastened properly, she threw it back into the river.

When the two women got back to the pub they found the tap-room full of strapping young Fenmen who were all looking sadly into empty quart pots. They were all very red in the face and sweating like anything because some of them had run a couple of miles across the fen when they'd heard the landlord fire two shots from his duck gun. He always did this to let his regular customers know that a drunken lighter crew were going to make a night of it and there'd be free beer for all. When the widow saw the pitiful look on the men's faces she asked the landlord what they were suffering from. He told her it was a complaint all hard-working men in the fen suffered from – a hell of a thirst and no money. So she threw down a sovereign and said that was for medicine to cure them; and it wasn't long before the medicine was doing those men a lot of good. They made such a noise that they woke young Tricky who, seeing a tallow dip stuck in the neck of an empty gin bottle, roared so loud that his mother had to fetch him down to get him to sleep again.

Suddenly the door flew open and in bounced Crafty Macraw. Now, he had been hidden in the long reeds by the river hoping for a shot at a snipe and he'd seen the two women by the stile and had wondered what they were doing there. So after they'd gone he went down to have a look and it wasn't long before he found the line and the leather bag. He was in a great stew over what he found inside the bag, so he cut it off the line and tied the ramrod of his gun in its place, then threw the line out again. Then he put a few sovereigns in his pocket and looked round for somewhere to hide the rest while he went to have a drink on his luck. He sneaked round the back of the pub where the landlord's straw stack stood, reached up as high as he could and pulled out some of the straw until he'd made a hole that went into the stack as far as his arm would reach. He put the bag in the hole, pushed the straw back so no one would know it had been touched, then rushed into the pub, threw a sovereign on the counter and said:

'That's what I pulled in today on my eel lines; there were so many of them it looked as if the river was running with them. I got rid of the catch in no time, so drink up and share my luck with me.'

As the men had never known Crafty stand anyone a drink, they emptied their mugs as quick as they could.

Well, what with the widow and Crafty trying to out-do each other in standing drinks, there soon came a time when the landlord said he'd have to close as he'd run out of beer. It was a good thing, too, as quite a few of the men's wives had come to fetch their husbands home because they knew what to expect when they heard the duck gun fired twice. It was the first time, though, they'd found they had to get their men away from two well-dressed women as well as the pub.

When everybody had cleared out, the landlady tidied things up a bit then took her two guests upstairs. Crafty hadn't gone as he was so tight he couldn't stand, so the landlord carried him into the cart shed and left him there to sleep it off. Next morning the landlord was up first and he got a proper telling-off from his wife for taking hot gin and water to wake the two women up with. When they came downstairs they asked the landlady if they could stay a day or two longer, but she shook her head and told them their room would be full of lightermen who would be pulling up at the pub that night.

After Tricky's mother and the widow had left, the landlord told his wife he'd have to ride into Ely to see if the brewers could rush a barrel out for the evening trade as there'd be hell to pay if those lightermen found there wasn't any beer. When he went outside to get his horse he saw Crafty walking round the straw stack, pushing his arm in here and pulling bits of straw out there; so he went up to him and asked him what the devil he thought he was doing and if he didn't clear off quick he'd pepper him with buck-shot. Then he went back into the pub and told his wife to keep an eye on that stack while he was away as he was afraid Crafty was trying to set fire to it.

So the landlord set out at a canter and wasn't long in coming up with the two women and he told them that if they were still set on spending a few days in the fen he could take them to his brother who kept the Rising Sun in Burnt Fen. They said they'd be glad of that, so off they went to the Rising Sun. When they got there the landlord told his brother he'd brought him a little gold mine and, seeing his brewery was at Littleport, he'd better cut off there and make sure the dray would be delivering to him every day for a week, as that little widow would buy him out in a week.

Never before or since has so much beer flowed in the fen and on the last night before the widow left, the men said they were going, in return for all she'd done, to make her a free-woman of the Fens. But this was a bit awkward to fix up, they said, because when a man was made a freeman, all they had to do was to stand him on his head and pour a pint of beer down each trouser leg. The widow said an honour like that she'd be proud to accept and she was certainly going to be made a freewoman. Then the men started a fight as to who was going to hold her while this was being done, but the landlady stepped in and said if there was any holding to be done then Tricky's mother would do it. So the widow was stood on her head, her dress was tied round her ankles and a funnel was pushed between her feet and a quart of beer poured into it. Then she was put right ways up and stood in the puddle of beer while all the men shouted: 'Long live the first freewoman of the Fens.'

Before the women left the Rising Sun Tricky's mother asked the landlady if, as the boy was so heavy to carry, she would keep him and look after him if she was paid well. The landlord was asked and he said he'd wanted for thirty-five years for his wife to have a baby so he thought it was a good idea to have one ready-made and with a bit of gold thrown in. Besides, he liked the little chap who showed signs of being a clever lad, small as he was, for show him a gin bottle and he knew what it was. So Tricky was handed over and his mother and the widow went back to Cambridge.

Back at the Dog and Duck Crafty was causing the landlord a lot of trouble for he would go into the pub, drink up a pint as quick as he could, then, before the landlord could stop him, he'd rush out and start pushing his hands into the straw stack. Then, one night, the landlady woke her husband saying she could hear someone shouting for help. Thinking somebody had fallen into the river, he got up and found Crafty, on his knees, with his hands together – just like that picture in Prickwillow Church – and he was muttering away to himself asking for someone to find a leather bag that was somewhere in that blasted stack. So the landlord went back to bed and told his wife it was only Crafty after some worms for his eel hooks, but he'd be much happier in his mind when those bullocks in the yard had trodden all that straw into muck.

Months went by and then the widow and Tricky's mother turned up again in the fen. They called at the Rising Sun to see the baby; the landlady said he was doing fine and had got on a lot since she'd knocked him off gin and put him on beer – there was no getting away from it, Cutlack's Littleport brew suited him a treat. He was crawling about all over the house and, when he wasn't doing that he spent the rest of his time sitting outside the cellar door, sniffing away as if he enjoyed the smell. She hoped they hadn't come to take him away as her husband was fond of the little chap and always let him take the top off a pint of beer before he'd touch it himself. The widow told her not to fret, it was only because she was running out of cash that they'd come, her bank being that way. So they thought they'd just drop in and leave the baby a present of a half-pint pewter mug. They weren't stopping as they wanted to go over to the Dog and Duck and have a drink there before they went back home.

At the Dog and Duck they made a good dinner off herring and bread, washed down with gin and water, then they went down to the stile and pulled in the line. Finding an iron rod instead of the bag, the widow gave a loud scream and fainted. When she came round she picked up the ramrod and went back to the Dog and Duck and asked the landlord if he knew whose it was.

'Why, that must be Crafty's ramrod,' he said. 'He told me he'd lost his when he borrowed mine.'

'Where does he live?' asked the widow. 'I'd like to take it to the old chap and tell him where I found it.'

The landlord said he lived a little over a mile down the drove and that she could see his house from the river bank. So she set off alone, telling Tricky's mother to stay behind as two were company but three weren't. The landlord was glad to have her stay behind because his wife was away for the day, so they had a good time together.

What happened in Crafty's house no one was ever told and, as he lived alone, there was no one to tell. It was two days afterwards that the baker came and looked through the window when he couldn't get an answer to his knocking on the door. He soon cut off and told everybody that he'd seen Crafty sitting in his chair with his throat cut from ear to ear. A lot of questions were put to the people in the fen but no one knew anything and, if they did, they wouldn't have said so. The landlord of the Dog and Duck was the only one who knew who'd been to see Crafty but he didn't say anything as he was scared to death that his wife would find out that Tricky's mother had spent the afternoon with him while she was away over in Isleham Fen for the day. It was a chap on a lighter who spilt the salt and brought bad luck to the widow. He said he'd pulled into the bank at Prickwillow and picked up a couple of well-dressed women; one was getting on a bit but the other was a fine, handsome wench who'd been very good company as far as Cambridge. The old one was very quiet, just as if she'd just lost her husband. He knew where they lived in Cambridge because they'd taken him home and wanted him to stay the night there, but he hadn't dared to do that as the boy who drove the towing horse was his son and he'd have been sure to tell his mother.

Well, the two women were run in and brought to Ely where the widow told the judge that Tricky's mother knew nothing about the murder. The landlord from the Dog and Duck, too, swore on the Book that when the widow went down into the fen, Tricky's mother had spent all the time with him. Even his wife spoke up for her, saying that bad a hussy as she might be, it wasn't right she should hang for something she never did. She could prove it, too, and she showed the court a garter she'd found in her bedroom on the day after she'd been down to Isleham Fen. The judge asked Tricky's mother if she could prove the garter was hers, so she pulled up her skirt and showed the other garter on one leg, while the other was tied with a piece of tape. So she was let off. The judge then told the widow she'd have to go and be hung and he said she'd be showing her garters, too, like her friend here, before she died. But she went to the scaffold with her stockings down, just to show that judge was a liar.

Tricky's mother took over the widow's house and, with the money she had left, she bought new curtains for the windows and furnished the rooms in style. An orphan girl came to live with her and Tricky's mother decked her out in starched collars and aprons and taught her what to say when anyone knocked at the door. After a fortnight of walking up and down King's Parade, Tricky's mother got to know so many of the college lads that soon she was able to stay at home in state like a real lady. She did so well that soon she had her own horse and cart and at Midsummer and Christmas she'd spend a few weeks at the Rising Sun with young Tricky, who was growing so fast that the landlord would have been out of pocket if his mother hadn't dropped a few sovereigns in his hand after her visits, because the little chap wouldn't touch a drop of beer unless it was a full pint pot. He was a little bit bandy-legged and he had the habit of walking with his head down and his hands behind his back; he had a mole, too, on his neck, as big as a florin.

One morning Tricky's mother woke up and remembered who it was that he looked like so, when he was eight years old, she took him back with her to Cambridge for a holiday. She wasn't long in telling the college chaps who the little fellow's father was – a well-known gent at the college where she'd been in service before he was born – and they all agreed that Tricky was a real chip off the old block. Some of the lads had a gown and cap made for him and soon the boy was walking about the town in them, a pint mug in one hand, the other behind his back and his head down as if he was looking for something. People often stopped him and asked if they could take a closer look at the mole on his neck, just for luck, and they'd put bits of silver in his mug so that, soon, Tricky was able to go round the back of a pub and buy his own beer. At last the man he so looked like came round to see his mother and asked how much she wanted to clear out of Cambridge. What he offered her was so good that she took the money, sold her furniture, put her horse in the cart and, with Tricky sitting beside her, drove off down to Burnt Fen.

They hadn't been there, at the Rising Sun, for many days when the landlord of the Dog and Duck asked her if she'd go and be his house-keeper as his wife had left him soon after the widow was hung, and he was sick of being on his own. She made up her mind to go and settled down quite happy, and before long some of the Cambridge lads were sailing down the river, staying at the pub for the night and sailing back next day, so these little breaks stopped her from feeling lonely in that rather quiet part of the fen.

As Tricky grew up, the bigger he got and the thirstier he always was, so that his foster father found out that instead of the pub keeping him he had to go out to work to keep the pub going. Then, one day, he found the till empty and Tricky brim full of beer, so he told him to clear out before he lost his temper. Tricky went over to the Dog and Duck and told the landlord he was coming to live there and would he mind if he called him Father? It was a funny thing, but those two got on really well together. Tricky always put it down to Hall's Ely Ales having more body in them than Cutlack's Littleport brew, but be that as it may, he was soon showing he wasn't afraid of work and he became a good, all-round chap on the land.

A few years afterwards he was harrowing a field one day, when he saw a leather bag caught in the tines of the harrow. Unhooking it he found it was half-full of sovereigns. Well, although he was a boozer he was honest, so he took it to the landlord who looked at it and said:

'Why, that's what Crafty must have put in the straw stack, years ago; it must have gone with the straw into the bullock yard and been carted out into the field with the muck. Well, two men have died for it and a woman's swung, so you and your mother and my brother and I had better share it out amongst ourselves.'

And they did, too. With his share Tricky bought a gang of lighters and made a good living carrying gault from the Rosswell Pits at Ely to build up the river banks. But as time went on the lighters went on, too, so Tricky turned them into cash and drank the lot. But, drunk or sober, he could always tell a good tale, but I don't know that his were any better than the one I've just told you.

* * * * *

Sylvia Townsend Warner (1893–1978): Soon after the publication of her first novel *Lolly Willowes* (1926), Warner stayed with the Bloomsbury writer David Garnett at Hilton Hall on the edge of the Cambridgeshire Fens. She went on to become a distinguished novelist, poet and prolific writer of short stories – nearly 150 throughout her life for the *New Yorker* – most of which have since been re-published in numerous collections. 'Poison', one of her earliest, appeared only in *Nine O'clock Stories* (1934) and may have been prompted by her visits to Hilton Hall or by holidays in Norfolk with her partner Valentine Ackland. 'A Stranger With A Bag' (p.187) is the title story of her 1966 collection.

Poison

SYLVIA TOWNSEND WARNER

The market was over, the town had grown so silent that one could hear very plainly the rain falling on the pavement as it had fallen all day. On the steamy windows the tracks of dribbling moisture left rivulets of crystal, and when the apprentice came in from putting up the shutters his spectacles clouded and the change of atmosphere set him yawning; for inside the shop it was extremely cosy, and the neatness, prettiness, and polish of the wares gave an impression of ladylike-ness – as though it were a parlour and not a chemist's shop.

Mr. Hawley looked up from the day-book and remarked that since the beginning of the year there had not been so great a sale of the cough-cure. As he spoke he coughed; he too had had influenza, though he had not taken to his bed for it, doctoring his temperature with quinine and salicylate. His voice was listless, even his cough had little energy. He had taken a great deal of quinine and it had lowered his vitality. The boy, responding, said that Mr. Hawley should go off to bed with something hot. It had been a day to tax any one, with so many people coming in and leaving the door open for the cold air to follow them. *Dogsnose*, he said; and fearing lest the advice should sound unprofessional he allowed the word to come out with blustering vehemence. For he was quite a young boy, his voice was still unruly to him.

As he spoke, the door was pushed open and a stranger entered. At least it was no one known to Mr. Hawley, though at the first glance it seemed to him that the face was familiar, that he had seen it, earlier in the day, flattened against the window, staring in past the bottles and the sponges and the display cards.

It was a striking face, striking and unpleasant – round as a platter, further extended by large out-standing ears, and bedizened (for really bedizened was the word) with a pair of pale shallow eyes. Bleached and

37

brilliant, they were like the eyes of a famished cat. The whole aspect of that face conveyed desperate hunger, though not the sort of hunger which can be appeased by a good square meal, for the facial bones were well-covered, there was plenty of flesh there. It was a hunger of the blood, more likely, some variety of chlorosis. Even now, in the midst of an influenza epidemic, to see a face so bloodless made Mr. Hawley's own blood run cold.

Walking up to the counter, leaning his elbow on the curved glass of the show-case, the stranger demanded something for a cold; something strong, a pick-me-up, he said, that he could toss off then and there. And while Mr. Hawley compounded the dose, choosing from this bottle and that, he remained leaning against the counter, his bright eyes flicking over the shelves, as though in search of some aspect of clear glass that could match their brilliancy.

The boy remained also, standing about as though it seemed to him that he might be needed. He was a good boy, a careful boy; Mr. Hawley dismissed him almost affectionately, for he had been touched by that recommendation of dogsnose, though he, an experienced chemist, could do better than that. What he now handed across the counter was stronger than any dogsnose. The man drank it off without comment, and asked for another.

To take at bedtime, Mr. Hawley suggested; but the man said he would take it now. It would not, he averred, be too strong for him. Nothing could be too strong for such a cold as his.

On the empty pavements the raindrops pattered like thin hurrying footsteps. Nodding towards the bottles of Special Influenza Mixture which stood prominently arranged on the counter the man said he supposed there was a brisk demand for that at this time of year. An unhealthy season, he added; and the chemist agreed.

'Not that that does you much harm, I suppose?'

'Well, no, sir. Though this year I've not been much of an advertisement for my own goods, for I've had a touch of the 'flu myself.'

The man laughed, showing his teeth. They were false teeth, and the coral red of his plate was in shocking contrast to his bloodless face and lips. Even in a healthy season, he went on to say, he would suppose this town to be sickly enough, mouldering away in the midst of the fens. In all his life he had never struck such a dead-alive place, a town with no life in it, with no possible future before it.

Mr. Hawley asked him if he travelled much. To hear the town thus abused distressed him: though indeed the words were true enough, for every year trade was dwindling and now the last factory was closing down.

The man did not trouble to answer. Boredom, not interest, it seemed, moved his glance hither and thither about the shop. He shivered, and pulled up his coat-collar, but made no move to go. When he spoke again it was to speak about chemists. He spoke ruminatingly, dispassionately, not at all as though he were addressing one who was a chemist himself. It must be a dreary life, he opined: the same old women with their interminable cancers and asthmas returning for their mixtures, or children wanting a pennyworth of liquorice. One might touch it up with face-powder and fancy soap for the young women, but that was only a top-dressing, and in a year or two the same young women would draggle in for teething powders and ringworm ointment. No, no, he said, coming suddenly out of his reverie, the only romance, the only redeeming excitement in a chemist's business was the traffic in poisons. That was something like. For one would have a queer, a fascinating sense of power, remembering that in a single bottle one had the wherewithal to send all one's neighbours to the churchyard. And a slip of the hand might do it, a moment's wavering of the memory.

It was not so easy as that, the chemist said. There were regulations, precautions imposed by law.

Yes, said the man, there would be. Nothing in life kept its sparkle of excitement for long. Regulations put on the damper, or if they did not, habit soon got the upper hand and made one thing as tame as another. And then still glancing over the shop with that bright blank gaze, he began to question Mr. Hawley about the regulations which rendered even possession of poisons a dull business, a mere routine.

There were three methods, the chemist explained. Poisons and dangerous drugs might be kept in a special cupboard, or secured on the shelves by a Tantalus-like device, making it impossible to take them down without a particular manoeuvre, as a minumum precaution they must be kept in bottles of a peculiar colour and surface recognisable to sight and touch.

And how did Mr. Hawley keep his, the stranger asked. 'In a cupboard?'
'In a cupboard.'
'Locked, of course?'
'Locked,' said Mr. Hawley, concealing a yawn of weariness. It was a dull enough conversation, to him at any rate; nor did the stranger seem to find

much interest in it either, asking questions only for the sake of asking them.

And yet, the stranger said, turning the emptied glass in his hands, poison was poison, when all was said and done. A chemist, a chemist with some incurable disease, or in trouble over money, or even tired, at last, of his dreary life and despairing of the future, might unlock that cupboard and help himself. He had his own death in his hands, no one could rob him of that.

'I have never heard,' said Mr. Hawley, speaking hurriedly, speaking emphatically, 'of a chemist who poisoned himself.'

'They know better, perhaps,' said the man. 'They've read up the symptoms.'

Putting down the glass he paid for his drinks, stared round once more, nodded casually, and went out. Mr. Hawley sat down with a groan of fatigue. This conversation, coming at the end of a hard day, had made him feel singularly dispirited; and it was a long while before he could rouse himself sufficiently to shut up the shop and retire to his solitary rooms above it.

In the morning the boy enquired how long Monsol had stayed, nodding towards the sneezing muffin-faced misery of the advertisement. It was to be hoped, he continued, that Monsol would not come in again, for a more unpleasant customer he had never set eyes on. Mr. Hawley said mildly that when the boy had seen as many customers as he had, one would seem much like another. Even as he spoke he remembered that the man overnight had implied as much; and he heard again that whining voice dwelling on the peculiar dreariness of being a chemist. He was glad to be interrupted by the voice of the boy, even though it spoke of the poor sale they had had for the new bath-cubes. In an unhealthy season, Mr. Hawley said, the demand for toilet luxuries alway lessened. The medicines, though, said the boy cheerfully, more than made up for that.

Mr. Hawley had a feeling that the man would come again. He did so, arriving at the same hour and asking, as before, for a pick-me-up. He left the door open, and the cold misty air, blowing in, roused up Mr. Hawley's neuralgia. Since it was obvious that the man had again come to linger, Mr. Hawley mentioned the neuralgia as a polite pretext for shutting the door. Strychnine, said the man was what he needed for that; nothing else on those shelves, over which his glance moved so disdainfully, would be strong enough. And as though released into his obsession he began to talk once more of poisons.

Poison

Poisons, sickness, death . . . these seemed to be the only things he cared to speak about, and yet he seemed with every word to flout the matter of his discourse, talking always with detachment and petulance, as though he were scornfully humouring the preoccupations of the man on the other side of the counter, as though poisons and sickness and death were Mr. Hawley's concerns only and nothing to him. It occurred to the chemist that a man so horribly pale, so ravaged by some strange fever of the wasting blood, should speak more seriously of sickness and death. But it was jauntily, confidently, that the man took his leave, saying that Mr. Hawley might expect to see him on the morrow.

'For I have taken a fancy to you,' he added. And as though to prove it he looked back through the glass door with an affable nod. Mr. Hawley remembered his impression of a face pressed to the window on market day. He had thought then that it might be imagination, for one often imagines things after influenza. But it was not.

He wished the stranger's fancy had pitched elsewhere, for he could not but dislike the man extremely; and the thought came to him that he might make his neuralgia a reason for spending the evening in the back shop and leaving the boy in charge of the counter. But that would not do. The boy was young, morbid conversation about poisons would do him no good; though an experienced chemist is well-salted to that aspect of his trade, young minds are easily infected with dangerous imaginings.

This time the stranger came to the point at once, asking the chemist what poisons he had sold that day; and with his customary scornfulness did not wait for an answer, going on to suppose that, in a one-horse town like this, ratsbane would be all that was demanded. A German rat-poison, he said, was the stuff; and he described how, when the lid was taken off, the paste smoked with a choking visible fume, so savagely ample was the amount of phosphorus. You spread it, he said, on bread and butter; and the rats who tasted it were instantly tormented with so burning a thirst that they would gnaw through leaden pipes to get at the water. Water – even a drop of water – would intensify their agony, hasten their death-throes. That was the cunning of it, he said; and his shallow colourless eyes grew rounder and rounder, and his breath, playing on Mr. Hawley's cheek, as he leaned so excitedly across the counter, seemed like the fumes, choking and visible, that wreathed up from the opened tin of rat-poison.

On leaving he repeated that he had taken a fancy to Mr. Hawley; and all that night and all the next day the chemist waited in heavy apprehension for him to come again.

He did not come.

Four days went by, and there was no sign of the stranger. Yet Mr. Hawley was little the better for it. It was as though the stranger's ghost walked in instead, for now, every evening at closing time, Mr. Hawley felt the oncoming of a fit of the horrors. Like a thick fog, gloom and weariness would overtake him, so that he could scarcely keep his eyes open while he made up the day-book and shut the shop. Too tired for supper, he would go to bed and fall into a leaden sleep. Out of this sleep he would awaken with the conviction of having made some fatal mistake in dispensing. At some time or other during the day, it seemed to him, he had put poison into a medicine. Sometimes he had done it by mistake, at other times, deliberately, not from any malice but with a malign indifference, as though a devil had possessed him and made him its conscious besotted tool. These were delusions, he knew, nothing but delusions. The attack of influenza had left him low, his persistent neuralgia was proof enough of that; horrors and bad dreams were only further signs of debility. So he would reason with himself in the midst of the dark night. But reasonings were of no avail; like the bursting of some subterranean flood the horror would rush over him again, wave after wave, and overwhelm him.

One night, during a moment when reason was uppermost, he got up and went down to the shop and opened the prescription book. There were the prescriptions he had made up during the day, and into no one of them did a poison enter. Even while he stood at the page the horror came back on him looking, a contemptuous voice saying that the prescription book was no register of his doings, for he would not be such a fool as to enter the details of the death poured into the bottle.

Out of these nights he would emerge broken and trembling, painfully sleepy and clumsy and forgetful. He would make mistakes in the change or hand customers the wrong article. His shaking hands knocked over the bottles on the counter or demolished the neat pyramids of soap and pill-boxes. He could no longer do up a parcel properly, the sealing-wax straggled over the white paper like smears of blood. He slopped the dispensing, though the drugs stood in their ordered positions on the shelves he could not find them. And all the while his neuralgia went nagging on. Strychnine, said a remembered voice, was what he needed for that; and on Sunday, in the closed and dusky shop, he set about compounding himself a strong tonic. But no sooner had he unlocked the poison cupboard and put forth his hand among the blue-ribbed bottles, recognisable to sight and touch, than such a horror overtook him that he slammed-to the door and fled. That night, awakening, he remembered that he had not stayed to lock the cupboard; but he dared not stir out of his bed, he must lie there, sick and trembling and in a cold sweat, till the harsh morning light brought some sort of astringent to his miserable mind.

Market day came round again, just such a day as the last, wet, cold, and foggy. He will come to-day, thought Mr. Hawley. As the clock jolted to the hour, and the shop emptied, and he could hear again the shutters being put up and the rain-drops tapping on the pavement he was ready to pray that the stranger might indeed come. Anxiously, snappishly, he bade the boy go home, and the boy went gladly enough, for he had no wish to prolong working-hours that had lately become so unpleasant.

Mr. Hawley waited. It was the hour when his horrors were due to begin. They came, but the stranger did not. To-night the horrors took a definite form. Mr. Hawley began to think of diseases of the brain. The ills of the flesh which his profession had made him so well acquainted with were bad enough, but madness was worse. There were no remedies, no palliatives, in his shop for that. Neurasthenia, he cried, it's only neurasthenia! There were dozens of patent medicines for neurasthenia; and he took up one of them and read the word, *phosphorus*.

When at last the stranger came quietly into the shop Mr. Hawley was standing before the opened poison cupboard.

'So you are having a look at it,' said the stranger.

The chemist shut the cupboard at his words, and locked it. Now, at the request for the usual pick-me-up, he laid the key on the counter, and turned in a flurry to find the various bottles he needed. The sal volatile . . . he could not find the sal volatile . . . the boy must have replaced it on the wrong shelf. While he was staring at the drug-jars the stranger picked up the poison cupboard key and dropped it into his pocket.

'Make it strong,' he said.

He certainly needed it strong. To-night he seemed more bloodless, more famishing, than ever before, his eyes, so round and pale and brilliant, were like pieces of glass set in a mask of white rubber.

He tossed off the pick-me-up, paid for it, and went away.

Mr. Hawley scarcely noticed his departure. Dragging his feet, only half conscious of the routine he performed, he shut and barred the door, put out the lights, and took himself to bed. With his hand on the switch he stood staring at the smooth mound of his pillow as if he had never seen a pillow before, or would never see one again. Bed had been a kind place, once, and he a dutiful contented man.

When he awoke, the light was still on, and this made the room look like a sickroom. But he had no mind for speculation now. Out of that pillow, so smoothly mounded, had sprung a new nightmare. He had dreamed that he had poisoned himself, that the poison was at this minute working in him, and that that was why he felt, as the rats did, such intolerable thirst. 'But now I am mad,' he said to himself, smoothly and reasonably. He had been already mad when he opened the cupboard to look in. Like the rats, frantic for the water which must complete their undoing, he, already poisoned in mind, must seek out the poison which should finish off his body. Then the stranger had come in, thwarting him. But now he was alone, there was nothing to stay him; and he got out of bed, put on slippers and a dressing-gown, and went downstairs.

Seeing the familiar shop, so cosy, so tidy and lady-like and parlour-like, he was seized with a piercing regret that he must leave it, end himself horribly, all for no reason. Fear leaped up in him, then common sense, awakening, overmastered fear. What he must do, what as a reasonable chemist suffering from neurasthenia consequent upon influenza, he must do, was to look this obsession in the face until it swayed him no longer. Yes, calmly and deliberately, he would open the poison cupboard, confront those bottled terrors, read their labels, handle them maybe; and then, having seen them for what they were, a dangerous but essential part of his stock-in-trade, familiar but disciplined perils, he would shut them away and go back to bed, his own man once more. The key was on the counter. He remembered leaving it there, and that showed the state he had allowed himself to get into; for such neglect was criminally careless.

The key was not on the counter.

He would not be foiled like that, death should not escape him so easily! Not for an accident of a key would he put off his desire, spend such another day of torment, go mad and be carried to an asylum. There were his dear poisons, his comforters, his dreadful and dear ones, waiting quiet as pigeons in a pigeon-cote. With his fist he smashed the cupboard door, chose, swiftly and unerringly, the bottle he wanted, poured out, deft with long habit, the strong, the sure dose into the measuring glass, and drank it off.

At the inquest the stranger was the chief witness. He told how he had gone to the chemist with a bad cold, how he had fallen into conversation with

44

him, how the chemist had spoken of the poisons in his charge. On subsequent visits Mr. Hawley had spoken after the same fashion, so markedly, so boastingly, that the stranger had surmised the existence of something like an obsession. He told, too, how, on his last visit, he had found the chemist standing before the opened cupboard, and how, on a sudden impulse, he had picked up the key and gone with it and his suspicions to the police station. A stranger to the town, he had been some little while finding his way thither; and in that interval the chemist was a dead man.

He was highly commended by the coroner for his humane and prudent behaviour.

The apprentice, who was also called as a witness, could not take his eyes from the stranger. All his pallor, all his famished looks were gone. His complexion was clear and ruddy, his voice was ringing, he seemed the picture of a well-nourished man. It was as though poor Mr. Hawley's death, thought the boy, had been the very pick-me-up his customer had needed, as though he had replenished himself with the dead man's blood; and his thoughts trudged between the dead man and the survivor, but could find no clue, no explanation.

On the following day the stranger left the town.

* * * * *

How They Buried Grandfather
CHAFER LEGGE

The tale I'm going to tell you goes back a long way and so does my family. I'm just over ninety, which means I was born in 1810; my grandfather was ninety-five when he died and before he did that he lived with us. I was a lad of eighteen when he died and I remember that he'd made Father promise that, come Hell or high water, he'd bury him in the corner of the garden because he'd be scared out of his wits if he knew the parson was going to stand over him and say what he liked about him when he wasn't able to answer back.

No one knew exactly when the old chap died; it was only after a piece of looking glass had been laid over his mouth all night and Mother had taken it away in the morning, and found no steam on it, that we knew that the gun which Grandfather had always promised me was now mine. Father went off to ask Mucky Porter, who made the coffins, to come and run his rule over Grandfather, while I was told to cut open an old sack and nail it over the window so as to make the room dark; that was a custom we had in the fen then, because most of the neighbours would want to bring their children along. You see, it was the proper thing in those days for the little ones to see as many dead folk as possible. The children were always a bit on the hungry side, and after being made to kiss the corpse for luck they'd be so scared that they wouldn't want any grub for a couple of days, which was a big saving where there was a large family and not much money coming in. And the women, too, wanted to hold a dead man's hand for a couple of minutes as this meant they wouldn't have another little one for a couple of years, which was another big saving when times were hard.

Well, Father didn't get back till it was dark, and he brought Mucky along with him and the coffin too. When he'd told Mucky what he wanted him for, Mucky had said it wasn't worth his while to go all that way just to measure Grandfather, so he'd made Father lie down on his bench while he ran his rule over him. Then he'd picked out some elm boards with a lot of knot holes in them and said that if he used them it would come a lot cheaper. So he'd marked the wood out there and then and told Father that if he sawed along the chalked lines for him he'd knock a bit off the price. So Father had set to and, with both of them on the job, the coffin was finished before the sun went down; if it hadn't been it would have had to wait till morning, and I'll tell you why.

It was reckoned that the tapping of a hammer on a coffin after dark brought the worst of bad luck because it disturbed the rest of those who'd been buried in the fen years ago. Folks round here tell how Mucky's father was working, once, late at night because he had a coffin to finish off in a hurry. Suddenly a blast of cold wind blew out his rushlight and his hammer was knocked out of his hand and he found himself pinned by a pair of hairy hands against his bench. After that night he was never able to use his hands again and for the rest of his life his grub had to be put into his mouth and he had to suck up his beer through a reed.

When Father got back he explained to Mother why he'd been so long; he'd have been back sooner, he said, if Mucky hadn't insisted on stopping at the Fleece and Plough because he knew the landlord's mother was in a bad way and he thought, if he showed a sample of his work he might get a job there when the time came. So he and Father had taken the coffin into the tap-room and put it on the floor, and then Spitter Osler, who was always a bit of a devil, had got into it just to see what it was like. Then Mucky had clapped the lid on and everyone who could get on to the lid had sat on it. Spitter was nearly gone when they lifted the lid to see how he was getting on, but he was all right again after a couple of pints, though he said the coffin would have been his for good if it hadn't had so many knot holes in it which had let through some air.

It was quite a job getting that coffin into our house, and when it was in there was nowhere to put it except on the table. The old handywoman stood on one side while Father lifted Grandfather into the coffin, and then it was found that it was too big, so I was told to get some hay which the handywoman stuffed into the sides. Then she took the form which was lying ready on the mantel shelf and put it on Grandfather's forehead. That form was called sin money and it was reckoned to show the Devil that it was no good coming as Grandfather's sins had been paid for. When all that was done, Father settled up with Mucky who only charged five shillings for the wood and half a crown for his time; he threw in the nails and the putty in return for Father's help.

Next morning Father went up to the parson's house, but the sexton told him that the parson was away in Cambridge and he didn't know when he'd be back, but before he went he'd told him that he'd arranged for the Lent services. The sexton told Father that he'd get the grave ready but said, if parson wasn't going to be home for a time, hadn't he better go over to the next village and get the parson there. Father said that as Grandfather had waited ninety-five years to die he wouldn't mind waiting another week or so.

You might like to know that, at that time, Father was mill-man at the big drainage mill near our house; he had three more mills in the fen to look after but, as they were small ones, it didn't mean much work. It was the big one, the one which threw the water into the river, that took up most of his time. She was a real powerful mill, the biggest, folks said, in the Fens, and when she was chopping off the wind with her sails in full swing, she shifted a lot of water in no time. There was a shed next to this mill full of lengths of timber which had been found drifting down the river or the main drain, and Father wasn't long in picking out some of these boards and in knocking up a coffin which was quite as good as the one Grandfather was already lying in.

While he was doing this, Mother was finding that Grandfather and his coffin were taking up too much room on the table, so Father put him underneath, which gave us more room to shift our elbows, but in a day or two we all knew it was time to put the lid on. So Father sent me round to Mucky who said he couldn't come as his chilblains were so bad; but he gave me a handful of nails to take back with me. The old handywoman came, too, and she picked up the sin money from Grandfather's forehead and clattered off to the young woman whose turn it was to have it because that form, you see, if the woman put it under her pillow, was reckoned to be powerful enough to stop her having any more children. But it never stayed long where she put it because, with beer at a shilling a gallon, her husband soon found the money and made good use of it, for a publican always gave nine pints to a gallon if he knew he was being paid with a sin florin. And the publican was very glad to have the coin because he knew that if it was put into a pot of beer and then stirred round with a black hen's wing feather, then that beer would calm down a fighting-mad customer in no time. I'm just telling you this to show you what fen folk believed in when Queen Victoria came to the throne; but now I'll get back to Grandfather.

Father and I dug a hole in a corner of the garden; we went down into the clay till the water seeped in faster than we could scoop it out, then we clambered out of the hole and waited till the water was about three feet deep. We went back into the house, moved Grandfather from Mucky's coffin into the one that Father had made, and nailed it down. Then Father called his old bitch in, lit a lantern and fastened it to her collar and then, with her in front and us two carrying the coffin behind, we went out into the garden and lowered Grandfather gently into the hole and watched until the water had covered the coffin. Then Father said:

'There you are, old 'un, I've done what I promised. You were never happy except when you were standing in water or sitting on it in a boat; now you're lying in it.'

We filled in the hole and, with the clay that was to spare, we filled the coffin which Mucky had made, nailed the lid on it and it was ready. But one thing we hadn't bargained for was the water in the clay which seeped through the knot holes in the bottom. Luckily Father was up first thing next morning and got the floor cleaned up before Mother came down; she was right pleased to see he'd swilled the floor bricks down, a thing he'd never done before.

Over a week had gone by when the sexton came along and said he was getting worried as the parson wouldn't be back for another three days. Father told him not to fret, everything was quite all right. When the parson did come home he came round to our house in a flaming temper and said the burial must take place next morning. Father said next day was Friday and surely Parson had lived long enough in the Fens to know that no one started on a long journey on that day of the week if he could help it. Parson told him that it was *his* churchyard and *he* always fixed the day and the time when people were put into it; but at last things were settled and Saturday was agreed on.

The bearers turned up at the time fixed and a few of the very old fenmen came along too, hoping to be picked for the job of carrying the trestles which the coffin would lie on while the bearers stopped for a rest and a drink; there was a nine gallon cask of beer, ready tapped, which was going to be pushed along in a wheel barrow to help everyone along on the two-mile walk to the church. Six strong men lifted the coffin on to their shoulders and started off, but they hadn't gone very far when they shouted for the trestles, saying they'd never had such a load; even old Boiler Bell, who'd weighed twenty-two stone, hadn't been so heavy. After a lot of arguing a chap went off to borrow Ratty Porter's donkey and cart, and then one of the trestle-carriers led the donkey which knew, to a step, where to stop for a rest as it had made the same journey dozens of times before. So, by easy stages, we all got to the churchyard gate where Parson was waiting, but as soon as the coffin was lifted out of the cart he turned his back on it and put his handkerchief over his nose saying that that coffin wasn't going to come into the church; when Grandfather was alive he hadn't been to church and he wasn't coming now.

'That's true enough,' Father whispered to me; so we all went over to where the grave had been dug, the coffin was lowered, Parson read out of his book and soon it was all over.

Next winter Father dug a may thorn out of the hedge and planted it over the spot where Grandfather had been put. The old cottage where I was born and brought up has been pulled down these last fifty years and the garden has gone too, most of it was taken in when the road was made. And what you call the 'Beggars' Bush' is that old thorn tree which Father planted; it's grown as big as a haystack now, and if you look under it most nights of the year you'll be sure to find a tramp or two there, fast asleep. Every one of them swears that there's no cosier place in the fen and they all say that, when their days are over, they'd like nothing better than a last resting place under that old bush, it's so quiet and peaceful; and so it ought to be.

* * * * *

Edna O'Brien: Irish novelist and short story writer brought up in County Clare. Much of her work, admired for its frank portrayal of female sexuality, is coloured by the lore and landscape of her youth. Having lived for many years in London, 'In the Hours of Darkness', from *Mrs Reinhardt and Other Stories* (1978), is a reminder that O'Brien's fiction is by no means restricted to her native country for either its inspiration or its sense of place. Her most recent novel, *The Light of Evening,* appeared in 2006.

In The Hours Of Darkness
EDNA O'BRIEN

On a stretch of road from London and not yet in sight of Cambridge, Lena suddenly remarked that it was like Australia. There was more than one reason for this: the physical loneliness was exactly like that she had experienced in the countryside above Sydney one warm intoxicating Saturday and the road itself, devoid of houses or tillage, suggested a depopulated land. Also the high grass on either side was tawny, bleached no doubt by the long phenomenal English summer. The bridges too that flanked the motorways were ugly and graceless and reminded her of that other time.

Her son Iain said that any minute they would see the spires of Cambridge and already her mind ran on to her first view of the old historic town, the various university complexes, the stout walls, the stained-glass windows and the overall atmosphere of studiousness. She was intrigued. She envisaged going into the hotel bedroom and drawing curtains – they would be dark red and once drawn she would click on a light and sit in an armchair to read some of Jane Austen in order to re-discover through that woman reserve and perseverance.

Her youngest son was going up to Cambridge and she was facing the predicament she had read about in novels – that of a divorced woman, bereft of her children, having to grow old without these beloved props, having in some indescribable way to take the first steps into loneliness as if she were a toddler again.

Two signposts read the same mileage for Cambridge even though they were miles apart and she said that was typical, then instantly decided that she was becoming a shrew. Soon maybe she would be questioning bills, talking to herself and finding fault with any services that were to be done to her house. To save face she remarked on the beauty of a fairly ordinary little village in which she noticed a post office, an ale house, whimsy-looking cottages and an antique shop.

The hotel at Cambridge was not what she had imagined. The entrance adjoined the car park and in the too huge lobby there were arrows pointing to several bars. Then hammering to testify that construction work was in progress. Would it stop at night? She was obsessed with noise and could, she believed, be wakened by an air bubble in her water pipes at night. She followed the porter and was dismayed to find that he lost his way. It was a big ramshackle place with various flights of stairs leading to different quarters. Her bed-room was on the first floor and just outside was a child's cot and a single mattress standing on its end. The room was everything she dreaded – a single bed with a stained orange coverlet, matching curtains, plastic lampshade, wardrobe with three empty metal hangers that moved slightly as if propelled by some shiver. The one summoning bell brought no response – no buxom girl, no doddery old man, no housekeeper with motherly smile came in answer to the ringing of the green oblong button. In fact there was no way of telling if it was connected, or if in fact a bell had rung somewhere in the bowels of that place and was being ignored with a shrug. 'Bad place to die', she thought, and as fervently as she had longed for the surprise and repose of that little room, she now longed to be out of it and safely at home.

She wanted tea. Her stockings were wet. She and Iain had had to walk the last bit of the journey carrying baskets, a record player, a drawing-board and loose bits of lighting flex. He had parked the car outside the town because it was against university rules to own one. On their walk it had begun to drizzle and by now it was raining heavily. Lifting the curtain she looked at the spatters as they crawled down the window-pane and lodged on the frame beneath. The view was of a football field empty except for its goal posts. She would make the best of it.

In the lobby the guests were being served with tea and everything about them suggested not an academic life but a life of commerce. She had to step over bags bursting with shopping, and at first glance every mouth seemed to be allied to a piece of oily chocolate cake. She sat at one empty table waiting for service, and in her restlessness began to eat the bits of damp ribbony lettuce that served as decoration on the plate of sandwiches that the previous occupant had devoured. The waiter strolled across and caught her in this nonsensical theft. She asked him to bring tea quickly as she was dining at seven. He spurned her to her face, he also spurned the entire human race and did both these offices in broken English.

Dinner was in one of the most esteemed of the colleges and they foregathered in a small overheated sitting-room, that was full of furniture and pieces of china. Her host, a professor, had invited a younger professor and two freshmen. They sat and awkwardly sorted each other out, the young men laughing lightly at everything and constantly interjecting their remarks with bits of French as they bantered with each other about their sleeping habits and their taste for sherry or classical music. It was stiff. Her son should have had a different introduction, something much less formal, a bit of gaiety. The conversation centred for a long time on a professor who had the nickname of a woman and who received students in his long johns and thought nothing of it. Incongruously he was described as a hermit even though he seemed to be receiving students most mornings in his cluttered room. It was stifling hot. To calm herself, Lena thought of the beautiful mist like fine gauze sparkling on the courtyard outside, and above it a sky perfectly pictorial with its new moon and its thrilling stars.

They went down a short flight of stairs and then climbed some other steps to their early dinner. The host had done everything to make it perfect – smoked salmon, grouse, chantilly, different wines for each course and all this printed alongside each person's nameplace. The old servant was so nervous that he trembled as he stood over her and kept debating with his long hands whether to proffer the entrée dish or the gravy jug. It was touch and go. His master told him for God's sake to put the jug down. A movement that caused his neck to tremble like that of a half-dead cockerel's. Yes, 'It was so' that students were sent down but they had to be awfully bad or else awfully unlucky and of course it was an awfully amusing thing. 'I am in a modern English play,' she thought, the kind of play that portrayed an intelligent man or woman going to seed and making stoical jokes about it. Academic life was not for her. She would rather be a barbarian. She sucked on the word as if it were sherbet. Barbarian.

The grouse was impossible to tackle. Everyone talked too much and tried too eagerly and this all-round determination to be considerate caused them instead to be distracted and noisy. Little bright jets of blood shot up as knives vainly attacked the game. To conceal his embarrassment the young professor said it was too delicious. The host said it was uneatable and if young Freddie's was delicious to give it to Lena since hers was like a brick. She demurred, said it was lovely, while at the same time resolved that she would eat the sprouts and would drink goblets of wine. A toast was raised to her son and he went scarlet as he heard himself being praised. Looking downwards she saw that the various plates contained a heap of little bones, decked with bits of torn pink flesh, and true to her domestic instinct she said they would make good broth, those leavings. A most tactless slip. Everyone raved over the nice raspberry chantilly and quite huge portions of it rested on the young men's dessert plates.

Having dined so early she felt it was appropriate to leave early. Earlier, her host had confessed to being tired and yet in his bedroom where she went to fetch her coat, she felt that he wanted to talk, that he was avid to tell some little thing. He simply said that he had never married because he could not stand the idea of a woman saying 'we', organizing his thought, his time, his suits of clothing and his money. It was a small functional room with a washstand, an iron bed with a frayed paisley robe laid across it. Staring from the wall was a painting of a wolf with a man's eyes and she thought this professor is not as mild as he seems. On an impulse she kissed him and he seemed so childishly glad that she then became awkward and tripped over a footstool.

Out on the street they lingered, admiring the courtyard, the stone archways, and the beautiful formidable entrance. The town itself was just shops, and shut cafés, with cars whizzing up and down as on any high street. At the hotel she bade Iain good night and knew that the hour had come when they were parting more or less for ever. They made light of it and said they would cruise Cambridge on the morrow.

As she approached her bedroom she began to remonstrate with herself, began to laugh. The music she heard was surely phantom music because after all she had been insistent about securing a quiet room. But as she proceeded down the corridor the sound increased in volume and pitch and she wondered if anxiety could play such a thorough trick. When she put the key in her own door and entered, the furnishings were shaking from the implosion of the noise and she looked instinctively for men in white coats with hair oil, which was her outdated version of the members of a dance band. Yes, a dance was in progress. The metal hangers which she had forborne to use were almost doing a jig. The hotel telephonist could do nothing, was not even sympathetic.

She took her key and went down the stairs, then crossed the street to the college where her son was. The porter directed her and seemed to sense her dismay because he kept repeating the instructions, kept saying, 'If you walk down now, towards the rectangular buildings, and take the first turning on the left you will find your son will be the fifth staircase along, and you will find him there.' Walking along she thought only of the sleep that would 'knit up the ravelled' day and hoped that in one of those buildings a bed awaited her, a bed, an eiderdown and total silence.

Coming towards her was a young man wearing a motorcyclist's leather jacket that was too small for him. Something about the way he walked reminded her of restless youths that she had seen in an American film, of gangs who went out at night to have fights with other gangs, and inventing as a reason for murder their virility or their honour. This boy reminded her of that group. She wondered who he would be, thought that probably he had put on the jacket to give himself an image, was looking for friends. Four or five hundred young men were now installed in that college and she thought of the friendships that would ensue, of the indifferent meals they would all eat, the gowns they would buy, the loves and hatreds that would flourish as they became involved. She was glad not to be one of them. Just before the figure came level with her she realized that it was Iain and that obviously he was going in search of adventure. She lost heart then and could not tell him of her plan to find a bed in his house. She joked, pretended not to know him, walked past with her hips out and then in an affected voice said, 'Haven't we met somewhere.' Then she asked him if he was enjoying it and he said yes, but he always said yes at an awkward moment. They walked towards the gates and he said that his name was painted at the foot of the landing, his and three other names and how he had a little kitchen with a fridge and that there was a note informing him of a maid who would be at his service on Monday. How she wanted to be that maid. They said good night again, this time a little more gamely since there was a mutual suspicion that they might meet a third time.

In the lobby some people had come out from the dance and a drunken woman was holding up a broken silver shoe asking if the heel could be mended. The dance would go on till two. Lena felt like crying. The manager asked if she would like another hotel and she said yes then ran to her room and packed things quickly, viciously. In the lobby yet again she felt herself to be conspicuous, what with half her belongings falling out of the bag and a look of madness. In the taxi she thought of warm milk laced with whisky. Vain thought. The porter in the new hotel was fast asleep and stirred himself only when the black Dalmatian dog bared his teeth at her legs which she quickly shielded with her suede bag. She had to pay there and then, and had to write the cheque by balancing the book against the wall as the counter space was taken up with various advertisement cards. Home, home, her heart begged. The last train for London had left an hour ago. She followed the porter down the corridor and herself let out a shriek when he admitted her to a room in which a shocked woman sat up in a bed-jacket screaming. In fact the two women's screams coincided.

'Sorry about that, Madam.' He had made a mistake. He made a similar mistake three times over, leaving some occupants of that wing in a state of anger and commotion. At last he conducted her to an empty room, that was weirdly identical to the one she had just vacated. He said not to open the window in case of burglary.

Such nights are not remarkable for their sound sleeping, but this one had extra impediments. The single bed was so narrow that each time she tried to turn over she had to stop herself from falling on to the floor. The tap let out involuntary groans and now and then the Dalmatian gave a watchdog's moan. She put her black cardigan over the telephone to blot out its faint luminous glow. She was fighting for sleep. She took two large two-toned capsules that were filled with barbiturate. Her son at that same hour had climbed up by means of scaffolding to the roof of Christ's College and with his friend was debating whether to pee on it or not, and make a statement that might result in their being rusticated. Up there they had brought the wine, the roast fillets of pork and the cheeses that she had given him for his first night's picnic. She could feel the sleeping pills starting to work as she put her hand out to assist herself in turning over. Nevertheless she tumbled, fell and conked her head on the bedside locker. It made her wide awake. The last sure little route to sleep was closed. It was a question of waiting till morning, so she dressed and then grappling with anger paced the room.

A hand-printed sign above the mirror caught her attention. It said, 'In the hours of darkness, if a client has an urgent need will he or she please ring *and wait* because due to security the night porter may be prowling the building and not find himself adjacent to the switch-board.' She took it down, re-read it with amazement, then wrote, 'You must be joking', and signed her name in full. Then she sank into the gaping armchair and waited stoutly for morning.

* * * * *

Elspeth Barker was married to the poet George Barker and lives on the Blickling estate in north Norfolk. Her first novel *O Caledonia*, published to great acclaim in 1991, was shortlisted for the Whitbread First Novel award and won the David Higham Prize. Two of her disturbing short stories appeared in *A Distant Cry* (2002), the first volume of East Anglian short stories from Black Dog Books. 'Down By The Sea' was commissioned for *Dead Men Talking*.

Down By The Sea
ELSPETH BARKER

Breathing heavily, the Morris Minor toiled over the crest of the coastal ridge. Mary gripped the steering wheel tight, veins bulging on her gnarled old hands, and inched cautiously onto the track ahead which glittered in frost light, straight as a Roman way far down to the cliff edge; beyond, sea and sky merged, grey into grey. Blanched by winter the headland grasses stood stiff and motionless. In summer this was a joyous landscape, a profusion of primary colours, crayon blue sea and azure sky, green cropped turf, scarlet poppies. Where did colour go? Once an emerald moth had balanced, quivering on her bedroom window frame, the purest, deepest translucent green, a platonically perfect green, fading imperceptibly through the days to pallid lettuce. Sorrow, like winter, leaches colour from the world. For a long time after Peter died, Mary moved in a blur of neutral tones, very occasionally offset by a bloody sunset. So it was today, sky and land and sea mournful, hushed, as though waiting for resolution. A storm cloud of lapwings lifted off the headland and darkened the air with omen.

Sidney's house was a garish brightness in the dreary day. He had painted it cornflower blue and it stood defiant on the edge of the high, crumbling cliff. Most of its garden had gone over years ago. Every now and then another yard or two would silently detach and plunge to the shingle sixty feet below. The lower parts of the cliff face had become gelatinous, involved in a mysterious marine process of liquefaction. Soon the house would go too. Sidney was untroubled by this prospect; he believed it would outlive him. Mary doubted this, but she too was untroubled. She saw herself floating downwards, like an inverted parasol, an airy scrap of flotsam, to be absumed by elemental wind and water. This was the brink of the world. Nothing but sky and sea, flint stone and the drifting sea birds. Fulmars nested in holes in the upper cliff face; they glided past, their flat faces enigmatic and preoccupied, the tips of their wings almost brushing the grasses. Sidney had called his house The Lobster's Return in anticipation of its watery destiny. Mary imagined the migrant lobsters even now marching in phalanxes over the murky ocean floor, through depths illuminated only by a shafting and fitful sunspot, guided by instinct towards their sunken palace.

Picking her way up the slippery garden path above the grind and groan of sea on shingle, she heard the urgent wails of Sidney's dogs. At once she wished she hadn't come. In the early morning she had been seized by a resentful need for the gardening books she had lent him perhaps four years ago, and had not even thought of since. Vengeful and waspish, she had set forth on a journey which she saw now was pointless. The return of borrowed books was no longer a matter of principle to her; nor was she, or Sidney, come to that, likely now to be planting any of those shrubs, bulbs, perennials, middle or back of the border subjects. *Heuchera Stormy Sea*, heliotrope, mulberry, quince or medlar; *rosa mundi, rosa versicolor, Belle de Crécy*, the strangely named masculine roses, *Parkdirektor Riggers, Rambling Rector*, or *Robert le Diable*, whom she had brought once as a gift for Sidney because it resembled him: 'procumbent in habit with a vinous flush'. The litany had lost its power to move her; those days were gone and her garden could go with them. How long before it reverted to bramble and nettle and wilderness, seeding grasses, dandelions, thistledown? Before Sidney's house went under the sea? Before her own demise?

She pushed the front door open. 'Come up to the drawing room,' cried Sidney from above. Warily she skirted the kitchen; it was worse than last time, with even more bread. Every flat surface was a litter of mouldering slices, crumpets lurid with verdigris, tureens and platters overspilling pockmarked loaves, carbonized toast, rolls turned to rock. She had asked him why he didn't throw it all out. 'I'm keeping it for the peacocks,' he said absently. The last peacock was long dead and the peacocks' tamarisk walk lay under water now. She pointed this out. 'Well, the birds then.'

But not even Sidney could wreck the drawing room. Three tall bay windows overhung the sea and on the walls between, great mirrors drew in the light so that at sunset the room was a spinning vortex of pink and gold and azure, and then a phoenix's nest of molten fire. In the cold gaze of this February morning a shift of clouds suggested changing weather, soothed her, confirmed the mutability of all things. Who should care about the bread and the birds?

Sidney hadn't done much about getting dressed. In his floor length red brocade dressing gown he tottered about the room looking for sherry glasses and wheezing. Mary declined the sherry and he ignored her. Dog hairs clung around the rim of her glass. She placed it on the nearest small table, one of a sequence which stood in inconvenient positions across the room, bearing tiny troops drawn up in battle formation, rearguards, vanguards, pincer movements, cavalry and infantry and artillery, awaiting their high command. 'Is it still Waterloo?' she asked politely. 'Absolutely not. Oudenard. If the dogs don't get in we could have victory by nightfall. And then I'm moving on to Malplaquet. What larks!' he said, rubbing his hands together. God, thought Mary. Five minutes more of this and she could go. There was precious little likelihood of victory by nightfall. The dogs had two purposes. One was to gallop about the headland, terrorizing ramblers; then they would collapse and sleep noisily in the back kitchen. But, when bored, they would work their door latch loose and come crashing up the stairs. Well, one of them crashed; the other scrabbled. Both were spoilers of the fortunes of war. With one mighty swinge of her tail, the Newfoundland despatched battalions piecemeal about the room; the Pekinese pounced among the fallen, snuffling and dismembering. Sidney would be lying helpless and breathless in his armchair, toppled by the Newfoundland's ecstatic greeting, high leap of embrace, fervent licks and jocular toss of the head. Stalactites of slobber slouched shining down the walls. When he had caught his breath, Sidney would make his joke. 'O, my America,' he gasped, 'my Newfoundland.' He had called the dog America for this purpose. The Peke was called Frean after Peek Frean, a biscuit firm which had long ceased to trade, so that no one was amused. Not that they would have been anyhow; and according to Sidney only two people had ever recognised the America allusion. He used it as an intellectual benchmark, he claimed, exonerating Mary's failure to respond by saying that in her very distant youth no girl would have been allowed to read a poem so shocking. Actually, Mary thought, he was even older than she was; and the close of girlhood did not signal an end to poetry reading. She intended now to leave before this all happened again.

As she drove down the coast road to Cromer, she realised that she had left all the books behind. She left the Morris tucked into the taxi rank by the church and hobbled through the great oak door. Bonily she settled into a hard, polished pew. She was tired and jangled. But then the familiar,

59

enfolding peace came upon her, conferred by high windows of sea water glass, through which she could just discern the shadow forms of pigeons tumbling from the tower. *A pigeon tumbling in clear summer air, a laughing schoolboy without grief or care*. She remembered that summer feeling from childhood, running with arms outflung through the silver birches, head back, eyes dazzled, almost flying. To swoop, to soar; all things then were possible. She closed her eyes and slept and dreamed of white feathers falling like winter round her.

Meanwhile Sidney, snugly wrapped against the cold, sits out on the cliff edge and stares at his soldiers. They lie in a heap of disorder on a folding table which is topped by an artful tray depicting Balmoral. He can think of nothing to do with them. Far below the sea prowls and sloughs over the shingle; the tide is full and the noise of sucking and disgorging drowns out the shrill yaps of the Pekinese and the baritone boom of the Newfoundland as they race about the headland, drowns out the working of Sidney's brain. He sips a gin and tonic and chews his lower lip. He gathers his coats and dressing gown about him; the late afternoon chill intensifies and the sky which for an hour had been a tender blue, a fickle promise of spring, has whitened. Time to go in, he thinks, heaving himself up. But it is already too late; the turf beneath his feet buckles and wrenches and slithers forward and downward. Sidney and his soldiers are gone, pitched in a headlong welter of earth and rock and sand and startled birds whose wing tips buffet him as he hurtles into darkness.

The dogs have noticed nothing, but after a comfortless night, tomorrow at low tide they will retrieve some of the soldiers and chew them up. Small children will find more and take them home in pockets clammy with sand and shells, dead crabs and starfish; but no one will find Sidney for a long time. He has been rolled far out on a rip tide, and will emerge, eyeless and shrouded in bladderwrack, one bright summer morning, miles down the coast on a Blue Flag beach, forever blighting the lives of a pair of ramblers.

* * * * *

Headlands

Virginia Woolf (1892-1941): 'A Simple Melody' appears to have been prompted by 'The school of Crome'. John Crome founded the Norwich School of Painting in the early 19th century, the most renowned regional group of landscape artists. A possible starting point for Woolf's story is John Sell Cotman's watercolour 'Mousehold Heath', c.1810. The story, written in the 1920s, did not appear until 1985 in *The Complete Shorter Fiction of Virginia Woolf*.

A Simple Melody
VIRGINIA WOOLF

As for the picture itself it was one of those landscapes which the unlearned suppose to have been painted when Queen Victoria was very young, and it was the fashion for young ladies to wear straw hats shaped like coal scuttles. Time had smoothed away all the joins and irregularities of the paint and the canvas seemed spread with a fine layer, here the palest blue, here the brownest shadow, of smooth lacquer-like glaze. It was a picture of a heath; and a very beautiful picture.

Mr Carslake, at least, thought it very beautiful because, as he stood in the corner where he could see it, it had the power to compose and tranquillize his mind. It seemed to him to bring the rest of his emotions – and how scattered and jumbled they were at a party like this! – into proportion. It was as if a fiddler were playing a perfectly quiet old English song while people gambled and tumbled and swore, picked pockets, rescued the drowning, and did astonishing – but quite unnecessary – feats of skill. He was unable to perform himself. All he could do was say that Wembley was very tiring; and that he believed it was not being a success; and things like that. Miss Merewether did not listen; after all, why should she? She played her part; she did one or two rather clumsy somersaults; skipping that is to say from Wembley to the character of Queen Mary, which she thought sublime. Of course, she thought nothing of the sort really. Mr Carslake assured himself of this by looking at the picture of the heath. All human beings were very simple underneath, he felt. Put Queen Mary, Miss Merewether and himself on that heath; it was late in the evening; after sunset; and they had to find their way back to Norwich. Soon they would all be talking quite naturally. He made not a doubt of it.

As for nature herself, few people loved her better than he did. If he had been walking with Queen Mary and Miss Merewether he would have been often silent; and they too, he was sure; calmly floating off; and he looked at the picture again; into that happy and far more severe and exalted world, which, was also so much simpler than this.

Just as he was thinking this, he saw Mabel Waring going away, in her pretty yellow dress. She looked agitated, with a strained expression and fixed unhappy eyes for all she tried to look animated.

What was the cause of her unhappiness? He looked again at the picture. The sun had set, but every colour was still bright, so that it was not long set, only just gone beyond the brown mound of the heath. The light was very becoming: and he supposed that Mabel Waring was with him and the Queen and Miss Merewether, walking back to Norwich. They would be talking about the way; how far it was; and whether this was the sort of country they liked; also, if they were hungry; and what they would have for dinner. That was natural talk. Stuart Elton himself – Mr Carslake saw him standing alone lifting a paper knife up in his hands and looking at it in a very strange way – Stuart himself, if he were on the heath, would just drop it, just toss it away. For underneath, though people seeing him casually would never believe it, Stuart was the gentlest, simplest of creatures, content to ramble all day with quite undistinguished people, like himself, and this oddity – it looked like affectation to stand in the middle of a drawing-room holding a tortoise-shell paper knife in his hand – was only manner. When they once got out on the heath and started to walk to Norwich this was what they would say: I find rubber soles make all the difference. But don't they draw the feet? Yes – no. On grass like this they're perfect. But on the pavement? And then socks and sock suspenders; men's clothes, women's clothes. Why, very likely they would talk about their own habits for a whole hour; and all in the freest, easiest way, so that suppose he, or Mabel Waring, or Stuart, or that angry looking chap with the tooth brush moustache who seemed to know nobody – wanted to explain Einstein, or make a statement – something quite private perhaps – (he had known it happen) – it would come quite natural.

It was a very beautiful picture. Like all landscapes it made one sad, because that heath would so long outlast all people; but the sadness was so elevated – turning away from Miss Merewether, George Carslake gazed at the picture – arose so plainly from the thought that it was calm, it was beautiful, that it should endure. But I cannot quite explain it, he thought. He did not like churches at all; indeed, if he said what he felt about the heath remaining and them all perishing and yet that this was right and there was nothing sad about it – he would laugh; he would dispose of that silly sentimental twaddle in a moment. For such it would be, spoken: but not, he felt, thought. No, he would not give up his belief that to walk over a heath in the evening was perhaps the best way of passing one's time.

One did come across tramps and queer people of course. Now a little deserted farm; now a man and a cart; sometimes – but this was perhaps a little too romantic – a man on a horse. There would be shepherds very likely: a windmill: or if these failed, some bush against the sky, or cart track which had this power – again he trembled on the silly words, – 'to reconcile differences – to make one believe in God'. It almost stung him that last! To believe in God indeed! When every rational power protested against the crazy and craven idiocy of such a saying! It seemed to him as if he had been trapped into the words. 'To believe in God'. What he believed in was a little simple talk with people like Mabel Waring, Stuart Elton, the Queen of England for the matter of that – on a heath. At least he had found great comfort in their having much in common – boots, hunger, fatigue. But then he could figure Stuart Elton, for example stopping, or falling silent. If you asked him What are you thinking about? perhaps he would say nothing at all, or something not true. Perhaps he would not be able to speak the truth.

Mr Carslake again looked at the picture. He was troubled by the sense of something remote. Indeed people did think about things, did paint things. Indeed, these parties on the heath do not annihilate differences, he thought; but he maintained, he did believe this – that the only differences remaining (out there, with that line of heath in the distance, and never a house to break the view) are fundamental differences – like this, what the man thought who painted the picture, what Stuart Elton thought about – about what? It was probably a belief of some kind.

Anyhow, on they went; for the great point of walking is that nobody can stand still very long; they have to rouse themselves up, and on a long walk fatigue, and the desire to end the fatigue, give the most philosophic, or those even distracted by love and its torments, an overpowering reason for setting their minds upon getting home.

Every phrase he used, alas, tinkled in his ears with a sham religious flavour. 'Getting home' – the religious had appropriated that. It meant going to Heaven. His thoughts could not find any pure new words which had never been ruffled and creased and had the starch taken out of them by others' use.

Only when he was walking, with Mabel Waring, Stuart Elton, the Queen of England and that fierce bolteyed looking uncompromising man there, this old melodious singsong stopped. Perhaps one was a little brutalised by the open air. Thirst brutalised; a blister on the heel. When he was walking there was a hardness and a freshness about things: no confusion; no wobbling; the division at least between the known and the unknown was as distinct as the rim of a pond – here was dry land, here water. Now a curious thought struck him – that the waters possessed an attraction for the people on earth. When Stuart Elton took his paper knife or Mabel Waring looked about to burst into tears, and that man with the tooth brush moustache glared, it was because they all wished to take to the water. But what was the water? Understanding perhaps. There must be someone who was so miraculously endowed, so fitted with all the parts of human nature, that these silences and unhappinesses, which were the result of being unable to fit one's mind to other people's, were all rightly understood. Stuart Elton dived in: Mabel dived. Some went under and were satisfied; others came gasping to the top. He was relieved to find himself thinking of death as a plunge into a pond; for he was alarmed at his mind's instinct, when unguarded, to rise into clouds and Heaven, and rig up the old comfortable figure, the old flowing garments and mild eyes and cloud-like mantle.

In the pond, on the other hand, were newts, and fish and mud. The point about the pond was that one had to create it for oneself; new, brand new. No longer did one want to be rapt off to Heaven, there to sing and meet the dead. One wanted something here and now. Understanding meant an increase of life; a power to say what one could not say; to make such vain attempts as Mabel Waring's – he knew her way of doing something suddenly quite out of her character, rather startling and dashing, [would] succeed – instead of failing and plunging her deeper into gloom.

So the old fiddler played his tune, as George Carslake looked from the picture at the people, and back again. His round face, his rather squarely built body expressed a philosophic calm which gave him, even among all these people, a look of detachment, of calm, of restfulness, which was not sluggish, but alert. He had sat down, and Miss Merewether who might easily have drifted off sat beside him. People said that he made very brilliant after-dinner speeches. They said he never married because his mother needed him. No one thought of him, however, as an heroic character – there was nothing tragic about him. He was a barrister. Hobbies, [tastes?], gifts over and above his able mind, he had none in particular – except that he walked. People tolerated him, liked him, sneered at him slightly, for he had done nothing that you could lay your hands on, and he had a butler who was like an elder brother.

But Mr Carslake did not bother his head. People were very simple – men and women much alike; it was a great pity to quarrel with anyone; and indeed he never did. That is not to say that his feelings were not sometimes hurt; unexpectedly. Living near Gloucester, he had an absurd touchiness about the Cathedral; he fought its battles, he resented its criticism as if the Cathedral were his blood relation. But he would let anyone say what they liked about his own brother. Also, anybody might laugh at him for walking. His was a nature smooth all over but not soft; and suddenly little spikes jutted out – about the Cathedral, or some glaring injustice.

The old fiddler fiddled his simple melody to this effect: We are not here, but on a heath, walking back to Norwich. Sharp, self-assertive Miss Merewether who said that the Queen was 'sublime' had joined the party on condition that she talked no more silly nonsense that she did not believe. 'The school of Crome?' she said, looking at the picture.

Very well. This being settled, they went on, it might be a matter of six or seven miles. It often happened to George Carslake; there was nothing strange about it – this sense of being in two places at once, with one body here in a London drawing-room, but so severed, that the peace of the country, its uncompromising bareness and hardness and [spirit?], affected that body. He stretched his legs. He felt the breeze on his cheek. Above all he felt, we are all of us, very different superficially, but now united; we may stray; we may seek the water; but it is perfectly true that we are all cool, friendly, physically easy.

Rip off all those clothes my dear, he thought looking at Mabel Waring. Make a bundle of them. Then he thought, don't worry, my dear Stuart, about your soul, its extreme unlikeness to anyone else's. The glaring man seemed to him positively amazing.

It was impossible to put this into words, and it was unnecessary. Beneath the fidgety flicker of these little creatures was always a deep reservoir: and the simple melody without expressing it, did something queer to it – rippled it, liquefied it, made it start and turn and quiver in the depths of one's being, so that all the time ideas were rising from this pool and bubbling up into one's brain. Ideas that were half feelings. They had that kind of emotional quality. It was impossible to analyse them – to say whether they were on the whole happy or unhappy, gay or sad.

His desire was to be sure that all people were the same. He felt that if he could prove it, he would have solved a great problem. But was it true? He kept looking at the picture. Was he not trying to impose on human beings who are by their very nature opposed, different, at war, a claim which is perhaps incongruous – a simplicity that does not belong to their natures? Art has it; a picture has it; but men do not feel it. These states of mind when one is walking, in company, on a heath, produce a sense of similarity. On the other hand, social converse, when everyone wants to shine, and to enforce his own point of view, produces dissimilarity; and which is the more profound?

He tried to analyse this favourite theme of his – walking, different people walking to Norwich. He thought at once of the lark, of the sky, of the view. The walker's thoughts and emotions were largely made up of these outside influences. Walking thoughts were half sky; if you could submit them to chemical analysis you would find that they had some grains of colour in them, some gallons or quarts or pints of air attached to them. This at once made them airier, more impersonal. But in this room, thoughts were jostled together like fish in a net, struggling, scraping each other's scales off, and becoming, in the effort to escape, – for all thinking was an effort to make thought escape from the thinker's mind past all obstacles as completely as possible: all society is an attempt to seize and influence and coerce each thought as it appears and force it to yield to another.

So he could see everyone now engaged. But it was not, strictly, thought; it was being, oneself, that was here in conflict with other beings and selves. Here there was no impersonal colouring mixture: here walls, lights, the houses outside, all re-enforced humanity, being themselves the expression of humanity. People pressed upon each other; rubbed each other's bloom off; or, for it told both ways, stimulated and called out an astonishing animation, made each other glow.

Whether pleasure or pain predominated, he could not say. On the heath, there would be no doubt about it. As they walked – Merewether, the Queen, Elton, Mabel Waring and himself – the fiddler played; far from rubbing each other's scales off, they swam side by side in the greatest comfort.

It was a beautiful picture, a very beautiful picture.

He felt a stronger and stronger wish to be there, on the Norfolk heath, indeed.

He then told Miss Merewether a story about his small nephew at Wembley; and as he told it she felt, as his friends always felt, that though he was one of the nicest people she had ever met, George Carslake was a dark horse, a queer fish. There was no saying what he was after. Had he any affections, she wondered? She smiled, remembering his butler. And then he made off, [that was all?] he said – went back to [Dittering?] tomorrow.

* * * * *

Mary Mann (1848-1941) achieved considerable success as the writer of romantic fiction but her many novels have long been out of print. During her years at Shropham in south Norfolk Mann was confronted by widespread deprivation that brutalised the rural workforce. Her observations inspired the remarkable collection of stories published in 1903 as *The Fields Of Dulditch*, tales of human endurance in a world of cruelty and superstition that stand alongside those of Thomas Hardy. 'Wolf Charlie' originally appeared in this collection.

Wolf-Charlie
MARY MANN

In a tumble-down cottage at one extreme end of the parish of Dulditch Wolf-Charlie lives. It is one of a couple of cottages in such bad condition that they are held past repairing. Year by year Sir Thomas threatens to pull them down, and year by year, merciful man that he is, holds his hand. For years he has received no rent; for years Wolf-Charlie and his old grandmother, who inhabits the other miserable edifice, have received notice to quit at Michaelmas – a notice always disregarded. In the one cottage the ground floor only is found to be habitable; in the other, by reason of the absence of door and window in the downstairs apartment, the grandmother has been compelled to take up her abode in the upper storey. With the broken panes from the window her great-grandchildren dig in the heaps of dust and rubbish where is their playground. The door was long ago broken up and converted into firewood.

The cottages are approached by a lane too narrow to admit of any vehicle wider than a wheelbarrow. It is a lane which leads only to these poor 'housen,' debouching on a melancholy space of grass and nettles growing above brick-bats, tiles, broken chimney-pots, refuse of all sorts, which space was once on a time the trim garden plots of the houses. Between the broken bricks of the little paved way before the doors a plentiful crop of sickly fungus grows.

More than once there has been illness among the children caused by impromptu feasts off the unwholesome growth. One child, rendered reckless by stress of hunger and indulging in a surfeit, gave the crown and glory to Wolf-Charlie's history by necessitating an 'inkwitch' in Dulditch.

He is called Wolf-Charlie, I suppose, by reason of the famished look in his melancholy eyes, of the way in which the skin of his lips, drawn tightly over his gums, exposes his great yellow teeth; by reason of the leanness of his flanks, the shaggy, unkempt hair about his head and face, the half fierce, half frightened expression. He is what is called in employers' parlance 'a three-quarter man,' receiving only three-fourths of the wages of the other labourers.

He has the use of his hands and feet; he is not a 'down fool' like 'Silly Solomon,' idiot *par excellence* of the parish, nor a cripple like Dan'l Luck, whose leg the Runwich Hospital authorities deemed it wise to leave dangling from his trunk after his accident, the foot turned the wrong way, so that for the honour of swinging the useless member he has to go on crutches for all his life. Wolf-Charlie is not specially afflicted in any fashion, yet he is in some indefinable way deficient. His fellow-labourers will not 'du' a harvest with him, and no farmer dares employ him to feed his cattle or to plough or drill.

Yet such labour as is entrusted to him he does with unfailing industry and a dogged, dull persistence. When the vapours hang white and ghost-like over the low-lying meadows, he stands all the day knee-deep in water 'ditching'; and he can always be trusted to 'top and tail' the turnips. In the winter, when work on the farm is only to be obtained by the best men, and such hangers-on as Wolf-Charlie are invariably among the first to be paid off, he sits patiently by the wayside breaking the stones of the road; or for a few pence he will trudge the seven miles to Runwich to fetch a sick neighbour's medicine.

His clothes are in rags, showing the poor flesh in many places which custom and comfort have ordained shall be hidden from view; his thin hairy chest is oftener bare than covered; of Sunday clothes he has none. When he sits on the long dank grass of the roadside bank, with his back to the wind and his shoulders pulled to his ears for warmth, and feels in the red and white bundle beside him for the midday meal which is to support him till he can look for his bowl of potatoes at night, he finds nothing but dry bread there. He does not even possess the 'shut knife' with which etiquette ordains the agricultural labourer shall carve his *al fresco* feast, but he pulls it to pieces, wolf-like, with claws and teeth, looking out with the fierce, yet melancholy gaze over the grey and shivering meadows as he drearily chews his food.

He is in a word the poorest of the poor – a most wretched and pitiable object.

Yet not so poor but that Wolf-Charlie, too, has had his romance. And here it is.

There was, some years ago, a winter longer and more cruel than any in Wolf-Charlie's experience; when a bitter frost bound the land in bands of iron, 'its rigid influence seizing Nature fast'; when the saddened sky looked down on a dead world wrapt in its winding sheet; when for even the valued hands no work could be found; and when the poor 'three-quarter man' was in every sense of the words out in the cold.

The Wolf was not a householder in those days, but shared bed and board with a family in exchange for the five shillings a week he paid them. For a couple of weeks not one of the five shillings was forthcoming.

The winter was hard in degree to all classes of the poor; no man dared to soften his heart toward his comrade; no woman ventured to give away bite or sup from the children's scanty meal.

There came a day when Wolf-Charlie, buckling the strap of his trousers tightly round his empty stomach, turned his back upon that poor table at which for long he had taken his place. The mother was doling out to her half-dozen little children the morning meal of bread soaked in hot water, peppered and salted; of this for the first time she ceased to offer the lodger a share. The poor fellow said no word of remonstrance, of appeal, of farewell even, but turned his back upon the place where his home had been and on the familiar faces, and took his way along a certain road. A road which the agricultural labourer and his wife travel (spiritually) in many a moment of depression and in their bad dreams; a road where surely no flower should grow, where the wayside grass and overhanging leafy trees should wither; a road paved with bitterness and hatred and a burning sense of injury and all evil thoughts and despair – the road to the workhouse.

No flowers were there to mock the passer-by on the morning when Wolf-Charlie sought the cold charities of the dreaded place; but the icy air cut his ill-protected body like a knife, the hard-encrusted snow of the road sounded like iron beneath his unwilling feet.

A taciturn man in company, the Wolf is given to talking a great deal to himself. As he trims the 'roots' for grinding, lops the overhanging branches of the trees, clears a way for the watercourse in the 'dekes,' his lips are always seen to move, and a low muttering issues forth. With such melancholy, indistinct murmurings, fit accompaniment to the vague, only half-comprehended bitterness and aching of his heart, Wolf-Charlie went his way and was swallowed up in the portals of the big whitewashed poorhouse. And in that village where hitherto his work was done he was seen no more.

In the springtime, when, as we are told, 'A young man's fancy lightly turns to thoughts of love,' and turns also, as we know in the case of our present hero, to possible odd jobs, easier to be come at in barley-sowing time and in the lambing season, Wolf-Charlie emerged from his place of retirement - not unaccompanied.

In spite of the warmth, regular food, and better clothing which he enjoyed in the workhouse, want of liberty had told sadly upon him. The strength of his longing and his misery had been too much for the body weakened by other privations, and Wolf-Charlie, who was not a favourite with the master, and whose sullen ways and uncomprehended mutterings made him obnoxious to the other officials, fell seriously ill. In this condition there was allotted him as nurse the woman who now issued with him from captivity.

She was a middle-aged woman, with a red and foolish face, with dust-coloured, dusty hair. She had a wooden leg and six children. She had been an inmate of the workhouse since the birth of her last, which toddled along, dragging on her skirts, a child of four.

So, boldly, Wolf-Charlie reappeared in that world which had not treated him too gently hitherto, bringing with him seven mouths to feed besides that capacious, never-satisfied one of his own. In such patriarchal fashion he made his entry into Dulditch, and, getting employment at the Brightlands Farm, installed himself and his tribe in the cottage above described.

It is probable that the idea of legalising the bond which bound the Wolf to the wooden-legged mother of six emanated from the rector. He found neither of the interested parties loth, and met with no such rebuff on the occasion as that with which Cyprian Crook answered a like appeal.

Crook is the village cobbler, a bad workman and a tipsy one. He does not come to church, and the rectory boots and shoes go to the next village, to be repaired there in the odour of sanctity.

'You don't employ me, why should I employ you?' Crook demanded of the rector, who had urged him to make the lady who resided with him as housekeeper his wife.

On the part of the Wolf and Wooden-leg no difficulties were made; the banns were duly asked, and all went merrily as the proverbial bell, until a report, speedily confirmed, was circulated through the village to the effect that Wooden-leg's husband, the father of the six, was still living, and not only living, but living in the adjoining parish.

Neither intending bride nor bridegroom was at all overcome by the announcement. The woman had known it all along – to the man it apparently made no difference. The idea of marriage having taken hold of their slow imagination, they would not relinquish it. Now that the 'crying' had made them celebrities in the place, they determined to accomplish that which they had publicly pledged themselves to perform. They would be married or perish in the attempt. They finally accomplished their purpose at the Runwich Registry Office. Having made all necessary and false declarations, they tramped off in the sunshine of an early summer morning, the six children, who could not with safety be left behind, trailing after them.

The bride, arrayed in her one frock – the old lilac print the matron had given her on her leaving the workhouse – hopped along bravely on her sound leg and that wooden substitute which, through use, had grown too short for her, causing her to walk with much pain and caution. The bridegroom, with his shaggy head sunk upon his breast, walked behind her, silent, his hands thrust in those slits in his trousers where his pockets had once been, gaping holes at his knees. So, with one shilling and twopence in hand to furnish forth the wedding feast, they tramped the seven miles.

So, having accomplished their object and expended their fortune, with the calm of satisfied ambition did they presently tramp home again – to the shelter of the filthy room with the empty cupboard, the bare table, the three broken chairs; to the connubial chamber where the big wooden bedstead filled all the space not occupied by the sacks of straw flung in one corner for the accommodation of the elder children. It swarmed with fleas, that gigantic couch; smelt abominably; its four great posts, undraped, used to reach to the ceiling and serve the children for impromptu gymnastic exercises until they were cut down, one at a time, in the first winter and converted into firewood.

On this wretched bed in the fulness of time a baby was born to the Wolf, and then another. Those few shillings which Wooden-leg picked up by gathering acorns for the farmers at sixpence a bushel, by picking stones, by singling beet, were stopped for these events; and at such times the family came dangerously near starvation. No nurse could be found, even if the necessary few shillings could have been scraped together to pay her; the eldest girl, thirteen years of age, was her mother's sole attendant for those few days she could lie beside her miserable baby before, with her hopping, painful gait, she must limp to her labour in the field once more.

As has been said, the Wolf's old grandmother lies bedridden next door. You mount to her room by an open flight of steps arising out of that ruined down-stair room, strewn with plaster falling from walls and ceiling, with the broken bricks kicked up from the floor. The old woman has not been down these steps for years, nor will descend them until she is carried down in her coffin; and because Wooden-leg cannot mount the unprotected, rickety stairway, the eldest girl is told off to wait on 'Gran'mawther'

Considering that the child is only thirteen years of age, that she has had the worst possible training, and that there is practically no supervision (for when 'Gran'mawther' grumbles from the bed Beatrice thinks it wiser not to hear), the work is done fairly well. A few favoured ones among the uneven boards are scrubbed; the bed-linen – the thread-bare blue counterpane, the cobwebby blankets, the yellow sheets – is neatly arranged; the chair and table dusted. When Beatrice is particularly energetic she spits upon the latter and polishes it to a quite cheerful shininess. The little nurse appears on the best of terms with grandmother.

The child receives, by family arrangement, the sum of sixpence weekly for services thus rendered. 'Gran'mawther' is not of a liberal turn of mind and has never been known of her substance to offer her small attendant bite or sup.

But at night when everything is still Beatrice noiselessly mounts the unsteady stairs, gently opens the door of the old woman's room, steals across the rotten boards, and with a deliberate, unwavering little hand robs her grandmother.

The poor old soul has but an allowance of a half-stone of bread, a weekly dole of two shillings and sixpence. Her coffers are not over full, her board is not too luxuriously spread, but to the famished set next door she is a feminine Croesus, a pampered being enjoying continual festival, diverting to her own selfish indulgence necessaries of life needed by far hungrier people.

The dark, still bright eyes of Gran'mawther open upon Beatrice, watch her as she appropriates the slice of cheese, the tallow candle, the lump of bread, which, with few variations, is the nightly toll she exacts. She watches that little marauder, but she says nothing. There is something uncanny to the imagination in the picture of the dauntless, small depredator at her nightly work, and the old woman, glib enough of tongue in the daylight, lying there, voiceless, to be robbed of her cherished store. It is almost as if that ugly grandchild in her scant and ragged chemise, barefooted, exercised some spell over the aged parent – as if supernatural agencies were at work.

But it is more the spirit of prudence than that of fear which strangles the curses on Gran'mawther's lips. She is entirely at the mercy of this abominable child, this unnatural descendant, who must have the elements of a conscience somewhere about her, as, up to the present, she has stayed her hand and left enough in the cupboard to preserve her relation from starvation.

Suppose that, night by night, the thievish imp made a clean sweep of the provender! Suppose, instead of coming with commendable regularity to 'redd up' her granny, she slunk out in the fields to play, and left the poor old soul to die of dirt and neglect?

In submission, it seems, Gran'mawther's chief safety lies. Her only chance of deliverance from such outrage is to give up her wretched bedstead, her round table, her couple of broken-seated chairs; to give up all her pride and her lifelong prejudices, and have herself carried to the workhouse. But Gran'mawther – who prays that she may not live long in loud monotonous petitions, which only cease when Beatrice is in attendance, and which are a sound as familiar to the household next door and as unregarded as the soughing of the wind in the broken chimney – would sooner endure ages of lonely, miserable days, centuries of horror-haunted nights, than face that indignity.

So from year to year the family of which Wolf-Charlie is the head goes on. They are scarcely, one may say, in fortune's power – they never can be poorer than they are; their cupboard is empty even of the skeleton of fear.

Yet often, perhaps, the thought of that other husband whose responsibilities he had taken on his own shoulders may have troubled the Wolf's slow brain. By the irony of fate it happened that this man, who had deserted his wife and children to follow a wandering life, settled for a time in the parish adjoining Dulditch (he had kept clear of the neighbourhood while the parish authorities were interested in his whereabouts). Fortune had smiled upon him and trade had prospered. He had lately started a donkey-cart, and was looked on as a well-to-do person. A buyer of rabbit skins, old bones, rags and papers, a vendor of dried herrings, tapes and cotton.

Often, as Wolf-Charlie sat by the roadside, breaking the stones on the heap before him, this hero would drive past in his pride and arrogance, belabouring his donkey, with not a thought or a look for that other poor bearer of other folks' burdens under the hedge.

The Wolf was not a speculative, nor an inquisitive, nor a ruminative person; his reasoning powers were of the smallest; yet surely in his half-awakened mind, in his twilight consciousness, there must have dwelt thoughts at such times which one would be curious to know.

Once, when the second baby was born – when winter was lying, dark, silent and sullen upon the land, when, tighten the trouser-strap round his shivering body as he might, drag the manure sack he wore as great-coat close as could be about his throat, he must yet suffer dismal pangs of hunger and of cold – these thoughts strove to become articulate.

Stooping over the beet which he was pulling in a field adjoining the road, he heard the well-known sound of the donkey-cart approaching. He stood, arrested in his work, his back bent, the beet he was in the act of pulling in his hand. The wheels of cart or carriage passing along the road never diverted him from his work; even when the traction engine panted slowly by, its fire gleaming redly in the gloom of the thick afternoon, he would not lift his head to look. But the donkey-cart was a different matter.

Presently he raised himself, and with a light of unlimited resolution in his eyes stood erect. The donkey-cart approached, and in the lightness of his heart and triumph of his fortune the owner whistled gaily as he rode along.

Suddenly, swinging the turnip in the air and holding it above his head as a signal, Wolf-Charlie hailed his rival.

'Hi! I say!'

The driver of the donkey-cart paused, looked beyond the hedge, saw the shaggy, ragged figure, the hungry, melancholy eyes, brightened by the unwonted fire of purpose.

'Hi!' the driver called back.

This did not look like a man with money to spare for bootlaces and such-like vain trifles. He did not have the air of a purchaser of red herrings even. The 'hi!' the trader gave was unexpectant, indifferent.

'I ha' got yar wife and child'un,' the Wolf shouted aloud to him.

The driver gazed for a moment at his wretched-looking rival, then turning back to his donkey belaboured it with a heavy stroke across its ribs.

'I don't keer whu th' devil ha' got 'em so long as I ha'n't,' he called out. And so, master of the situation, drove off.

After that rebuff the Wolf made no further effort to detach from himself the burden he had hung about his neck, neither does he make complaint. With an intelligence not much removed from that of the beasts of the field, he is patient and uncomplaining as they.

And the children in some mysterious way seem to thrive on their half rations of bread, cunningly soaked in hot water to make the allowance appear more, their random dessert off hedge berries, wild apples, and the fungus from the doorstep. They are ragged and they are filthy, it is true, but they are not particularly thin or pitiable-looking; they inherit their mother's complexion of brick red; their hair, which one would not care too closely to inspect, seen from a safe distance is a luxuriant growth. Perhaps out of their potsherds, their bits of window-glass, their 'rubbage' heaps, and that most prized and precious plaything, the especial property always of the youngest, a rusty key attached by a filthy string to the half of a pair of scissors, they get as much pleasure as happier-circumstanced children may from a nursery over-crowded with toys.

There is something too melancholy in the history of such sordid lives. One stands aghast for the moment, frightened at the privation which those fashioned like ourselves in outward seeming can bear and live, shrinking from the recital. It is only from such a 'perhaps' as that above we can regain ease of mind and conscience and go on our way comfortably indifferent once more. Perhaps the toys suffice; perhaps, never having had enough to eat, Wolf-Charlie does not understand how bad it is to be hungry; perhaps, educated in the school of hardship, Wooden-leg does not feel pain and weakness and privation as gentler nurtured women must; perhaps their lot, if one could see from the inside, as it were, is a happy one after all.

> *Poor and content is rich, and rich enough,*

says Shakespeare.

It is comforting to reflect that if Wolf-Charlie is not thoroughly contented, he at any rate does not complain.

* * * * *

Philip Hensher: Critic and novelist was born in London where he now lives. He is the author of four novels, *Other Lulus* (1994), *Kitchen Venom* (1996) which won the Somerset Maugham Award, *Pleasured* (1998) and most recently *The Mulberry Empire* (2002). 'In the Net' is from his collection of short stories, *The Bedroom of Mister's Wife* (1999).

In The Net

PHILIP HENSHER

Matthew was forty-seven when his heart, as they say, was broken. His wife died, with no more than the usual inadequate warning, and he decided to go and live as a widower in a Suffolk village.

He could quite imagine it, a widower in a Suffolk village, living behind a kempt front garden, a regimented frontage. For the first time, he would occupy a position in society. A Suffolk widower; it was a position secure, and as little needing explanation to the world as a vicar, an MFH, a prostitute. He made his decisions; to go and live in Suffolk, and to live and announce himself as a widower. And he made them, understanding that, from now on, this was how his life was going to be. Things had turned out oddly for him, all in all, turning him into a widower killing his wife off like that. It was not the first time he had declared himself a widower. A more pensive man might have wondered whether this was the role the world had decided upon for him; decided upon it before his wife had been killed, before he married her, decided upon it long before he had even declared himself bereaved of the wife who, as yet, did not exist.

Matthew had not married Catherine until he was almost forty-five. He was an academic who, for thirty years, had lived in London, in various districts south of the River: SW2 SW4 SW8 SW9 SW11, a whole narrative of slow improvement in the green flat suburbs, like a planned history, like a logical series of numbers, 2, 4, 8, 9, 11. It had always seemed as if the next number in the series would tell him what his future might hold, and now he knew that had not been the case.

An anthropologist he was, who for nearly thirty years had worked on nothing but matrilinearity in the Hindu Kush. Field trips occupied more than half his time, and he had not married. Three times he had perceived the growing irritation in a girl's letters; on each occasion (girl one, girl two,

79

girl three) it had been a girl he had loved, and on each occasion, he had asked her to release him from his obligations, in nineteenth-century fashion. He had not married, in fact, until he had given up the idea of publishing anything more substantial than an article, and given up the idea of greatness which, when he had been twenty, had so fired his ideas, so lit up his eyes; and, giving up all his ideas of greatness, he had met Catherine.

In London he had hardly ever given a thought to his unmarried status. But, on his trips to the Hindu Kush, the universal question 'Are you married?' was quickly followed by the question 'Why not?' And perhaps they were right to express a bafflement, which, as he grew older, became more extravagant in its expressions. His training as an anthropologist made him disinclined to snub the serious and intelligent men in their drab clothes, wrapped up as if in puttees, holding their machine guns at the dinner table, who always asked him the question, and looked at him seriously, as if it were more than small talk. And perhaps it was not a case of the incompatibility of cultures; perhaps here was a question which could reasonably be asked of him even in London. Why not, indeed? So once, sitting in the grand house of a village elder thousands of metres up, trying neither to shiver nor to think about the rather lardy feast he had just forced down with all the usual expressions of over-whelmed retching gratitude, he replied that he was not married, because his wife had died. The resulting narrative improvisation, incredible as it had seemed to him, had successfully filled the increasingly cold evening; his listeners were gripped by his fictitious marriage, the hopes he and his fictitious wife (named after girl two) had held, the terrible tragedy of his wife's giving birth and killing herself and the child in the process. The village elders nodded, unsurprised, and there he was, a widower. He reminded himself that a wife dead in childbirth was not as remarkable a biographical fact among the Afghans as it was in Parson's Green, and made an academic mental note to examine the mortality rates of childbirth, infant and mother, in urban and rural Afghanistan.

Widower was an odd term. He hardly thought of it in his own context. Academically, he could place the bereaved; he could say something unsympathetic and accurate about the place a society halfway up a mountain in the Hindu Kush would find for a man whose wife had died in childbirth, and, on paper, it would be interesting and abstract and thoroughly footnoted.

So it was odd, beyond anything he had considered, when it happened to him. Odd, when he returned from a trip and bumped into a girl he knew – she was not an anthropologist, but the dined-with cousin of someone he remembered from Cambridge, a lawyer who asked him to dinner once every eighteen months, on average. Odder when, a year later, she had no stated objection to him, nothing of sulk, nothing beyond a kindness and an interest and a respect he had never thought might form part of his relations with a woman, and they found themselves marrying; and he looked at her, and saw her happiness, and saw, in a way, his own feelings, reflected, improved upon, made perfect in her perfect eyes; and oddest beyond anything when, two years after that, Catherine was cycling down the road for some trivial purpose, no reason at all, and was hit by a car, and killed.

He met the driver of the car, who had been talking on his mobile telephone, and felt nothing towards him, watched his ugly screwed-up pained face trying to be sorry enough, and just wanted to bring the poor man's ordeal to an end. 'Who were you talking to, on the telephone?' he asked. The driver said nothing, just looked at him, having no answer, and not seeing that, if your wife had been killed, if your wife's skull had been crushed by a lump of metal under the control of another human being, if in a moment your wife, who had been a living woman, her eyes blue and her hair dark and a magical unique unforgettable superorbital ridge, a magical unique unforgettable way of raising the eyebrow, always, mysteriously, the left eyebrow, a woman with her own thoughts and her own voice and her own way, unforgettable, her own way of walking, had been turned into heavy unmoving flesh, you too would want to know why, to inquire into the circumstances and find out what you would rather be ignorant of. And then he was a widower.

He thought of his status as he had thought of previous attained and incredible states of being; just as, at eighteen, he had locked the bathroom door and gazed at his face, and mouthed an incredible sentence, I have been given a scholarship by Trinity, or, later, I am a member of the Apostles, I am an Apostle; just as he had thought of himself, with thrilled observation, as a husband, and looked forward to becoming a father. He was a widower, and that was all there was to it. Yes, he said, looking, somehow, for the right bathroom mirror to mouth into, yes, I am a widower.

'Are you sure?' his friend and colleague Conrad said. They had known each other for years. He had not got as far as Matthew had. His career had shifted restlessly from Chinese court rituals, to structures of society in American fraternity houses, to Swedish warlocks, and he had never quite established a clear reputation for anything but niceness, never quite made a mark beyond the department they both worked in. Matthew had just announced to him his intention to go and live in Suffolk.

Matthew finished his glass of wine. The bottle was not quite empty, but he would wait to be offered the last inch. He took off his spectacles, held them up to the light. 'It seems,' he said, 'like the right sort of thing to do. I feel very uncomfortable, to be honest, in London. I mean in our house. And there's nothing much to keep me here.'

'The teaching – '

'The teaching can easily be done in one day a week. I'm not going to the ends of the earth. Even in Suffolk there's a telephone, a fax, the post. I might even get on that E-mail thing, the Net. Once you start to think, to be honest, I just wonder what I'm doing here. Why does anyone want to stay here?'

Conrad looked at him, quite soberly. They were in a slightly unexpected bar; not one near the college, not in any sense an academic bar where they might be disturbed by the sight of students, or have to nod civilly at tactful anthropologists across the way, but a chrome and green-painted bar in the West End where the transient clientele of theatre-goers, the brisk noise and the anonymous crowds of media boys awarded them an unobtrusive privacy. The wine, Matthew had noted, was half as expensive again as it was in the usual haunt just east of the Museum.

'I don't quite know,' Conrad said finally. 'I mean, I know why I stay here. I like it. Some people don't need green space – Hyde Park is about as much as I can cope with. Do you really know the country? Do you really have any idea what it's like, living outside London?'

'Of course I do,' Matthew said. 'Come on. It's not so terrifying. Going to live in Suffolk, it's not like setting off on field work, and knowing you're going to have to struggle along with your subjects for months with no one to have a laugh with. London's no good for me.'

'Well, go back to Afghanistan,' Conrad said.

'Suffolk is easier,' Matthew said.

'I don't know about that,' Conrad said.

'Easier for solitude,' Matthew went on. He wasn't going to turn this into a joke; it was what he wanted to do, and what he was going to do. 'Living in the country, it's good for solitude. And of course I know what it's like. I grew up there. It's my parents' house I'd be going to live in. I never had much of an idea what to do with the house after they died – I was going to sell it three years ago, but, you know, the state of the market – and now I might as well go and live in it.'

'But do you really think this is such a good idea?' Conrad said. 'Cutting yourself off from friends? I know, I'm just being selfish. But you and me, seeing each other, every single day. You put up a good front of coping, but what is it going to be like without – you've been through –'

'I know,' Matthew said, heavily. He looked at the crowded and crowing bar; too crowded, too loud, too full, too London. He wanted to sit in silence, and look at nothing very much. That would be good. He could not quite express the fear that he had, that the consolation his friends offered was another means of renewing the grief. 'Yes, I know. You've been good through all this. It's not far. I'll be in London every week, more, as often as you like.'

'As often as you like.'

'Thank you. And there's E-mail.'

'I love the thought of you on E-mail.'

'Yes,' Matthew said. 'I thought it was really about time. I thought the fax machine would see me out, but –'

'I know a very good man,' Conrad said briskly. 'He'll set you up, won't frighten you. He's used to dealing with terrible old Luddites like you. God, going off and living some joke Marie Antoinette existence in Norfolk or Suffolk or wherever.'

'Suffolk,' Matthew said. He smiled. 'You're right. I need to change. This is a good change.'

Conrad, supportive as he was being, would not quite assent to this, but, in any case, Matthew would go on seeing him at least once a week. The course of his life, and its value did not depend on what his friends thought of it. And there was always the Net, or E-mail, which, if you believed what people said, had opened up the world, and would bring the world even to Suffolk. The world was on E-mail, and the world had become E-mail, a great floating invisible rippling grid of individuals talking, of unknowable extent, of incomprehensible nature. There was no telling the people he would, instantaneously, be able to talk to, no imagining the voices he would be able to access, who, in turn, would seek him out and find him. His mind turned from the specific and distant – the subcontinental universities he used as his bases, his Iranian correspondents, perhaps even his Kabul informants – to the intangible, the inconceivable, the thrillingly unknown, materialising from the ether.

Voices from the ether, like the first days of wireless, appearing, and talking calmly to you, just voices, just talking.

He left the professional removers to box up the books, and went to the house in Suffolk. It was not much like moving. He had no desire to replace the ancient and familiar properties of his parents' rooms with his possessions and their now unwelcome associations. Apart from removing the books, he left the London house as it was, thinking that he would decide what to do with it when his life had clarified a little, and drove out, one Tuesday morning. It was a clear April day. The roads were rather better than usual, and unconvincing as it was, it was hard to resist the banal idea that a new beginning was upon him. In the clear empty light, he drove down the clean roads, wondering what, in all correctness, he ought to feel.

The village was neither picturesquely rural nor coherently urban, and the house fell similarly between categories, neither a sombre and unique manor house nor a cottage. The notion of a cottage interested Matthew only professionally, and not much even then. There was nothing pastoral or sentimental in his character, and he responded hardly at all to the urbanite fantasies of a mushroom-squat house with a five-foot door, a rose-crawling facade and a fat rosy farmer with a herd of geese. Still, he felt, stopping outside his parents' old house, there was something unduly severe about the bleak little village. It had a sort of green, with a couple of ducks shivering by a murky pond. A group of teenagers, drunk, smacked-out or just bonelessly limp with boredom, swayed on the fence outside the less respectable of the two pubs. No doubt they came from the forty houses of the brick development at the far end of the village, which, though it had proved a trial to his father as he entered his letter-writing dotage, echoed, when viewed in purely aesthetic terms, the bleak uneyebrowed frontages of the little eighteenth-century market-place, so approved of by the gentry, behind one of which he must now begin to live.

Matthew had warned nobody that he was coming back to the village, having nobody to warn, and, as he opened the door, a cold ghostly smell damped his face, the cool and vacant smell of cement dust. He stood there for a moment, trying to summon a feeling of homecoming, of returning to the place he had begun from and a place he could set out from again, ignoring the narrative of love and marriage and bereavement which had intervened. It did not come, the feeling. He wondered why he had ever thought it would.

The shop in the village was open these days only three days a week, and it had been thirty years since there had been a market in the market-place, so Matthew had brought a big bag of food from London. He unpacked it in the cold kitchen. Bachelor food, really, he thought, as he put it into the fridge, because if there was such a thing as food appropriate to a widower, he did not care to imagine it. The fridge smelt odd; there was nothing rotting in it, but it had been kept closed and had been preserving the air and the shelves, nothing more. He unpacked, anyway, his bachelor shopping; ready-prepared dishes in white plastic tubs, things eloquent of incapacity. Chewing them, he thought of nothing.

The next day was better. Conrad's sympathetic man turned up with the computer Matthew had ordered, and connected the whole thing up. He was younger than Matthew had thought he would be, and more professional; Matthew had expected, in some vague way, a sort of workman in overalls, and hardly knew how to deal with a bright young man who talked to him with patient sympathy instead of deference. He wondered what kind of tip-off the man had been given, or if, perhaps, this particular brand of kindness was a prerequisite for the job. He stayed most of the afternoon, showing Matthew one trick after another, and bewildering him. Afterwards, Matthew found himself wanting to stroke the blank machine, looking forward to a good day exploring the recesses of the little white object and discovering for himself what the man had already shown him. Not quite a pet, something more than merely a utility, he wanted to delay the moment he sat down and really talked to it, really talked through it to the vast listening world.

The next morning, he sent a message to Conrad.

Good morning Conrad. I'm not quite sure if this is going to work, but I'll send it to you anyway. Let me know if you get this – it will give me some confidence. Your man was very helpful, so thank you for that, but I expect I'll be struggling with it for weeks to come.

Conrad replied an hour or so later.

How amusing to be talking to you like this. How is Cold Comfort Farm? Incest still the favourite occupation of the rural classes? When are you coming back – I'm sure you're beginning to miss London already. So pleased that Johnny was helpful.

They sent messages back and forth for most of the day, saying almost nothing. Before Matthew started, he had imagined that they would type for a while and then, bored of an artificial means of communication, they would simply pick up the telephone and talk. But they didn't, and after a while he began to see that this was a way of talking just like any other; a way of talking which allowed him a little space; allowed him a moment of thought, permitted him a little freedom from the pressure of people's voices, the pressure of other people's feelings. He could see the point of it; and the point, perhaps, was silence. Communication, and silence; communication, perhaps, in silence, and a virtuous solitude.

Matthew spent the afternoon going through his address book, and letting various academic contacts know that he was now on the system. In a couple of weeks, this would be ordinary. For the moment, he let his arms tingle at the idea of the ether, the magical compressor of distance, the instantaneous traveller, summoning the world to his study. He finished, and looked up; he had not quite perceived that the room had grown dark around the bright computer screen. He extracted himself from the system, switched the machine off. The house was cold; he felt an abrupt hunger.

He went for a long walk the next day. The wind was up, blowing against his face, and quickly the sense of the pointlessness of walking in Suffolk settled on him. Without hills, in a place where the walker cannot see where he is going, nor where he has been, but is just walking, as if in an empty unmarked landscape; he could see little point to it. In Suffolk, there was no companion to walk with; in Suffolk, there was no work for him to mull over, no questions of Afghan matrilinearity to sort out; in Suffolk, he started to think, there was no point to him. In the end, his planned whole morning's walk dwindled into an hour and a half. He came back, and drove to Ipswich to buy groceries. When he returned, he put them on the kitchen table. But instead of putting them away, he sat down and looked at them. He lit a cigarette; something he had never done, here, when his parents were still alive, and as he began to smoke, he felt, not as if he were claiming the house for himself, but that he was an improper and undetected intruder. He had no idea what he was doing; he had no idea what he should do in this empty place, and it came to him that it had been four days since he had spoken to another human being. It hardly mattered any more.

When he switched on the computer it winked at him. It was a moment before he understood that someone had sent him a message. He entered the box; there was no name, just a string of numbers indicating the caller.

You've been on edge. Don't be edgy. You always had too much of an edge, a sort of sharp one, rough and hard. You cut me, you know. Do you know who this is? Can you guess where I'm speaking from, how I found you? But didn't you always know that I would always manage, somehow, to find you? Didn't you always know that?

He looked at the word **edge**. It was so strange, unlike an ordinary word, and he watched it behind the blinking cursor. That *d*, that *g*, banging against each other, so strange. He knew the word, he understood the expression **on edge**, but now he felt it as alien. There was no way of knowing when the message had been sent; it might have been waiting for him for hours, but he felt a certainty that the sender was there, at the other end, waiting for his response. He opened a file to reply, and laid his hands on the keyboard, like a relaxed alert virtuoso about to begin to play the piano. In the end he took his hand from the keyboard and placed it, flat, against the screen of the computer. He had nothing to say.

Memory was the worst thing, in the house, just as it had been on his field trips. On field trips, the memory of food, of English cheese and apples, of the tones and timbres of the voices of friends, had always had the power to bring pain into his head; once in the Hindu Kush, a taste, in a high mountainous feast for the honoured guest, had shocked him with its unmistakable school-taste of Lancashire hot-pot, and he had had to thank his Afghan hosts too effusively, afraid that he was about to start crying, and have to explain why. And here it was as if he had left everything, not as if everything that mattered had left him. He had left the London house, fearing to be reminded of Kate in an object of hers, in a corner of a room where he could see her standing, and, in this Suffolk house, a place they had infrequently visited and never lived in, she was everywhere. The silence of the dour village invited only the memory of a dear laugh; the food he made do with only summoned up the food, so different, she liked to eat. A cup of coffee; a flower; a blank wall; the white sheets and the white pillow on which no pained pale face rested; they were all filled with her, all seemed to form some tiny fragment of her giant Arcimboldo-face, within which, he began to understand, he now lived. He went from room to room, not knowing what to do, not knowing what not to do. His lack of effort; the effort they made with each other, all the time, every day. Every second a new reminder. He sat at his desk; he switched on, he switched off the computer, its hum and click like a slow rhythm, a natural rhythm insensitive to, indifferent to his existence.

There had been a party, for instance; so characteristic that now he could not remember what it was for, but only her, standing there, with her slight foot-shifting nervousness, and all the time she seemed to be holding the thing he had said to her, when they were alone, before people came; you'll be fine. He watched her, and she was fine, of course she was, because nobody could not love her, whatever this party was for: engagement, marriage, his birthday, a first anniversary, perhaps, in the course of their brief life together. She had greeted the guests, and talked to them, and made a good effort not to look at him for approval. In turn, he respected her, and made an effort not to look at her, out of his love and concern, and only once did he listen to what she was saying. 'Thank you very much, thank you very much indeed,' she was saying, 'for making the effort to come all this way', and his heart filled with her kindness, knowing that thank you was so inadequate for the gratitude she so ordinarily felt that it had to be filled out with *very much* and *very much indeed*, and they looked at each other, two hosts of a party, and shared their silent pleasure, for one moment, for just one moment.

He turned the computer on, and it was waiting for him, in the same patient kindness.

You didn't reply, the computer said. Don't worry. It doesn't really matter. I'm here for you anyway, whether you want to talk to me or not. I'm watching over you. You have a nice view there, you know. You don't know it, but you do. In one direction, you can see as far as the blue. If you look straight up, you can see the blue. The sky there, it's so big, it's enough of a view for anyone. When you go out, isn't it just like being on the top of a great big dome, doesn't it feel as if the horizon is beneath you? And no hills and no land-marks and nothing but wind, all the way to the sea? Isn't that good? And what did you go to Suffolk to look at? Did you think you might escape something? Maybe you did. But it isn't really working. I know you think about me, as much as I think about you. I'll come for you, one day, I promise. You know that, Matthew, don't you? I'm going to come for you, and I know you'll be waiting for me, and thinking about me as much as I think about you. You'll be waiting for what I've got for you. Because you know what I've got for you. You know it.

He read it, and he read it again. He reached forward to touch the screen of the computer. He was convinced that now, something extraordinary was about to happen. He felt that the surface of the screen, as he touched it, would not be cold hard glass, but something soft and warm and yielding, that a hand would mould itself around his, and take firm hold, and tug. But it was with no dread that he reached forward, and he felt only a small disappointed shock when there was nothing, after all, there, that the glass barrier remained as it was. He pulled his hand back from the cold screen, and began to type. Who are you, he tried to type, who are you. But something had happened to the computer. He pressed down each key in turn, with increasing slow deliberation, but nothing changed on the screen. The screen displayed only the message he had received, and would not register his question. Who are you, he typed again, and again, but nothing came up. Only the message he had received, and the cursor, blinking; and though he knew perfectly well that the cursor could only blink at the rate it was set at, it seemed to slow, a slow slow throb which his heart effortlessly doubled. He could send nothing; he could only wait for the next message, and he sat, looking at the screen, waiting for the machine to speak to him. Nothing came. The voice was gone, and the invisible magical net roamed through the electronic sea, and caught nothing.

The next morning Matthew got up and drove to Cambridge, very early. He got there before nine, and left his car at the railway station. He telephoned Conrad from a payphone, and explained that he was coming to London to sort out some dull things, and, if he had nothing better to do –

'Lunch?' Conrad interrupted.

'Why not,' Matthew said.

'You sound a bit strange.'

'It's a bit early, isn't it,' he said. 'I haven't – '

'Yes?'

'I mean, I haven't really been speaking to anyone much for a few days. I've been reading nothing but Persian tracts. Perhaps I've forgotten how to. How to speak English, I mean.'

'Well, make an effort to remember by lunch.'

They arranged a place, and he went to buy a ticket. He had a segment of the train to himself. He bought the *TLS*, and a junk paperback. Reading matter; he did not want his head to be unoccupied for a moment before he saw Conrad. He did not think; he only read. That was best. He wanted not to think about the place he found himself in; he wanted not to think about the story he found himself in.

The green fields passed, the lines of rain marking the window. Matthew had been a student in Cambridge, and a doctoral student, and had held a junior research fellowship there. He had spent over ten years of his life in the town, and for most of that decade had gone either in one direction, to his parents' house, or in another, towards London. He found it inexplicable that both these routes, without his constant use, were as they had been, that the railway line still pursued the same dull slow route into East London, past the dull flat countryside with the flat-faced animals. He had changed, and the world had changed with his perception of it. But the ways of escape and entrapment were as they were, as they had always been.

He had never thought to find himself in a ghost story. He knew how ghost stories started; they started with a communication, in daylight, from a voice long thought silenced. And that had happened. If he did not know where the voice came from, from what part of the vast invisible world, that was because he did not care to look. The world was out there, the invisible world which the linking hands of the Net, like a seance of the ignorant many, had accessed for him, and now it gathered round his little computer, around his little hurting head, and tormented him. He knew how ghost stories began. He knew, too, how they ended: with the solitary widower in the solitary house, his arm chewed off, a look of inexpressible unearthly terror on his face in the locked room. He said to himself, as the train rolled over the points, don't be stupid, don't be stupid. He looked out at the land, and sitting in the empty carriage, he was only calm. There were explanations. There were always explanations. A friend might be sending them, these messages – a friend who thought he had understood quite well who it was – out of kindness, or some complicated malice. Or it could be her. Yes, he thought, looking out with a tranquillity he would never have been able to predict as he accepted the worst thing of all; it could be her, speaking to him across insubstantial space.

Unexpectedly, Conrad was there before him. It was a restaurant they had often passed, and often vaguely promised each other that they would try, in a street by the Museum. Its calm white walls and discreet waiters – and its cost – were satisfyingly unlike the usual Museum cafés, but its proximity to learning inoculated it against any fashion, against – it was a phrase, a shorthand for vulgarity and noise the two of them used – against expense-account. Conrad had ordered himself a Bloody Mary, elaborately structured with celery and a floating detritus of black pepper.

'You look well,' Matthew said. 'Am I late?'

'Not at all,' Conrad said. 'I had nothing to do this morning and got here early out of boredom. Actually, I have nothing to do this afternoon, so I plan to get rather drunk. If you don't object.'

'Not in the slightest,' he said. 'It's been so long since –'

He stopped. In fact, it had not been long at all.

'I'll tell you,' Conrad said, sipping his drink, taking up the conversation from the awkward gap. 'I'll tell you what has been a long time. It's been years and years since I finished a book and had no idea what I was going to start working on next. It's quite a nice feeling.'

'Finished with those boring warlocks?'

'They were terrible, in the end,' Conrad agreed. 'I might come out with you to your murderers. That might be fun.'

Matthew nodded, smiling, having nothing to say to this. They looked at their menus for a while.

'It looks good, doesn't it?' Conrad said. 'What would you like?'

'I'm not sure, Matthew said. 'But you mustn't –'

'I mustn't?'

'You mustn't buy me lunch, really.'

'I had no plan to,' Conrad said. Matthew looked up. Perhaps he had misunderstood what Conrad had meant.

'I'm sorry,' he said. 'I thought you said – I mean. I was going to buy you lunch, in fact.'

'Well,' Conrad said. 'I'd rather you didn't.'

'I'm sorry,' Matthew said, trying to get to the end of the conversation. 'I thought you said something. I thought you said, what would you like, and I thought, I thought you were saying that this one was on you. I misunderstood. I was going to buy you lunch. I mean I still am.'

'I'd rather you didn't,' Conrad said. 'Let's order.'

'What are you thinking of working on?' Matthew said, more or less at random.

'I really don't know,' Conrad said. 'There are a lot of things I feel vaguely interested by, but nothing is striking me with any enthusiasm at the moment. I might just teach for a bit and see if something comes up out of the blue.'

'Or,' Matthew said, 'you might just go back to something you've worked on before. I think – well, I've never worked on anything but my boys, you know, for nearly thirty years now, it just gets more and more fascinating.'

'Anthropologists,' Conrad said after a moment, 'they come in so many different shapes and sizes, don't they.'

The waiter came to take their order.

'How is the computer?' Conrad said when he had gone.

'Fine,' he said. 'Yes, fine. I worked out the E-mail system. Oh, you know I have. I was talking to you on it.'

'Yes, indeed,' Conrad said. 'Are you getting much use out of it?'

'Yes,' Matthew said. 'You know, something odd happened.'

'Yes?' Conrad said. 'Things often go wrong at first.'

'Yes, they do,' Matthew said. He let it drop for a moment. 'Do you – do you get messages from strangers, ever?'

'What sort of messages?'

'About you. I mean personal messages. Do you ever get anonymous messages from people who know about your life?'

'I don't remember having one,' Conrad said. He looked oddly at Matthew. 'I don't think it's as easy as all that to find someone's E-mail address. Have some more wine.'

The lunch went on. The food was quite good; perhaps not quite as excellent as they had imagined, but quite good enough, and it went on until the restaurant was almost empty. In Conrad's face was a tense expression, as if wondering why Matthew had asked him there, and, answering the questioning look, Matthew felt a need to produce a request.

'I wonder,' he said in the end. 'I wonder if I could ask you a favour.'

'Anything,' Conrad said, warmly.

'You know Kate,' Matthew said. 'I mean, you know her clothes.'

Conrad looked at him, nodding faintly.

'And you know women,' Matthew said. 'A lot more than I do, I expect. Well, I was just going through things the other day, and there are really a lot of Kate's clothes in the wardrobe still. I wondered if you knew any women who might have some use for them. Of course, I haven't given them away, don't really have anyone to give them to, or –'

He stopped. Perhaps this was a strange thing to ask someone.

'Of course,' Conrad said. 'Of course, I'll take them and give them to charity shops. Of course it isn't good for you to have them around.'

'No,' Matthew said. 'No, I wasn't saying that, I just wondered if you knew any women who would like any of them. Some of them are probably quite good, and she didn't wear them, or anything.'

'Matthew,' Conrad said. 'I'll take them to a charity shop. You wouldn't like it if you had lunch with the librarian and she was wearing an old dress of Kate's. Don't worry. I know what to do. I'll arrange the whole thing.'

He nodded, knowing from the tone of Conrad's voice that he was right. He put his coffee spoon down in the saucer. 'I am a widower,' he said. 'My wife died.' He looked at Conrad. Oddly, it was not the first time he had declared himself a widower.

'I'm sorry,' Conrad said, and there was feeling, unfeigned in his eyes.

Matthew nodded.

'You knew that, though,' he said.

'Yes,' Conrad said. 'Of course I knew.'

'I just thought,' Matthew said. He gulped. Here in this restaurant, this unfamiliar good restaurant, something was sticking in his throat. It was not emotion, but only, he was sure, food. He wanted to say something, and could only say what everyone knew. He wanted to say something truthful, and food, surely, was getting in the way, some lump of bread, some fishbone.

'Are you all right?' Conrad said.

'Yes,' Matthew said. 'It was nothing. I can't remember what I was going to say.'

'No one's sending you messages, are they?' Conrad said. 'Offensive messages?'

'No,' Matthew said. 'No, nobody. It doesn't matter.' Sometimes you understand events as they happen; sometimes you understand too late to respond to them and have to live with your understanding. Lunch was over. They got up.

The Persians sewed mirrors into their hunting nets, and caught small birds with their own reflections. And this Net too, was mirrored. He had thought that he was looking at the world, and beyond this world, and all the time, like a trapped and fluttering lark, he had only seen himself, and the fluttering and brilliant sudden movements which had appeared to him were only his own last movements, bringing not freedom, nothing new, no change, but the last desperate gestures of one confined and caught.

He made his way back to Suffolk. He took a taxi to the station, making no communication with the driver. He got on the train to Cambridge, and noticed only that it was full at the beginning and emptied slowly at each stop, like a full stage gradually revealing the protagonist of the drama. He got in his car, at Cambridge, and drove. The whole journey took three hours. He stopped his car outside the blank house, and got out. The sky was blackening with clouds, black and weighted as zinc. He stood there for a moment. The house was empty, and night was coming on, and, as he stood, a light in an upstairs room flicked on. It was the timer switch, but it made him jump. The house, empty, had its own life now. It would continue with its on and off, indifferent to human presence or absence. He went towards the front door, having nowhere else to go, and as he put his hand on the doorknob, there was a thunderous certainty in him that here was no ghost, here was no torturing outside presence, but only himself.

In his house, and in his head. No ghost, nothing but the great mirrored Net, seeming to offer him the thought of possibilities, of other torments which might have been spared him, and showing him only himself. In his head and his house, there would always be the pain, the grief, the truth, and he contemplated the consolation of a ghost with the unarguable knowledge that there was nothing as good and kind as that here; the unarguable familiarity with the unnameable thing which could search the great invisible universe, and, in less than a second, infallibly find him.

* * * * *

Ronald Blythe was born in Suffolk and is best known for *Akenfield* (1969), his remarkable study of change in the English village. His output ranges through poetry, fiction and essays including *From The Headland* (1982) and the highly acclaimed *Wormingford Trilogy* (1997-2005), the village in the Stour valley where he lives in an old farmhouse once home to the painter John Nash. Blythe has always been intrigued by the cultural life of the region, and its provincial dramas are the subject of 'Everything a Man Needs' (p.154) and 'Shadows of the Living', inspired by the fate of a 17th century Suffolk clergyman. Both first appeared in *The Stories of Ronald Blythe* (1985).

The Shadows Of The Living
RONALD BLYTHE

The activity, both inside and outside Springwaters, had been immense. Springwaters, because the source of the broad, short, sluggish Bourton river literally sprang from the rough pasture just behind the house. Faulkner had watched all the preparations with his usual oblique gaze, keeping them at bay, as it were, and not allowing them his full interest.

He was in the study doing the farm accounts but the door was ajar and he could see all the to-ing and fro-ing; Sophie heaving the furniture about and Mrs Blanch helping her. They were making a space in the library so that seventeen clergymen, including a bishop and an archdeacon, might robe. Through a series of doorways like those in a Velásquez, Faulkner was able to see the darting movement in the Great Hall as the village ladies spread an enormous parish tea.

'What can I do?' he had offered.

Sophie had not needed to consider the question. 'You can keep out of the way, that's what you can do.'

The upheaval was bothering him, he realized. There was something overreaching about it; a sense of going too far. Some kind of mis-judgment, not so much of the occasion but of the person who was central to it. Once, he had got as far as the 'field of operation', as Sophie called it, to suggest some kind of calming-down in all the preparations. It was, after all, the induction of the new rector, not a hunt ball they were about. But the women wove around him, like ants round a stone, impervious to everything except their tasks and burdens. So now he ran his fat old-fashioned Parker up and down the feed bills, trying to concentrate, trying, too, to take the day in his stride. After all, parsons came and went, and Mr Deenman would be no exception.

Staring straight ahead, Faulkner saw the familiar heart of the village, the huge shapeless green, its little paths busy with people, its surround of lanes glittering with cars and vans. The embryonic river trickled through it and children sailed over it on the swings which he and Sophie had given to commemorate the Festival of Britain. What had somebody said – quoted – when looking at the same scene from the Hall? 'And all shall be well, and all manner of things shall be well.' Well he certainly hoped so! Church and Hall shone towards each other in the late April light, as they had done for centuries.

A figure dramatically appeared on the top of the tower and soon the patronal flag hurled on the wind, a vivid cross on a white field, a scaffold as a matter of fact, thought Faulkner, surprising himself. A peculiar stomach-fluttering wax smell drifted through the room. 'Blasted polishing and cleaning!' he grumbled to the sleeping dog. 'What's it all about, eh? You tell me, boy!' It's about God, he thought morosely. It's either about God or it's about nothing. The alternatives see-sawed in his subconscious. If I believe, then *what* do I believe? he wondered. 'Sophie!' he shouted.

She put her head round the door.

'Sophie, I was thinking, something has happened to us, hasn't it? To us and to our world. God isn't here as He was, well, when grandfather was here, is He? It's the truth, isn't it? It should make us scared or sad, yet it doesn't. Think how big God was when the men built the church and how little He is when you cut sandwiches for Terence!' Terence was the Bishop.

'I refuse to think anything of the sort,' said Sophie. 'You look a bit pale; are you all right?'

'I'm O.K. It's that damn floor polish. It seems to upset me.'

'Darling, nobody has been polishing anything, and don't complain. Why don't you pack those accounts in if you don't feel like it? Go and do something in the garden for an hour – you've got time before lunch.'

'I'm your tiresome little boy, aren't I?'

'You're my dear old boy,' she said, kissing his thinning hair.

The gules and martlets and lozenges in the armorial window were caught in sunlight and spattered the pair of them with gaudy shadows. A few minutes later, Faulkner was happily walking through the orchard, noting the swollen buds and disturbing the finches. The smell of wax persisted but it no longer upset him. On the contrary, it seemed to lift and strengthen him. And when the first tentative sounds of the practice peel broke from the church tower he felt a return of ease which was almost as good as a return of certainty. What a relief! How could he have explained to Sophie – to anyone – that there had been moments during the past month when he had heard (although that was too strong and definite a word, maybe) the tumult of a destroying force making its relentless way towards the village, and seen whisps of smokey darkness, and had known the taste of substances which drew the lips back from the tongue in gagging refusal? Strolling back to the house, he heard the pips for the World at One and Mrs Blanch calling, 'Colonel! – her Ladyship, says "Lunch and hurry!"'

Sitting with the two women at the great scrubbed kitchen table, Faulkner ate quickly, as though solid food could fill what pockets of emptyness might remain within him. He thought, as he frequently did, though without rancour, of that enviable thing in most people's eyes, his inheritance, and how much better his life would have been without it. All the rooms and acres and farms, and the duties that festooned them, the local bench, the committees and, of course, the church. He and Sophie were museum-keepers, both in the metaphysical as well as in the material sense. Lumbered! He might, with a bit of conniving, heave the house and its contents into the lap of the National Trust but he could scarcely shed his duties. Not at his age. But he wished that life had provided him with more than merely a decent response to social obligations. It would have been nice to have been clever like Sophie, or really good like Mrs Blanch. The trouble was, he never did have much imagination.

He rose and freed a butterfly which was beating its wings against a pane. A gust of over-hot air burst at him through the momentarily open window. He almost said, 'It's going to be a scorcher,' then remembered the date, the fourteenth of April. A jet from the nearby American airbase screamed across the garden, spinning a rope of smoke behind it. The power and the glory, thought Faulkner, what did that mean now?

Both Bishop and clergy arrived promptly at 2.30. Mattock, the new young constable, fussed their cars over the cattle-grid into the park. Most of the cars stopped just inside the gates to let wives and other passengers get out and walk across the green to the church. Faulkner met everybody on the terrace, drawing them through the hall in the courteous way which seemed to make his house their property for the time they were there. His hospitality was his special genius, though he had no knowledge of this.

The little Bishop was merry. For someone who slaved fifteen hours a day at an administrator's desk, such functions as introducing a new priest to one of these beautiful time-lost country places lying in the wilds of his diocese came more into the category of recreation than work. He wandered happily from group to group. The response to him, Faulkner observed, was a pleasure verging on radiance. The older clergy seemed to lose their staleness when he chattered to them. As for the young men, they noticeably gained in spiritual confidence or authority. Or something. Faulkner watched with a mixture of embarrassment and longing. God flickered in his brain like a neon sign, one minute with total definition, the next without form and substance.

The Bishop, looking at his watch, said, 'Not a sign of him yet, Colonel! I hope that old bus of his hasn't had a breakdown.'

Faulkner's confusion was obvious.

'Your new Rector, Colonel – remember?' said the Bishop with mock severity.

Mr Deenman: it was true, the curious, unsettling appointee had clean gone from Faulkner's mind. 'The man of the moment!' he smiled – 'And me forgetting him!' The gaunt untidy figure rushed into his consciousness; the odd harsh voice, so compelling yet so difficult to understand at times, suddenly filled his ears. Deenman had been the Bishop's nomination after a year had passed without another soul applying for the living. The Bishop was speaking to him again, although now his words contained an underlying seriousness.

'You won't forget him, I'm sure, Colonel.' He was really saying, 'Deenman is a lonely, wifeless man who is going to need a bit of unobtrusive help and encouragement.'

'He'll be all right, Terence. Never fear.'

Why did the Bishop insist on their calling him by his Christian name and yet continue to address him as Colonel?

'I expect he's gone straight to the church,' said the Bishop. 'We may as well go too, I think.. We can wait at the back until he turns up.'

The impressive little procession, headed by the blacksmith's teenage son carrying a tall brass cross he had made for his apprenticeship exams, wound its way darkly over the green, Faulkner and the other churchwarden attending the Bishop with wands and solemn steps. Cars were lined up in rows round the churchyard wall and the dead seemed to be slickly wrapped in tinfoil. It was what Faulkner called a good turnout. Except that the bellringing bothered him by its resonance. He thought that it was probably something to do with the wind – although he had never known such nerve-touching sounds before. Each bell seemed to skilfully slide away from its true note and produce a deliberate travesty of what was expected. The clashing was being built up to some sort of climax. Faulkner's bewilderment changed to anger. As the procession entered the churchyard, the last vestige of shape vanished from the peal and a chaotic shaft of percussive noise took over. 'What the hell . . .?' He turned a half-apologetic face to the Bishop, only to glimpse the serene smile and the silver flash of the crozier. Faulkner's worried glance passed on to Robarts, the people's warden. Robarts was a ringer and had been a tower-captain in his day. But the old shepherd was shambling forward in his usual manner, his features as expressionless as he could make them. You couldn't get anything out of Robarts, thought Faulkner, even if the world was coming to an end. Which was what it sounded like.

They were about to enter the porch when the huge old 1950s Humber which Faulkner had last seen when Mr Deenman had arrived at the Hall for his interview, and smothered in what appeared to be an entire winter's mud, lurched into view and shook itself to a standstill at the very entrance to the churchyard. He's not going to leave the thing there! Faulkner thought incredulously. Right bang in the way!

The procession had stopped and in a few seconds, bowing in that strangely excessive way of his, Mr Deenman strode through it to his place at the front of the nave. No 'good afternoons.' Just a gaunt dipping of the large head in its crushed and dusty Canterbury cap. No smile. Once inside the church, however, Mr Deenman's odd rushing confidence seemed to desert him; the huge strides slowed down and the tall solitary figure passed through the dense congregation with an awe which silenced the whispering. The first notes of the introit, piercingly grave, added to the drama. Nerves, thought Faulkner, rather relieved. Deenman's behaviour up to this moment was beginning to overwhelm him. He saw the new Rector's glance pass from object to object in the chancel. It was as though he were checking an inventory, making sure that everything remained as he had left it.

Scarcely moving his head, Mr Deenman's gaze fell on carved angels and devils, the Mothers' Union banner and all the other ornaments and fittings, while the altar candles blazed in his spectacles, filling the dark eyes with reflected fire. Faulkner remembered now that this was the first time Deenman had seen the church. He recalled how surprised he had been – even a little hurt – when, at the interview, he had offered to show him over it and the new Rector had said, 'No, not now. Not yet.' Adding stiffly, 'I thank you.' 'He talks rather old-fashioned-like,' 'Shepherd' Robarts had said approvingly.

The induction went faultlessly, the clever Bishop manipulating the best instincts of the laity. Tolerance and love were manifest. The ancient revolutionary argument of Christ's philosophy was heard plain and clear. Mr Deenman played his part to perfection and emerged as an undeniably holy man. He was led by the churchwardens to the door, the font, the lectern and the altar in turn, and making great promises all the way. Finally, he was taken to his rectorial stall, this being the first in a row of magnificent fifteenth-century misericords on the right of the chancel. A curious hesitation occurred at this point, a flight of confidence not unlike that which had affected him when he had first entered the building. He almost sat in the correct seat, then slipped quietly into that next to it. The archdeacon, who was still holding his hand, grinned and insisted on the official stall, and Deenman accepted it, though so gingerly, Faulkner had remarked to Sophie afterwards, 'You'd have thought it was the hot seat!' While they sang the *Te Deum*, Mr Deenman remained hunched in his place, his eyes fixed on the great painted oak angels roosting in the roof. The time then came for him to make the customary brief speech of thanks. The first few sentences were conventional enough, although Faulkner was once again struck by the rich, rough voice with its unplaceable accent. It was only necessary to say a few polite words. It was obvious that the new Rector realized this but that he also was struggling with a compunction to add something personal. This obviously got the better of him for, to the controlled astonishment of the packed church, he replaced his cap and began to preach. The magnificently spoken words were crammed together in complicated phrases which were often hard to follow, though the reason for the outburst was plain enough – accusation. Wrath. Faulkner listened, fascinated but made slightly sick, as one listens to a gale.

'What is this that Peter said?' demanded the new Rector. 'Wash both feet, hands and head? Verily to open the matter clearly unto you, by these hands are understood *opera hominis* – the works and deeds of man! For the hands are the principal instruments whereby man does his work and labour.'

Here Mr Deenman held up his hands which Faulkner saw with distaste were extremely dirty, brown and strong but with blackened, broken nails.

'Therefore by the hands are understood words and deeds. . .' The Rector was now staring at the hands of the people in the front pews, his look passing from one to the other, rather like an officer at an army inspection. When he reached Faulkner, he spoke straight at him and pointing. 'These thy evil works must be washed clean by penance ere thou go to the great maundy of God, or that thou receive thy Maker!' And he swung round to the altar.

'He can't mean that he is going to refuse me Communion!' thought Faulkner. 'Why? What on earth have I done? What the hell is he getting at? The man must be mad!' He looked at the Bishop for support but he sat on his uncomfortably carved chair with all his usual implacable sweetness.

'And not only thy hands, thy works, but also thy head,' continued the Rector, 'whereby is understanding of all thy five senses, thy five wits . . . There is thy sight, thy hearing, thy smelling, thy tasting and thy touching. These senses otherwise called thy five wits must also be by penance washed!' Leaning over the partition made by the sawn-off stump of the rood, he looked into Faulkner's amazed face and said, almost conversationally, *'Thy hands, thy hands that did it, they must be by penance washed!'* . . .'

He now turned to the assembled clergy in the choir, then to the long rows of politely listening faces in the nave, and said simply, his hand indicating the apparent peacefulness of the scene, *'Haec requies mea.* This was my rest. This was my place of quiet. I was to be happy here as long as I lived. But what followed? *Nulla requies* – no rest. . .'

A few minutes later, everybody was strolling across the green to the parish tea which had been laid out in the Hall, while the bells rang with perfect precision. Mr Deenman was shuffling along with the other clergy and carrying his surplice over his arm. Sophie saw that it had a large tear near the hem.

'You know that we're expecting you for dinner tonight, Rector!' she cried. She wanted to add, but who is going to get your meals and look after you in the future? How are you going to manage in that big old rectory? 'He's going to be a bit of a problem', she whispered to Faulkner. 'Darling, are you all right? Is it your funny tummy?'

A boy flying a kite was so absorbed that he seemed unaware of the surge of churchgoers. 'I won't let you go, I won't let you go,' he was muttering over and over to himself as he clung to the string of the desperately straining pink shape.

A few weeks later Faulkner bumped up the Rectory drive with some papers for Mr Deenman's signature. The barren-looking house with its curtainless, ogling black windows no longer worried him. The new Rector had made himself comfortable in a two-roomed den adjacent to the kitchen and simply ignored the rest of the building. A massive table, a few books, his clothes on hangers dangling from the picture-rail, a stiff little iron bed standing on a square of brown drugget and a prie-dieu with a padded kneeler appeared to be his total household goods. After his initial shock, Faulkner found himself rather approving this austerity. Why should a nuclear age parson be obliged to set himself up in Victorian domestic style? He glanced around and, seeing that a spade and barrow had been left in the courtyard, wandered off in search of Mr Deenman, now and then shouting, 'Rector!' The neglect in the garden really did rather upset him. It worried him to see the untouched lawns and weedy beds. Yet he was determined not to criticise. Things had been easier since he had made up his mind to accept the Rector as he was. 'Just let him get on with things in his own way,' Sophie had said. 'He is so *good* – everybody says so.'

Following the sound made by a machine, Faulkner came across the Rector just beyond where the formal garden ran into a large rough ridge of ground, dense with grass and gorse, and treacherous on the north side with a blackthorn hedge. He had cleared some of the scrub with a scythe and was now trying to plough the clearing with a rotavator. In spite of the modem machine with its cheerful green paint and shining gadgets, there was something in the bowed, fatalistic attitude of its operator which suggested to Faulkner a scene he had witnessed in France, a solitary peasant, chipping away in a vast Norman field with a short-handled hoe, who had seemed to him the essence of everlasting human toil.

The Rector was dressed in old battledress trousers held up with a wide leather belt, a flannel shirt and his clerical collar. The rotavator was either jammed or the Rector did not understand the working of it, for after a yard or two's straight ploughing it seized the initiative and swung the heavy figure round in a mad uncontrolled arc, churning up haphazard scraps of root and gravel. When Faulkner hurried over and switched the thing off, the Rector looked as if he had reached breaking point. His hands trembled and he was almost in tears.

'My dear man, why wear yourself out on this dreadful old bit of ground? It's part of the glebe but nobody has touched it in my lifetime. It's just a donkey acre. If you *must* have it ploughed, then I'll ask Arnold to bring a tractor up and see what can be done. Though take my word – it's useless.' (Why was the silly ass fooling around up here anyway when there was a beautiful bit of kitchen garden simply begging to be dug?)

'Perhaps you're right,' said Mr Deenman. He was making a great effort to recover his dignity, or maybe (thought Faulkner) simply not to show anger and frustration. 'It seems a pity, that's all. Not to mention having to give up part of my vocation!' He gave one of his rare smiles.

'Oh come now, Rector! We don't expect you to farm as well as preach!'

'You don't?' Mr Deenman was clearly astonished.

'Why, no,' replied Faulkner uncertainly. What was the chap driving at?

He changed the subject. 'Sophie says I'm to bring you back to supper.'

'And am I to bring you back to God.'

For a moment Faulkner could scarcely believe his ears. To 'get at him' here, out in the garden, to swing the conversation over like that – it was the limit! All his suppressed dislike of the priest rushed to the surface; he could taste its putrescence in his mouth, it burned like acid in the corneas of his eyes, it soaked out of his palms and glutted his stomach. His loathing of Deenman was blind and desperate, like the loathing he had had for a rat which would not die, *would not die*, though he had beaten his walking-stick into a paroxysm of revulsion. *He* had died, for an entire abyss-like minute, but the rat had dragged its frightful wounds away. Deenman was touching him! Jesu . . . Jesu . . .

'I thought you were going to catch your foot on that stump. I shall have to dig it out. We'll go over to the church and say the office, then have tea. Call it a day.'

'What office?'

'I'm not certain. Perhaps you'd like to choose – it's the feast of St Alban.' He fumbled in the pocket on the front of the battledress trousers and withdrew a Bible. 'That's right – Ezra. They are laying the foundations of the temple. "The people could not discern the noise of the shout of joy from the noise of the weeping . . ." Well, that's life for you.'

'I think I should go home,' said Faulkner. 'I told Sophie I wouldn't be long.'

'You won't be long – I can promise you that.'

'Perhaps I should have said that I'm not very good at this sort of thing – saying offices and all that. I'm just a once-a-weeker I'm afraid.'

'Don't worry,' answered the Rector. 'None of us is very good at it. Here, half a sec, I'll get my cassock.'

Again Faulkener noticed the double language, as if two time-divided colloquialisms had joined each other. Then he remembered that Mr Deenman knew endless unusual things about the Reformation, odd little scraps of social information, customs and the like. He had conducted a party of local historians round the cathedral and Faulkner and Sophie, dutifully trailing in his wake, had been amazed.

The Rector returned from the house with the cassock untidily flung on him and attempting to fasten its many buttons as he half-walked, half-ran to where Faulkner waited. His movements, too, were contradictory, alternating as they did between clumsiness and grace. The cassock heaved around the thick body, a horrible garment, Faulkner decided. Looked as though it had been slept in, or under. Yet it was plain that the Rector assumed it with a sense of honour.

They left the Land Rover in the drive and walked to the church. Mrs Howe, cleaning the altar brass, looked up and said, 'Rector, Colonel.' The building, as usual, was freezing cold and smelled cosily of vermin. Faulkner imagined Mrs Howe going home to tell her family about him being on his knees on a Wednesday afternoon and her husband carrying the news to the pub that evening.

The Rector, after giving the dismantled altar a stare, turned into the Faulkner chapel and plunged before the gaudy tomb of a Robert Faulkner who had died in 1641. An aquamarine light from the east window bathed the alabaster face.

'All that – will have to be shifted,' said the Rector conversationally. 'He's in the altar space.'

He spread his books on a chair and knelt. Faulkner crouched a little to his right. Mrs Howe watched with an expressionless face, her hands continuing to polish at a tremendous rate. For a while the Rector muttered his way through Evensong and Faulkner managed to say the responses. The devotion soon became something normal and ordinary, and his cool English worship gave way to an uninhibited contact with God. As the service proceeded he rationalized all the difficulties which had arisen between himself and the new Rector. They stemmed, surely, from their degrees of belief. The Rector was God-possessed, while he was, well, God-acquainted. He tried to pray. Not to say words but to break through the decent Anglican formula and reach God's ear. A silence. A universe of flint. Sentences which not only fell short of their target but which returned to him like spit in the wind. He was soiled by his own prayer. It didn't work for him and, if he was honest, it had never worked. Being Robert Cosgrave Faulkner, J.P., T.D., hadn't worked either. His life was trivial. It was trivial because it was nothing more than a packet of unexamined gestures. The gesture he made towards heaven was the worst. God was so sick of it that he had sent him a slight coronary (over a year ago now and no further effect) and he had sent him Mr Deenman. It was time the Rector rose from his knees. Faulkner felt giddy. He was also quite unmistakably aware of a rank odour coming from the cassock and that the bulging shape which pushed through the broken boot in front of him was Mr Deenman's bare foot.

As if conscious of Faulkner's doubt, the Rector half-turned in his direction and whispered, 'We are like women who have a longing to eat coals and lime and filth. We are fed with honour and ease and wealth, yet the gospel waxeth loathsome and unpleasant in our taste, so how can we feed others with what we cannot fancy ourselves?'

Faulkner leaned forward until the large ear with its whorl of red hair was almost touching his mouth and said, slowly and distinctly, 'They burnt the parson of this parish. They burnt him on the green. It was a long time ago. His name was Daneman – John Daneman.'

'Blessed John Daneman?'

'I don't care about that. *But I think you ought to know.*'

Mr Deenman said, 'My strength hath been my ruin and my fall my stay. I was in danger, like a chased bird. Yet who would wish to remain in a misshapen or ruined nesting hole?'

'*I think you should go.*'

'Where should the frighted child hide his head, but in the bosom of his loving father?'

Faulkner got to his feet. His head throbbed and there was an ache in his eyes which made the late afternoon sun unbearable. He half-dragged the Rector to the varnished board containing the list of the incumbents and jabbed at a name about halfway down, 'John Daneman – suffered 1554.'

'And it wasn't Bloody Mary,' said Faulkner. 'It was the village. They did it off their own bat, on the green. *That* green!' And he pointed through the open door at the endlessly swinging children and the bus crawling to a stop and women with prams and three old men waiting for death on the jubilee seat. He saw the slight greying of the Rector's swarthy face, and was satisfied. 'So I think you ought to go,' he repeated.

'I think I should, too,' said Mr Deenman. 'That is, if I'm to tidy up in the garden and get changed for this evening. Please do thank Lady Sophie for her invitation – it really is most kind.'

Faulkner walked back to the Rectory in order to pick up the Land Rover. Neither of them spoke. Mr Deenman was strolling in a concentrated sort of way, eyes on the ground, arms folded and when people said, 'Good afternoon', Faulkner was obliged to reply for both of them. The air made him feel better every minute.

As the year wore away, Mr Deenman came less and less to the Hall. It was not so much a question of his refusing invitations as something implicit in his manner which forbade Sophie to offer them. She was rather pleased about this. It meant that the Rector's way of life was a deliberately chosen independent thing and not in need of her carefully concealed props. Faulkner, on the other hand, felt oddly affronted by such independence.

105

But both of them, like the rest of the village, got used to the unkempt Rectory and to the sight of the massive figure bent over a book in an uncurtained room or futilely slaving away in the garden. Doors and gates were never shut, and a naked bulb was often seen burning throughout the night. The services were taken with a mixture of stillness and commotion. The congregation seemed to have adapted itself to the passionate tirades which occasionally broke into an otherwise conventional sermon, though for Faulkner it was like waiting for a bomb to go off, disappointing when it did not, terrifying when it did.

Once or twice he had sounded the local opinion regarding the Rectory. Decently, of course – the Hall had always been a place where the gossip stopped. To his astonishment, he discovered a good deal of admiration for the grubby clergyman. 'He's a funny old bugger all right, but he'll give anybody a hand,' was the verdict at the pub. This was praise.

But one Saturday in September, Faulkner took the letters to the post and fancied he saw a very different reaction. It was a hot day but summer was ebbing nonetheless. The baked elms, their green fronds fading into ultramarine shadows, had no illusions about it and rustled with dissolution. The harvest had been snatched up by mechanical grabbers before anyone had realized there had been a harvest and from the high land surrounding the village, already stripped down for the plough, there came a warm and mocking wind which spelt no good. Or so Faulkner believed. He wasn't well; there was no longer the faintest doubt about it. It was not what his doctor said but what he himself knew. Because there was no pain or discomfort, the unusual thing which was happening to him – he had never before had actual, unmistakable illness, the state which alters life or ends it – was novel – almost luxurious. It was the feeling of pure sorrow which he found so acceptable, an acknowledgment of his own personal grief for something within himself which he could not name. He and Sophie had had a holiday in Crete, enjoyed a good summer, in fact. But it was the intensification of the rather ordinary views within walking distance of the Hall which had fascinated him ever since they had returned. A group of trees, a pasture, the home woods which he must have seen countless times now burst against his vision in a climax of beauty. At such moments he was praying, though he never knew it.

It was while he was taking one of these last-of-summer walks that he passed by the field where the village football team was playing a visiting side, and that he saw amongst the gaggle of spectators the awkward figure of the Rector. The match ended just as Faulkner was approaching and players and spectators swirled around the tall clergyman, who smiled and nodded. To Faulkner's surprise (to his satisfaction, he was inwardly bound to confess) these nods and smiles were returned by hostile glances or at the best indifference. It gave Faulkner a curious thrill to see the hurt on Mr Deenman's face when this happened. An overpowering emotion caught at him; the kind of blood-triumph which used to sweep him across the hunting-field in his youth leaped in him with a forcefulness he had long forgotten. What he remembered was Mr Deenman's remark – 'I was in danger, like a chased bird' – and he saw a great squawking crow, winged and unable to soar, tumbling desperately over the furrows and himself in pursuit of it. 'Get him, sir! . . . Get him, sir!' the villagers were howling. The footballers and their girls began to drift homewards, Mr Deenman with them. Faulkner could hear the distinctive voice but not the words. Now and then there was laughter, and at the gate, raised arms. Waves? 'I must get back too,' thought Faulkner. Sophie had arranged for the whole houseparty to go to the Boulez concert at Cheltenham.

They were still having tea in the garden when he returned.

'These constitutionals of his, they really do wonders for him,' said Sophie. 'Just look at him! – he looks fit to kill!'

The days which followed were extraordinarily full. The activities which Faulkner and Sophie had put off on account of their long holiday – five weeks – and the harvest, crowded one upon the other. This busyness did not make life run fast, as it is supposed to do, but expanded it. London meetings, a Northumberland shoot, an unusual amount of time at his club and the like, took him for a while out of the direct village orbit. Mrs Blanch's descriptions of what had been going on in his absence left him only politely interested. The truth was that when he was away from home he no longer felt or glimpsed the end approaching. On the other hand, nothing that he did outside the village gave him the extreme, almost ecstatic, happiness which he now drew from this familiar place. It had to be gradually, deliciously enjoyed: every hour with it was like a bite of the cherry and the time would come when he had devoured it all and he would no longer exist. This remained inconceivable.

'Let's go away again after Christmas, Sophie.'

'Marvellous! Where?'

The way she agreed to his every whim bothered him. She might have wrangled as she usually did; it would make things more normal. She never had possessed subtlety, only a big dull good heart. She had bored the passion out of their marriage.

'I don't know yet. Somewhere warm.'

After tea he walked to the post office and was kept waiting while a huddle of boys bought fireworks and Guy Fawkes masks. A few large leaves had trodden into the shop and the sweet smell of decay from the lanes and gardens infiltrated the cluttered room.

'Days drawin' in, sir – Colonel,' said the postmaster.

'They must,' replied Faulkner. He had not meant to sound either gnomic or vague but at that moment he had witnessed something very strange. The boys who had bought the masks had just got them on when the Rector passed. Waggling their heads and laughing, they were flattered by his elaborate fright, eyes rounded, mouth horrified. But Faulkner, hidden behind racks of groceries, was able to see a spasm of true terror take hold of Mr Deenman and shake him as if he were in the maw of a fiend. His own heart thudding with excitement, he greeted the Rector and accompanied him on the way home. He took the path which led to the waste at the back of the green and it was as he thought. A huge pile of faggots, straw, cardboard boxes, old tyres and other rubbish stood waiting for the fifth.

'I – I didn't think I had better come this way, if you don't mind,' said Mr Deenman.

'Then you know this way?'

'No – yes of course I know it.'

'Of course you do.'

Faulkner heard the fear and could smell the disgusting evidence of it.

'It's all pretty barbarous, don't you think?' said the Rector.

'I don't know . . .' considered Faulkner. 'Old customs and all that. Fire cleanses you know.'

'Well, it certainly will in this instance,' said the Rector, pointing at the heap of rubbish.

Joking, thought Faulkner. Nervous reaction. He was about to destroy Mr Deenman's confidence with a further threat when he felt his arm taken and himself led rapidly away from the bonfire. A voice inside him shrieked with loathing at the contact but the words – if words they were – vanished in the harsh talk. And what a freak the man was! Scuffed boots, old army trousers, stink and hair everywhere! Christ! they would have known what to do with him in the regiment old days!

Some children arrived, their arms filled with sticks. 'Remember! Remember!' they cried.

'We cannot forget, can we, Rector? Ever.'

Mr Deenman made one of his strange lunging movements, head

swivelling forward on a powerful neck, trunk twisted to the side but legs somehow immobilized. It was the trapped gesture which Faulkner found so exciting. When it came to the point the Rector was not the kind of quarry which ever got away. In such a fix, it was natural that he should roar. The words erupted over Faulkner but, expected as they were, their force rocked him.

'You do what you do, not for our Saviour, but for sport. You are like Leviathan in the sea without a hook in his nostrils, a Behemoth without a bridle. *I know thy ways.* I see thy painlusting arm. Smoke always goes before fire, to declare that fire is in kindling, and a sickness before the tempest to tell that the storm is in breeding. You mouth Christ while you play the hobgoblin. You parade virtue while you lurk under a hollow vault. You sent me out of this dear world as a cinder in His dear Name. It was your pleasure – *your pleasure only*. My flame was by the hour, yours shall be by the eternal clock. I am ash but you are anathema!'

Suddenly, the Rector's voice changed, his body regained its normal gaunt height and he asked, 'How long?'

'Three days – Thursday.'

'Just after All Souls?'

'1 suppose it is; I hadn't thought about it.'

'You poor creature,' said the Rector gently.

'I?' Faulkner was genuinely astonished.

Mr Deenman just smiled. 'We part here, don't we?'

'He's taking it pretty well,' Faulkner thought, watching the confident figure stride away into the dusk.

The fifth was a full day for both of them. Sophie's day for the Bench and his for the County Council. Then they both had to be together in Tewkesbury for a meeting about forestry, as well as do some shopping. Sophie insisted on doing the driving, saying that she liked it, though Faulkner knew that this was one more of her none too subtle ploys to make him ease-up. It was ridiculous really. He felt so strong, at least in that sense. The weather was perfection. A spell of sunshine was coming to a close and the hint of a drastic change – gales, even early snow showers had been mentioned in the television bulletins – made the last lavishly summery hours precious.

Sophie, when they had collected everything, had some tea and delivered a boot-full of iris roots to her cousins in Kingham – trailed home, as she described it. Faulkner, normally a bad passenger, sat docilely

109

beside her, watching the yellow-glaring trees, the small massive stone houses and the ancient white road. He imagined his ancestors, nearly five hundred years of them according to the local historians, using this same path whenever they journeyed west. Not that he was often given to such ideas. Of course it was something – even in 1970 – to be a Faulkner, but family in this sense had never meant much to him. Partly because he was rather a dud at history, he supposed. 'You'll have to ask my wife,' he said when people enquired about the great-something-grandfather who had fought with Monmouth or written 'The Testament of Huntsmen'. Once, when his father had been alive, some Catholic priests had arrived to collect information about the Faulkner who had signed the warrant sending Father Daneman to the stake. They were so embarrassed that it amused his father. When the old man had said, 'Other days, other ways,' they looked a bit offended, as though time had nothing to do with it. All the same, Faulkner continued to wish that he had not been born in this kind of estate-prison, that he had been free as most men are, to go and do what he liked where he liked. No arms, no armour. Nothing of that kind left over to anchor him.

A pale rocket tongued its way up the sky and feebly burst. 'Oh, look!' cried Sophie. 'I'd forgotten. How pretty.'

'They should have waited until it was dark.'

'Do you remember our firework parties, darling? When was the last – when Rodger was young, I suppose.'

'Rodger's twenty-first.'

'Of course. What ages ago! We're getting on – do you realize that?'

He did not reply. She chattered on, driving slowly but well, pointing at obvious things, missing things which really interested him, being Sophie. A top-drawer Earth Mother.

More sporadic fireworks went off, mostly a long way away, odd flashes and sparks neutered by the westering sun. 'Pretty'! They filled him with sorrow. It was about six-twenty when they reached home.

Half an hour later, while Sophie was in the bath and Mrs Blanch was laying the table, he heard the first shouts. He hurried from the house at once, taking the path through the kitchen garden which came out near to the piece of rough ground where they had built the bonfire. Other people were scurrying in the same direction. He could hear their quick tread, their urgent voices, even at times their breathing. Above this confused, thick but modulated sound rose the howls of imprisoned dogs, also other massively fretful noises which he took to be panic in the factory farms.

A homing bomber, a cross of lights, passed to the American airfield, adding its throb to the uproar. A group of men ran from the pub and the main road was ablaze with cars and motor-cycles. Isolated bangs gave the turmoil a curious stateliness, like minute guns announcing some great solemnity.

Faulkner could see the unlit bonfire now, tall as a house and immensely ritualistic. The crowd already gathered round it was restless but at the same time restrained. Children twittered in the darkness like disturbed birds. A bull, scenting danger, began a regular bellowing on some unseen field; the row created a brief mirth, then a crude acceptance. Faulkner pushed his way to the bonfire and touched it with his foot. He was near to worship, to love maybe, something overwhelmingly exultant, like a coming to life.

He looked at his watch. Seven-thirty. Then at two young man standing slightly apart.

'Right. Let's go and get him.'

The taller of the young men stared at Faulkner and then at his friend.

'We can't start without the Rector, can we?'

Faulkner's playful words produced a cautious grin.

'He'll come when he's ready, I expect, Colonel,' answered Mamby, the thresher's son. He continued to look at Faulkner uneasily, his fingers playing with a medallion which hung from his neck.

'He'll come when we tell him to. Come on.'

Followed by the couple, Faulkner saw the gleamingly curious eyes of the crowd and felt the heavy expectancy.

'Not long now, eh!' he called out to a group of women, some with small children in their arms. The women replied with shrill, hooting laughs.

As usual, the naked light burned in the uncurtained Rectory window and, in spite of the sudden drop in the temperature, the front door stood half open. Faulkner walked boldly up to the window and saw Mr Deenman. He was praying. He knelt at the prie-dieu with his hands clasped in the most extraordinary manner, on the top of his bowed head, the fingers making a tense arch above the wild grey hair. He was wearing his cassock and was very still. Mamby and his companion were clearly shocked and after the first glance into the room backed away.

'We'll give him another couple of minutes,' said Faulkner. 'Do the right thing, what!'

The boys scarcely heard him. They had retreated to the overgrown lawn and did not know what to do. Faulkner remained at the window taking in every detail of the scene, the neat bed, the teapot and cups on the scrubbed table, the letters waiting to be posted, the open book – Teilhard de Something – he couldn't quite see. Also *The Times* open at the Court page and a sleeping cat. Mr Deenman himself was motionless. Faulkner looked once more at his watch then strode into the house.

'Daneman - we're ready.'

His hand grasped the cassock and shook it. Mr Deenman rocked slightly then toppled crazily from the prie-dien. The young men heard the confusion and rushed forward. They saw the body of the Rector sprawling on the floor, the eyes fixed in terror and a great bare white leg exposed by his disordered robe. And at the same moment there was a *boom!* as the bonfire was ignited and a long, wailing roar of relief.

'Christ, oh Christ . . .' murmured the boy with the medallion.

It seemed extraordinary that on November 12th, the day of the funeral, the garden should be full of roses. The mild autumn had produced a massive second flowering. The flagged terrace was drenched in their scent. The Bishop trailed up and down after Sophie, listening to her rose-talk and thinking about the service he had just taken. Faulkner had driven straight back to an interrupted farming conference at Oxford. What a tower of strength the man was!

'I hear the Colonel did everything that could be done.'

Sophie snipped a fat, dew-logged Zephrine Druin with her secateur. 'Well, you know what Robert is,' she answered loyally. 'He's only sorry that he got there too late . . .'

* * * * *

George Ewart Evans (1909-88): On arriving in a remote Suffolk hamlet just after the war Evans was unaware that his new friendship with elderly neighbours would lay the foundations of what has become known as Oral History. *Ask The Fellows Who Cut The Hay* (1956), a celebrated tribute to the people of Blaxhall, was followed by a series of remarkable books that explore the traditional rural culture of East Anglia. In 1973 Evans returned briefly to fiction with the publication of *Acky*, a collection of gently subversive stories about a wiley old horseman living on the edge of a broad heath that catches perfectly the language and humour of Suffolk. 'The Coin' is one of those stories.

The Coin

GEORGE EWART EVANS

After Acky Flatt retired from the farm he spent a good deal of his time walking round the Common. He was up there so often with his old lurcher he called *Bundler* that he became known as the *Keeper*; and they used to say there wasn't a caterpillar up there he didn't know well. He'd be there just after dawn, and again in the evening, often standing against an old elder bush, as still as a stone, watching what was going on, and sizing up the birds, the rabbits and an occasional hare that came out after dusk. On his way up to the heathland he passed the school; and he would often stop to have a chat with the schoolmaster, Mr Robertson, whenever he happened to be out in the schoolhouse garden.

The schoolmaster was a Scot and interested in the new area he had come to: he liked talking to Acky about the farming customs he knew in Scotland when he was a boy. Acky had frequently mentioned him to Sarah:

'That there Mr Robertson is some clever. He read a rare lot o' books; and he's allus asking questions. But he's a-willing to larn; and it's a right pleasure to hev a word or two with him now and again.'

'I hope you not a-telling him a lot o' that old squit you try to load off on to me!'

'Now then!' Acky answered. 'Don't you git windy over nawthen! I allus tell him what I know – leastways, most of it. He's on about the owd farming, and I'm of the same mind as him there. They don't farm like they used to, he say; and I tell him the way they're a-going on now will soon be the ruination o' the land.'

'It 'pears to me,' said Sarah, 'you together is like an open-air sewing meeting, going at it like a pair o' milliners. It's a pity Mr Robertson don't do more digging and less talking. He's not got his garden round yet.'

'You must ha' got up the wrong side o' the bed this marning, gel. Give

113

the man time! He's only been here a year, and he got suthen else to see to asides his garden. But do you know what he say to me? He's allus polite and he call me Mr Flatt. Howsomever, he say to me last week: "Akerman, that's a very interesting name; a rare name and a very old one," he say. And I towd him:

'"I reckon it is. It were my grandfather's second name; and he weren't born yesterday!"

'"Well," he say, "it's a name that's six or seven hundred year old. I see it writ in the documents."'

Sarah looked at him severely.

'You're romancing again, Acky! You better keep to boasting about your owd yard to Mr Robertson, and steer away from books and all thet.'

'Ma heart alive!' said Acky 'If you were a man, us together would have to call you Thomas! Here it is!' he added, taking a grubby piece of paper out of his pocket. 'He writ it down for me. He say he seen it in a Latin document, whatever that is. Here it is: here!'

He handed the paper to Sarah who put on her spectacles and peered at it suspiciously

'*Akermanni et Carucarrii*. Whatever gibberish is this?'

'Latin, didn't I now tell you, gel! And there's the English for it underneath: *Acremen and ploughmen*. And he say that an *akerman* were a man who had an acre o' land let to him while he done work for the lord.'

'For the Lord! For the Charch you mean?'

'No, no, no, gel. Not Him up there. Him who say he own the land; the lord o' the manor! Mr Robertson, he reckon my name were handed down from them folks. What do you think o' thet, gel?'

But Sarah didn't seem impressed and asked coolly:

'And what did you say to him?'

This was the question that Acky needed.

'I made him laugh, gel. He laugh so much he fare double up over his spade.

'"Akerman," I say; "well, my grandfather and a' them must ha' been some careless, or thet owd lord must ha' been some sly I reckon. For some'un has been nibbling at my acre good tidily; 'cos all I got left on it now is less than a quarter-acre. And if they build that new road they're a-talking about, I'll hardly have enough land to grow a bit o' mint for ma sauce."'

'Sauce! You got a rare lot too much o' that already,' said Sarah. 'But you better be some careful how you talk to thet schoolmaster. He'll have you in atween the covers of a book afore you know what's happened to you. And how will you fare then? You'd be in a right pickle then!'

'Oh I wouldn't mind about thet! I allus got a fancy to git my name into the papers. And a good name it is, too; like I say.'

But Acky's talk with the schoolmaster made him return to a problem that had taken up most of his real thinking during the greater part of his life: how to get a fair piece of land that he could work on and call his own. That was the mainspring of all his striving: his keeping of pigs, his poaching, his grubbing around doing small jobs – the whole of his saving; it was to get enough money to rent or buy a piece of land that he could farm as his own. Now that he had retired he had more time for thinking; and this small piece of land was always the bed and bottom of his thoughts. He'd often looked at the Common outside his own *yard*, or allotment, with a speculative eye. But there was, he knew well, little chance of an answer to his problem in that direction.

Then one Sunday morning he was walking across the Common when he noticed a party by the old mound or tumulus that was near the centre of the stretch of heathland. They were bending over something; from a distance it looked as if two or three of them were digging. Acky first got Bundler to heel and then strolled across. As he approached he recognised the schoolmaster who called out:

'We've got a spare spade here, Mr Flatt, if you'd care to feel the handle of it.'

But Acky was too wily a bird to be taken in by such an invitation, and he answered cheerfully:

'Thank you kindly, Mr Robertson; but my owd back don't fare to be what it should this morning.' And after he'd watched the three men and a girl digging away for a few minutes he called Bundler and continued on his walk.

The same afternoon Acky was standing at the gate of his cottage at the other end of the Common when Tom Downey passed. He was driving the Firtree cattle down to the marshes. He stopped and asked:

'What are they a-doing on up there on the Common, Acky? They're a-digging up there as if meant it.'

'That they are!' Acky agreed. 'After history, so they tell me, Tom – to see if they cin find ruins or suthen.'

'Ruins! Thet's a rum thing to go a-diggin' for,' Tom Downey grunted, as he prodded one of the heifers. 'If they want some diggin' I got a tidy piece of ma owd yard that I haven't started on yet. Thet could do with some diggin'!'

Acky nodded; but when Tom Downey had gone, a certain light came into his eye. Tom wasn't a beetle-head after all: there was some good sound sense in what he was saying. What a waste of good digging energy to go spending it all on ruins! He went to his allotment at the side of his house. A turn round his *owd yard*, as he called, helped him in his thinking. He walked slowly to the bottom, fingering one of his ear-rings and looking thoughtfully out on to the bit of Common on the other side of the fence. Then he suddenly hurried into the house; put on his jacket and walked purposefully up to the village.

His broad face was shining when he came to the cottage of old Silas Crosby who had once been a horseman with him on Firtree Farm. Silas was sitting outside peeling a few potatoes for his evening meal. He was a tricky old man, but Acky went straight to the point:

'You recollect thet owd coin you turn up, Silas?'

'Which 'un were that?' the old man asked, looking at Acky shrewdly 'I turned up a rare lot o' coins in my time, I have.'

'You know the one I mean. This 'un were some owd – all wore up. You shew it me. On Schol'us Walk you plough it up, weren't it?'

The old man dropped the potato-knife into the bowl:

'Now that were a whoolly fine coin that were. Worth a lot more'n those ear-rings o' yourn, I reckon, Acky.'

'I don't doubt it – but I thought you'd recollect it, Silas. You don't fare to have it somewhere about, do you?'

'Maybe I have, maybe I haven't,' the old man answered, with a sly look at Acky before picking up his knife and turning his attention to the bowl of potatoes.

But Acky was man enough for old Silas; and it wasn't long before the coin was in his pocket and he was walking straight over to call on the schoolmaster. As it happened he was working in his garden.

'Evening, sir,' Acky called out. 'I brought something maybe you'd like to have a look at.'

He produced the coin, and immediately the schoolmaster leaned his hoe against the fence: 'This is interesting. Very interesting indeed,' he said quickly. 'Where did you get it from, Mr Flatt?'

'Picked it up the day afore yesterday on that bit o' the Common ahind my own yard. A bit o' ground were disturbed like. Bundler, ma owd dog,

116

must ha' scrabbled it up.'

Acky told his story without a blink. But in any case, the schoolmaster was too interested in the coin to pay much attention to Acky.

'If I'm not mistaken this is a second-century Roman coin. Do you mind if I keep it a day or two to get this confirmed?'

'Keep it! Keep it, you,' Acky said generously, 'until you get it properly fixed. I know you'll be looking arter it. Maybe there's some more where this 'un came from.'

Acky went home feeling very pleased with himself. So far his scheme had gone well; but he told Sarah very little about it. But she knew his views: it was a shame not to make use of that bit of Common behind the cottage. He'd had his eye on it for some time; only he dare not move his fence forward an inch to take in any of the land. He knew he'd have the whole pack of village lawyers down on him like a shower of acorns on a windy day in October. And Joe Easy the parish clerk, would be at the head of them. The time he planted a few gooseberry bushes on the wrong side of the fence, they were after him as though he had committed some great crime.

'Gooseberries on the Common this year, and gooseberries in your own yard the next, Acky!' Joe Easy had lectured him. 'We weren't born yesterday, bor. And most of us have got something else between our ears asides stuffin'.'

But, thought Acky, this here looked a more promising scheme altogether; and it would give him a great lift to get round Joe Easy and all the other lawyers.

The following week-end a digging party turned up in full strength to explore the piece of Common where Acky was supposed to have found the coin. He was in tremendous spirits.

'Come to the window, gel,' he told Sarah, after he'd explained a little of what was happening. 'Do you see that 'un with the glasses? He don't fare to look a likely one, do he? But you wait! He can handle a wheelbarrow half tidy once he gits a-going.'

By Sunday evening the piece of Common had been cultivated as well as if it had been done by a pair of horses; and Acky was rubbing his hands with the success of his plan. Although the digging party had found nothing, the schoolmaster didn't seem very much put out.

'We'll be back next week-end. We need patience for this job, Mr Flatt.'

'We whoolly do, Mr Robertson,' Acky agreed. Then he added: 'Don't you think we'd better have a bit o' nettin' put round where you been a-digging; a fence of some sort. That trench there . . . it'll be kinda dangerous in the dark. Now I got a bit of spare wire here. I shouldn't mind . . .'

'Yes, yes,' Mr Robertson said, 'you do that. That's an excellent idea. I'll fix it with the parish council. There'll be no trouble at all.'

That was good enough for Acky. Within a couple of days there was a neat wire fence around the bit of Common, neater in fact than he had round his own chicken-run.

The digging party started early on the following Saturday morning. Acky didn't interfere. He settled down to smoke a pipe by his back door. He calculated that they would have covered most of the piece by evening; and then, having found nothing, they would pack up their tools; and it was unlikely that they'd ever return. As he enjoyed the sun and kept half an eye on the diggers, Acky went through his plan again: he'd let a few weeks go by then he'd level off the ground; and in the spring he'd sow a handful or two of oats. In the following year he'd maybe give it a trial with a bit of sugarbeet. That would give him a start. He'd fix Joe Easy and his gang this time. He had thought out what he was going to tell him, and quietly rehearsed it:

'This here is a historical piece of land, Joe; and that fence has got to stay up. We got to be some careful with this land while those clever fellers are a-thinking what they're going to do about it. And the best way to look after it and keep it private like is to have something a-growing on it.'

Acky had it all beautifully set out. He could see the wilderness blossoming coins; but not the sort that fool the schoolmaster was looking for. The future opened up for him. He'd take a farm and soon Fenhall would be too small to hold him.

His castle-building was disturbed by a shout from the Common. Mrs Robertson was waving her arms about as though a bull had got loose in the yard; and the spectacled chap was hopping about like a sparrow after a thaw. The schoolmaster was down in a trench; and it was plain that he had found something. Acky hurried across to find out the cause of the excitement. All he could see was a lot of black earth and what looked like a charred bit of an old tree stump.

In a short time the diggers uncovered a considerable area near the post. The digging revealed some charred and rounded stones, pieces of pottery and three more stumps similar to the one already uncovered. Acky watched gloomily and stayed long enough to hear Mr Robertson's opinion that they had come across the site of an early British settlement.

'Early British conglomification!' Acky muttered disgustedly as he got back to his cottage. 'It's all them books thet schoolmaster's been a-reading; must be, to git ideas like that! Well, that's cooked our little scheme, gel. We got as much chance now o' growing anything on that bit o' land as the man in the moon's got o' raising cabbages.'

For a couple of days Acky couldn't bear to look at the piece of Common. But one morning he was surprised by a big car full of people turning up and asking for the site of the excavations. Later that morning two cars arrived. Soon there were reporters and camera-men and two experts from London roaming all over the patch.

As Acky stood watching from his back window his eyes lit up once more as he fingered one of his ear-rings:

'Why! I got it, gel! Can't you see, we're becoming famous. Who's got that tea-urn they used to have at the Women's Institute? Hold on while I go after it. And you git all the kettles a-boiling; and hunt up a piece of flannin to wrop the tea in. We're going into the caff business, gel. Fivepence a cup, it'll be – the same as on the railway. And it'll be better tea than the brew you get with them. The water out here fare to have a lot more body in it to start with.'

Before the morning was out Acky and Sarah were serving cups of tea as fast as they could hand them out of the window.

'We'll have to lay in the stocks, gel. I hear that bloke with the beard say it's an important find, if you can fathom the meaning o' that. But we can expect some more wisitors. Not so much milk in the cups, gel. They don't give you quarter o' that on the railway.'

Within a few weeks the tea business was thriving; and Acky had appointed himself more or less 'official' guide to the excavations; and he was talking about Ancient Britons as familiarly and as knowledgeably as if they'd been his neighbours for most of his life. The only wrong note was the schoolmaster who would keep returning to the coin, and worrying over it like a dog over a bone that wouldn't yield him its marrow.

'I can't understand it,' he said. 'What is a Roman coin of the second century doing in such an early settlement as this? And on its own! There's not a sign of anything else Roman. It's a complete mystery.'

But Acky reassured him blandly:

'Oh, don't you worry about that, Mr Robertson. Them Romans were a sociable lot, you ma' depend. Seemingly, one o' them dropped that coin while he was out a-wisiting. But you don't want to fret about that, sir. Strange things have been happening in Fenhall, ever since I can recollect; and some stranger things were a-going on when them Romans were about. A rare lot o' rum 'uns those Romans were, you ma' depend.'

* * * * *

D J Taylor: Born in Norwich where he and his family now live, Taylor has written several studies of modern British fiction, a biography of Thackeray and most recently an acclaimed *Life* of George Orwell (2003). His novel *The Comedy Man* (2001), set partly in Great Yarmouth, has been re-released as part of the trilogy *Returning* (2007). Taylor's historical novel *Kept* appeared in 2006 and *Bright Young People* is out later this year. Several short stories with an East Anglian setting appear in his collection *After Bathing at Baxter's* (1997). 'Cranked up Really High' first appeared in *The Mail on Sunday* in 2001.

Cranked Up Really High

D J TAYLOR

Beyond the kitchen door the lawn descended into sunlight. Coming from twenty feet away, still deep within the house, the fat man's voice – was his name Roger? Or Jeremy? – seemed curiously disembodied, hanging in the air above the trails of Virginia creeper and the outsize plant pots.

'Of course there are things we ought to have done to the place, I don't deny . . . But when it comes down to it, I mean, in the end you've got to *live* in a house haven't you?'

Ignoring the voice, to the extent that its brisk, man-to-man bark was ignorable, Julian stared critically across the grass. A hundred feet, perhaps, or a hundred and twenty. Where the lawn ended there was a cluster of miniature outbuildings: two sheds, a ramshackle summerhouse, what looked like a compost heap trammelled behind wooden bars.

The voice was drawing nearer again. Close up it seemed less substantial, somehow ghost-ridden. 'As to the garden, there's a bit of a stench first thing in the morning. Down-wind of the local pig farm, I'm afraid. But if you want to live in the country, then really that's the kind of thing that . . .'

Turning back on his heel Julian watched the fat man come lumbering through the doorway, two coffee mugs sunk into the red flesh of his fists, half-smoked cheroot still dangling from the fingers of his right hand. The fat man's name, he now remembered – and this kind of confusion was endemic to serial house inspection – was Hugo. Despite the open-necked shirt and the bare, plump feet crammed into espadrilles, the adjective that suggested itself was 'soldierly'. You could visualise Hugo in battledress commanding the prow of a tank, giving orders to Gurkha riflemen.

They set off across the lawn – Hugo determinedly, as if he was shouldering his way through bracken – past an apple tree and an oak bench lightly dusted with powdery green lichen. Here the small, red-

121

haired girl that Hugo had shooed briskly out of the hall when they arrived was sitting with a pile of windfalls in her lap. Hugo's expression, which had been proprietorial in the dining room and bored in the kitchen, now registered simple annoyance.

'I don't think' he said solemnly, 'that we want any of *that.*'

'Sorry, daddy.'

'You know you're not supposed to eat the windfalls, darling. Now, go and put them in the box in the scullery so that mummy knows where they are.'

'All right.'

'Otherwise there won't be any to make into preserve, will there?'

'I suppose there won't.'

Julian watched the girl skidding back across the grass, apples gathered in the crooked knot of her arms. Hugo was looking at the cluster of outbuildings, momentarily baffled, like an actor robbed of a vital cue. Then his face brightened.

'Now, if you're a gardening man, well, here's something that really, I mean . . .'

The something turned out to be a motorized lawn-mower with a defective rotor blade that Hugo proposed to 'throw in with the house.' Standing by the doorway of the shed, in the shade of the mighty cypress trees that bordered the fence ('Cost you three hundred a year to trim, of course, but there's a chap two doors down who, I mean . . .') Julian wondered, as he usually did on these real estate tours, what Hugo did for a living. Even with people called Hugo, who lived in moss-covered rectories out in the Norfolk wild, it was sometimes difficult to tell. There had been a mass of sailing charts strewn over the deal table in the study, but that didn't prove anything. Remembering the black stuff gown that meek-eyed Mrs Hugo had been commanded to carry away out of the lobby along with other weekend detritus, he marked him down as a barrister.

'Good solid pinewood, that fence' Hugo chipped in, taking this moment of reflection as waning interest. 'So if you wanted to prune back the hedge, you could . . .'

Two months into the search for a house, Julian was familiar with this kind of language: the language of uplift, exhortation, limitless possibility. Rock gardens just waiting to be turned into swimming pools. Dowdy attics craving the coat of paint that would transform them into playrooms, studies and guest annexes. Somewhere in this world of ritualized embellishment, moral obligation lurked.

'Any particular reason why you're selling?' he wondered as they trekked back uphill over the scree of windfalls. Hugo, looking slightly more affronted than most vendors allowed themselves to be by questions of this sort, muttered something about schools, wives and proximity to work. It was eleven in the morning now, and hot. Looking up at the house (*a highly desirable rectory conversion on the edge of this much-loved village*) he saw his own wife silhouetted against one of the upstairs windows, the agents' brochure fanned out beneath her gaze. Mary would be half-way through her check-list by now: roof; drains; village school's position in the OFSTED table; bus service; danger of flooding; local burglary statistics; neighbours. Curiously, people answered these questions with an unfailing patience. The protocols and assumptions of house purchase – common ground, inches offered and received – appealed to them. Watching Mary bob her head in answer to some response from Mrs Hugo – invisible behind curtains – reminded him that starker realities lay at hand. 'If we don't get this one' she had said in the car earlier that morning, hand poised over the mobile phone in her lap, 'it'll mean another six month let. Five thousand out of the capital. Just think about it.'

Julian thought about it, as they wandered back inside. Hugo was staring suspiciously at the corpse of a gigantic slug that lay suppurating on the mat. 'Bloody cats' he pronounced. 'They just bring every bit of wildlife they can find indoors, and, I mean, it's not as if . . .' Julian wondered if he left his sentences unfinished in court. 'Last week I found a dead *weasel* on the landing' Hugo went on. From the tail of his eye Julian saw the red-haired girl issuing secretively through the hall and heading towards the staircase. 'Look' said Hugo. Julian saw that he had straightened up from the mat and resumed the demeanour of someone who seriously wants to sell his house. 'This is rather fun.'

Julian examined the miniature pulley system suspended above their heads, from which various hooks and wires hung down.

'What does it do?'

'What does it do? Well, you stick something on one of these hooks – like this, see? – and then you just, I mean . . .'

Some way above, footsteps could be heard moving over an uncarpeted floor. With elephantine precision Hugo put an ashtray onto the wire cradle and sent it chugging over to the other side of the ceiling. Julian had a sudden vision of him as a serious-minded boy unpacking train sets, whisking toy cars round their circles of track. 'I'd very much like to see upstairs' he said, 'see if Mary's come up with anything.' 'Actually' Hugo riposted, flipping the ashtray neatly out of its cage, 'we'll probably be taking this with us, that and the, I mean . . .' By degrees, and by way of an inspection of the scullery damp course, they beat a path back to the dining room, where there was a sideboard supporting decanters and a line of family photographs: a younger Hugo with slightly longer hair in rugby kit; Mr and Mrs Hugo on their wedding day; a recent Hugo staring peevishly at something feathery and dead sticking out of a labrador's muzzle. Beyond the door, at the foot of the staircase, the red-haired girl was sitting on the bottom-most step crooning softly to herself and plucking clothes pegs one by one out of a vermilion bag.

'Darling. Annabel. Darling. We've had this conversation before.'

'What conversation daddy?'

'The conversation about not leaving things on the staircase. About what would happen if anyone fell over them.'

'Yes.'

Halfway along the upstairs landing, dwarfed by a giant representation of some Monet waterlilies, Mary and Mrs Hugo were huddled over a sheaf of architect's drawings. As he approached to greet them Julian thought he heard the words 'extension over the garage roof.' Seeing her husband, Mrs Hugo announced, not without all signs of trepidation, 'They want to see the loft.'

'The *loft*?'

'That's right, you see . . .'

'No. That's fine. That's absolutely fine. Darling. I'll just get the, I mean, and they can . . .'

Unhooked by means of a long silver pole, the loft trap-door fell open. Further tugging realised a patent ladder that Hugo managed to unfurl to within an inch or two of the carpet. Silently they clambered up, the small red-haired girl leading the way. It was a spacious loft, Julian divined, the best they had seen: fifty feet long, boarded, with storage cupboards, and capable of fulfilling his solitary criterion for house purchase, which was a study-cum-bookroom. They hovered about for a moment while Mary got out her tape measure and Julian tried not to notice, or to be seen to have noticed, that one of the books in the pile of paperbacks spilled over the floor was called *High Jinks in a Women's Prison*. Hugo, he saw, was looking pleased, like some schoolteacher whose most backward pupil has, against all odds, managed to recite a poem or conjugate a French verb.

'What's behind this curtain?' Mary wondered. She gestured in the direction of a kind of tarpaulin slung over one of the furthermost beams.

'That?' Hugo looked affronted again. 'Some nonsense of Annabel's. I don't know. Actually, though, there's a lot more space there than, I mean, perhaps we ought to . . .'

'Daddy, it's not nonsense.' Julian saw that the red-haired girl had suddenly materialised beside them, at once hugely animated and bitterly upset.

'Darling. Daddy is trying to show Mr and Mrs . . . Mr and Mrs . . . and really . . .'

'Daddy, you mustn't let them see.' There was something quite desperate in the girl's face, Julian saw: lost, worn-out, end-of-tether.

'Hugo . . .'

'No, darling, really don't see why I can't . . .' Hugo was calling back over his shoulder as he foraged through the heaped-up boxes. What followed Julian remembered only as a tableau of noise and colour: Hugo's beetroot face, dust motes hanging in the bright air, the surprisingly loud slither that the tarpaulin made as it hit the floor, the pink, glassy faces of the rows of dolls revealed behind it; the whole perfectly unsinister apart from Annabel's banshee wail as she threw herself forward in their defence.

Back in the car ('Some bloody nonsense, no idea why she, carrying on like that, I mean . . .' Hugo had confided on the journey downstairs) they drove through back lanes crowded out with loosestrife and cow parsley. 'Well?' Mary said expectantly. 'What did you think?'

'Not terribly exciting' he said, keeping it non-committal despite his fury. 'What about you?'

'Dream house. Just ravishing. Apparently he's been made redundant, so they're desperate to sell. And Mrs Warren says they'd let us have eight off for the state of the roof.'

Julian thought about Hugo being made redundant, the pink face growing steadily pinker as sentence was pronounced. 'Well, we're not buying it.' He was quite surprised at the sound of his voice, the memory of the small girl's face suddenly streaking into tears. 'Not if it was the last house in Norfolk.'

There was silence for a moment. Signposts flicked by to Holkham and Wells-next-the-Sea. 'You're cranked up pretty high aren't you?' Mary wondered in faint bewilderment. It was an old, pet phrase they had, from years back, denoting sudden access of emotion, loss of temper.

'I'm sorry' he said. 'Really, I am.'

125

That night, while Mary slept in front of the rented TV, he wrote out the cheque to the letting agency. Later, in his dreams, the red-haired girl ran on blithely over endless tropical dunes while, far below on the beach, Hugo lay up to his shoulders in sand as the apes, capering with glee, threw ripe fruit at his head. There were ways of behaving, he thought, whole worlds that existed beyond the arc of red-faced barristers and their silent wives, sides that needed to be taken, even here amid the crawling ivy and the distant, shimmering lawns.

* * * * *

Elizabeth Bowen (1899–1973): Eminent Anglo-Irish novelist whose fiction was strongly influenced by both modernism and her own powerful sense of place. She is best known for her novels of the 1930s, especially *The House in Paris* (1935) and *The Death of Heart* (1938) with their acute observations of upper middle class sensibility and neuroses. Place and transience, evident here in 'Look At All Those Roses' from her *Collected Stories* (1980), are recurring motifs in much of her work.

Look At All Those Roses
ELIZABETH BOWEN

Lou exclaimed at that glimpse of a house in a sheath of startling flowers. She twisted round, to look back, in the open car, till the next corner had cut it out of sight. To reach the corner, it struck her, Edward accelerated, as though he were jealous of the rosy house – a house with gables, flat-fronted, whose dark windows stared with no expession through the flowers. The garden, with its silent, burning gaiety, stayed in both their minds like an apparition.

One of those conflicts between two silent moods had set up, with Lou and Edward, during that endless drive. Also, there is a point when an afternoon oppresses one with fatigue and a feeling of unreality. Relentless, pointless, unwinding summer country made nerves ache at the back of both of their eyes. This was a late June Monday; they were doubling back to London through Suffolk by-roads, on the return from a week-end. Edward, who detested the main roads, had traced out their curious route before starting, and Lou now sat beside him with the map on her knees. They had to be back by eight, for Edward, who was a writer, to finish and post an article: apart from this, time was no object with them. They looked forward with no particular pleasure to London and unlocking the stuffy flat, taking in the milk, finding bills in the letter-box. In fact, they looked forward to nothing with particular pleasure. They were going home for the purely negative reason that there was nowhere else they could as cheaply go. The week-end had not been amusing, but at least it had been 'away'. Now they could foresee life for weeks ahead – until someone else invited them – the typewriter, the cocktail-shaker, the telephone, runs in the car out of London to nowhere special. Love when Edward got a cheque in the post, quarrels about people on the way home from parties – and Lou's anxiety always eating them. This future weighed on them like a dull burden . . . So they had been glad to extend today.

127

But under a vacant sky, not sunny but full of diffused glare, the drive had begun to last too long: they felt bound up in the tired impotence of a dream. The stretches of horizon were stupefying. The road bent round wedges of cornfield, blocky elms dark with summer: for these last ten miles the countryside looked abandoned; they passed dropping gates, rusty cattle-troughs and the thistly, tussocky, stale grass of neglected farms. There was nobody on the roads; perhaps there was nobody anywhere . . . In the heart of all this, the roses looked all the odder.

'They were extraordinary,' she said (when the first corner was turned) in her tired, little, dogmatic voice.

'All the more,' he agreed, 'when all the rest of the country looks something lived in by poor whites.'

'I wish we lived *there*,' she said. 'It really looked like somewhere.'

'It wouldn't if we did.'

Edward spoke with some tartness. He had found he had reason to dread week-ends away: they unsettled Lou and started up these fantasies. Himself, he had no illusions about life in the country: life without people was absolutely impossible. What would he and she do with nobody to talk to but each other? Already, they had not spoken for two hours. Lou saw life in terms of ideal moments. She found few ideal moments in their flat.

He went on: 'You know you can't stand earwigs. And we should spend our lives on the telephone.'

'About the earwigs?'

'No. About ourselves.'

Lou's smart little monkey face became dolorous. She never risked displeasing Edward too far, but she was just opening her mouth to risk one further remark when Edward jumped and frowned. A ghastly knocking had started. It seemed to come from everywhere, and at the same time to be a special attack on them. Then it had to be traced to the car's vitals: it jarred up Lou through the soles of her feet. Edward slowed to a crawl and stopped. He and she confronted each other with that completely dramatic lack of expression they kept for occasions when the car went wrong. They tried crawling on again, a few tentative yards: the knocking took up again with still greater fury.

'Sounds to me like a big end gone.'

'Oh my goodness,' she said.

All the same, she was truly glad to get out of the car. She stretched and stood waiting on the grass roadside while Edward made faces into the bonnet. Soon he flung round to ask what she would suggest doing: to his surprise (and annoyance) she had a plan ready. She would walk back to that house and ask if they had a telephone. If they had not, she would ask for a bicycle and bicycle to the place where the nearest garage was.

Edward snatched the map, but could not find where they were. Where they were seemed to be highly improbable. 'I expect you,' Lou said, 'would rather stay with the car.' 'No, I wouldn't,' said Edward, 'anybody can have it . . . You like to be sure where I am, don't you?' he added. He locked their few odd things up in the boot of the car with the suitcases, and they set off in silence. It was about a mile.

There stood the house, waiting. Why should a house wait? Most pretty scenes have something passive about them, but this looked like a trap baited with beauty, set ready to spring. It stood back from the road. Lou put her hand on the gate and, with a touch of bravado, the two filed up the paved path to the door. Each side of the path, hundreds of standard roses bloomed, over-charged with colour, as though this were their one hour. Crimson, coral, blue-pink, lemon and cold white, they disturbed with fragrance the dead air. In this spell-bound afternoon, with no shadows, the roses glared at the strangers, frighteningly bright. The face of the house was plastered with tea-roses: waxy cream when they opened but with vermilion buds.

The blistered door was propped open with a bizarre object, a lump of quartz. Indoors was the dark, cold-looking hall. When they had come to the door they found no bell or knocker: they could not think what to do. 'We had better cough,' Lou said. So they stood there coughing, till a door at the end of the hall opened and a lady or woman looked out – they were not sure which. 'Oh?' she said, with no expression at all.

'We couldn't find your bell.'

'There they are,' she said, pointing to two Swiss cow-bells that hung on loops of string by the door she had just come out of. Having put this right, she continued to look at them, and out through the door past them, wiping her powerful-looking hands vaguely against the sides of her blue overall. They could hardly see themselves as intruders when their intrusion made so little effect. The occupying inner life of this person was not for an instant suspended by their presence. She was a shabby amazon of a woman, with a sculptural clearness about the face. She must have lost contact with the outer world completely: there was now nothing to 'place' her by. It is outside attachments – hopes, claims, curiosities, desires, little touches of greed – that put a label on one to help strangers. As it was, they

129

could not tell if she were rich or poor, stupid or clever, a spinster or a wife. She seemed prepared, not anxious, for them to speak. Lou, standing close beside Edward, gave him a dig in a rib. So Edward explained to the lady how they found themselves, and asked if she had a telephone or a bicycle.

She said she was sorry to say she had neither. Her maid had a bicycle, but had ridden home on it. 'Would you like some tea?' she said. 'I am just boiling the kettle. Then perhaps you can think of something to do.' This lack of grip of the crisis made Edward decide the woman must be a moron: annoyance contused his face. But Lou, who wanted tea and was attracted by calmness, was entirely won. She looked at Edward placatingly.

'Thank you,' he said. 'But I must do something at once. We haven't got all night; I've got to be back in London. Can you tell me where I can telephone from? I must get through to a garage – a good garage.'

Unmoved, the lady said: 'You'll have to walk to the village. It's about three miles away.' She gave unexpectedly clear directions, then looked at Lou again. 'Leave your wife here,' she said. 'Then she can have tea.'

Edward shrugged; Lou gave a brief, undecided sigh. How much she wanted to stop. But she never liked to be left. This partly arose from the fact that she was not Edward's wife: he was married to someone else and his wife would not divorce him. He might some day go back to her, if this ever became the way of least resistance. Or he might, if it were the way of even less resistance, move on to someone else. Lou was determined neither should ever happen. She did love Edward, but she also stuck to him largely out of contentiousness. She quite often asked herself why she did. It seemed important – she could not say why. She was determined to be a necessity. Therefore she seldom let him out of her sight – her idea of love was adhesiveness . . . Knowing this well, Edward gave her a slightly malign smile, said she had far better stay, turned, and walked down the path without her. Lou, like a lost cat, went half-way to the door. 'Your roses are wonderful . . .' she said, staring out with unhappy eyes.

'Yes, they grow well for us, Josephine likes to see them.' Her hostess added: 'My kettle will be boiling. Won't you wait in there?'

Lou went deeper into the house. She found herself in a long, low and narrow parlour, with a window at each end. Before she could turn round, she felt herself being looked at. A girl of about thirteen lay, flat as a board, in a wicker invalid carriage. The carriage was pulled out across the room, so that the girl could command the view from either window, the flat horizons that bounded either sky. Lying there with no pillow she had a

130

stretched look. Lou stood some distance from the foot of the carriage: the dark eyes looked at her down thin cheekbones, intently. The girl had an unresigned, living face; one hand crept on the rug over her breast. Lou felt, here was the nerve and core of the house . . . The only movement was made by a canary, springing to and fro in its cage.

'Hullo,' Lou said, with that deferential smile with which one approaches an invalid. When the child did not answer, she went on: 'You must wonder who I am?'

'I don't now; I did when you drove past.'

'Then our car broke down.'

'I know, I wondered whether it might.'

Lou laughed and said: 'Then you put the evil eye on it.'

The child ignored this. She said: 'This is not the way to London.'

'All the same, that's where we're going.'

'You mean, where you were going . . . Is that your husband who has just gone away?'

'That's Edward: yes. To telephone. He'll be back.' Lou, who was wearing a summer suit, smart, now rather crumpled, of honey-yellow linen, felt Josephine look her up and down. 'Have you been to a party?' she said, 'or are you going to one?'

'We've just been staying away,' Lou walked nervously down the room to the front window. From here she saw the same roses Josephine saw: she thought they looked like forced roses, magnetized into being. Magnetized, buds uncurled and petals dropped. Lou began to wake from the dream of the afternoon: her will stirred; she wanted to go; she felt apprehensive, threatened. 'I expect you like to lie out of doors, with all those roses?' she said.

'No, not often: I don't care for the sky.'

'You just watch through the window?'

'Yes,' said the child, impatiently. She added: 'What are the parts of London with most traffic?'

'Piccadilly Circus. Trafalgar Square.'

'Oh, I would like to see those.'

The child's mother's step sounded on the hall flags: she came in with the tea-tray. 'Can I help you?' said Lou, glad of the interim.

'Oh, thank you. Perhaps you'd unfold that table. Put it over here beside Josephine. She's lying down because she hurt her back.'

'My back was hurt six years ago,' said Josephine. 'It was my father's doing.'

Her mother was busy lodging the edge of the tray on the edge of the tea-table.

'Awful for him,' Lou murmured, helping unstack the cups.

'No, it's not,' said Josephine. 'He has gone away.'

Lou saw why. A man in the wrong cannot live where there is no humanity. There are enormities you can only keep piling up. He had bolted off down that path, as Edward had just done. Men cannot live with sorrow, with women who embrace it. Men will suffer a certain look in animals' eyes, but not in women's eyes. And men dread obstinacy, of love, of grief. You could stay with burning Josephine, not with her mother's patient, exalted face . . . When her mother had gone again, to fetch the teapot and kettle, Josephine once more fastened her eyes on Lou. 'Perhaps your husband will be some time,' she said. 'You're the first new person I have seen for a year. Perhaps he will lose his way.'

'Oh, but then I should have to look for him!'

Josephine gave a fanatical smile. 'But when people go away they sometimes quite go,' she said. 'If they always come back, then what is the good of moving?'

'I don't see the good of moving.'

'Then stay here.'

'People don't just go where they want; they go where they must.'

'Must you go back to London?'

'Oh, I have to, you know.'

'Why?'

Lou frowned and smiled in a portentous, grown-up way that meant nothing at all to either herself or Josephine. She felt for her cigarette case and, glumly, found it empty – Edward had walked away with the packet of cigarettes that he and she had been sharing that afternoon. He also carried any money she had.

'You don't know where he's gone to,' Josephine pointed out. 'If you had to stay, you would soon get used to it. We don't wonder where my father is.'

'What's your mother's name?'

'Mrs Mather. She'd like you to stay. Nobody comes to see us; they used to, they don't now. So we only see each other. They may be frightened of something – '

Mrs Mather came back, and Josephine looked out of the other window. This immediate silence marked a conspiracy, in which Lou had no willing part. While Mrs Mather was putting down the teapot, Lou looked round the room, to make sure it was ordinary. This window-ended parlour was lined with objects that looked honest and worn without having antique grace. A faded room should look homely. But extinct paper and phantom cretonnes gave this a gutted air. Rooms can be whitened and gutted by too-intensive living, as they are by a fire. It was the garden, out there, that focused the senses. Lou indulged for a minute the astounding fancy that Mr Mather lay at the roses' roots . . . Josephine said sharply: 'I don't want any tea,' which made Lou realize that she would have to be fed and did not want to be fed in front of the stranger Lou still was. Mrs Mather made no comment: she drew two chairs to the table and invited Lou to sit down. 'It's rather sultry,' she said. 'I'm afraid your husband may not enjoy his walk.'

'How far did you say it was?'

'Three miles.'

Lou, keeping her wrist under the table, glanced down covertly at her watch.

'We are very much out of the way,' said Mrs Mather.

'But perhaps you like that?'

'We are accustomed to quiet,' said Mrs Mather, pouring out tea. 'This was a farm, you know. But it was an unlucky farm, so since my husband left I have let the land. Servants seem to find that the place is lonely – country girls are so different now. My present servant is not very clear in her mind, but she works well and does not seem to feel lonely. When she is not working she rides home.'

'Far?' said Lou, tensely.

'A good way,' said Mrs Mather, looking out of the window at the horizon.

'Then aren't you rather . . . alone? – I mean, if anything happened.'

'Nothing more can happen,' said Mrs Mather. 'And there are two of us. When I am working upstairs or am out with the chickens, I wear one of those bells you see in the hall, so Josephine can always hear where I am. And I leave the other bell on Josephine's carriage. When I work in the garden she can see me, of course.' She slit the wax-paper top off a jar of jam. 'This is my last pot of last year's damson,' she said. 'Please try some; I shall be making more soon. We have two fine trees.'

'You should see mother climb them,' said Josephine.

'Aren't you afraid of falling?'

'Why?' said Mrs Mather, advancing a plate of rather rich bread and butter. 'I never eat tea, thank you,' Lou said, sitting rigid, sipping round

133

her cup of tea like a bird.

'She thinks if she eats she may have to stay here for ever,' Josephine said. Her mother, taking no notice, spread jam on her bread and butter and started to eat in a calmly voracious way. Lou kept clinking her spoon against the teacup: every time she did this the canary stared and fluttered. Though she knew Edward could not possibly come yet, Lou kept glancing down the garden at the gate. Mrs Mather, reaching out for more bread and butter, saw, and thought Lou was looking at the roses. 'Would you like to take some back to London?' she said.

Josephine's carriage had been wheeled out on the lawn between the rosebeds. She lay with eyes shut and forehead contracted, for overhead hung the dreaded space of the sky. But she had to be near Lou while Lou cut the roses. In a day or two, Lou thought, I should be wearing a bell. What shall I do with these if I never do go? she thought, as she cut through the strong stems between the thorns and piled the roses on the foot of the carriage. I shall certainly never want to look at roses again. By her wrist watch it was six o'clock – two hours since Edward had started. All round, the country under the white, stretched sky was completely silent. She went once to the gate.

'Is there any way from that village?' she said at last. 'Any 'bus to anywhere else? Any taxi one could hire?'

'I don't know,' said Josephine.

'When does your servant come back?'

'Tomorrow morning. Sometimes our servants never come back at all.'

Lou shut the knife and said: 'Well, those are enough roses.' She supposed she could hear if whoever Edward sent for the car came to tow it away. The car, surely, Edward would not abandon? She went to the gate again. From behind her Josephine said: 'Then please wheel me indoors.'

'If you like. But I shall stay here.'

'Then I will. But please put something over my eyes.'

Lou got out her red silk handkerchief and laid this across Josephine's eyes. This made the mouth more revealing: she looked down at the small resolute smile. 'If you want to keep on listening,' the child said, 'you needn't talk to me. Lie down and let's pretend we're both asleep.'

Lou lay down on the dry, cropped grass alongside the wheels of the carriage: she crossed her hands under her head, shut her eyes and lay stretched, as rigid as Josephine. At first she was so nervous, she thought the lawn vibrated under her spine. Then slowly she relaxed. There is a moment when silence, no longer resisted, rushes into the mind. She let go, inch by inch, of life, that since she was a child she had been clutching so desperately – her obsessions about this and that, her obsession about keeping Edward. How anxiously she had run from place to place, wanting to keep everything inside her own power. I should have stayed still: I shall stay still now, she thought. What I want must come to me: I shall not go after it. People who stay still generate power. Josephine stores herself up, and so what she wants happens, because she knows what she wants. I only think I want things; I only think I want Edward. (He's not coming and I don't care, I don't care.) I feel life myself now. No wonder I've been tired, only half getting what I don't really want. Now I want nothing; I just want a white circle.

The white circle distended inside her eyelids and she looked into it in an ecstasy of indifference. She knew she was looking at nothing – then knew nothing . . .

Josephine's voice, from up in the carriage, woke her. 'You were quite asleep.'

'Was I?'

'Take the handkerchief off: a motor's coming.'

Lou heard the vibration. She got up and uncovered Josephine's eyes. Then she went to the foot of the carriage and got her roses together. She was busy with this, standing with her back to the gate, when she heard the taxi pull up, then Edward's step on the path. The taxi driver sat staring at the roses. 'It's all right,' Edward shouted, 'they're sending out from the garage. They should be here any moment. But what people – God! – Look here, have you been all right?'

'Perfectly, I've been with Josephine.'

'Oh, hullo, Josephine,' Edward said, with a hasty exercise of his charm. 'Well, I've come for this woman. Thank you for keeping her.'

'It's quite all right, thank you . . . Shall you be going now?'

'We must get our stuff out of the car: it will have to be towed to the garage. Then when I've had another talk to the garage people we'll take this taxi on and pick up a train . . . Come on, Lou, come on! We don't want to miss those people! And we've got to get that stuff out of that car!'

'Is there such a hurry?' she said, putting down the roses.

'Of course, there's a hurry . . .' He added, to Josephine: 'We'll look in on our way to the station, when I've fixed up all this, to say goodbye to your mother.' He put his hand on Lou's shoulder and punted her ahead of him down the path. 'I'm glad you're all right,' he said, as they got into the taxi.

135

'You're well out of that, my girl. From what I heard in the village –'

'What, have you been anxious?' said Lou, curiously.

'It's a nervy day,' said Edward, with an uneasy laugh. 'And I had to put in an hour in the village emporium, first waiting for my call, then waiting for this taxi. (And this is going to cost us a pretty penny.) I got talking, naturally, one way and another. You've no idea what they said when they heard where I had parked you. Not a soul round there will go near the place. I must say – discounting gossip – there's a story there,' said Edward. 'They can't fix anything, but. . . . Well, you see, it appears that this Mather woman. . .' Lowering his voice, so as not to be heard by the driver, Edward began to tell Lou what he had heard in the village about the abrupt disappearance of Mr Mather.

* * * * *

M R James (1862–1936): Son of a Suffolk clergyman, James established a brilliant reputation as a medievalist at King's Cambridge. He eventually became University Chancellor but is best remembered for the ghost stories he wrote to amuse fellow students. The wooded park and mere of Castringham Hall in 'The Ash Tree' may owe something to Livermere Hall (since demolished) near Bury St Edmunds – James was brought up in the rectory on the edge of the park. The story appears in his *Collected Ghost Stories* (1933).

The Ash Tree

M R JAMES

Everyone who has travelled over Eastern England knows the smaller country-houses with which it is studded – the rather dank little buildings, usually in the Italian style, surrounded with parks of some eighty to a hundred acres. For me they have always had a very strong attraction with the grey paling of split oak, the noble trees, the meres with their reed-beds, and the line of distant woods. Then, I like the pillared portico – perhaps stuck on to a red-brick Queen Anne house which has been faced with stucco to bring it into line with the 'Grecian' taste of the end of the eighteenth century; the hall inside, going up to the roof, which hall ought always to be provided with a gallery and a small organ. I like the library, too, where you may find anything from a Psalter of the thirteenth century to a Shakespeare quarto. I like the pictures, of course; and perhaps most of all I like fancying what life in such a house was when it was first built, and in the piping times of landlords' prosperity, and not least now, when, if money is not so plentiful, taste is more varied and life quite as interesting. I wish to have one of these houses, and enough money to keep it together and entertain my friends in it modestly.

But this is a digression. I have to tell you of a curious series of events which happened in such a house as I have tried to describe. It is Castringham Hall in Suffolk. I think a good deal has been done to the building since the period of my story, but the essential features I have sketched are still there – Italian portico, square block of white house, older inside than out, park with fringe of woods, and mere. The one feature that marked out the house from a score of others is gone. As you looked at it from the park, you saw on the right a great old ash-tree growing within half a dozen yards of the wall, and almost or quite touching the building with its branches. I suppose it had stood there ever since Castringham ceased to be a fortified place, and since the moat was

137

filled in and the Elizabethan dwelling-house built. At any rate, it had wellnigh attained its full dimensions in the year 1690.

In that year the district in which the Hall is situated was the scene of a number of witch-trials. It will be long, I think, before we arrive at a just estimate of the amount of solid reason – if there was any – which lay at the root of the universal fear of witches in old times. Whether the persons accused of this offence really did imagine that they were possessed of unusual powers of any kind; or whether they had the will at least, if not the power, of doing mischief to their neighbours; or whether all the confessions, of which there are so many, were extorted by the mere cruelty of the witch-finders – these are questions which are not, I fancy, yet solved. And the present narrative gives me pause. I cannot altogether sweep it away as mere invention. The reader must judge for himself.

Castringham contributed a victim to the *auto-da-fé*. Mrs. Mothersole was her name, and she differed from the ordinary run of village witches only in being rather better off and in a more influential position. Efforts were made to save her by several reputable farmers of the parish. They did their best to testify to her character, and showed considerable anxiety as to the verdict of the jury.

But what seems to have been fatal to the woman was the evidence of the then proprietor of Castringham Hall – Sir Matthew Fell. He deposed to having watched her on three different occasions from his window, at the full of the moon, gathering sprigs 'from the ash-tree near my house.' She had climbed into the branches, clad only in her shift, and was cutting off small twigs with a peculiarly curved knife, and as she did so she seemed to be talking to herself. On each occasion Sir Matthew had done his best to capture the woman, but she had always taken alarm at some accidental noise he had made, and all he could see when he got down to the garden was a hare running across the park in the direction of the village.

On the third night he had been at pains to follow at his best speed, and had gone straight to Mrs. Mothersole's house; but he had had to wait a quarter of an hour battering at her door, and then she had come out very cross, and apparently very sleepy, as if just out of bed; and he had no good explanation to offer of his visit.

Mainly on this evidence, though there was much more of a less striking and unusual kind from other parishioners, Mrs. Mothersole was found guilty and condemned to die. She was hanged a week after the trial, with five or six more unhappy creatures at Bury St. Edmunds.

Sir Matthew Fell, then Deputy-Sheriff, was present at the execution. It was a damp, drizzly March morning when the cart made its way up the rough grass hill outside Northgate, where the gallows stood. The other victims were apathetic or broken down with misery; but Mrs. Mothersole was, as in life so in death, of a very different temper. Her 'poysonous Rage,' as a reporter of the time puts it, 'did so work upon the Bystanders – yea, even upon the Hangman – that it was constantly affirmed of all that saw her that she presented the living Aspect of a mad Divell. Yet she offer'd no Resistance to the Officers of the Law; onely she looked upon those that laid Hands upon her with so direfull and venomous an Aspect that – as one of them afterwards assured me – the meer Thought of it preyed inwardly upon his Mind for six Months after.'

However, all that she is reported to have said was the seemingly meaningless words: 'There will be guests at the Hall.' Which she repeated more than once in an undertone.

Sir Matthew Fell was not unimpressed by the bearing of the woman. He had some talk upon the matter with the Vicar of his parish, with whom he travelled home after the assize business was over. His evidence at the trial had not been very willingly given; he was not specially infected with the witch-finding mania, but he declared, then and afterwards, that he could not give any other account of the matter than that he had given, and that he could not possibly have been mistaken as to what he saw. The whole transaction had been repugnant to him, for he was a man who liked to be on pleasant terms with those about him; but he saw a duty to be done in this business, and he had done it. That seems to have been the gist of his sentiments, and the Vicar applauded it, as any reasonable man must have done.

A few weeks after, when the moon of May was at the full, Vicar and Squire met again in the park, and walked to the Hall together. Lady Fell was with her mother, who was dangerously ill, and Sir Matthew was alone at home; so the Vicar, Mr. Crome, was easily persuaded to take a late supper at the Hall.

Sir Matthew was not very good company this evening. The talk ran chiefly on family and parish matters, and, as luck would have it, Sir Matthew made a memorandum in writing of certain wishes or intentions of his regarding his estates, which afterwards proved exceedingly useful.

When Mr. Crome thought of starting for home, about half-past nine o'clock, Sir Matthew and he took a preliminary turn on the gravelled walk at the back of the house. The only incident that struck Mr. Crome was this: they were in sight of the ash-tree which I described as growing near the windows of the building, when Sir Matthew stopped and said:

'What is that that runs up and down the stem of the ash? It is never a squirrel? They will all be in their nests by now.'

The Vicar looked and saw the moving creature, but he could make nothing of its colour in the moon-light. The sharp outline, however, seen for an instant, was imprinted on his brain, and he could have sworn, he said, though it sounded foolish, that, squirrel or not, it had more than four legs.

Still, not much was to be made of the momentary vision, and the two men parted. They may have met since then, but it was not for a score of years.

Next day Sir Matthew Fell was not downstairs at six in the morning, as was his custom, nor at seven, nor yet at eight. Hereupon the servants went and knocked at his chamber door. I need not prolong the description of their anxious listenings and renewed batterings on the panels. The door was opened at last from the outside, and they found their master dead and black. So much you have guessed. That there were any marks of violence did not at the moment appear; but the window was open.

One of the men went to fetch the parson, and then by his directions rode on to give notice to the coroner. Mr. Crome himself went as quick as he might to the Hall, and was shown to the room where the dead man lay. He has left some notes among his papers which show how genuine a respect and sorrow was felt for Sir Matthew, and there is also this passage, which I transcribe for the sake of the light it throws upon the course of events, and also upon the common beliefs of the time:

'There was not any the least Trace of an Entrance having been forc'd to the Chamber: but the Casement stood open, as my poor Friend would always have it in this Season. He had his Evening Drink of small Ale in a silver vessel of about a pint measure, and to-night had not drunk it out. This Drink was examined by the Physician from Bury, a Mr. Hodgkins, who could not, however, as he afterwards declar'd upon his Oath, before the Coroner's quest, discover that any matter of a venomous kind was present in it. For, as was natural, in the great Swelling and Blackness of the Corpse, there was talk made among the Neighbours of Poyson. The Body was very much Disorder'd as it laid in the Bed, being twisted after so extream a sort as gave too probable Conjecture that my worthy Friend and Patron had expir'd in great Pain and Agony. And what is as yet unexplain'd, and to myself the Argument of some Horrid and Artfull Designe in the Perpetrators of this Barbarous Murther, was this, that the

Women which were entrusted with the laying-out of the Corpse and washing it, being both sad Persons and very well Respected in their Mournfull Profession, came to me in a great Pain and Distress both of Mind and Body, saying, what was indeed confirmed upon the first View, that they had no sooner touch'd the Breast of the Corpse with their naked Hands than they were sensible of a more than ordinary violent Smart and Acheing in their Palms, which, with their whole Forearms, in no long time swell'd so immoderately, the Pain still continuing, that, as afterwards proved, during many weeks they were forc'd to lay by the exercise of their Calling; and yet no mark seen on the Skin.

'Upon hearing this, I sent for the Physician, who was still in the House, and we made as carefull a Proof as we were able by the Help of a small Magnifying Lens of Crystal of the condition of the Skinn on this Part of the Body: but could not detect with the Instrument we had any Matter of Importance beyond a couple of small Punctures or Pricks, which we then concluded were the Spotts by which the Poyson might be introduced, remembering that Ring of *Pope Borgia*, with other known Specimens of the Horrid Art of the Italian Poysoners of the last age.

'So much is to be said of the Symptoms seen on the Corpse. As to what I am to add, it is meerly my own Experiment, and to be left to Posterity to judge whether there be anything of Value therein. There was on the Table by the Beddside a Bible of the small size, in which my Friend – punctuall as in Matters of less Moment, so in this more weighty one – used nightly, and upon his First Rising, to read a sett Portion. And I taking it up – not without a Tear duly paid to him which from the Study of this poorer Adumbration was now pass'd to the contemplation of its great Originall – it came into my Thoughts, as at such moments of Helplessness we are prone to catch at any the least Glimmer that makes promise of Light, to make trial of that old and by many accounted Superstitious Practice of drawing the *Sortes*: of which a Principall Instance, in the case of his late Sacred Majesty the Blessed Martyr King *Charles* and my Lord *Falkland*, was now much talked of. I must needs admit that by my Trial not much Assistance was afforded me: yet, as the Cause and Origin of these Dreadful Events may hereafter be search'd out, I set down the Results, in the case it may be found that they pointed the true Quarter of the Mischief to a quicker Intelligence than my own.

'I made, then, three trials, opening the Book and placing my Finger upon certain Words: which gave in the first these words, from Luke xiii. 7, *Cut it down*; in the second, Isaiah xiii. 20, *It shall never be inhabited*; and upon the third Experiment, Job xxxix. 30, *Her young ones also suck up blood.*'

This is all that need be quoted from Mr. Crome's papers. Sir Matthew Fell was duly coffined and laid into the earth, and his funeral sermon, preached by Mr. Crome on the following Sunday, has been printed under the title of 'The Unsearchable Way; or, England's Danger and the Malicious Dealings of Antichrist,' it being the Vicar's view, as well as that most commonly held in the neighbourhood, that the Squire was the victim of a recrudescence of the Popish Plot.

His son, Sir Matthew the second, succeeded to the title and estates. And so ends the first act of the Castringham tragedy. It is to be mentioned, though the fact is not surprising, that the new Baronet did not occupy the room in which his father had died. Nor, indeed, was it slept in by anyone but an occasional visitor during the whole of his occupation. He died in 1735, and I do not find that anything particular marked his reign, save a curiously constant mortality among his cattle and livestock in general, which showed a tendency to increase slightly as time went on.

Those who are interested in the details will find a statistical account in a letter to the *Gentleman's Magazine* of 1772, which draws the facts from the Baronet's own papers. He put an end to it at last by a very simple expedient, that of shutting up all his beasts in sheds at night, and keeping no sheep in his park. For he had noticed that nothing was ever attacked that spent the night indoors. After that the disorder confined itself to wild birds, and beasts of chase. But as we have no good account of the symptoms, and as all-night watching was quite unproductive of any clue, I do not dwell on what the Suffolk farmers called the 'Castringham sickness.'

The second Sir Matthew died in 1735, as I said, and was duly succeeded by his son, Sir Richard. It was in his time that the great family pew was built out on the north side of the parish church. So large were the Squire's ideas that several of the graves on that unhallowed side of the building had to be disturbed to satisfy his requirements. Among them was that of Mrs. Mothersole, the position of which was accurately known, thanks to a note on a plan of the church and yard, both made by Mr. Crome.

A certain amount of interest was excited in the village when it was known that the famous witch, who was still remembered by a few, was to be exhumed. And the feeling of surprise, and indeed disquiet, was very strong when it was found that, though her coffin was fairly sound and unbroken, there was no trace whatever inside it of body, bones, or dust. Indeed, it is a curious phenomenon, for at the time of her burying no such things were dreamt of as resurrection-men, and it is difficult to conceive any rational motive for stealing a body otherwise than for the uses of the dissecting-room.

The incident revived for a time all the stories of witch-trials and of the exploits of the witches, dormant for forty years, and Sir Richard's orders that the coffin should be burnt were thought by a good many to be rather foolhardy, though they were duly carried out.

Sir Richard was a pestilent innovator, it is certain. Before his time the Hall had been a fine block of the mellowest red brick; but Sir Richard had travelled in Italy and become infected with the Italian taste, and, having more money than his predecessors, he determined to leave an Italian palace where he had found an English house. So stucco and ashlar masked the brick; some indifferent Roman marbles were planted about in the entrance-hall and gardens; a reproduction of the Sibyl's temple at Tivoli was erected on the opposite bank of the mere; and Castringham took on an entirely new, and, I must say, a less engaging, aspect. But it was much admired, and served as a model to a good many of the neighbouring gentry in after-years.

One morning (it was in 1754) Sir Richard woke after a night of discomfort. It had been windy, and his chimney had smoked persistently, and yet it was so cold that he must keep up a fire. Also something had so rattled about the window that no man could get a moment's peace. Further, there was the prospect of several guests of position arriving in the course of the day, who would expect sport of some kind, and the inroads of the distemper (which continued among his game) had been lately so serious that he was afraid for his reputation as a game-preserver. But what really touched him most nearly was the other matter of his sleepless night. He could certainly not sleep in that room again.

That was the chief subject of his meditations at breakfast, and after it he began a systematic examination of the rooms to see which would suit his notions best. It was long before he found one. This had a window with an eastern aspect and that with a northern; this door the servants would be always passing, and he did not like the bedstead in that. No, he must have a room with a western look-out, so that the sun could not wake him early, and it must be out of the way of the business of the house. The housekeeper was at the end of her resources.

'Well, Sir Richard,' she said, 'you know that there is but one room like that in the house.'

'Which may that be?' said Sir Richard.

'And that is Sir Matthew's – the West Chamber.'

'Well, put me in there, for there I'll lie to-night,' said her master. 'Which way is it? Here, to be sure'; and he hurried off.

'Oh, Sir Richard, but no one has slept there these forty years. The air has hardly been changed since Sir Matthew died there.'

Thus she spoke, and rustled after him.

'Come, open the door, Mrs. Chiddock. I'll see the chamber, at least.'

So it was opened, and, indeed, the smell was very close and earthy. Sir Richard crossed to the window, and, impatiently, as was his wont, threw the shutters back, and flung open the casement. For this end of the house was one which the alterations had barely touched, grown up as it was with the great ash-tree, and being otherwise concealed from view.

'Air it, Mrs. Chiddock, all to-day, and move my bed-furniture in in the afternoon. Put the Bishop of Kilmore in my old room.'

'Pray, Sir Richard,' said a new voice, breaking in on this speech, 'might I have the favour of a moment's interview?'

Sir Richard turned round and saw a man in black in the doorway, who bowed.

'I must ask your indulgence for this intrusion, Sir Richard. You will, perhaps, hardly remember me. My name is William Crome, and my grandfather was Vicar here in your grandfather's time.'

'Well, sir,' said Sir Richard, 'the name of Crome is always a passport to Castringham. I am glad to renew a friendship of two generations' standing. In what can I serve you? for your hour of calling – and, if I do not mistake you, your bearing – shows you to be in some haste.'

'That is no more than the truth, sir. I am riding from Norwich to Bury St. Edmunds with what haste I can make, and I have called in on my way to leave with you some papers which we have but just come upon in looking over what my grandfather left at his death. It is thought you may find some matters of family interest in them.'

'You are mighty obliging, Mr. Crome, and, if you will be so good as to follow me to the parlour, and drink a glass of wine, we will take a first look at these same papers together. And you, Mrs. Chiddock, as I said, be about airing this chamber . . . Yes, it is here my grandfather died . . . Yes, the tree, perhaps, does make the place a little dampish . . .No; I do not wish to listen to any more. Make no difficulties, I beg. You have your orders – go. Will you follow me, sir?'

They went to the study. The packet which young Mr. Crome had brought – he was then just become a Fellow of Clare Hall in Cambridge, I may say, and subsequently brought out a respectable edition of Polyaenus – contained among other things the notes which the old Vicar had made upon the occasion of Sir Matthew Fell's death. And for the first time Sir Richard was confronted with the enigmatical *Sortes Biblicae* which you have heard. They amused him a good deal.

'Well,' he said, 'my grandfather's Bible gave one prudent piece of advice – *Cut it down*. If that stands for the ash-tree, he may rest assured I shall not neglect it. Such a nest of catarrhs and agues was never seen.'

The parlour contained the family books, which, pending the arrival of a collection which Sir Richard had made in Italy, and the building of a proper room to receive them, were not many in number.

Sir Richard looked up from the paper to the bookcase.

'I wonder,' says he, 'whether the old prophet is there yet? I fancy I see him.'

Crossing the room, he took out a dumpy Bible, which, sure enough, bore on the flyleaf the inscription: 'To Matthew Fell, from his Loving God-mother, Anne Aldous, 2 September, 1659.'

'It would be no bad plan to test him again, Mr. Crome. I will wager we get a couple of names in the Chronicles. H'm! what have we here? 'Thou shalt seek me in the morning, and I shall not be.' Well, well! Your grandfather would have made a fine omen of that, hey? No more prophets for me! They are all in a tale. And now, Mr. Crome, I am infinitely obliged to you for your packet. You will, I fear, be impatient to get on. Pray allow me – another glass.'

So with offers of hospitality, which were genuinely meant (for Sir Richard thought well of the young man's address and manner), they parted.

In the afternoon came the guests – the Bishop of Kilmore, Lady Mary Hervey, Sir William Kentfield, etc. Dinner at five, wine, cards, supper, and dispersal to bed.

Next morning Sir Richard is disinclined to take his gun with the rest. He talks with the Bishop of Kilmore. This prelate, unlike a good many of the Irish Bishops of his day, had visited his see, and, indeed, resided there for some considerable time. This morning, as the two were walking along the terrace and talking over the alterations and improvements in the house, the Bishop said, pointing to the window of the West Room:

'You could never get one of my Irish flock to occupy that room, Sir Richard.'

'Why is that, my lord? It is, in fact, my own.'

'Well, our Irish peasantry will always have it that it brings the worst of luck to sleep near an ash-tree, and you have a fine growth of ash not two yards from your chamber window. Perhaps,' the Bishop went on, with a smile, 'it has given you a touch of its quality already, for you do not seem, if I may say it, so much the fresher for your night's rest as your friends would like to see you.'

'That, or something else, it is true, cost me my sleep from twelve to four, my lord. But the tree is to come down to-morrow, so I shall not hear much more from it.'

'I applaud your determination. It can hardly be wholesome to have the air you breathe strained, as it were, through all that leafage.'

'Your lordship is right there, I think. But I had not my window open last night. It was rather the noise that went on – no doubt from the twigs sweeping the glass – that kept me open-eyed.'

'I think that can hardly be, Sir Richard. Here – you see it from this point. None of these nearest branches even can touch your casement unless there were a gale, and there was none of that last night. They miss the panes by a foot.'

'No, sir, true. What, then, will it be, I wonder, that scratched and rustled so – ay, and covered the dust on my sill with lines and marks?'

At last they agreed that the rats must have come up through the ivy. That was the Bishop's idea, and Sir Richard jumped at it.

So the day passed quietly, and night came, and the party dispersed to their rooms, and wished Sir Richard a better night.

And now we are in his bedroom, with the light out and the Squire in bed. The room is over the kitchen, and the night outside still and warm, so the window stands open.

There is very little light about the bedstead, but there is a strange movement there; it seems as if Sir Richard were moving his head rapidly to and fro with only the slightest possible sound. And now you would guess, so deceptive is the half-darkness, that he had several heads, round and brownish, which move back and forward, even as low as his chest. It is a horrible illusion. Is it nothing more? There! something drops off the bed with a soft plump, like a kitten, and is out of the window in a flash; another – four – and after that there is quiet again.

146

The Ash Tree

'Thou shalt seek me in the morning, and I shall not be'

As with Sir Matthew, so with Sir Richard – dead and black in his bed!

A pale and silent party of guests and servants gathered under the window when the news was known. Italian poisoners, Popish emissaries, infected air – all these and more guesses were hazarded, and the Bishop of Kilmore looked at the tree, in the fork of whose lower boughs a white tom-cat was crouching, looking down the hollow which years had gnawed in the trunk. It was watching something inside the tree with great interest.

Suddenly it got up and craned over the hole. Then a bit of the edge on which it stood gave way, and it went slithering in. Everyone looked up at the noise of the fall.

It is known to most of us that a cat can cry; but few of us have heard, I hope, such a yell as came out of the trunk of the great ash. Two or three screams there were – the witnesses are not sure which – and then a slight and muffled noise of some commotion or struggling was all that came. But Lady Mary Hervey fainted outright, and the housekeeper stopped her ears and fled till she fell on the terrace.

The Bishop of Kilmore and Sir William Kentfield stayed. Yet even they were daunted, though it was only at the cry of a cat; and Sir William swallowed once or twice before he could say:

'There is something more than we know of in that tree, my lord. I am for an instant search.'

And this was agreed upon. A ladder was brought, and one of the gardeners went up, and, looking down the hollow, could detect nothing but a few dim indications of something moving. They got a lantern, and let it down by a rope.

'We must get at the bottom of this. My life upon it, my lord, but the secret of these terrible deaths is there.'

Up went the gardener again with the lantern, and let it down the hole cautiously. They saw the yellow light upon his face as he bent over, and saw his face struck with an incredulous terror and loathing before he cried out in a dreadful voice and fell back from the ladder – where, happily, he was caught by two of the men – letting the lantern fall inside the tree.

He was in a dead faint, and it was some time before any word could be got from him.

By then they had something else to look at. The lantern must have broken at the bottom, and the light in it caught upon dry leaves and rubbish that lay there, for in a few minutes a dense smoke began to come up, and then flame; and, to be short, the tree was in a blaze.

The bystanders made a ring at some yards' distance, and Sir William and the Bishop sent men to get what weapons and tools they could; for, clearly, whatever might be using the tree as its lair would be forced out by the fire.

So it was. First, at the fork, they saw a round body covered with fire – the size of a man's head – appear very suddenly, then seem to collapse and fall back. This, five or six times; then a similar ball leapt into the air and fell on the grass, where after a moment it lay still. The Bishop went as near as he dared to it, and saw – what but the remains of an enormous spider, veinous and seared! And, as the fire burned lower down, more terrible bodies like this began to break out from the trunk, and it was seen that these were covered with greyish hair.

All that day the ash burned, and until it fell to pieces the men stood about it, and from time to time killed the brutes as they darted out. At last there was a long interval when none appeared, and they cautiously closed in and examined the roots of the tree.

'They found,' says the Bishop of Kilmore, 'below it a rounded hollow place in the earth, wherein were two or three bodies of these creatures that had plainly been smothered by the smoke; and, what is to me more curious, at the side of this den, against the wall, was crouching the anatomy or skeleton of a human being, with the skin dried upon the bones, having some remains of black hair, which was pronounced by those that examined it to be undoubtedly the body of a woman, and clearly dead for a period of fifty years.'

* * * * *

Nicci French is the writing partnership of Nicci Gerrard and Sean French. They published their first Nicci French thriller, *The Memory Game*, in 1997. Since then they have written six further best-selling novels together. Their most recent novel is *Catch Me When I Fall* (2005). 'Overlooked' was first broadcast on Radio 4 in 2005. They are married and live in Suffolk with their four children.

Overlooked
NICCI FRENCH

She cycled up the long hill ahead of me, under the dusty canopy of trees. The dappled light flickered over her and I saw how thin her shoulders were, how there was a dark V of sweat on her pink tee-shirt, how the muscles in her calves flexed as she pedalled. I imagined the expression on her face: frowning, determined, a lick of nearly-black hair snaking over her smooth cheek.

'Turn left at the top,' I called.

From here, you could just glimpse the sea, usually grey and furrowed but today a smooth blue. Wordlessly Maddie swung her bike down the tiny sunken lane and I followed her, free-wheeling past the field of cows, past the dead oak tree, the stubby church with its wooden spire and its crowd of faded, mossy gravestones, until we came to meadow and the hidden pond.

'Here we are,' I said, a bit too brightly maybe. I was finding it hard to get the tone right today. 'The perfect place.'

Still Maddie didn't say anything, just dismounted from her bike and leaned it against the stone wall. I unhooked the panier with our picnic in it and led the way through the meadow, the long grass scratching our bare legs. The pond was covered in duckweed. There was a smell of decay in the air. It was a dank, moist, secret place in the middle of summer.

'I bet it's good for mushrooms in the autumn,' I said. 'It's a pity we'll be gone by then.'

Maddie didn't reply. She sat down, curling her long legs up under her, and sighed. There was a bead of sweat on her upper lip. I persevered.

'It feels ancient here, doesn't it?' I said. 'That's what everyone told me before we came here: just a thin skin between the past and present. It was somewhere near here that Lizzie died. The summer of 1654.' I picked up a small branch and chucked it into the pond; the duckweed closed over it immediately; it didn't even send out a ripple. 'Maybe even in this very pond,' I said with a small shiver.

'I'm sitting on a bloody thistle,' said Maddie.

Lizzie Sammond was the reason we were here – well, Lizzie and the messy break up of my marriage and then my growing anxiety about Maddie, my silent, beautiful, sixteen-year-old daughter who seemed to have a whole world going on inside her head that I no longer had access to. But it was Lizzie who had brought me to this particular corner of Suffolk, a 'land full of the damned breed of witches' as the paper that I'd read yesterday in the Public Records Office had said. In flight from the pain of being left for a woman nearer Maddie's age than my own, and from London whose crowded streets and tall buildings I suddenly, desperately, needed to escape, I had fetched up on the eastern edge of England, where the owls shrieked at night.

Lizzie had been killed 350 years ago for being a witch, for laying a curse on her community. There was never a trial. No church authority, no witchfinder general was involved. She was killed by her neighbours, her fellow villagers. The details were confused and contradictory but there were claims that she had given local people the evil eye. Milk had turned sour, young men's genitals had shrivelled. She had a mark on her body and a butterfly for a familiar. A crowd of local people had seized her and drowned her in a pond. Perhaps this one. I imagined the scummy green weed in her open, calling mouth, in her long hair, between the fingers of her flailing hands. A justice of the peace had reported on the case with much distaste for local lawlessness and superstition.

I'd first read about Lizzie years ago, but I forgot about her, let her go, until Lewis had left me and I'd found myself wondering what I should do next with my life, where I should go. Lizzie was my research project, my convenient symbol of female oppression and female wisdom, my next historical novel, my excuse for dragging Maddie away from the hot, throbbing city to a cool, green place, far from anywhere. I'd rented a cottage for the summer, on the edge of the village where she had lived and died. It was narrow, with a blue door and a steep staircase, windows that looked out over fields and woods. At night time it was so quiet I could hear my own heart beating, and so dark that the stars felt large and bright and close.

I read books and pamplets with titles like Sacrilege Arraigned, The Displaying of Supposed Witchcraft, A Sermon Concerning the

Punishment of Malefactors but they didn't give me what I needed. I wanted to believe that there were things forgotten in the ancient forests and pathways and burial grounds of East Anglia and that Lizzie Samond had heard them and that if I walked the paths she had walked, I would hear them too. I trudged along the mud flats under the grey shafts of light, heard the lonely curlews cry and heard the wind blow down from the north and I wondered: is that it?

While I was waiting for this woman to inhabit my book, I was all the time aware of Maddie, curled in her room eating apples and reading romantic novels, or sometimes slipping out of the house, her bag slung over her shoulder and lipgloss on her mouth. She didn't tell me where she was going and I didn't ask. For the first time I noticed how the men that we met looked past me, at my daughter.

'Cheese or tuna fish?' I asked.

'No thanks.'

'Crisps?'

'No thanks.'

'You didn't have breakfast. Or supper last night,' I added.

'I'm not hungry.'

'But . . .'

'You promised not to pester me about food. You said you'd trust me.'

She leaned forward and took a peach from the pannier, and as she did so her pink shirt rode up and I saw an inky mark on her hip bone.

'What's that?'

'Nothing.'

She pulled her shirt down further.

'What is it?'

She bit into the peach: white teeth and juice dripping down her chin.

'Maddie?'

"Nothing,' she repeated.

'Where did you get it done? Why? You have to be careful with the needles. . . .'

'How old was she?'

'Who, Lizzie? Young. Sixteen or seventeen. A girl really.' I nearly added, "like you", but thought better of it.

'Why did they think she was a witch?'

'They thought she cursed them with her touch and by a kind of mysterious emanation from her eyes. They called it being fascinated or "overlooked".'

151

'Overlooked?' Maddie giggled. 'You mean she ignored them?'

'No,' I said. 'It was the opposite. She looked at them. Maybe she looked at them too intensely.'

'It was all about sex then?'

'Not exactly,' I said.

'Do you miss Daddy?'

The abruptness of the question ambushed me.

'Yes,' I said, before I had time to say no.

'I have dreams about him being with us again,' she said.

'Oh Maddie,' I said.

'Don't worry, I know it won't happen.'

A cloud slid across the sun and suddenly it was cold. There were goosebumps on my legs.

'There's something I want to ask you,' I began, cautiously. 'When you go out by yourself, where do you go?'

'Different places.'

'Who do you go with? That girl down the road and her boyfriend, what's his name . . . ?'

'Not her. She hates me.'

'I'm sure that's not true.'

'Anyway, he's not her boyfriend anymore.'

'Carla in the shop said you were hanging around in the car park.' I hesitated, and added, 'With the dealers.'

'Dealers?' she said, repeating the word as if it were comical.

'I think I'm quite liberal as a mother,' I continued. 'And after all, when I was not much older than you . . .'

'Yeah, yeah, I know, you were a teenager once.'

'I'm worried,' I said. 'I'm worried you're doing something more serious.'

'You don't need to worry.'

'So you're not?'

'I told you. You don't need to worry.'

'The people you meet, who are they? Maddie? You're only sixteen.'

'Old enough to overlook people and be stoned and drowned.'

'Don't.' I said sharply. 'This isn't funny.'

She suddenly softened, leaning across our picnic to give me a little hug. Sharp bones, smooth skin, a smell of coconut and sweat.

'I'm not a little girl any more,' she said, still close to me. 'It must be hard for you to lose two people at once. First Daddy and now me.'

'Am I losing you?'

'Every mother has to lose her daughter,' she said, ironically, as if she was quoting something she had read. 'Every daughter has to leave.'

Suddenly she stood up and, still in her shoes, stepped calmly into the pond, slithering down the bank until she found a steady footing. The water came up just below her shoulders. The ends of her black hair floated on the thick water. I stared at her, quite unable to speak or scream. She lifted an arm and stirred the water with her hand, leaving momentary little runes on the scummy surface.

'It's not too bad in here,' she said. 'Muddy and warm.'

She clambered out and stood dripping on the bank beside me, panting slightly, her mouth open. I could see her pink tongue. There were flecks of green all over her skin and her shirt rode up slightly and clung to the contours of her body. This time, I saw the mark on her exposed hip bone clearly: a small tattoo of a butterfly, whose wings moved as she did.

'You can write your book now,' she said. 'Now that you know.'

* * * * *

Everything A Man Needs
RONALD BLYTHE

Margery Nethersole had confidence, self-assurance, call it what you will. Her poise was obvious and challenging, and people and arguments less poised, although not necessarily wrong, collapsed at her approach. Sheer presence allowed her to win usually half the battle, occasionally all of it. It was something, of course, which one would get used to after fifty-odd years and Margery had got used to it. When life was rough, she was shining and smooth, like a lighthouse in a gale. She had always been called reliable and now that springy grey curls advanced across the still mainly chestnut masses of her hair her role of wise woman increased. The demand for her services on committees and in personal difficulties grew. There was no problem, great or small, on which she withheld her advice. Her method was to beam a powerful common sense on every complexity, with the result that she scarred not a few lives whose terrors called for a less drastic approach. In any case, people never blamed her when her *mana*, as she liked to call it, didn't work; they blamed themselves for lack of faith or for not understanding her instructions. And so her name remained the natural conjunctive to any emergency in central Suffolk.

A problem shared is a problem halved was one of Margery's favourite axioms and all round Ipswich there could be seen faces entirely concerned with these half-problems on the one hand, and the fact that Mrs Nethersole knew the whole secret on the other. To do her justice, there was no need for this latter anxiety. Information where she was concerned was a strictly one-way traffic. She collected confidences as other people collected rare or strange objects and was congenitally incapable of giving them away. Experiences and confessions were packed inside her like shale, an instant stoniness fossilizing them the minute she received them. It was strange that there were those who doubted her discretion, though less strange, perhaps, that those whom she had helped should hate her, as one sometimes hates a seducer. 'You can tell me *anything*,' Margery would say, fumbling in her bag for a Goldflake and coughing comfortably, and, amazingly enough, people did. They talked, she listened. If she saw herself as anything it was as the local sin-eater, but a growing number of people saw her as a kind of walking file in which, in a moment of madness, they had thrust their reputations. An inescapable O.B.E. for social services did nothing to lessen the fact that she was human and one victim of her charity had a recurring dream in which Margery appeared as a piggy-bank from which he could only regain what was once his alone with a knife.

Only one person understood Margery's secretiveness and this was Perpetua Cranmer, her friend-housekeeper since before the war. They had actually met on Abdication Day in the Charing Cross Hotel, recognizing in each other the peculiar happiness which follows a blessed release.

'I thought it was for the King,' said Perpetua, indicating Margery's black.

'Heavens, no!' smiled Margery. 'It's for Alfred. Or was. But I'm wearing it today because it suits me.'

'Alfred?'

'My husband.'

'Oh, I am sorry. Was it a happy release?'

'I expect so. It is usually reckoned to be, isn't it?'

'I didn't wear black for Mummy,' said Perpetua. 'She asked me not to – to save the money, you know.'

'Do go on,' said Margery.

'I shouldn't be telling you all this. It is such an imposition. I mean you don't know me . . .'

'But I do know you,' said Margery. 'Besides, it helps to talk and you can say things to a stranger which you cannot say to even the dearest friend.'

'How understanding you are,' said Perpetua, and she then told all there was to know about herself, which was very little. She then ordered more hot water and invited Margery's confidences in return.

'But I wouldn't dream of boring you with them,' cried Margery. And she never did. They had shared Penault Fayre, their house on the edge of Ipswich, for thirty years and all this time the only things which Perpetua had been able to discover about her friend had been such odds and ends as had accidentally sagged into view, like the hem of the oyster silk slip which Margery inevitably wore under her tweeds. Naturally, Alfred provided the greatest mystery. Who was he . . . *who*?

'He worked in Dunbury, Fife and Loman's.'

'A solicitor?'

'Just. He died before he began really to earn.'

'He must have been young?'

'Oh, he was – we both were.'

'He must have been, well, more than just a solicitor,' persisted Perpetua. She had lived with Margery for years before daring to hold this conversation. At first she had imagined that the subject filled her friend with pain but there was soon plenty of evidence to prove that this wasn't so.

'He was just a young man,' said Margery. 'They're all much of a muchness, you know!'

Perpetua refused to believe this, but having no evidence to support an argument, she broke a cotton indignantly against her teeth. She wanted to say, an ordinary photograph would tell me all I need to know. Your wedding picture, Marge. But years of reserve prohibited any reasonable discussion of the subject and Perpetua was left, more often than not, with a miserably embarrassing flush induced by a special look, half-playful and entirely too knowing, which her friend turned on her when she stumbled into talk about men. Sometimes she thought of Alfred *with* Margery – no, she didn't mean just that, but simply the two of them, young and companionate. And Alfred sitting for his finals. Fancy having to do that the year one died! Time heals, they say, and time had healed the place where Alfred had been in Margery's life so totally that there wasn't a sign left of his existence. Not a snapshot nor a collar-stud. Perpetua had looked, not once but scores of times, turning over the papers and oddments in Margery's desk and hoping to see his signature. Margery bore his name of course, and no wonder, for else she would have had to revert to Miss Catt.

'He was part of you,' said Perpetua accusingly. She was suddenly Alfred's champion, his remembrancer.

'Don't be too sure of that!'

'Oh?'

But Margery was not to be drawn. She stood up, banging threads and fluff from her thick skirt with the hand upon which Alfred's rings glittered feebly.

'Come on, Perp. Get the booze out – and stop ferreting.'

They drank their sherry like medicine and then went into the kitchen to begin the dinner. The kitchen was warm and lofty, with a scarlet rug in front of the Aga and a buttoned Victorian armchair full of sleeping kittens. Old wooden cream platters were heaped with withered Cox's Orange Pippins and flaking ropes of onions swung from bacon hooks. There were endless labelled canisters, all of them containing what they said they did, and in generous quantities. A *jardinière*, besides its usual burden of plants, held a load of freshly made marmalade and a torpid cat. Crates of beer and wine lay under the dresser and a huge straw-coloured table whose pale sweet grain eddied in the lamplight stretched itself purely across the scrubbed brick floor.

'Mmmm!' murmured Perpetua appreciatively, entering her kingdom.

'We live well, is that what you mean?' asked Margery. Her friend thought she noticed a change of inflexion; some clouding or maybe brightening in Mrs Nethersole's voice, causing it to sound like the voice of a stranger. The eyes, too, while retaining both their customary shape and expression, contained some new intelligence which Perpetua could not fathom. Surprisingly, it occurred to her that the sensible, practical front had slipped and that she was looking at a revealed, an exposed Margery. It was the merest momentary displacement, rather like when one of their colour-slides went crooked into the projector and brought the garden out flaring like Africa on the screen.

'As some kind of compensation, perhaps?'

The non-typical sharpness of this brought the familiar Margery hurriedly into focus.

'Maybe. But we don't have to go into it. After all, we are not the usual kind of women who, er, share, are we . . . ?'

It was more a statement than a question.

'No, we are not,' said Perpetua so distinctly as to make it clear that, this hitherto tacit fact having been uttered, there was no need ever to mention the subject again. She was stripping a chicory head leaf by leaf and now she rejoiced in the mutual silky coolness of her fingers and the plant. Behind her, she could hear Margery laying the table, bonking down their heavy silver on the spotless wood, chinking glasses, sounding slapdash but achieving perfection. Order! I love it! That was what Margery said – this, in fact, was her creed. Alfred, the marriage, it had all been tidied away. Order. This was all it was. Perpetua had pondered that it might be so before but now it convinced her. She could have hugged Margery, except they never hugged. Or touched. Or even shook hands. Order. Sweet, immaculate order. Feeling happy, she leaned over and switched on the kitchen wireless. It was the same instrument on which they had listened to Churchill and ITMA. A group thumped way. Shopping around she found an announcer offering selections from *The King and I*.

'That's better,' cried Margery, 'let's have some real music!'

She had finished laying the table and was crouched over a big Boot's diary on the dresser, checking over tomorrow's engagements. The Bench in the morning. School governors at two. Then nothing until six, which was Library Committee. One got a fairly clear day like that sometimes; she wondered what she would do. Perpetua, glancing round her, saw only the stalwartness, the large beam and the contradictorily small, pretty feet. Margery's face was in the shadows. It hung down over the page, the faintly swarthy flesh pulling away from the bone and creating soft fresh planes. Her mouth in this absorbed, leaning-forward stance was pouched and greedy like a child's. Her thick lustreless hair swung out in fat scimitars which hid her earrings. Body at this moment was definitely one thing, and mind, indicated by the ballpoint with which Margery was scrawling in further appointments, another. Bare neck and arms flowed out of sight with great richness. Something in the very reality of such an ignored corporeal wealth proclaimed an unlooked-for and unthinkable defeat of an intelligence which had hoarded it so matter-of-factly. There was no surface tremor, no discomfort as it is so curiously called. Nothing to suggest to Margery or to anybody else that she would act as indomitably out of character as in it.

Two days later Margery returned from Ipswich with a pile of shopping which included some garment or other, judging by the softness. Breathing heavily and carefully, like a singer, she whipped it open and tossed what it contained over to Perpetua, who caught it with a little scream of pain.

'Sorry, I forgot. Men's shirts are always full of pins.'

Perpetua spread the shirt on her lap with one hand and sucked her finger. The heavy salty taste of blood filled her mouth. The small, decided injury, the shirt and Margery's ordinary face left her feeling more stupid than astonished.

'I just went in and bought it,' said Margery like a teacher chivvying a child in the direction of the required answer.

'Compulsion . . .perhaps?' asked Perpetua in an attempt to say what she imagined Margery would have said had she done such a thing.

Margery laughed (her safe old laugh). 'I didn't lift it, love. I went into Whithers and asked for a man's shirt, size fifteen, and bought it.'

Subsequent action and its sharp corollaries stem from a small moment when conspirators decide to see eye to eye. Perpetua did not say 'Why?' She said, 'Whithers – isn't that the outfitters near the bus station? They don't know you there.'

'That's right, they don't.'

A long pause while Perpetua's blood flowed, disgustingly filling her nail.

'It's for – Alfred?'

'Alfred's dead, isn't he?'

Teacher was back again.

'Oh, I don't know!' said Perpetua crossly. 'Who then?'

'That is exactly what we have to decide. Who and what, though chiefly who.'

Perpetua's tight, waxy face relaxed.

'Oh, Marge, it's a game!'

'If it is, I've had my turn,' said Margery.

Perpetua thought hard, like when she played Scrabble. Her first move would show at once whether she understood the rules. 'I'll put it in his room shall I?' she said.

'Whose room?'

'Thomas's.'

This time she scarcely had to think at all.

'Thomas's room will do,' said Margery, adding, 'Only knock before you barge in.'

Perpetua hesitated then left the kitchen and went upstairs. The bedroom doors were shut all round the landing, her door, Margery's door, the bathroom, the guest-room. He wouldn't be in the guest-room if he actually lived with them, would he? There were two more spares. She chose the first.

'He was out,' she announced, returning slightly puffed.

'Never mind,' said Margery. 'He won't always be.'

About a week later, Perpetua went into the spare room to air it and noticed the shirt lying on the bed. It was slightly damp and the room itself ached with its sealed uselessness. The curtains were faded on the folds and the leather buttons on the rolled-up mattress were curled and wrinkled like perished flowers. There was a thin, pervasive smell which she could not name. It was the smell of poverty. At first she only put the shirt in a drawer, opened the windows and laid the mattress flat. Then came sheets and pillows; a great Turkestan rug for a bedspread and the duelling prints from the top of the stairs where they could not be seen. Hangers in the

159

wardrobe. A lamp. Some books. She was like a child playing houses and dashing off to fetch a thing the moment she thought fit. She was putting the finishing touches when Margery arrived. She was carrying something in her hand and appeared more surprised to see Perpetua than the transformed room. She laid it on the dressing-table.

'What is it?'

'Shaving soap.'

Perpetua's face set up a desperate fluttering, like a bird on the point of being dispatched. Making a room comfortable in one's own house, that was one thing, but to buy shirts and shaving soap . . . Then Margery looked at her with that steadying, special look which was full of the wise, broad view of things, and which she usually reserved for youths she was about to sentence to three years' Borstal training, and Perpetua understood. She opened the little drawer under the looking-glass and displayed her father's set of razors, seven in a blue velvet case, one for each day of the week.

'Very thoughtful, dear,' said Margery, 'except a young man of twenty-four is bound to use a safety.'

Not long after this, perhaps not more than a month, Thomas was safely confined within the margins of a game. The actual rules remained implicit, mostly because both Margery and Perpetua disliked the idea that they were playing to rule, although it was hard to see how else they could play at the moment. Besides, the excitement came only in moments of over-play. Breathless after such a moment, and with a little creeper of veins suddenly appearing on the sides of her emphatic white nose, Perpetua would exclaim, 'What a couple of fools!' Meaning the two of them with whatever it was delivered to the room, which stayed damp and strictly uninhabited so far as it was concerned. During this time, each of them learned the great importance of the casual move. After all, Thomas was not a doll to be shaped and stuffed and attired, although it was his clothes which presented his first great test of faith. Their cost. It was scarcely credible. The Oxfam baby thrust at Margery with his broomstick legs and, with an urgency not entirely despicable, her car called for an exchange. There was money in the bank but there were also priorities.

Perpetua thought she was just being logical when she declared, 'If he is – you know what I mean, Marge – *if* he is, he would come first. Naturally.'

Margery flew at her.

'If! If?'

Perpetua flinched and then had a brainwave.

'I know! He can have some jeans and pullovers from Marks and Sparks.'

'Who can?'

'Tom. You know, that young man we've got upstairs. Also, we'll have to get him a record-player and a motor-bike and . . .'

'You've made your point, Perpetua. Tom or Thomas, we don't get him for nothing, is that it?'

Perpetua did not answer. She was staring at her friend with the large faded eyes in which the vitality came and went like a faulty street sign. 'Marge,' she whispered, 'I've got to know something. Thom . . . as, is he . . . ' Her brain began to throw out words for Thomas and one of them rolled straight off her tongue. '*Is he a gigolo?*'

There was a second when it looked as though Margery's stern hand would strike Perpetua. Instead, her head bent down and down until her face was so close to Perpetua's that all she could see was a pouch of powdered fur. The pouch was open and through the crimson slit she was screaming at Perpetua under her breath, a sound so thin with temper that it hardly had the strength to be heard. She imagined something like 'dirty bitch', except who could believe that Margery would say words like that? Yet Margery had got to be made upright and audible again. The slap set Perpetua's hand stinging as if she had pushed it into nettles and all her fingers had left a birthmark-pink negative on Margery's cheek. There was lots of life in Perpetua's eyes now and a wonderful energy in her painful hand. She would have liked to have slapped Margery again and only kept herself from doing so with great difficulty. After falling back in a chair in a frumpish sitting position, Margery rose, looked at her watch and went out to the garage. The car crunched round under the window and, whether out of saintliness or habit, Margery toot-tooted. The pink fingers on her face had turned into a kind of dahlia.

She drove to Hunter's right in the middle of the town and bought a two-piece suit off the hook. Her behaviour was superb. She was refusing to cheat, even when there was no one to watch her. She took her time. She did not say it was for her nephew, nor did she flinch when the proprietor, who was a colleague on the Library Committee, bustled over to give her his special attention. From her handbag she took a card on which were the sizes of an eleven-stone man which she had copied from the Ideal Weight Chart in a colour supplement.

'He really is stock!' remarked the assistant. 'They're usually just stocky when they think they're stock, but he's *stock*, your friend – husband, madam.'

She went on buying, shoes, socks, pyjamas, underwear, just one of everything. The proprietor passed and repassed with professional indifference. The assistant now and then ran his tongue along the edge of his top teeth. When she had finished he stuck down the packages with Scotch tape on which was printed 'Everything a man needs.'

'There, everything,' he said.

She drove home and Perpetua helped her put the clothes away in Thomas's room. They worked silently in an atmosphere which was stifling at first but which later grew more and more lax, until by the time they returned to the warm drawing-room their peace had reached the stage of a delicious nervelessness. In the midst of tea, Perpetua, thinking of the pale colours, the fresh blues and greys, said,

'He's fair then?'

Margery nodded and answered, 'Is that all right?'

'Oh, perfectly,' said Perpetua. 'Marvellous,' she added.

'All so excellently fair!'

'Is that a quotation?'

'Coleridge,' said Margery. Swallowing a mouthful of cake and staring at Perpetua with eyes which said, nosey-parker-there-won't-be-any-peace-until-I-tell-you, she murmured, 'Alfred was small and dark.'

'None of Thomas's things would have fitted him, then?'

'No,' answered Margery. Her voice rose and broke on the word. It seemed to fill her with tumultuous relief. The cruel double-vision of the past few weeks (of which she had bravely not complained to a single soul) vanished as she spoke this resolute syllable and she was back once more to the big plain outline which constituted her usual view of life. Could it be the Change? If it was, she did not intend to tell Perpetua. And even if some such logical excuse for her recent behaviour was not forthcoming, what was there to get upset about? She thought she had been using her imagination in helping others but it was obvious now that some other faculty had been involved all these years and that imagination, or whatever one liked to call it, had been suppressed, causing it to burst out now. These and other arguments for her conduct raced through her mind while, at the same time, she heard her tongue carrying on a reasonable conversation with Perpetua. She had frankly changed the subject and was describing that morning's embarrassment when Dr Cleary's wife had appeared before her for shoplifting, but Perpetua's huffiness and displeasure could be felt long before Margery got to the part about the court's civilized attitude to the tragedy.

162

'What's wrong?' she demanded, halting the recital and similarly bringing the analyses, all various, of why she should have gone into the village shop, of all places, and bought a dozen handkerchiefs initialled T, to a standstill.

'I know what you're getting at,' said Perpetua. 'I'm not a fool. But just speak for yourself – that's all!'

'I'm speaking about poor Mrs Cleary.'

'Are you – are you sure?'

It was on the tip of Margery's tongue to have the matter settled there and then, but this seemed too harsh in view of what had happened. What had happened? A psychiatrist or a parson could offer a thesis if they were asked, no doubt, but what was the use of this when she had the answer within herself and only needed the courage to exhume it! She had been off her chump and old Perp had been damned decent about it. She'd find out why if it meant digging down to Australia! Excelsior! She leaned over and patted her friend on the knee. 'Don't worry, it's all right!' Her big smile ruled everything. '*It's all right . . .* '

In her room that night she delved into what she supposed would be termed her subconscious. It was a process or deed which she found quite repulsive but she did it gladly, knowing now that she did it for others. A banana-like moon dangled outside the window, picking out the furniture with its feeble mocking light. Now, what is it all about? Margery asked herself. It was 16 April, 1936, wasn't it? Yes. Why should you be so certain of this – because it was the day after . . . (Yes, go on) after Alfred's funeral. (Doesn't that explain it? Who behaves normally after their husband's funeral; you were not yourself.) I *was* myself, my dreadful, dreadful self! (Nonsense!) No nonsense about it; I obliterated him. (But men don't live on in their 'effects', as the law describes them. You could have given his clothes to a tramp – plenty of tramps in 1936 – but they would have gone just the same. Why are you accusing yourself?) I'm not accusing myself, I'm seeing myself. (You looked a bit daft, that was all. I looked . . . I looked wicked . . . (Oh, for God's sake!) I *did*!

'Did you call?' asked Perpetua through the closed door.

'Goodnight.'

'Goodnight . . . !'

Then it was the day after Alfred's funeral and she was in the semi-detached in Reading, opening windows at first to get rid of the stench of the wreaths and then opening Alfred's wardrobe, and his chest of drawers, and his stud-box, and his Minty bookcase, where his school prizes were

163

only separated from Roman Law by a run of Sappers, and then she was carting all this stuff into the garden in order to get it *out of the house*. There was a mountain of it. She had to run backwards and forwards half the day before Alfred was out, all out. Marrying her and then dying! Dying all the time they were married and then – dead. And all this stuff to hide his flimsiness: golf clubs, and fishing rods, and the Hilary term photograph with Alfred fourteenth along in the back row, and, help! one of those B.S.A. bicycles with a laced-up chain case – what on earth was she to do with that? Oh, the horror of seeing his suits in flames and his braces jumping in the heat like snakes. His shoes sizzled like meat and his umbrella burned like a martyr, cloth first then ribs. The explosion of his watch in the incandescent glory which such mediocre possessions had so strangely created really did mark the end of Alfred. It was beautiful, poetic! Margery had told herself at the time. Although it could not have been, for else how could she have spent thirty years repenting her bonfire? She now forced herself to recall every memorable minute of it with such completeness and totality that she was left charred and ashen herself. Poor Alfred! He had made her put it all back. Had haunted her, she supposed. She tried to think of him, of what he looked like, but all she could see were a pair of rather stubby hands and heavy shaving shadow. Pig! she told herself. She must sleep now. Tomorrow she must talk to Perpetua.

Her intention had been an honest confrontation, a clean break, but these were checked by the daring of Perpetua's latest move. She had picked up the letters from the mat in the usual way and was waiting for Margery to sit down at the breakfast-table before sorting them out. Margery sat, her relief smothered in foreboding. The bulk of the letters were for her, as usual. Two were for her friend but there were two more, and these Perpetua placed against the toast-rack. Her brow was shiny with achievement and a pulse throbbed busily in her naked throat.

'Oh, no!'

Margery's despair sounded like wonder to Perpetua; that was the way; she was thinking. 'Of course, I had to give him a surname first,' she said.

The letters were circulars from *Reader's Digest*, and the National Gardens Scheme, and they were addressed to Thomas Home, Esq., Penault Fayre, Flint Drive, Ipswich.

'But what the hell will the postman think?'

'Its pronounced Hume.'

'Perp, concentrate!' Margery's disappointment was making her shout.

'What are they going to say at the Post Office when they sort my letters and then, er, his?'

'What does Mrs Ellis say when you buy all the pipe tobacco?'

'He is going to give up smoking,' said Margery meanly. And we are going to give Thomas up, she longed to add, but she needed time to explain all this and she had to be in the centre of the town by nine-thirty. I'll tell her tonight, she thought. She was sitting in the car and rubbing a space in the dust on the windscreen with Kleenex when Perpetua's leading face appeared.

'Smoking is one of his few pleasures,' she said accusingly.

Margery did her best to see beyond the mask – it must be mask, surely? – Perpetua was a bit withdrawn, as they called it, but she wasn't daffy. Nothing showed. It was Perpetua's ordinary bare morning face before she covered it up with cosmetics.

'But the expense, darling . . . '

'He can afford it. You seem to forget he earns two thousand a year.'

'At twenty-four?'

'Yes. It's great, isn't it! He's going a long way, that boy. You'll see!'

'I must get on, too,' said Margery, tugging at the choke.

'What am I going to do?' she asked the Golly mascot bobbing against the window. 'I don't know what to do!' She felt ponderous and stupid. This feeling reminded her of her childhood and the dismal realization of being too big to join the game. She drove past the old part of the cemetery where the gravestones staggered about like bad teeth. That was what Alfred's grave was like she imagined. She had not been near it since the day of the funeral, although she had got them to put up a cross. She could be a sentimental old hypocrite and go and see it, she supposed. Perpetua needn't know. And, anyway, it would get her away from the house. The idea hardened into an intention. The uproar in her head died down. The policeman on traffic control saluted her trimly and received her commending nod. I acknowledge you, too, Alfred, she thought. I do – Guide's honour!

That evening she explained her plan with deliberate vagueness to Perpetua.

'Just a couple of days in Berkshire, you know. Take the car, look around . . .'

'Visit old haunts?' added Perpetua. 'Oh, I don't mind, I've got lots to do I'm out all Saturday evening, anyway. They're doing *The Knack* at the Rep. Thomas is going to be away too.'

'Is he?' said Margery with automatic interest. She could have bitten off her tongue. She heard Perpetua telling her, with incredible elaboration and conviction, how Thomas was going bird-watching at Minsmere and how pleased he was with his new field-glasses.

'How much were they?' she asked shakily.

'It's no use having a cheap pair,' countered Perpetua.

'How much?'

Perpetua was offended. 'You'd better ask Thomas.'

'Listen – listen! You've got to listen. There isn't a Thomas. Do you understand? *No Thomas*. He doesn't exist, he didn't exist. Ever.'

'I understand all too well,' answered Perpetua coldly. 'You decide when people exist and when they don't – or even if they ever did. Like your husband.'

Margery felt the raw blush eating its way up her neck and across her face, making her ridiculous and hideous. It was the 'your husband', the implacable relationship between Alfred and herself. Perpetua saw the ugly blood-flooded skin and was immediately shocked and contrite. She couldn't apologize: her lips twitched soundlessly. But her eyes were strained with regret and her hand flew out to Margery's like a cold white bird and held it awkwardly. Margery squeezed it. How were you to know where the most naked nerve lay? She was telling her friend in this rare contact. She went upstairs to pack. What on earth did one wear for a night in Reading? She would drive out to the Downs afterwards or perhaps to Windsor and look at the Castle. When she got home on Sunday she would set to work on the whole problem, even if it meant talking to Dr Healey.

The drive down was easy, miraculously easy, taking her a little under four and half hours to reach April 1936. For the dim road took the same twists to the cemetery and the weathercock on the chapel spire caught her eye just as it had then. The evergreen smell and the sharp gravel under foot were identical. Countless little numbers on tabs shaped like the ace of clubs sprouted in the grass, making her think, as she had then, in big, sad, obvious and satisfying terms of mortality. She made her way instinctively, pride refusing to let her inquire at the office as to the whereabouts of the grave. She remembered it as being a long way and she also recalled passing a remarkable stone, a kind of undertaker's Rock of Ages which looked as though it weighed a ton. And there it was, only riven. Or something had happened to it. It was fallen on its back with its wet base stuck with snails for all to see. Other monuments were cavorting themselves with equal abandon. They had toppled and cracked or simply gaped, as at the Resurrection. And suddenly the cemetery was not silent any more but was full of struggling, gesticulating men, talking and writing things down. Bewildered, her heart thudding, Margery walked through their midst to Alfred's grave. His cross had snapped off and the marble wound shone frostily in the sun. A fringe of sour grass hid Alfred's name. She knelt and pulled it up by the roots. 'Alfred Nethersole,' she read. Said. Many times. The men clambering about near her drew back. They included two policemen and a photographer. It's all right, Alfred, thought Margery, they think I'm praying, I expect. But I'm apologizing. I'm sorry. She tried to remember Alfred's face and a vacant splodgy horrible thing wordlessly introduced itself. She saw for the first time the extent of her destruction. Pity struck her like a brand.

'Alfred!'

A policeman and a workman were leading her to a seat. They guided her feet round scattered lumps of granite and through crushed flowers. She could hear the larks singing against a babble of indignation.

'What happened?' she asked.

'Vandals,' said the policeman shortly.

'Must want a job!' said the workman. 'I mean desecrating the dead, what could be worse than that?'

Perpetua began to dress for the theatre at six. Margery always laughed at this 'dressing' which wasn't dressing in fact but a glorified fixing and arranging of Perpetua's ordinary quiet clothes, and the addition of a gold bangle and a fob watch, plus her mother's rings. 'All for Ipswich!' she would mock, only kindly. What she failed to realize was the importance to Perpetua of what preceded the dressing, her spoiling, as she liked to describe it to herself. She bathed and did her nails and pumiced the little depilated patches on her legs. She took her time to fix her well and carefully dyed hair – tinted, she called it – in a clever facsimile of Katherine Mansfield's fringe and chignon. They could have been sisters, somebody once said years and years ago. But mostly she sank into a leisurely and unconceited appraisal of her own flesh. Its contours beneath the blanched, glowless skin had an arrested, immaculate quality. The immutability made her so grateful. None of the taken-for-granted things had happened to it. Women of her age – fifty-three – resigned themselves to appendicitis scars, Caesarean puckers, limp breasts and livid groups of vaccination marks but she was untouched. She wore a sleeveless navy-blue sheath and her three-strand pearls. She felt – it was one of her favourite words – svelte.

The novelty of being alone at Penault Fayre pleased her. She walked about trimly in her high court shoes putting out lights and checking the heating gauges. A mackintosh hanging in the hall made her think, 'Thomas!' Her cool and certain feeling at once left her and a troubled exciting sensation took its place. Her eyes widened and her hand reached for her necklace in a swift guarded gesture. She could feel her breasts against her bare arm; they disturbed her by their new sense of obvious largeness and warmth. She was no longer svelte, with its concomitant reassurances of grace and restraint, she was perspiring freely and her suspender-belt seemed to drag and claw at her legs. Thomas's room was dank – it was always dank, whatever one did to it. It was on the sad side of the house. She opened the lower sash and the early spring-night smell came pouring in. A pair of tangerine-coloured pyjamas lay on the bed. She tucked them under the pillow to keep them from getting damp. The open book on the bedside table was *Born Free*. She closed it, marking the place with an envelope. At the bottom of the long drive, just before she turned to walk up the lane to the bus-stop, she glanced back and thought how lonely the house looked and yet how rarely she left it. 'I don't touch it, somehow,' she told herself. 'But Thomas does – he's there all the time, even when he is at Minsmere. I know it and Margery knows it . . .'

The Rep let her down – or she let it down, what did it matter, the fact was that what she had come for and what she was offered bore no relationship in her mind – and this was a habit it tended to repeat. She felt stupid sitting in the front stalls with a group of mostly middle-aged women with blued hair and powdered necks, and watching a boy and a girl in jeans bickering on a mattress. She had 'gone to the theatre'. Such an action suggested some kind of magic and beauty in return for her money but the girl, who was grubby and plain, was shrilling, 'Rape! Rape! Rape!' like an ululating native. At least Margery wouldn't be waiting with the Horlick's all ready and a 'I can't think why you go if you don't like it' and her own mean answer of 'If I stop going to the Rep I wouldn't go anywhere!' She smiled her way through the departing regulars in the foyer and got a taxi. The short drive home was the biggest treat of the evening. Instead of Horlick's, she gave herself a whisky, then made up the Aga. A hint of the happiness she had felt earlier on returned. It was a joy and a privilege, as her mother would have said, to have a real home. Not a flat or one of those estate developer's boxes but Penault Fayre on its tree-swathed hill with its rich Victorian decorations and silence.

Silence. That was because of no Margery and thus perfectly understandable. And no Thomas. Only herself. She filled a hot-water bottle and went upstairs. Owly was calling – she must tell Margery. Pussies were sound asleep. That *daft* play – and after all those marvellous reviews she had read! There was a scraping noise and then a creak. She listened intently and heard it again. Thomas's window! She'd left it open. With the zip of her dress open at the side to reveal a long petal-like slash in the tight silk, she hurried next door.

The light blazed before she touched the switch. She saw the pyjamas first, more and more of them until their waving brilliance seemed to fill the room, and then the door slammed behind her and her head was being thrust back into the choking folds of the dressing-gown hanging against it. 'Thomas! Thomas! Thomas!' she shrieked against a barrier of gagging wool. What was the use? she asked herself, just as she thought she would faint. Who could hear? Then her face was free and she was panting and gulping in the close stale air, and words, like a whispered shout, were beating against her ear.

'How did you know? How did you find out? Who told you? *Who told you?*'

'Thomas . . .' she gasped weakly.

'You heard it on telly, didn't you? Didn't you?'

Oddly enough, the blow steadied her. She struggled up from the floor with an elaborate knowledge of what she was doing. She heard Thomas say, 'I'm sorry about that, missus, but you asked for it and you got it.' She could see his face now, fair and damp and rather tired. His hair stood up in a ferocious spike and his blue eyes maintained a constant vivid motion. He was nearly pretty but hard. 'Now, missus,' he was saying.

'Miss – Miss Cranmer.'

'Listen, old doll, how'd you find out? Tell me.'

'This is Thomas's room and so you are Thomas.'

The blue eyes ceased their mad dancing and became fixed and still. She returned their flat concentration and repeated, 'You-are-Thomas. Aren't you?'

'I see,' he said, his voice quiet and drifting now. 'I'm Thomas and this is my room, is that it? Let's get things right. Is that it? Is it?'

She nodded, relieved. She had subsided into a crouched sitting position at the foot of the bed.

'And what happens in Thomas's room, eh? I bet you haven't seen Thomas lately, have you?' He laughed. His mouth with its wet red flesh

169

and fine teeth hanging over her had the richness of a cave. The laugh stopped abruptly and her head was being forced to look down at something which lay in the palm of Thomas's hand. It was one of her father's razors. It was open and rocked lazily to and fro against the life-line. 'Just so you realize,' Thomas told her. 'Because I've got to eat and if you touch the phone or call out . . .' and he drew the blade in a flashing little arc just above her pearls. What would Margery do? She wondered. She knew what Margery would say – something sensible.

'Get back into bed,' she said. 'You're getting cold.'

'Or cool, perhaps. Like you, eh?'

He put the dressing-gown on and then the slippers. The clothes pulled him together somehow.

'Are you an American?' she asked. His accent slipped about and worried her, the voice avoiding identity, as it were.

He looked vaguely pleased and said, 'Lead the way, lady,' like a Hollywood gunman.

She broke two eggs into the pan. 'Go on until I say when,' he murmured, standing close behind her. She broke another and he said, 'When.' She also cooked some bacon and fried bread. The greasy breakfast smell in the middle of the night – it was only a little after eleven, actually, but the twin sensations of strain and ordinary behaviour reminded Perpetua of the war, which always went on most after bedtime – revolted her. She had to make a great effort not to be sick. The heat from the Aga met her in waves and she gripped the rail unsteadily. When he first touched her she thought it must be to stop her from falling. Then she felt the hand inside her dress, rapid, searching.

'Don't,' she breathed.

'Not now – later? Is that what you mean?'

She remained rigid, hardly able to create a pulse-beat. That this could – would – *must* happen to her was unbelievable. Had never entered her thoughts. She must protest, explain. He had to understand! She turned and shook her head soundlessly. He kissed her and wiped his mouth on his cuff.

'Say thank you,' he said. '*Say thank you!*'

'Thank you.'

She watched him eat. The eggs disappeared in halves and afterwards he ate a lot more bread and a whole pile of fruit. Perpetua had never seen anyone eat so in her life before; it was animal but it wasn't ugly. The cats had woken up and sat blinking and detached. He threw them scraps and they ignored them.

'This is a nice loving house,' he said, 'a real nice loving house.'

She sat staring, sometimes at the young man, sometimes at the grain ridges of the table, wondering what to say. Now and again he caught her look and once he winked, an incredibly coarse gesture in the context of his rather blank good looks. She picked up his plate and carried it to the sink. She had fastened her dress and now she began to wash up with mechanical efficiency. He sat watching her with languid patience but when she turned to the Aga with a damp cloth, he dragged it from her hand and said,

'Uh-uh! That's enough.'

She flew at him. Her hands thumped against his chest, making his laughter jerky and breathless. 'No-no-no-no-no!' she was shouting, just like somebody she had heard recently. It was the heroine in the play. He caught both her wrists at last and held her away from him, easily and conceitedly, without apparent effort. Speaking quietly and in a natural Midlands voice, his mouth parted in a deliberately sweet smile, he said, 'Listen, doll. Who came into Thomas's room stinking of scent and whisky with her dress all undone? But never mind that. Who is stupid enough to let a scared old girl go charging off to the neighbours? – that is what we have to consider.'

'I wouldn't betray you, Thomas.'

'You won't get the chance to, doll.'

Grasping her shoulder with one hand, he switched off the lights and, in a dream, she accompanied him up the stairs and into the spare room. He transferred the key and locked the door. Then he pulled off the dressing-gown and slid into bed. 'I leave at six,' he said. 'What are you going to do?'

Perpetua stood looking down at him, quite motionless. She was conscious of the cold stippling the skin on her arms and of a sour distinctive smell from which there was no escape. Disturbed birds scuttered in the guttering outside. The young man breathed with a profound regularity and depth which suggested near-sleep; it was nearly one o'clock. I can't just stand here, she thought. I can't just stand in this room for five hours! Her fear had gone and she now felt the incredulous annoyance of someone who had lost the last train and for whom there was no other choice but to sit on a bench until it was light. Her unbelief communicated itself to the young man and he grinned. Then he put an arm outside the bedclothes and patted the space by his side. Total refusal seemed to make her enormous. She thought she must look absurd, horrible, and bent forward in a mixed gesture of attempted recovery and extenuation. His hand reached out and grasped her arm.

'You *can't* stand there all night, can you now?' he said.

She shook her head. She couldn't. For one thing there was the terrible light bulb swooping out of the ceiling and almost hypnotizing her with its harsh filament, though most of all there was the cold. There was, too, her draining will-power which was reducing her reactions to a puppet's responses. This could not be happening to her, *it could not*, thus how could she greatly care? She switched off the light and lay beside him. All the landmarks of her conscious identity were obscured. She was crashing through a black and fantastic forest where tense and unwanted sensations were thrust upon her. Her hair was torn and pressed across her face and sometimes she was eating it. There was invasion and outrage and sometimes the most ordinary conversation as though nothing had happened – was happening – at all. For instance he said, 'I shall have to change sides, my arm has gone to sleep,' and she said, 'I'll put the hot-water bottle on the floor; that'll give us more room.' The birds chuck-chucked and clawed the eave the whole time. The room wasn't properly dark because the grey night seeped through the comfortless unlined curtains. She could see her pearls, phosphorescent on the dressing-table, and her stockings, pale as dust. She could not sleep – wouldn't ever sleep again – but he slept. He hissed faintly and sadly and occasionally caught his breath in a muted sob like a baby. The hours dawdled by, taking every second of their time and with them wandered the vast unwanted leisure of her thoughts. No recollection of any happening in her life occurred to her without a full-scale analysis becoming attached to it. Margery appeared and reappeared in her relentlessly exposed confidence as a great shutter, a wall, a dense hedge, a swooping baton commanding her occasionally ranging free-notes to cease. There was no longer anything to feel grateful for. She ate, breathed, that was all. So did a maggot.

Cocks were crowing now. How medieval that sounded and who ever listened? The morning lay deserts of time away and so far without a hint of an horizon. Where their bodies touched there was careless moist agreement, the kind of humanity which the flesh itself took for granted. Not because of this but because her tumbling dreams made her uneasy, she dragged herself up into a sitting position, saw, incredibly, her breasts like suns and snuggled down again. She could see him lying in profile with his lips slightly parted and silver spit glittering as he whispered his way through sleep. He smelled, acrid, institutional. Where had she noticed this odour before? In a class-room? No, in Nissen huts during the war. That was it. During the war and during the year she spent in the.W.A.A.F. before Margery got her out with 'pull'.

'What are you doing?' he asked without moving, without opening his eyes.

'Only getting comfortable.'

'I was asleep.'

'I'm sorry'

'You keep on being sorry, don't you? Life is just life. You don't change it or stop it by being sorry.' His eyes were still closed. The mouth was hardly enough awake to frame the words.

'I'm sorry . . .' she began before she could stop herself.

He giggled, turned to her and pulled her against him.

'There you go.'

'Are you never sorry then?'

There was a pause this time, not his usual snap response. 'Not now – not yet, is what I mean. But I will be. I mean you can't live and sit still, and if you live you make things happen. Funny things sometimes. Good things and bad things.'

'You're quite a philosopher,' she said without irony. Yet the remark displeased him. He turned from her abruptly and even in the uncertain glaucous haze of earliest morning, with the things in the room mere hulks of darkness, she caught the look on his face as a hardening of the mouth and eyes thinned the expression down to the mean and glinting one she had seen in the kitchen. But now, instead of fear, she felt pity. She patted his shoulder and then his hair. Awkwardly.

'Go to sleep,' he said. 'You got what you wanted, didn't you?'

Incredibly, she did sleep. The merciless images chasing one after the other through her brain tore away into blankness like a fractured film. She awoke to the inconsiderate sound of the bath running and of drawers being opened and slammed shut. He was robbing, of course. She clutched her hands together and felt the rings. Her necklace and her watch lay where she had left them. What was it then?

'What are you looking for?' she called.

'Blades.'

'They're here – in the little drawer under the mirror.'

He chatted while he dressed.

'You'll be on that buzzer to them the minute I've gone, won't you, doll?'

'The . . . police?'

'The police,' he mimicked. He was pulling clothes out of the wardrobe, feeling the material of the suit, choosing socks. She might not have been present. 'And then,' he said, 'when you've told them all they'll want to know, you will be a very interesting lady in the neighbourhood. You think about that, doll. Think of the look on the beak's face!'

'Where will you go?' she asked.

'Harwich, maybe: get a boat.' He put on the jacket and turned to face her. 'There now, how do I look? More like Thomas?' He looked transformed.

'Things could be better for you if you got abroad.'

'A new start?' he mocked. 'But better than never making a start, eh? Poor old doll!'

Her eyes filled with tears. She lay there letting them roll to the sides of her upturned face. She had not removed her make-up and scraps of it still adhered to her skin with cruel irrelevance.

'Poor old doll . . .' he repeated thoughtfully, staring down at her. He left the room and returned with her handbag. He must have noticed it lying on the dresser last night, she told herself. 'Now I *am* sorry about this,' he said, handing it to her, 'but we can't spoil the sailor for a ha'p'orth of tar, can we?' She gave him five pounds. 'I'd better have a spot of loose, too,' he said. 'For the bus.'

'There's some silver in the baker's jar on the dresser.'

'Thanks.'

She looked past him, deliberately not seeing him.

'I did ask,' he reminded her. 'I asked, you asked . . . for what was there for the asking.'

'Go away –*go!*'

She heard the back door bang and hurried to the window. He was swinging down the drive. After a few yards she saw him stop, glance back at the house and shake his head incredulously. She went into the bathroom. There was water everywhere, grey suddy water in the primrose basin and still steaming water in the bath itself. Blobs of shaving soap spattered the floor. Her immediate thought was to clear everything up before Margery returned – in time for lunch, she said. What was she going to tell her when she discovered that the clothes had gone? What was she going to tell her anyway? Would Margery go to the police? In a way she was the police. Her imagination reeling, Perpetua began to clean and tidy, at first with a certain plodding efficiency but after a little while with an unnatural rush which made her clumsy and confused. Soon she was running about the place, frenziedly putting it to rights. She was brought to a halt, not by the actual surprise, but by the harsh confirmation of the bundle which lay under the bed. The shoes were worn down at the heel and the trousers and jacket of thick grey flannel were each stencilled on the inside with 'Thomas, J.N.' and his prison number. There was a striped, collarless shirt and a pair of grey socks with reddish sweat-stained soles. She carried them into the garden, holding them away from her. Her face was now dragged into a knot of hysterical loathing. That it was of herself merely intensified the revulsion. She envied the brilliant simplicity with which the foul things and the foolish things, the prison uniform and what was left of 'Thomas', pulverized in the flames. The bed-clothes roared their purification and blazed thankfully in a tent of light. When it was over, when the room was stripped and it and her strength had been crushed, Perpetua crouched in it. Her mother's rings itched on her scorched hands and ashes powdered her brow. She wasn't weeping when Margery found her. Just sitting still and thinking that there was no substance in her life to burn anyway.

Margery looked at the smuts, looked at the hollow spaces and then saw the murderous smoke blowing outside in the garden.

'Alfred . . . Alfred . . .' she said.

* * * * *

Clive Sinclair: Novelist and critic. 'Bedbugs', the partly autobiographical title story of his 1982 collection of short stories, was written in Bury St Edmunds while the author was working on his doctorate at UEA and teaching English to German students in Cambridge.

175

Bedbugs
CLIVE SINCLAIR

During the night I have a vision of bedbugs in congress. A concrescence of male and female. The polluted mass pulsates, masculine organs pullulate, grow into dangerous spikes that, blinded by passion, miss the proffered orifices and stab deep into the soft bellies of their consorts. While I thus dream my blood is sucked and the satiated bugs, too bloated to return to their hiding places, excrete their waste upon the sheets and make their getaway. When I awake I observe the tell-tale black stains and become conscious of new islands of itchiness erupting upon my body. Life has taken a turn for the better for the dispossessed bedbugs, homeless since the demolition of the ancient slums, with the construction of the concrete college. Here at last the flat-bodied bugs have found sanctuary in the snug crevices, and plenty of food in the beds. Even during the long summer vacation, when the abandoned beds are filled by foreign students and their teachers; the former having come to Cambridge to improve their English, the latter to improve their finances. I am among the latter.

Some weeks previously I had been telephoned by a director of Literature & Linguistics Ltd, hitherto unknown, and been offered a job as a tutor at their Cambridge Summer School, held annually in the vacated university. He was frank. He said that they had been let down at the last minute and that someone had given him my name; he apologized for the short notice and enquired if I knew anything about the poets of the Great War, the course set by the deserter, for which books had already been purchased and despatched to the students; he added that these students tended to be young, German, intelligent, fluent, and – with a chuckle – female; he said by way of conclusion that Literature & Linguistics Ltd was a reputable company and that the salary was equally respectable. I promised to let him know the following day. Here was irony! Teaching First World War poetry to Germans, who had cut short the careers of most of the poets. Being Jewish I also felt a more personal thin-skinned irony. But was such irony justified? After all neither I nor the students were even born in the days of the Third Reich, so could I blame them for the fact that had their parents proved victorious I would never have been born at all? Easily. Then what made me take the position? Money? Of course. But even more persuasive was Isaac Rosenberg. On account of a little known biographical detail: his affair with my grandmother. He was ten and she was seven. They kissed one fine afternoon outside the Rosenbergs' house in Stepney, a few doors down from my great-grandfather's green-grocery. Furthermore, when Rosenberg decided to enlist he ran away from home and joined a bantam battalion in Bury St Edmunds. You can see his barracks from our bedroom window. The grotesque red-brick pastiche of a castle looms over me as I call the director to announce my acceptance. I do not mention that I have re-named the course Rosenberg's Revenge.

However, the German girls completely disarm me. They are charming, receptive and funny. Above all they seem so innocent. Our first class began in a tentative way, polite, giggly, until one of the girls demanded to know why we were studying such poetry. 'The concerns of the poets are out of date, they do not mean anything to us,' she said, 'especially since we are mostly girls here and not interested in war one bit. So why do you make us read about these horrible things?' Other girls snorted, to be interpreted as derisive. In that parallel course running in my head, Rosenberg's Revenge, I rubbed the cow's nose in Nazi atrocities, but in our Cambridge classroom I was patient, persuasive. I did not mention the pink stain on her neck which I took to be a love bite, sign of her preoccupations. 'Why? Because the poetry transcends its environment,' I said. 'War becomes the inspiration. A source of destruction, but also creation. A paradox to contemplate. The proximity of death added to the intensity of the poet. Their minds were consecrated wonderfully.' My allies moved in to attack. Women not interested in war? What nonsense! War involves everybody. My enemy was routed, isolated, leaving the rest of us clear to commence the course. In that introductory meeting relationships were established, and I was pleased to note that foremost among my supporters was the most attractive girl in the room. Vanity also is an inspiration.

There are two tutors for the twenty students; myself for literature, the other for linguistics, with composition shared. Although Bury St Edmunds is only thirty miles from Cambridge I am expected to sleep in the college, since my duties include evening entertainment. Tonight my colleague is giving a lecture on phonemes, freeing me to telephone my wife. As I listen to the ringing tone I consider the fact that while each peal is identical, subsequent conversation gives it a retrospective value; from phony, wrong number, to euphony for a lover. 'Hello love,' says my wife, 'miss me?' 'Lots,' I say. So our catechism continues, a pleasant exchange of self-confidences, until I realize with alarm that my answers are counterfeit. I am not thinking about her. I do not miss her. I am a liar. Second sight suddenly reveals this peccadillo as prophetic and I foresee the wreck of our marriage. Doubtless this is a romantic fallacy to be dismissed as easily as the psychosomatic cramp that has gripped my stomach. What harm can there be in euphemism if it makes her happy? 'Sleep well,' says my wife, 'sweet dreams.'

But the belly-ache won't go away. Back in my room I stretch upon the bed. My room is modernistic, without extraneous matter; for example, there are no handles on the drawers, just holes for fingers to pull them open. Being double the room is a duplex, and in the steps that connect the levels the style reaches its apotheosis. Granted that only 50 per cent of a regular staircase is used, since just one foot presses on each step, what does the architect do? Lop off the redundant half, of course. Leaving steps that alternate, right, left, right, left, etcetera. True the residents have tried to impress their personalities upon this chamber, by decorating the walls with posters, but in their absence, devoid of their possessions, these emphasize the emptiness. Nor are there any books on the shelves, save my war poems, and a book marked with a single yellow star. The ghetto journal of a Warsaw Jew. The diary was discovered after the war, his body never was. Actually, I did not bring the book along to read, rather as a reminder of an evil that cannot be exorcized. Nevertheless, flat out with colic I read it from cover to cover. What can I say? In class we talk of literature, but this is not art. The writer chronicles everything as dispassionately as possible, a record for future historians, until in the end he can restrain himself no longer. 'Daughter of Germany!' he curses. 'Blessed is he who will seize your babes and smash them against the Rock!'

Sweet dreams! I dream of flesh in torment and awaken to find my body in a rash. No stranger to hives I blame my brain, never suspecting the true culprits. But instead of fading the hives swell so that by mid-morning, my class in full swing, they are throbbing in sympathy with the soldiers in the trenches. Fighting the temptation to scratch I ask my enemy to read Rosenberg's *Louse Hunting*. Blushing she begins,

Nudes, stark and glistening,
Yelling in lurid glee. Grinning faces
And raging limbs
Whirl over the floor on fire;
For a shirt verminously busy
Yon soldier tore from his throat
With oaths
Godhead might shrink at, but not the lice . . .

And gets no further. Bursting into tears she cries, 'You mock me! You see the bites on my neck and you think I am dirty! But only here have I got them! There are bugs in my bed!' 'She means Franz,' says someone, referring to my only male student, likewise bitten. 'My dictionary tells me that a bug is a ghost, a bogeyman, a night prowler,' says another, 'so Franz could be defined as a bed-bug.' 'But they are not the only ones who have been bitten,' I say, 'look at my arms.' Whereupon my enemy regards me with something like gratitude. 'You see,' I say, 'the poems are relevant to our condition after all.'

Tonight it is my turn to amuse the students. So I have arranged a visit to the Cambridge Arts Theatre. Since the play is Ionesco's *The Lesson*, which ends with the pedagogue stabbing his pupil and donning Nazi uniform, we have made attendance voluntary. In the event I am accompanied only by my erstwhile enemy, Franz, and my most attractive acolyte. Naturally I am curious to see how my charges will react to the drama. Franz and Monika fidget as the dead girl drops immodestly into a chair and her professor pulls on his swastika armband. On the other hand Inge is impressed. 'Such a play explains much about fascism,' she says, 'and about Germany.' 'Perhaps Germany as it was,' says Franz, 'but today things are different.' 'Nonsense', says Inge, 'we remain a nation of *hausfraus* who thrive on order. We didn't like the Jews so we made them disappear. Just like dust. We were frightened by the Baader-Meinhof gang so we killed them. Pouf! No more terrorism. We adore neatness. That is why Monika is horrified by her bed-bugs. They leave marks. So she cannot forget them. She cannot sweep them under the carpet – is that what you say?' 'Suicide,' says Franz, 'they killed themselves.' 'That is what we are told,' says Inge, 'what you are pleased to believe.' Monika looks at Franz. 'We must go,' he says, 'we are tired.' 'Not me,' says Inge, 'the play has given me an appetite.'

The Castle, an unexceptional pub on the road back to college. We request drinks and curries. The landlord motions us to a table. It is midweek and the pub is deserted save for a couple sitting in a darkened corner. The man is not in his right mind. 'Tell me, George,' he says to the landlord, 'now the season is a fortnight old what do you think of our esteemed football team?' 'My name is not George,' says the landlord. 'No spunk, that's their problem,' he says, 'not enough aggression.' 'They've only lost two games,' says the landlord. 'But how many more?' says the man. 'Listen, George, you know everyone in Cambridge. You tell the manager I've got some advice for him. A bastard I may be, pardon my French – father was killed in the war before he had time to do the honourable thing – but I'm related to lords, the highest in the land. Therefore the manager will listen to me. Did you hear about that Aussie coach who showed his team newsreels of Nazi war crimes before a big match? That got their blood up! Went straight out and thrashed the opposition. I've plenty of ideas as good as that. I'm counting on you, George. Tell the manager the bastard wants to see him.' 'Wash your mouth out,' shouts the landlord, 'I won't have bad language in this pub. Not when there's ladies present. If you won't behave you can clear off.' But Inge is not embarrassed. 'That was a fine play we saw tonight,' she says, 'perhaps we could produce something like that in our composition class?' 'Good idea,' I say, 'but it will be difficult with so many people. You and Monika will never agree about anything. You'll argue over every word and nothing will get written.' 'You are right of course,' says Inge. 'Maybe we could do something with a smaller group,' I say, 'you, me and one or two others.' 'But then those who are left out might become envious,' says Inge, 'they will accuse us of elitism.' 'Then we must arrange a cabaret for the last night,' I say, 'everyone will be invited to help. I'll advertise for poets, singers, even stripteasers. Our contribution will be the play.' Inge laughs. Her shoulders tremble. Not for the first time I observe the body beneath the shirt.

Two plates of curry stand in the serving hatch growing cold. We watch them while the landlord sulks. Finally I deliver them myself. But before we can begin our meal the loony snatches Inge's plate and scurries to his table. 'You've taken our dinner,' he yells, 'we were here before you!' His companion looks miserable, but remains silent. As if awaiting this opportunity the landlord reappears. 'You have gone too far,' he bellows, 'apologize to these people at once!' The man is outraged. He puckers his lips as if about to blow a kiss. 'Sir,' he says, 'it is they who should apologize to us for stealing our food.' The landlord's wrath descends upon the lunatic who flees for his life. 'I might be illegitimate,' he cries into the night, 'but I do not copulate with Germans.' Now I am angry. But I am a hypocrite, the half-wit is a prophet.

Brushing my teeth in preparation for bed there is a knock on the door. Foaming at the mouth I admit Inge. 'This afternoon I purchased equipment to purge your bedbugs,' she says, 'I planned to tell you after the theatre but the events in the pub drove it from my mind.' I rinse out the toothpaste. Inge meanwhile is crumbling a firelighter into a large metal fruit-bowl, and mixing the fragments with charcoal chips. The result is ignited. Flames leap from the bowl like tongues ravenous for bedbugs. 'Now we must wait,' says Inge, 'until the charcoal becomes red hot.' We sit looking at one another. 'You are married?' says Inge. 'Yes,' I say. 'I am not married, though I have a man in Germany,' she says, 'here I am free, there I am a prisoner. You understand? Always we must do what he wants. Do you know the word "eudemonism"? It means you act for another's happiness. It is your moral duty. That is always the role of women, don't you think? Your wife, does she work?' 'No,' I say. 'Why not?' says Inge. 'She was pregnant,' I say, 'but she lost the baby. She is going back to work soon.' 'Is she – how do you say? – in a depression?' asks Inge. 'She is over it now,' I say, 'we don't talk about it any more.' We feel the heat from the glowing coals. 'Let us hope the bowl does not crack,' says Inge, 'it isn't mine, it comes from my room.' As if casting a spell she pours yellow powder on to the embers. Asphyxiating fumes immediately fill the room. 'Sulphur,' she says, 'the gas it makes will kill all the bugs.' Coughing I lead her upstairs.

We stare into the underworld. 'Look,' says Inge, 'as I said.' Sure enough, bugs are dropping lifelessly from crannies in the ceiling. Suddenly an unexpected twang! The bowl has split. 'Oh no,' cries Inge. Brilliant as the steps are in conception it is dangerous to descend them at speed, as Inge learns. She tumbles, hits the floor with a thump, and remains utterly inert. Spreadeagled, supine. There is no blood, but I do not know if this is a good or a bad sign. Her hand is limp. I feel for the pulse, but it is either stopped or I have my thumb in the wrong spot. Her heart. Situated, of all places, beneath her left breast. It is warm certainly. But I can feel no heartbeat, though the nipple tantalizingly hardens. However, for all I know this may be a posthumous reflex action or even the beginnings of *Rigor mortis*. I am no doctor. At a loss I rock forward upon my knees and part her lips with my tongue, intending to administer the kiss of life. But as I begin to blow into her mouth I feel Inge's right arm curl around my neck. And as she presses me closer I realize that my hand is still upon her breast.

Bugs continue to fall as Inge glides out of her pants. Possessed now, I turn out the light so that Inge's naked body is illuminated only by the smouldering charcoal, a serpentine shape, splashed with red, an undulant stream of lava into which I fling myself. 'Take me,' hisses Inge, 'here, as I am, on the floor.' While the madness lasts I pump my body into her, aware only of our sweat and the uncontrollable pleasure, dimly conscious of the mocking parody the dying embers cast upon the wall. Spent, prone upon Inge's salty body, I gasp for breath in the sulphurous air. 'Please,' whispers Inge, 'I am not finished.' She directs my hand down her belly to a damper place. Slowly my senses settle as I watch Inge's spectre writhe, and listen to her ecstatic groans, which dissolve as a deeper voice fills my ear:

> *Soon like a demons' pantomime*
> *This plunge was raging.*
> *See the silhouettes agape,*
> *See the gibbering shadows*
> *Mix with the baffled arms on the wall.*

A man emerges from the shadows. He is dressed in khaki and puttees, but looks too delicate to be a soldier. 'Do you like my poem?' he says. 'Yes,' I say, 'you were a genius.' 'Tell that to the Germans,' he says. I nod. I am. 'Do you hate them?' I ask. 'You cannot hate the dead,' he says, 'and you lose touch with the living.' Inge, oblivious, cavorts on the end of my finger. 'I'm doing this for you,' I say. He shrugs. 'Why bother with humbug when you've got bedbugs?' he says. 'Jews, Germans, we're all the same to them. They have cosmopolitan sympathies. We destroy one another and the bedbugs take revenge.' 'Not here,' I say, 'they're all dead.' 'So am I,' he says. 'Do you remember my grandmother?' I ask. 'Eva Zelinsky, she lived near you in Oxford Street.' 'What does she look like?' he asks. 'An old lady, white hair, in her eighties,' I say. He smiles. 'Everything changes,' he says, 'except the dead.' 'Aaaaaaaah!' cries Inge. She comes, he goes. There is quiet in the room. Inge is drowsy with delight. The charcoal has burned itself out. 'Come,' I say, 'let's go to bed.' During the night I have a vision of bedbugs in congress.

   Throughout the day Inge wears a silk scarf to conceal the bites upon her neck. Likewise, when I telephone my wife, I hide the truth from her.

Better keep quiet and skip the consequences. In two weeks Inge will be back in Germany with her jailer. At the moment, however, she is in my room again. We are awaiting another girl, selected to complete our playwriting team. 'When you took off your clothes,' says Inge, 'I saw something. That you are a Jew. Please, you must tell me. When you fucked me, was it for revenge?' I shake my head. 'No,' I say, 'I did it because I wanted you. I forgot you were a German.' 'I am glad,' says Inge. 'You know, I have always admired the Jewish people. You have read Martin Buber?' 'Buber? Sure,' I say. 'I know my melancholy fate is to turn every *thou* into an *it*, every person into a thing. Last night you were a *thou*, this afternoon already you are an *it*, last night we had intercourse, a real spiritual dialogue, this afternoon we must write dialogue.' Inge grins. 'And do you have any ideas?' she says. 'No,' I say, 'I am the producer. Ideas are not my responsibility. Do you?' 'Only simple ones,' she says, 'like a husband and wife, eating dinner, watching television, talking but not communicating. Just one twist, a girl will be the husband and you must play the wife.' The other girl arrives and accepts the idea with enthusiasm. We work on the play through the evening and into the night. The other girl goes. Inge stays. Martin Buber? A *boobe-myseh!*

On the last Saturday I escort all the students to Bury St Edmunds. A coach has been hired and I sit up beside the driver holding a microphone. As we approach the town along the Newmarket Road I indicate, to the left, the barracks where Rosenberg trained, on the right, my house. The coach halts in the large square at the top of Angel Hill. 'Okay,' I say, 'I'll tell you what there is to see in Bury St Edmunds. Opposite are the walls of the Abbey, behind are the ruins and a park. There is a cathedral. Go up Abbeygate Street and you'll come to the market. Fruit. Vegetables. Junk. Beyond the market is Moyses Hall. Built by a Jew in 1180. Unfortunately for him all the Jews were expelled from Bury in 1190. Now off you go. Back here at three o'clock.' Gradually the others slip away until I am left with only Inge for company. It is a hot day, dusty with heat. The locals look white and sweaty, like creatures unused to the light. The women wear drab moth-proofed frocks that show off the freckles on their breasts; the men roll up their shirt-sleeves to reveal the tattoos upon their arms. It is a mystery, this abundance of sample-book tattooing, all of course applied by choice. By contrast Inge's spectacular sexuality stops people in their tracks; her black scarf, her red tee-shirt, clinging like a second skin, her denim shorts and – this I know – no underwear. 'I feel so good today,' says Inge, 'I should like a souvenir. Is there perhaps a booth where we can have our photograph taken together?' 'There's one in Woolworth's,' I say. A photograph! Thus far the affair has been vague, nothing to do with my real life, as insubstantial as a dream. It will be a simple trick to persuade myself that it never happened. But a photograph! Our faces fixed, cheek by cheek, our relationship projected into the foreseeable future. Proof snatched from the lethal fingers of time.

The booth is already occupied by three small boys. We can see their legs, and hear their excited giggling. Then as the first flash fades we hear, above their laughter, the screech of a creature in terror. Inge tears back the curtain and exposes the boys, including one who is dangling a kitten by its tail in front of the camera. The kitten flails about uselessly, tensing and squealing with horror at each flash, only to redouble its efforts in the lacuna. 'You monsters,' cries Inge, 'stop torturing that poor animal.' The boys grin. The kitten swings. Faster and faster. Until the boy lets go. The kitten lands on Inge's shoulder. Seeking to steady itself it raises its paw and sinks its claw into her ear. Inge gently lifts the kitten so her ear is not torn although the lobe is pierced and bleeding profusely, staining her tee-shirt a deeper red. I give her my handkerchief to press against the wound. 'It looks worse than it is,' says Inge, 'it does not hurt.' 'Nevertheless, you must come back to our house,' I say, 'you must wash and change. You can't go around covered in blood.' Once again a curious accident has left me with no choice. Inge will meet my wife.

We surprise my wife sunbathing naked in the garden. 'Hello love,' she says, 'I didn't know you were bringing somebody back with you.' 'Only one of my students,' I say, 'she's been wounded.' My wife, wrapping a towel around herself, approaches Inge and leads her off to the bathroom. They reappear in identical cotton shirts, bargains from the market. A stranger might take them for sisters. I cook omelettes for lunch, with a few beans from the garden, and serve them on the lawn where my wife had been alone less than an hour before. I am astonished how relaxed we all are. Inge rattles off examples of her lover's male chauvinism. We all laugh. I feel no guilt, my wife feels no pain. She suspects nothing. She waves the flies from our food and throws breadcrumbs down for the sparrows. 'Are you enjoying the course?' she asks. 'Very much,' says Inge, 'especially our little playwriting group. Has Joshua told you about our play? Yes? Of course. You must come to our cabaret and see it performed.' 'I shall look forward to that,' says my wife. She removes the plates and returns with a bowl of peaches. They are sweet and juicy and attract many wasps. Our fingers become sticky. 'I am glad everything is going so well,' says my wife, 'without any problems.' 'Only the bedbugs.' I say, 'look what they've done to my arms.' 'Poor thing,' says my wife, 'can't you move into a different room?' 'No need,' I say, 'they've been exterminated.' My wife smiles. What contentment! I realize now why I feel so untroubled; I do not really believe that I have made love to Inge. She is what she seems, just a visitor. My wife is my wife. We belong. Cambridge is a foreign city. To which I must return, however. I kiss my wife. 'See you on Wednesday,' I say. 'What a nuisance,' says Inge as the coach passes our house, 'I have left my scarf behind.' 'Never mind,' I say, 'I'll pick it up on Wednesday. Besides you can hardly see the bites now.'

On Tuesday we complete the play. In the evening the heatwave breaks with a tremendous storm. Knowing how much my wife dreads thunder I telephone her. She does not answer. Later, when the rain has stopped, Inge and I stroll to the Castle to toast our success. Afterwards we return to my room, where Inge now sleeps as a matter of course. In the morning I telephone my wife again. No reply. Probably shopping. Lunch over, teaching being at an end, I drive home to collect her. There are three milk bottles on the doorstep, the first already sour. Its top is off, filling the stagnant air with its nauseous odour. Within is a different smell, naggingly familiar. I shout my wife's name. But there is no response. The house seems deserted. Bedrooms, bathroom, dining room, all empty. On the table is Inge's black scarf, neatly folded, and a note:

> Don't forget this, Love Rachel
> PS. Hope the bedbugs have stopped biting Inge.

Then in the kitchen I realize what the smell reminds me of. A butcher's shop. Naked, legs splayed, my wife sits upon the kitchen floor with the wooden handle of our carving knife protruding from her belly. Her back rests against the wall, her arms hang stiffly down, her eyes are open wide. The blood is dry. It flowed down from her wound, between her thighs, and formed puddles on the floor. The only sound is the buzzing of flies. They walk upon her breasts, mass around her vagina where the hair is matted with blood. This horror is too shocking to be true! It is a phantasmagoria produced by my conscience. Art, not life.

'Your face is very white,' says Inge, 'is everything all right?' 'I'm just nervous about this evening,' I say. We have gathered all the props we require; cutlery, crockery, sauce bottles, and a starting pistol loaded with

185

blanks. And while Monika – of all people – strips down to her underwear in front of the directors of Literature & Linguistics Ltd Inge and I exchange clothes. A suit and tie for her, a dress for me. 'This is Cambridge,' I think, 'this is my life. There is nothing else.' We hear Franz sing his folk songs. Then applause. We are joined by the third member of the cast. We walk out to cheers and laughter. 'Your wife is in the audience?' asks Inge. 'I hope so,' I say, 'she is coming by train.' The play begins.

Inge – my husband – is a bank clerk. I am a housewife. The other girl is a television set. Inge orders me to switch her on. We hear the news. I serve dinner to my husband and our two children who are invisible. An argument develops between us over the boy's long curls. 'You'll turn your son into a pansy with your ways of bringing him up,' yells Inge. 'They're always my children when there is something the matter,' I shout, 'I don't think you really wanted them. I won't forget how you treated me when I was pregnant. You didn't even try to hide your disgust. But you're the one who's disgusting!' What am I talking about? Why am I pretending to be my wife? Wife? I have no wife. How these silly words have confused me! What next? Oh yes, I am supposed to take the gun from my handbag. I point the gun at Inge. Why? Because I hate her. But why? Because she seduced me? Because she murdered my wife? Wife? I can't even remember her name. With her shirt and tie and pencil moustache Inge looks like a creature from pre-war Berlin. I hate her because she is German. A Nazi! I fire the gun. The blast fills my head. 'Daughter of Germany!' I scream. 'Daughter of Germany!' I shoot at her until the gun is empty.

* * * * *

A Stranger With a Bag
SYLVIA TOWNSEND WARNER

After three years as a travelling salesman Clive Peters supposed he knew every detail of the East Anglian landscape he covered, whether he went southward to Bungay and Beccles or inland through the Cambridgeshire fens. The firm that employed him was old-fashioned and without enterprise; he only went out two days a week, working the rest of the time in the office as a clerk. The landscape through which he travelled, going by local trains – for the previous salesman had met his death in a car accident, for which Mr. Ingham, a paternal employer, had never ceased to blame himself – from one market town to another, was not the sort of landscape in which details escape one's attention. If a new milking shed were built or an old barn pulled down or a tree uprooted by the gales that blew in from the North Sea Clive would have noticed it and marked it down in his memory as an event and something to speculate about. But now, glancing out of the train window, he saw a house that had never been there before. Square and sombre and planted massively behind a screen of overgrown laurels and tossing ilexes, it looked as though the time of the year had put it there, a corroboration of the dark waterlogged November fields and the dull sky.

But really it was just that he had never happened to notice it before. It was quite an old house; it must have been there for years. It stood about half a mile from the track – too far to see it as more than a picture. He had an instant conviction that it was uninhabited, which on examination he traced to the fact that though this was a Monday there was no washing out. It was a house in which there would be no place for a spin dryer. Everything would be done in the old way: the washing pegged to a line, the pork meat for pies and galantines chopped with a sharp knife on a wooden board, the carpets swept with tea leaves. The spell had fallen on him so completely that simultaneously he knew the house to be uninhabited and knew all about its former inhabitants: chapelgoers; up-right, hard-working, close-fisted, bleakly suspicious of all customs but their own, yet secreting a kind of sturdy cosiness, bred of duty and self-satisfaction. While they lived there, the core of the house was safety and prosperity. Now they were gone, and the house remained for his possession – a solemn plaything.

The house slid out of sight but remained solidly in his mind. He saw himself approaching it, the figure in the foreground. Presently he was near enough to hear the swish of the ilexes, the laurels' dry rattle. In the garden, hoary gooseberry bushes were laced with strings of last summer's bindweed; trailing brambles caught at his feet but did not delay him. The house was certainly empty. Sure enough, on its weather side a back door had rotted from its hinges. He walked in, meeting the raw smell of a cold hearth, a smell mixed of soot and rusty iron. He went up the stairs and wandered from room to room. In one of them a discolouring illuminated text flapped on the wall, stirred by the wind blowing down the chimney. 'Be Ye Also Ready.' In a garland of wheat and poppies.

He was too deeply absorbed to notice the train slowing down. Now it stopped. The station was called Yetton Halt; he had never known the train to stop there before. He heard a voice say 'Here you are, Bill' and a heavy parcel thrown down on the platform. Before he knew what he was doing he got out, carrying his bag of samples. Before he could think better of it the train was moving on. Bill was walking away with the parcel; there was no one else about. Clive thought, If I am killed, there will be no one to give evidence that I left the train at Yetton Halt. The thought pleased him. In his regular days between work and home, there was no room for even a possible anonymity. Outside the station a road branched east and west, and he turned eastward.

Though he was uncertain how far away the house might be he judged it could not lie more than three or four miles back. Standing alone and within sight of the railway it should be easy to find; if he guided himself by the railway he must hit it, sooner or later. For a mile or so the road kept level with the railway, then it veered suddenly and went under the track by a tunnel. It would be fatal to get on the wrong side of the track, so he retraced his steps to where he had noticed a lane which branched off in the direction he wanted. The lane ran zigzagging between tall hedges; he soon lost his sense of orientation, and whenever he came to a left-hand gate and looked hopefully over it, some obstacle, a further hedge or a stand of tall winter kale, interposed itself between him and any chance sight of the railway telegraph poles. But he kept on, and felt a kind of obstinate enjoyment. He was splashed with mud, his arms ached from the weight of the bag, it was nearly half past two and he had left his parcel of sandwiches in the train, he was behaving like a madman and would have to account for it; but it was a break, and worth it.

He was still obstinately enjoying himself when he heard an engine whistle. With a burst of joy that denounced his previous enjoyment, he scrambled through the hedge and began to run across country. He ran on and on, scattering a herd of bullocks, setting up a flock of curlews feeding in a marshy meadow. He swung himself over a gate into a rickyard where blown chaff streamed across his vision like a sallow snowstorm. He stooped under a strand of barbed wire, stood up, dizzied with breathlessness, and saw the row of telegraph poles and the railway track. The train had vanished, but the smell of coal smoke remained.

So now he had only to find the house. He walked on soberly, in line with the railway track, and presently, as in a dream, the house reappeared, and was instantly recognizable, though, as in a dream, it looked quite different. Seen from ground level it lacked the compactness and drama of its first presentation and had an upstart, ungainly appearance, its chimneys too tall, its roof too sharply pitched and furbelowed by ornate bargeboards. It was smaller, too, than he had supposed.

It was not so easy of access, either. The ilexes and laurels were fenced in by a railing of tall iron spikes and he had to walk to the farther side before he found the gate, which was approached by a track across a muddy pasture – branching off, no doubt, from some farm lane, for he could hear the shouting voice of a man driving cows. The gate was of iron, like the fencing, and with the same air of having been brought from a town. Beyond the gate a path, running between a laurel hedge and a shaggy lawn on which there were some rabbit hutches, led to the front door and on round the corner of the house. Clive followed it, because in his imagined house the door rotted from its hinges had been a back door. The compulsion of the imagined house was stronger than the disenchantment of what he saw; and it still seemed to him that if he went on he would find the door rotted from its hinges, and make his

189

way into that other house and go upstairs and read the text bordered with wheat and poppies. Meanwhile the rational part of him continued to make the rational assertion that, having come so far, it would be poor-spirited to give up his intention just because the house turned out to be uninviting and rather pretentious with its lowering barge-boards and oversized sash windows. Looking with sidelong distaste at one of these windows he saw a boy, whose pale face was pressed to the glass, whose eyes were fixed on him. A moment later the vision disappeared, for the boy's breath had been released and misted over the pane. A skinny hand wiped the mist away and the face looked out once more, with the stare of a full moon emerging from a cloud.

As though the staring gaze had shown it to him, Clive saw what the boy was looking at. A stranger, carrying a bag. Of course, that was the answer. He smiled at the boy, who did not return his smile, walked back to the front door, mounted its pretentious steps and pulled the bell handle. He heard no footsteps, but presently the door opened and the boy stood on the threshold. He looked to be about ten years old, very near the age of Clive's own son, but small for his age.

'Anyone in, Sonny?'

'Be,' said the boy, who had a cold in his head.

'I wonder if I can interest you in these samples of floor and furniture polish.' Clive opened the bag. 'All made locally, with real beeswax. You don't find many polishes nowadays with the real beeswax. Perhaps if I leave this card, you could tell your mother.'

'I habn't got a bother now. She went away last Tuesday, with Jib Bason. I saw theb go off together, on his botor bike. And Dad says he won't hab her back, not if she came on her bended knees.'

Shaking off the impression that there must be something superlatively appealing about a mended knee, Clive said, 'Oh dear!' and then, 'I'm sure I'm sorry.'

'So ab I. I liked Jib. He bade me laugh.'

Clive looked at the skinny, unappetizing child, framed against the recession of that long, dark passage and the stairway ascending under the bleak glare of another of those oversized windows, and thought that Jim Mason must have talents for the impossible. One could imagine a woman's laugh flaring out in such a house; but not the laughter of a child. And there was nothing he could do about it. And pity was unavailing.

'You mustn't stand here, Sonny. You'll make that cold of yours worse.

And I must be going.'

He stooped and fastened the bag. A stranger with a bag. Well, at least he had supplied a brief diversion, an incident in a winter afternoon.

'Cub in,' said the boy.

'Why, Sonny, that's very nice of you. I wish I could. But I'm on my rounds, you see. And I've got a long way to go yet.'

'Cub in,' the boy repeated.

'And what would your dad say? I don't suppose he'd approve of you asking strangers into the house.'

'*Cub in*' The boy's voice, which his cold rendered totally expressionless, rose to a peremptory shriek.

'Cub in, cub in, cub in!' His hands fastened on Clive's wrist like pincers, like red-hot pincers, for they were burning with fever.

'Well, for two minutes, then. Just to settle you back by the fire and see that you're comfortable.'

The boy flitted down the passage before him and opened a door into a high-ceilinged room. It was cold and cavernous and the glow of a small electric heater darkened it rather than warmed it.

'Is this where you've been sitting all this afternoon?'

The boy was shaking up a cushion and did not reply.

'Dull work, having to nurse a cold, isn't it? Still, better indoors than out on a day like this. What rain we've been having! And gales, too.'

A train was passing; the reverberation in the chimney seemed to decant it into the room. But he's too old for trains now, thought Clive.

'Though I don't suppose gales mean much to you in a house like this. It looks uncommonly solid. Built to last.'

The boy was still fidgeting with the armchair. Having beaten up its cushions, he was now diving into the cranny between the back and the seat. Clive walked about the room, trying to make conversation.

'Are those your rabbits, in the hutches near the gate?'

'They were.' After so long a silence it was almost disconcerting to be answered. 'But now we hab eaten theb. We ate old Roger yesterday.'

The statement was so flat that it was not even unfeeling.

'When I was your age, I had a tame rat. I used to take it to school with me, in my pocket, and one day – I say, Sonny, what's that? Take care you don't cut yourself.'

The boy had somehow produced a carving knife and was fingering the blade.

'And that's not the way to handle it, running your finger across its

191

edge. You must use your finger and thumb if you want to feel how sharp it is. I'll show you.' He took the knife and demonstrated. 'Sharp as a razor. Let me tell you, you were very lucky not to give yourself a nasty cut. Well, here you are. Be more careful next time.'

The boy put his hands behind his back and shook his head vehemently. 'No! It's for you.'

'But, Sonny, I don't want a carving knife.'

'It's for you.'

Half mad with loneliness, thought Clive. His mother's gone off with a man, his rabbits are eaten, he's got nothing to care for; then I come along, a romantic stranger.

'I want you to burder Dad.'

'What!'

'I want you to burder Dad,'

'Is that what you asked me in for?' said Clive, after a pause.

The boy nodded. A delicate pink colour had come into his cheeks; his eyes glittered.

Clive laid the knife on the table and sat down in the armchair. It was a more fatherly attitude – and his knees were shaking. 'Now, look here, Sonny. This sort of thing won't do. I suppose you've been watching the tellie.'

'We habn't got a tellie. Dad wouldn't get one. We neber hab anything like other people do. Burder hib, burder hib! It's all he's good for.'

'Blow your nose,' said Clive. 'What, lost your handkerchief? Have mine, then. Now, listen to me. I'm not going to murder your dad. Neither are you. Murder's a fool's game – not to mention a crime. Do you ever feel afraid?'

The boy glanced at the black mouth of the chimney, then out of the window at the tossing ilexes.

'I can tell you this. Whatever you may feel afraid of, a murderer feels ten times more afraid, a million times more afraid. And because he's a murderer, he's afraid of everything, everyone he meets, every knock at the door, every noise –'

The noise was quite perceptible, and was the noise of a bicycle being wheeled along the path. 'There's Dad,' said the boy.

Clive leaped up. The bicycle was being wheeled past the window; presumably there was a shed at the back of the house. There was still time for him to get away. At the same moment, the boy switched on the light. It lit up the small, dejected figure of a man with a pointed beard.

He turned and saw Clive standing by the window. His look of oppression deepened. He attempted to prop the bicycle against a bush. At each attempt, the bush gave way and the bicycle subsided. Finally he left it lying, and turned towards the front door. While the door was opened and carefully closed again, and a swishing mackintosh shaken and hung on a peg, and a tread that would have better matched a larger man came along the passage, Clive avoided looking at the boy.

'Hullo, Tony! I see you've got a visitor.'

Clive began to explain, reopening the bag and drawing out a couple of tins to substantiate his words. The sound of his voice embarrassed him – it was so full and ringing, so grossly unlike the flat, dejected tones that replied.

'Hmm. Yes, I see. Very kind of you, I'm sure. But I'm afraid I don't want any polish just now.'

'No, no! Of course not. I quite understand.'

The words were no sooner spoken than Clive realized their appalling appropriateness. He hurried on. 'And I'm sure it's a reward in itself to be asked in so kindly by Sonny here.'

Mentioning the boy, he dared to glance towards him, and saw the knife still lying on the table. 'To tell the truth, I've always been rather interested by this house. I often notice it from the train. Quite a period piece, isn't it? Puts one in mind of Dickens – Pickwick, and What-d'you-call-it Hall, and that house in the marshes where the old lady lived.'

'Yes. They don't build such houses nowadays. It's got the date over the door – I don't know if you observed it. 1887. Same date as Queen Victoria's Jubilee. You could call it historic.'

'Neber had an alteration since,' interposed the boy, as though repeating something known by rote.

'Yes, it has, Tony. You know it has. It's got the electricity. And I've a good mind to take it out again – nothing but trouble from first to last. I don't know why anyone should complain of a house like this. It's a splendid house; everything of the best, and built by an Indian colonel to retire to. Got its own water supply, and a patent pump to raise it, and a game larder, and any number of cupboards, and a marble pedestal basin in the downstairs lavatory. You'd think anyone would be happy to live in such a house. So they would be, if they feared God and knew what was best for them.'

'The rats do! They know what's best for theb. That's why Bother slept with be – to keep the rats off. But now I'b going to tabe theb. I'b going to hab billions and billions of tabe rats. This man said he had a tabe rat and he took it to school with hib in his pocket.'

The chin beard, as though it had a life of its own quite independent of the meagre flesh it was fastened in, suddenly bristled.

'So it's you that have been putting ideas into the boy's head, is it? That's what you've been coming here for, whenever my back was turned? I knew it, I knew it! But I tell you, I've had too much of that sort of thing. First there's Jim Mason going off with my wife, now it's you, sneaking in after my boy. And what's that knife meant for, lying there on the table? There you were in the dark, waiting to get me as soon as I came into the room. You and your polishes! You and your soft sawder about books you've never read in your life. No need to read nowadays you can see it all on the tellie. Yes, and pick up those clever ideas about carving knives. But two can play at that game!'

He snatched the knife, and attacked. Clive caught up a chair to defend himself.

'I'll get you, I'll get you!'

Lunging at Clive, he became entangled in the legs of the chair and fell, pulling the chair down with him. The knife was jolted from his grasp; he lay sprawled face downward, gasping for breath. A small trail of blood appeared on the carpet.

The boy darted forward, light as a ferret. 'He's bleeding! He's dying!'

'He's hit his nose against the chair,' Clive said. 'And presently, I suppose, *he'll* be wanting a handkerchief, too. Well, I can't oblige him, that's all. Here, take that knife and for God's sake put it back where it belongs. I'm sick of the pair of you.' It seemed to him that he had invaded a very disagreeable family.

After a minute the man sat up. He was weeping, and mopped his eyes and his nose alternately. 'I can't go on, I just can't go on,' he lamented. 'God knows I've always done my best – and look what happens to me. I love my wife, I don't look at another woman, I take her out of Woolworth's and put her in this splendid house and make a lady of her, I slave to keep the roof over our heads – and she goes off to live in a bungalow with a motor mechanic! I do everything I can for the boy, I keep a smiling face for his sake, I get up in the middle of the night to boil milk for him – and he hates me! And today, when I go to see my lawyer, first he keeps me waiting for nearly an hour, and then he tells me I can't ask for damages, not for the wife of my bosom, because it's common knowledge how unkindly I treated her. Unkindly! What about the way she's treated me? And there you stand, grinning. Grin on, grin by all means! Your time hasn't come yet.'

'I wouldn't dream of laughing at you,' Clive said. 'I'm sure I'm very sorry for you.' But he knew that he had smiled. For the man's nose, rapidly swelling, made him talk just as the boy did, and the words 'get up in the biddle of the night to boil bilk' had been too much for him.

The boy had opened a book and feigned to be absorbed in it. His hate no longer warmed him; he sat hunched up and shivering – a sickly child, in terror of rats and dark corners and swaying trees. But suffering and depravity had put their aristocratic stamp on his pallid face; there could be no doubt which of these two would be master.

Dad was now on his feet, rubbing his shins and groaning. 'You don't happen to have such a thing as a bottle of liniment in that bag, I suppose?'

'I'm afraid not.'

'I might have known it!' He spoke as though this were the culmination of his misfortunes and injuries.

'And I really must be getting on,' Clive said. 'Good night. Don't trouble to show me out. I know the way.'

He saw the beard begin to bristle again, and the fury of suspicion mounting. The boy must have seen it too, though he continued to read. A smile crossed his face as though something in the book had amused him.

'Tony!' the man said. 'Where are your manners? Get up and say good night.'

The boy rose, and bowed with formality. 'Good night.'

'Just in time,' said Clive, slamming the door behind him and running down the path. 'Whew! Just in time.' At the same moment, the laurel hedge caught him in a dragonish embrace and remembering the rabbit hutches he went on more cautiously. It was the ambiguous interval of winter nightfall when one seems to be wading through darkness as through knee-high water while there is still light overhead. But soon it would be unequivocally dark and though he was out of that nightmare house he had still to find his way home. Ahead of him was the lane where he had heard the man shouting at cows. It seemed likely that this was a continuation of the lane he had followed so patiently and which would have brought him here if he had not left it at the call of the engine whistle. His best hope would be to turn to the right and follow its windings till it joined the road he had taken from Yetton Halt. He did so, and had walked for what seemed quite a long way when a picture came into his mind's eye of himself sitting at Yetton Halt watching trains that didn't stop there go by. But how to get home wasn't his only trouble. He must also decide on a story that would somehow account for him being so muddy and so belated, a story that would satisfy Ella tonight and Mr.Ingham tomorrow – for Ella being Mrs. Ingham's niece he could not expect the story to remain under his own roof. 'I tripped and wrenched my ankle.' But if he had tripped anywhere on the path of duty there would have been a telephone within reach. 'I got into the wrong train at the junction.' But the train would not have carried him into a ploughed field and muddied him to the knees. 'I heard there was a family who had just moved into an old manor house with masses of oak panelling.' But Mr. Ingham had little sympathy for enterprise, and would have even less for an enterprise that had not resulted in as much as an order for a three-shilling tin of Busy Bees Household Wax – their cheapest line. So what was he to say? And which way should he turn in order to say it? As he stood hesitating and hearing the wind mutter along the hedge, he saw a shaft of light and heard the approach of what must be a very old and slow car. The slower the better. He might thumb a lift. The car, bouncing and rattling, seemed to be close at hand, but its light travelled onwards. There must be a crossroads. If it were enough of a crossroads, it would have a signpost. He hurried on.

There was a signpost, but he had to swarm up it before he could read by the flicker of his cigarette lighter that to his left was Branham, five miles, and to his right Yetton St. Gabriel, two miles. Branham had it. He knew Branham, it was a place on his rounds. He lit a cigarette, knocked the worst of the mud off his shoes and set off again, this time on a good hard-surfaced road that rang reassuringly under his tread. Now all he had to think of was his story. Why not, after all, include a measure of the interesting truth, leading up to it by that hearsay manor house? He was on his way to the manor house, which was much farther off than it had been reported to be, when he noticed a solitary house which stood a little back from the road and had a sort of moat round it. The strange thing was that even before he drew level with it, he felt as though the house had a call for him. If it had not been for one lighted-up window, he would have supposed it was empty and deserted. Then, glancing through the lighted window, he saw a man with a knife in his hand chasing a little boy round a table. Not wasting a moment, he jumped the moat, ran to the window and banged on it, shouting, 'You leave that child alone!' The man threw open the window and leaned out, saying, 'Mind your own business!' 'Just what I mean to do,' retorted Clive, and sprang in over the window sill. At this point Mr. Ingham's voice interposed itself, exclaiming, 'It's a case for the Prevention of Cruelty Society, Peters, if not for the police. We'll report this right away,' while Mrs. Ingham cried, 'You tell me where he lives, Clive, and I'll teach him something about carving knives, that I will!' So no sooner was Clive in the room than the man's whole demeanour changed; dropping the knife he came up to Clive and wrung his hand, saying, 'God must have sent you, God must have sent you! What mightn't I have done otherwise?' And then, bit by bit, it all came out: how the man's wife had left him that same morning, how when he got back from market he had found her gone and a letter saying she wanted an easier life with a younger man, how he had found the child cold and hungry and crying for his mammy, and how, in his desperation, he had decided to put an end to himself – but first he must take the child with him. Clive, feeling that he had indeed been called, realized that there was nothing for it but to give up all idea of the manor house and stay with the frantic husband till he calmed down again. ('Quite right, Peters, quite right.') So he quickly kindled up a nice wood fire, and there they sat, going into it all, till it was time to turn on the news. This helped to clear the air, and after a little more chat Clive rose to depart, seeing that his work was done. 'I don't suppose we'll ever meet again,' were the man's last words. 'But I'll remember you in my prayers for the rest of my life.' Deeply religious, which made the wife's action an even crueller blow, he was more to be pitied than blamed.

More to be Pitied than Blamed. Pom! More to be Pitied than Blamed. Pom! Marching to the rhythm of the words, carried on towards Branham by their asseveration, Clive felt that he had got both truth and fiction safely under his control. The story was certainly a case of making a silk purse out of a sow's ear, but he had managed it; the purse was constructed, and ought to satisfy everybody. All that remained was to put the true afternoon firmly out of his mind and rehearse the fictional one till he was word-perfect in it. Manor house to house, not forgetting the premonition, then the lighted-up window, then the man with the carving knife and the terrified child dodging him round the table, then the banging on the window and the window thrown up and his retort (another touch not to forget) and his entry. . . . Suddenly and appallingly, Ella's voice broke in. 'But what about the poor little boy, Clive? Didn't you do anything for him? Didn't either of you men think of giving him his supper? You said he was hungry.' The sow's ear bristled out of the purse, the real child started up before him, dancing like a ferret at the sight of his father's blood. No wonder he had shirked facing the issue of the fictional child. He, too, was the father of a son.

* * * * *

Rose Tremain: Distinguished novelist whose works include *Restoration*(1989), shortlisted for the Booker Prize, the highly acclaimed *Sacred Country*(1992), both set in East Anglia and *Music And Silence* which won the 1999 Whitbread Novel Award. More recent novels include *The Colour* (2003) and *The Road Home* (2007). 'Peerless' is from *The Darkness of Wallis Simpson* (2005) the latest of several collections of short stories. Tremain lives near Norwich with the biographer Richard Holmes.

Peerless

ROSE TREMAIN

His parents had christened him Broderick, but for as long as he could remember, he'd always been known as 'Badger'. He spent his life feeling that Badger was a fatuous name, but he couldn't stand Broderick either. To him, the word 'Broderick' described a *thing* – possibly a gardening implement or a DIY tool – rather than a human being. Becoming an animal, he decided, was better than remaining a thing.

Now, because he was getting old, it worried Badger that the hours (which, by now, would have added up to years) he'd spent worrying about these two useless names of his could have been far better spent worrying about something else. The world was in a state. Everybody could see that. The north and south poles, always reliably blue in every atlas, now had flecks of yellow in them. He knew that these flecks were not printers' errors. He often found himself wishing that he had lived in the time of Scott of the Antarctic, when ice was ice. The idea of everything getting hotter and dirtier made Badger Newbold feel faint.

Newbold. That was his other name. 'Equally inappropriate,' he'd joked to his future wife, Verity, as he and she had sat in the crimson darkness of the 400 Club, smoking du Maurier cigarettes. 'Not bold. Missed the war. Spend my days going through ledgers and adding up columns. Can't stand mess. Prefer everything to be tickety-boo.'

'Badger,' Verity had replied, with her dimpled smile, with her curvy lips, red as blood, 'you seem bold to me. Nobody has dared to ask me to marry them before!'

She'd been so adorable then, her brown eyes so sparkly and teasing, her arms so enfolding and soft. Badger knew that he'd been lucky to get her. If that was the word? If you could 'get' another person and make them yours and cement up the leaks where love could escape. If you could do that, then Badger Newbold had been a fortunate man.

All his friends had told him so. He was seventy now. Verity was sixty-nine. On the question of love, they were silent. Politeness had replaced love.

They lived in a lime-washed farmhouse in Suffolk on the pension Badger had saved, working as an accountant, for thirty-seven years. Their two children, Susan and Martin, had gone to live their lives in far-off places on the other side of the burning globe: Australia and California. Their mongrel dog, Savage, had recently died and been buried, along with all the other mongrel dogs they'd owned, under a forgiving chestnut tree in the garden. And, these days, Badger found himself very often alone.

He felt that he was waiting for something. Not just for death. In fact, he did nothing much except wait. Verity often asked him in the mornings: 'What are you going to do today, Badger?' and it was difficult to answer this. Badger would have liked to be able reply that he was going to restore the polar ice cap to its former state of atlas blue, but, in truth, he knew perfectly well that his day was going to be empty of all endeavour. So he made things up. He told Verity he was designing a summer house, writing to the children, pruning the viburnum, overhauling the lawnmower or repairing the bird table.

She barely noticed what he did or didn't do. She was seldom at home. She was tearing about the place, busy beyond all reason, trying to put things to rights. She was a volunteer carer at the local Shelter for Battered Wives. She was a Samaritan. Her car was covered with 'Boycott Burma' stickers. Her 'Stop the War in Iraq' banner – which she had held aloft in London for nine hours – was taped to the wall above her desk. She sent half her state pension to Romanian Orphanages, Cancer Research, Greenpeace, Friends of the Earth, Amnesty International, Victims of Torture and the Sudan Famine Fund. She was never still, always trembling with outrage, yet ready with kindness. Her thick grey hair looked perpetually wild, as though desperate hands had tugged it, in this direction and that. Her shoes were scuffed and worn.

Badger was proud of her. He saw how apathetic English people had become, slumped on their ugly, squashy furniture. Verity was resisting apathy. 'Make every day count' was her new motto. She was getting old, but her heart was like a piston, powering her on. When a new road threatened the quiet of the village, it was Verity who had led the residents into battle against the council – and won. She was becoming a local heroine, stunningly shabby. She gave away her green Barbour jacket and replaced it with an old black duffel coat, bought from the Oxfam shop. In this, with her unkempt hair, she looked like a vagrant, and it was difficult for Badger to become reconciled to this. He felt that her altered appearance made him seem stingy.

The other thing which upset Badger about the new Verity was that she'd gone off cooking. She said she couldn't stand to make a fuss about food when a quarter of the world was living on tree bark. So meals, in the Newbold household, now resembled post-war confections: ham and salad, shop-bought cake, rice pudding, jacket potatoes with margarine. Badger felt that it was unfair to ask him to live on these unappetising things. He was getting constipated. He had dreams about Béarnaise sauce. Sometimes, guiltily, he took himself to the Plough at lunchtime and ordered steak pie and Guinness and rhubarb crumble. Then he would go home and fall asleep. And in the terror of a twilight awakening, Badger would berate himself for being exactly the kind of person Verity despised: apathetic, self-indulgent and weak. At such times, he began to believe it was high time he went to see his Maker. When he thought about heaven, it resembled the old 400 Club, with shaded pink lights and waiters with white bow ties and music, sad and sweet.

One spring morning, alarmingly warm, after Verity had driven off somewhere in her battered burgundy Nissan, Badger opened a brown envelope addressed to him – not to Verity – from a place called the Oaktree Wildlife Sanctuary. It was a home for animals that had been rescued from cruelty or annihilation. Photographs of peacefully grazing donkeys, cows, sheep, geese, chickens and deer fell out from a plastic brochure. Badger picked these up and looked at them. With his dogs, the last Savage included, Badger had felt that he had always been able to tell when the animals were happy. Their brains might be tiny, but they could register delight. Savage had had a kind of grin, seldom seen, but suddenly there in the wake of a long walk, or lying on the hearthrug in the evenings, when the ability to work the CD player suddenly returned to Verity and she would put on a little Mozart. And, looking at these pictures, Badger felt that these animals (and even the birds) were in a state of contentment. Their field looked spacious and green. In the background were sturdy shelters, made of wood.

Inside the brochure was a letter in round writing, which began:

Dear Mr Newbold,
I am a penguin and my name is Peerless.

At this point, Badger reached for his reading glasses, so that he could see the words properly. Had he read the word 'Peerless' correctly? Yes, he had. He went on reading:

... I was going to be killed, along with my mates, Peter, Pavlov, Palmer and Pooter, when our zoo was closed dowm by the Council. Luckily for me, the Oaktree Wildlife Sanctuary stepped in and saved us. They've dug a pond and installed a plastic slide for us. We have great fun there, walking up the slide and slipping down again. We have a good diet of fish. We are very lucky penguins.

However, we do eat quite a lot and sometimes we have to be examined by the vet. All of this costs the Sanctuary a lot of money. So we're looking for Benefactors. For just £25 a year you could become my Benefactor. Take a look at my picture. I'm quite smart, aren't I? 1 take trouble with my personal grooming. I wasn't named 'Peerless' for nothing. Please say that you will become my Benefactor. Then, you will be able to come and visit me any time you like. Bring your family.

With best wishes from Peerless the Penguin.

Badger unclipped the photograph attached to the letter and looked at Peerless. His bill was yellow, his coat not particularly sleek. He was standing in mud at the edge of the pond. He looked as though he had been stationary in that one place for a long time.

Peerless.

Now, Badger laid all the Sanctuary correspondence aside and leaned back in his armchair. He closed his eyes. His hands covered his face.

Peerless had been the name of his friend at boarding school. His only real friend.

Anthony Peerless. A boy of startling beauty, with a dark brow and a dimpled smile and colour always high, under the soft skin of his face.

He'd been clever and dreamy, useless at cricket, unbearably homesick for his mother. He'd spent his first year fending off the sixth-formers, who passed his photograph around until it was chewed and faded. Then, Badger had arrived and become his friend. And the two had clung together, Newbold and Peerless, Badger and Anthony, in that pitiless kraal of a school. Peerless the dreamer, Badger the mathematical whiz. An unlikely pair.

No friendship had ever been like this one.

'Are you aware, Newbold, that your friend, Peerless, has been late for games three times in three weeks?'

'No, I wasn't aware, sir.'

'Well, now you are. And what do you propose to do about it?'

'I don't know.'

'I don't know, sir!'

'I don't know, sir.'

'Well, I think I know. You can warn Peerless that if he is ever – *ever* – late for cricket again, then I, personally, will give *you* a beating. Do you understand, Newbold? I am making you responsible. If you fail in your task, it will be you who will be punished.'

Peerless is in the grounds of the school, reading Keats. Badger sits down by him, among daisies, and says: 'I say, old thing, the Ogre's just given me a bit of an ultimatum. He's going to beat me if you're late for cricket practice again.'

Peerless looks up and smiles his girlish, beatific smile. He starts picking daisies. He's told Badger he loves the smell of them, like talcum powder, like the way his mother smells.

'The Ogre's mad, Badger. You realise that, don't you?' says Peerless.

'I know,' says Badger. 'I know.'

'Well, then, we're not going to collude with him. Why should we?'

And that's all that can be said about it. Peerless returns to Keats and Badger lies down beside him and asks him to read something aloud.

"*. . . overhead – look overhead*
*Among the blossoms white and red – *'

*

When Verity came back that evening from wherever she'd been, Badger showed her the photograph of Peerless the Penguin and said: 'I'm going to become his Benefactor.'

Verity laughed at the picture. 'Typical you, Badger!' she snorted.

'Why typical me?'

'Save the animals. Let the people go hang.'

Badger ate his ham and salad in silence for a while; then he said: 'I don't think you've got any idea what you've just said.'

There wasn't a moment's pause, not a second's thought, before Verity snapped: 'Yes, I do. You're completely apathetic when it comes to helping people. But where animals are concerned, you'll go to the ends of the bloody earth.'

'Perhaps that's because I am one,' said Badger. 'An animal.'

'Oh, shut up, Badger,' said Verity. 'You really do talk such sentimental bollocks.'

Badger got up and walked out of the room. He went out on to the terrace and looked at the spring moon. He felt there was a terrible hunger in him, not just for proper food, but for something else, something which the moon's light might reveal to him, if he stayed there long enough, if he got cold enough, waiting. But nothing was revealed to him. The only thing that happened was that, after ten or fifteen minutes, Verity came out and said: 'Sorry, Badger. I can be a pig.'

Badger wrote to Peerless and sent his cheque for £25. An effusive thank-you note arrived, inviting him to visit the Sanctuary.

It wasn't very far away. But Badger's driving was slow, these days, and he frequently forgot which gear he was in. Sometimes, the engine of the car started screaming, as if in pain. It always seemed to take this screaming engine a long time to get him anywhere at all. Badger reflected that if, one day, he was obliged to drive to London, he would probably never manage to arrive.

He drove at last down an avenue of newly planted beeches. Grassy fields lay behind them. At the end of the drive was a sign saying 'Welcome to Oaktree Wildlife Sanctuary' and a low red-brick building with a sundial over the door. It was an April day.

At a reception desk, staffed by a woebegone young man with thick glasses, Badger announced himself as the Benefactor of Peerless the Penguin and asked to see the penguin pool.

'Oh, certainly,' said the young man, whose name was Kevin. 'Do you wish to avail yourself of the free wellingtons service?'

Badger saw ten or eleven pairs of green wellingtons lined up by the door.

He felt that free wellingtons and new beech trees were a sign of something good. 'Imagination,' Anthony Peerless used to say, 'is everything. Without it, the world's doomed.'

Badger put on some wellingtons, too large for his feet, and followed the young man across a meadow where donkeys and sheep were grazing. These animals had thick coats and they moved in a slow, unfrightened way.

'Very popular with children, the donkeys,' said Kevin. 'But they want rides, of course and we don't allow this. These animals have been burdened enough.'

'Quite right,' said Badger.

And then, there it was, shaded by a solitary oak, a grey pond, bordered by gunnera and stinging nettles. At one end of it was the slide, made of blue plastic, and one of the penguins was making its laborious way up some wide plastic steps to the top of it.

'So human, aren't they?' said Kevin, smiling.

Badger watched the penguin fall forwards and slither down into the muddy water of the pond. Then he asked: 'Which one's Peerless?'

Kevin stared short-sightedly at the creatures. His gaze went from one to the other, and Badger could tell that this man didn't know. Someone had given the penguins names, but they resembled each other so closely, they might as well not have bothered. It was impossible to distinguish Pooter from Pavlov, Palmer from Peter.

Badger stood there, furious. He'd only sent the damn cheque because the penguin was called Peerless. He'd expected some recognisable identity. He felt like stomping away in disgust. Then he saw that one of the penguins was lying apart from all the others, immersed in the water, where it lapped against the nettles. He stared at this one. It lay in the pond like a human being might lie in a bed, with the water covering its chest.

'There he is,' said Kevin suddenly. 'That's Peerless.'

Badger walked nearer. Peerless stood up and looked at him. A weak sun came out and shone on the dark head of Peerless and on the nettles, springy and green.

'All right,' said Badger. 'Like to stay here a while by myself, if that's OK with you.'

'Sure,' said Kevin. 'Just don't give them any food, will you? It could be harmful.'

Kevin walked away over the meadow where the donkeys wandered and Badger stayed very still, watching Peerless. The other penguins queued, like children, for a turn on the plastic slide, but Peerless showed no interest in it at all. He just stayed where he was, on the edge of the pond, going in and out, in and out of the dank water. It was as though he constantly expected something consoling from the water and then found that it wasn't there, but yet expected it again, and then again discovered its absence. And Badger decided, after a while, that he understood exactly what was wrong: the water was too warm. This penguin longed for an icy sea.

Badger sat down on the grass. He didn't care that it was damp. He closed his eyes.

It's the beginning of the school term and Badger is unpacking his trunk. He's fourteen years old. He lays his red-and-brown rug on his iron bed in the cold dormitory. Other boys are making darts out of paper and chucking them from bed to bed. Peerless's name is not on the dormitory list.

The Ogre appears at the door and the dart-throwing stops. Boys stand to attention, like army cadets. The Ogre comes over to Badger and puts a hand on his shoulder, and the hand isn't heavy as it usually is, but tender, like the hand of a kind uncle.

'Newbold,' he says. 'Come up to my study.'

He follows the Ogre up the polished main stairs, stairs upon which the boys are not normally allowed to tread. He can smell the sickly wood polish, smell the stale pipe smoke in the Ogre's tweed clothes.

He's invited to sit down in the Ogre's study, on an old red armchair. And the Ogre's eyes watch him nervously. Then the Ogre says: 'It concerns Peerless. As his friend, you have the right to know. His mother died. I'm afraid that Peerless will not be returning to the school.'

Badger looks away from the Ogre, out at the autumn day; at the clouds carefree and white, at the chestnut leaves flying around in the wind.

'I see,' he manages to say. And he wants to get up, then, get out of this horrible chair and go away from here, go to where the leaves are falling. But something in the Ogre's face warns him not to move. The Ogre is struggling to tell him something else and is pleading for time in which to tell it. I may be 'the Ogre', says the terrified look on his face, but I'm also a man.

'The thing is . . .' he begins. 'The thing is, Newbold, Peerless was very fond of his mother. You see?'

'See what, sir?'

'Well. He found it impossible. Her absence. As you know, he was a dreaming kind of boy. He was unable to put up any resistance to grief.'

That evening, Verity made a lamb stew. It was fragrant with rosemary and served with mashed potato and fresh kale. Badger opened a bottle of red wine.

Verity was quiet, yet attentive to him, waiting for him to speak to her. But for a long time Badger didn't feel like speaking. He just felt like eating the good stew and sipping the lovely wine and listening to the birds fall silent in the garden and the ancient electric clock ticking on the kitchen wall.

Eventually, Verity said: 'When I said what I said about you letting people go hang, Badger, I was being horribly thoughtless. For a moment I'd completely forgotten about Anthony Peerless.'

Badger took another full sip of the wine, then he said:

'It's all right, darling. No offence. How were the Battered Wives?'

'OK. Now, I want you to tell me about the penguins. Are they being properly looked after?'

He knew she was humouring him, that she didn't care one way or the other whether a bunch of penguins lived or died. But the wine was making him feel cheerful, almost optimistic, so he chose to say to her: 'The place is nice. But the penguin pool's not cold enough. In the summer, they could die.'

'That's a shame.'

'I won't let it happen. I've got a plan.'

'Tell me?' said Verity.

She poured him some more wine. The stew was back in the oven, keeping warm. Mozart was softly playing next door. This was how home was meant to be.

'Ice,' said Badger. 'I'm going to keep them supplied with ice.'

He saw Verity fight against laughter. Her mouth opened and closed – that scarlet mouth he used to adore. Then she smiled kindly. 'Where will you get that amount of ice from?'

'The sea,' he said. 'I'll buy it from the trawlermen.'

'Oh,' she said. 'Good idea, Badger.'

'It'll be time-consuming, fetching it, lugging it over to the Sanctuary, but I don't mind. It'll give me something to do.'

'Yes, it will.'

'And Peerless . . .'

'What?'

'He seems to suffer the most with things as they are. But the ice should fix it.'

'Good,' said Verity. 'Very good.'

He lined the boot of his car with waterproof sheets. He bought a grappling hook for handling the ice blocks. He christened it 'the Broderick'. Despite the sheeting, Badger's car began to smell of the sea. He knew the fisherman thought he was a crazy old party.

But at the pond, now, when the penguins saw him coming, lugging the ice on an ancient luge he'd found in the garage, they came waddling to him and clustered round him as he slowly lifted the end of the luge and let the ice slide into the water. Then they dived in and climbed up on to the ice, or swam beside it, rubbing their heads against it. And he thought, as he watched them, that this was the thing he'd been waiting for, to alter the lot of someone or something. All he'd done was to change the water temperature of a pond in the middle of a Suffolk field by a few degrees. As world events went, it was a pitiful contribution, but he didn't care. Badger Newbold wasn't the kind of man who had ever been able to change the world, but at least he had changed this. Peerless the penguin was consoled by the cool water. And now, when Verity asked him what he was going to do on any particular morning, Badger would be able to reply that he was going to do the ice.

From this time on, in Badger's nightmares, the death of Anthony Peerless was a different one . . .

Peerless has come to stay with him in Suffolk. There are midnight feasts and whispered conversations in the dark.

Then, one morning, Peerless goes out alone on his bicycle. He rides to the dunes and throws his bicycle down on to the soft sand. He walks through the marram grass down to the sea, wearing corduroy trousers and an old brown sweater and a familiar jacket, patched and worn. It's still almost summer, but the sea is an icy, meticulous blue. Peerless starts to swim. His face, with its high colour, begins to pale and pale until he's lost in the cold vastness. He floats serenely, silently down. He floats towards a vision of green grass, towards the soft smell of daisies.

> *. . . overhead – look overhead*
> *Among the blossoms white and red.*

* * * * *

Tidelines

Charles Dickens (1812-70): For admirers of Dickens Yarmouth will always be associated with the opening chapters of *David Copperfield* (1849-50), the author's veiled autobiography. Davy's decision to invite his schoolfriend Steerforth to Yarmouth leads to disaster. Ham is about to marry Little Em'ly when she agrees to run away with Steerforth who later abandons her. Like most of Dickens' novels it was first published in instalments and in 'The Tempest' Yarmouth becomes the setting for one of the great melodramatic episodes in Victorian fiction.

The Tempest

CHARLES DICKENS

I now approach an event in my life, so indelible, so awful, so bound by an infinite variety of ties to all that has preceded it, in these pages, that, from the beginning of my narrative, I have seen it growing larger and larger as I advanced, like a great tower in a plain, and throwing its forecast shadow even in the incidents of my childish days.

For years after it occurred I dreamed of it often. I have started up so vividly impressed by it, that its fury has yet seemed raging in my quiet room, in the still night. I dream of it sometimes, though at lengthened and uncertain intervals, to this hour. I have an association between it and a stormy wind, or the lightest mention of a sea-shore, as strong as any of which my mind is conscious. As plainly as I behold what happened, I will try to write it down. I do not recall it, but see it done; for it happens again before me.

The time drawing on rapidly for the sailing of the emigrant ship, my good old nurse (almost broken-hearted for me, when we first met) came up to London. I was constantly with her, and her brother, and the Micawbers (they being very much together); but Emily I never saw.

One evening, when the time was close at hand, I was alone with Peggotty and her brother. Our conversation turned on Ham. She described to us how tenderly he had taken leave of her, and how manfully and quietly he had borne himself – most of all, of late, when she believed he was most tried. It was a subject of which the affectionate creature never tired, and our interest in hearing the many examples which she, who was so much with him, had to relate, was equal to hers in relating them.

My aunt and I were at that time vacating the two cottages at Highgate – I intending to go abroad, and she to return to her house at Dover. We had a temporary lodging in Covent Garden. As I walked home to it, after this evening's conversation, reflecting on what had passed between Ham and myself when I was last at Yarmouth, I wavered in the original purpose I had formed, of leaving a letter for Emily when I should take leave of her uncle on board the ship, and thought it would be better to write to her now. She might desire, I thought, after receiving my communication, to send some parting word by me to her unhappy lover. I ought to give her the opportunity.

I therefore sat down in my room, before going to bed, and wrote to her, I told her that I had seen him, and that he had requested me to tell her what I have already written in its place in these sheets. I faithfully repeated it, I had no need to enlarge upon it, if I had had the right. Its deep fidelity and goodness were not to be adorned by me or any man. I left it out, to be sent round in the morning, with a line to Mr. Peggotty, requesting him to give it to her; and went to bed at daybreak.

I was weaker than I knew then; and not falling asleep until the sun was up, lay late, and unrefreshed, next day. I was roused by the silent presence of my aunt at my bedside. I felt it in my sleep, as I suppose we all do feel such things.

'Trot, my dear,' she said, when I opened my eyes, 'I couldn't make up my mind to disturb you. Mr. Peggotty is here; shall he come up?'

I replied yes, and he soon appeared.

'Mas'r Davy,' he said, when we had shaken hands, 'I giv Em'ly your letter, sir, and she writ this here; and begged of me fur to ask you to read it, and if you see no hurt in't, to be so kind as take charge on't.'

'Have you read it?' said I.

He nodded sorrowfully. I opened it, and read as follows:-

'I have got your message. Oh, what can I write, to thank you for your good and blessed kindness to me!

'I have put the words close to my heart. I shall keep them till I die. They are sharp thorns, but they are such comfort. I have prayed over them, oh, I have prayed so much! When I find what you are, and what uncle is, I think what God must be, and can cry to Him.

'Good-bye for ever. Now, my dear, my friend, good-bye for ever in this world. In another world, if I am forgiven, I may wake a child and come to you. All thanks and blessings. Farewell, evermore.'

This, blotted with tears, was the letter.

'May I tell her as you don't see no hurt in't, and as you'll be so kind as take charge on't, Mas'r Davy?' said Mr. Peggotty, when I had read it.

'Unquestionably,' said I; 'but I am thinking – '

'Yes, Mas'r Davy?'

'I am thinking,' said I, 'that I'll go down again to Yarmouth. There's time and to spare for me to go and come back before the ship sails. My mind is constantly running on him, in his solitude. To put this letter of her writing in his hand at this time, and to enable you to tell her, in the moment of parting, that he has got it, will be a kindness to both of them. I solemnly accepted his commission, dear good fellow, and cannot discharge it too completely. The journey is nothing to me. I am restless, and shall be better in motion. I'll go down to-night.'

Though he anxiously endeavoured to dissuade me, I saw that he was of my mind; and this, if I had required to be confirmed in my intention, would have had the effect. He went round to the coach-office, at my request, and took the box-seat for me on the mail. In the evening I started, by that conveyance, down the road I had traversed under so many vicissitudes.

'Don't you think that,' I asked the coachman, in the first stage out of London, 'a very remarkable sky? I don't remember to have seen one like it.'

'Nor I – not equal to it,' he replied. 'That's wind, sir. There'll be mischief done at sea, I expect, before long.'

It was a murky confusion – here and there blotted with a colour like the colour of the smoke from damp fuel – of flying buds tossed up into most remarkable heaps, suggesting greater heights in the clouds than there were depths below them to the bottom of the deepest hollows in the earth, through which the wild moon seemed to plunge headlong, as if, in a dread disturbance of the laws of nature, she had lost her way and were frightened. There had been a wind all day; and it was rising then, with an extraordinary great sound. In another hour it had much increased, and the sky was more overcast, and it blew hard.

But as the night advanced, the clouds closing in and densely overspreading the whole sky, then very dark, it came on to blow harder and harder. It still increased, until our horses could scarcely face the wind. Many times, in the dark part of the night (it was then late in September, when the nights were not short), the leaders turned about, or came to a dead stop; and we were often in serious apprehension that the coach would be blown over. Sweeping gusts of rain came up before this storm, like showers of steel; and, at those times, when there was any shelter of trees or lee walls be got, we were fain to stop, in a sheer impossibility of continuing the struggle.

When the day broke, it blew harder and harder. I had been in Yarmouth when the seamen said it blew great guns; but I had never known the like of this, or anything approaching to it. We came to Ipswich – very late, having had to fight every inch of ground since we were ten miles out of London – and found a cluster of people in the market-place, who had risen from their beds in the night, fearful of falling chimneys. Some of these, congregating about the inn-yard while we changed horses, told us of great sheets of lead having been ripped off a high church tower, and flung into a by-street, which they then blocked up. Others had to tell of country people, coming in from neighbouring villages, who had seen great trees lying torn out of the earth, and whole ricks scattered about the roads and fields. Still, there was no abatement in the storm, but it blew harder.

As we struggled on, nearer and nearer to the sea, from which this mighty wind was blowing dead on shore, its force became more and more terrific. Long before we saw the sea, its spray was on our lips, and showered salt rain upon us. The water was out, over miles and miles of the flat country adjacent to Yarmouth; and every sheet and puddle lashed its banks, and had its stress of little breakers setting heavily towards us. When we came within sight of the sea, the waves on the horizon, caught at intervals above the rolling abyss, were like glimpses of another shore with towers and buildings. When at last we got into the town, the people came out to their doors, all aslant, and with streaming hair, making a wonder of the mail that had come through such a night.

I put up at the old inn, and went down to look at the sea; staggering along the street, which was strewn with sand and seaweed, and with flying blotches of sea-foam; afraid of falling slates and tiles; and holding by people I met, at angry corners. Coming near the beach, I saw, not only the boatmen, but half the people of the town, lurking behind buildings; some now and then braving the fury of the storm to look away to sea, and blown sheer out of their course in trying to get zigzag back.

Joining these groups, I found bewailing women whose husbands were away in herring or oyster boats, which there was too much reason to think might have foundered before they could run in anywhere for safety. Grizzled old sailors were among the people, shaking their heads, as they looked from water to sky, and muttering to one another; shipowners, excited and uneasy; children, huddling together, and peering into older faces; even stout mariners, disturbed and anxious, levelling their glasses at the sea from behind places of shelter, as if they were surveying an enemy.

214

The tremendous sea itself, when I could find sufficient pause to look at it, in the agitation of the blinding wind, the flying stones and sand, and the awful noise, confounded me. As the high watery walls came rolling in, and, at their highest, tumbled into surf, they looked as if the least would engulf the town. As the receding wave swept back with a hoarse roar, it seemed to scoop out deep caves in the beach, as if its purpose were to undermine the earth. When some white-headed billows thundered on, and dashed themselves to pieces before they reached the land, every fragment of the late whole seemed possessed by the full might of its wrath, rushing to be gathered to the composition of another monster. Undulating hills were changed to valleys, undulating valleys (with a solitary storm-bird sometimes skimming through them) were lifted up to hills; masses of water shivered and shook the beach with a booming sound; every shape tumultuously rolled on, as soon as made, to change its shape and place, and beat another shape and place away; the ideal shore on the horizon, with its towers and buildings, rose and fell; the clouds flew fast and thick; I seemed to see a rending and upheaving of all nature.

Not finding Ham among the people whom this memorable wind – for it is still remembered down there, as the greatest ever known to blow upon that coast – had brought together, I made my way to his house. It was shut; and as no one answered to my knocking, I went, by back ways and by-lanes, to the yard where he worked. I learned there that he had gone to Lowestoft, to meet some sudden exigency of ship-repairing in which his skill was required, but that he would be back to-morrow morning, in good time.

I went back to the inn; and when I had washed and dressed, and tried to sleep, but in vain, it was five o'clock in the afternoon. I had not sat five minutes by the coffee-room fire, when the waiter coming to stir it, as an excuse for talking, told me that two colliers had gone down, with all hands, a few miles away; and that some other ships had been seen labouring hard in the roads, and trying, in great distress, to keep off shore. Mercy on them, and on all poor sailors, said he, if we had another night like the last!

I was very much depressed in spirits, very solitary, and felt an uneasiness in Ham's not being there disproportionate to the occasion. I was seriously affected, without knowing how much, by late events; and my long exposure to the fierce wind had confused me. There was that jumble in my thoughts and recollections, that I had lost the clear arrangement of time and distance. Thus, if I had gone out into the town,

I should not have been surprised, I think, to encounter some one who I knew must be then in London. So to speak, there was in these respects a curious inattention in my mind. Yet it was busy, too, with all the remembrances the place naturally awakened; and they were particularly distinct and vivid.

In this state, the waiter's dismal intelligence about the ships immediately connected itself, without any effort of my volition, with my uneasiness about Ham. I was persuaded that I had an apprehension of his returning from Lowestoft by sea, and being lost. This grew so strong with me, that I resolved to go back to the yard before I took my dinner, and ask the boatbuilder if he thought his attempting to return by sea at all likely? If he gave me the least reason to think so, I would go over to Lowestoft and prevent it by bringing him with me.

I hastily ordered my dinner, and went back to the yard. I was none too soon, for the boatbuilder, with a lantern in his hand, was locking the yard-gate. He quite laughed when I asked him the question, and said there was no fear; no man in his senses, or out of them, would put off in such a gale of wind, least of all Ham Peggotty, who had been born seafaring.

So sensible of this, beforehand, that I had really felt shamed of doing what I was nevertheless impelled to do, I went back to the inn. If such a wind could rise, I think it was rising. The howl and roar, the rattling of the doors and windows, the rumbling in the chimneys, the apparent rocking of the very house that sheltered me, and the prodigious tumult of the sea, were more fearful than in the morning. But there was now a great darkness besides, and that invested the storm with new terrors, real and fanciful.

I could not eat, I could not sit still, I could not continue steadfast to anything. Something within me, faintly answering to the storm without, tossed up the depths of my memory, and made a tumult in them. Yet, in all the hurry of my thoughts, wild running with the thundering sea – the storm and my uneasiness regarding Ham, were always in the foreground.

My dinner went away almost untasted, and I tried to refresh myself with a glass or two of wine. In vain. I fell into a dull slumber before the fire, without losing my consciousness, either of the uproar out of doors or of the place which I was. Both became overshadowed by a new and indefinable horror; and when I awoke – or rather when I shook off the lethargy that bound me in my chair – my whole frame thrilled with objectless and unintelligible fear.

I walked to and fro; tried to read an old gazetteer; listened to the awful noises; looked at faces, scenes, and figures in the fire. At length, the steady ticking of the undisturbed clock on the wall tormented me to that degree that I resolved to go to bed.

It was reassuring, on such a night, to be told that some of the inn-servants had agreed together to sit up until morning. I went to bed, exceedingly weary and heavy; but, on my lying down, all such sensations vanished, as if by magic, and I was broad awake, with every sense refined.

For hours I lay there, listening to the wind and water – imagining, now, that I heard shrieks out at sea; now, that I distinctly heard the firing of signal guns; and now, the fall of houses in the town. I got up several times and looked out; but could see nothing, except the reflection in the window-panes of the faint candle I had left burning, and of my own haggard face looking in at me from the black void.

At length my restlessness attained to such a pitch that I hurried on my clothes, and went downstairs. In the large kitchen, where I dimly saw bacon and ropes of onions hanging from the beams, the watchers were clustered together, in various attitudes, about a table, purposely moved away from the great chimney, and brought near the door. A pretty girl, who had her ears stopped with her apron, and her eyes upon the door, screamed when I appeared, supposing me to be a spirit; but the others had more presence of mind, and were glad of an addition to their company. One man, referring to the topic they had been discussing, asked me whether I thought the souls of the collier-crews who had gone down were out in the storm?

I remained there, I dare say, two hours. Once, I opened the yard gate, and looked into the empty street. The sand, the seaweed, and the flakes of foam were driving by, and I was obliged to call for assistance before I could shut the gate again, and make it fast against the wind.

There was a dark gloom in my solitary chamber when I at length returned to it; but I was tired now, and, getting into bed again, fell – off a tower and down a precipice – into the depths of sleep. I have an impression that for a long time, though I dreamed of being elsewhere and in a variety of scenes, it was always blowing in my dream. At length I lost that feeble hold upon reality, and was engaged with two dear friends, but who they were I don't know, at the siege of some town in a roar of cannonading.

The thunder of the cannon was so loud and incessant, that I could not hear something I much desired to hear, until I made a great exertion, and awoke. It was broad day – eight or nine o'clock, the storm raging, in lieu of the batteries; and some one knocking and calling at my door.

'What is the matter?' I cried.

'A wreck! Close by !'

I sprung out of bed, and asked, what wreck?

'A schooner, from Spain or Portugal, laden with fruit and wine. Make haste, sir, if you want to see her! It's thought, down on the beach, she'll go to pieces every moment.'

The excited voice went clamouring along the staircase; and I wrapped myself in my clothes as quickly as I could, and ran into the street.

Numbers of people were there before me, all running in one direction – to the beach. I ran the same way, outstripping a good many, and soon came facing the wild sea.

The wind might by this time have lulled a little, though not more sensibly than if the cannonading I had dreamed of had been diminished by the silencing of half a dozen guns out of hundreds. But the sea, having upon it the additional agitation of the whole night, was infinitely more terrific than when I had seen it last. Every appearance it had then presented bore the expression of being *swelled*, and the height to which the breakers rose, and, looking over one an other, bore one another down, and rolled in, in interminable hosts, was most appalling.

In the difficulty of hearing anything but wind and waves, and in the crowd, and the unspeakable confusion, and my first breathless efforts to stand against the weather, I was so confused that I looked out to sea for the wreck, and saw nothing but the foaming heads of the great waves. A half-dressed boatman, standing next me, pointed with his bare arm (a tattooed arrow on it, pointing in the same direction) to the left. Then, O great Heaven, I saw it, close in upon us!

One mast was broken short off, six or eight feet from the deck, and lay over the side, entangled in a maze of sail and rigging; and all that ruin, as the ship rolled and beat – which she did without a moment's pause, and with a violence quite inconceivable – beat the side as if it would stave it in. Some efforts were even then being made to cut this portion of the wreck away; for, as the ship, which was broadside on, turned towards us in her rolling, I plainly descried her people at work with axes, especially one active figure with long curling hair, conspicuous among the rest. But a great cry, which was audible even above the wind and water, rose from the shore at this moment: the sea, sweeping over the rolling wreck, made a clean breach, and carried men, spars, casks, planks, bulwarks, heaps of such toys, into the boiling surge.

The second mast was yet standing, with the rags of a rent sail and a wild confusion of broken cordage flapping to and fro. The ship had struck once, the same boatman hoarsely said in my ear, and then lifted in and struck again. I understood him to add that she was parting amidships; and I could readily suppose so, for the rolling and beating were too tremendous for any human work to suffer long. As he spoke, there was another great cry of pity from the beach: four men arose with the wreck out of the deep, clinging to the rigging of the remaining mast – uppermost, the active figure with the curling hair.

There was a bell on board, and as the ship rolled and dashed, like a desperate creature driven mad, now showing us the whole sweep of her deck, as she turned on her beam-ends towards the shore, now nothing but her keel, as she sprung wildly over and turned towards the sea, the bell rang; and its sound, the knell of those unhappy men, was borne towards us on the wind. Again we lost her, and again she rose. Two men were gone. The agony on shore increased. Men groaned, and clasped their hands; women shrieked, and turned away their faces. Some ran wildly up and down along the beach, crying for help where no help could be. I found myself one of these, frantically imploring a knot of sailors whom I knew not to let those two lost creatures perish before our eyes.

They were making out to me, in an agitated way – I don't know how, for the little I could hear I was scarcely composed enough to understand – that the lifeboat had been bravely manned an hour ago, and could do nothing; and that as no man would be so desperate as to attempt to wade off with a rope, and establish a communication with the shore, there was nothing left to try; when I noticed that some new sensation moved the people on the beach, and saw them part, and Ham come breaking through them to the front.

I ran to him, as well as I know, to repeat my appeal for help. But, distracted though I was by a sight so new to me and terrible, the determination in his face, and his look out to sea – exactly the same look as I remembered in connection with the morning after Emily's flight – awoke me to a knowedge of his danger. I held him back with both arms, and implored the men with whom I had been speaking not to listen to him, not to do murder, not to let him stir from off that sand!

Another cry arose on shore; and looking to the wreck, we saw the cruel sail, with blow on blow, beat off the lower of the two men, and fly up in triumph round the active figure left alone upon the mast.

Against such a sight, and against such determination as that of the

219

calmly-desperate man who was already accustomed to lead half the people present, I might as hopefully have entreated the wind. 'Mas'r Davy,' he said, cheerily grasping me by both hands, 'if my time is come, 'tis come. If't an't, I'll bide it. Lord above bless you, and bless all! Mates, make me ready; I'm a-going off!'

I was swept away, but not unkindly, to some distance, where the people around me made me stay – urging, as I confusedly perceived, that he was bent on going, with help or without, and that I should endanger the precautions for his safety by troubling those with whom they rested. I don't know what I answered, or what they rejoined; but I saw hurry on the beach, and men running with ropes from a capstan that was there, and penetrating into a circle of figures that hid him from me. Then I saw him standing alone in a seaman's frock and trousers, a rope in his hand, or slung to his wrist, another round his body; and several of the best men holding, at a little distance, to the latter, which he laid out himself, slack upon the shore, at his feet.

The wreck, even to my unpractised eye, was breaking up. I saw that she was parting in the middle, and that the life of the solitary man upon the mast hung by a thread. Still, he clung to it. He had a singular red cap on – not like a sailor's cap, but of a finer colour; and as the few yielding planks between him and destruction rolled and bulged, and his anticipative death-knell rung, he was seen by all of us to wave it. I saw him do it now, and thought I was going distracted when his action brought an old remembrance to my mind of a once dear friend.

Ham watched the sea, standing alone, with the silence of suspended breath behind him, and the storm before, until there was a great retiring wave, when, with a backward glance at those who held the rope which was made fast round his body, he dashed in after it, and in a moment was buffeting with the water – rising with the hills, falling with the valleys, lost beneath the foam, then drawn again to land. They hauled in hastily.

He was hurt. I saw blood on his face, from where I stood; but he took no thought of that. He seemed hurriedly to give them some directions for leaving him more free – or so I judged from the motion of his arm – and was gone as before.

And now he made for the wreck, rising with the hills, falling with the valleys, lost beneath the rugged foam, borne in towards the shore, borne on towards the ship, striving hard and valiantly. The distance was nothing, but the power of the sea and wind made the strife deadly. At length he neared the wreck. He was so near that with one more of his vigorous strokes he would be clinging to it – when a high, green, vast hillside of water moving on shoreward from beyond the ship, he seemed to leap up into it with a mighty bound, and the ship was gone!

Some eddying fragments I saw in the sea, as if a mere cask had been broken, in running to the spot where they were hauling in. Consternation was in every face. They drew him to my very feet – insensible – dead. He was carried to the nearest house, and, no one preventing me now, I remained near him, busy, while every means of restoration were tried; but he had been beaten to death by the great wave, and his generous heart was stilled for ever.

As I sat beside the bed, when hope was abandoned and all was done, a fisherman, who had known me when Emily and I were children, and ever since, whispered my name at the door.

'Sir,' said he, with tears starting to his weather-beaten face, which, with his trembling lips, was ashy pale, 'will you come over yonder?'

The old remembrance that had been recalled to me was in his look. I asked him, terror-stricken, leaning on the arm he held out to support me, –

'Has a body come ashore?'

He said, 'Yes.'

'Do I know it?' I asked then.

He answered nothing.

But he led me to the shore. And on that part of it where she and I had looked for shells, two children – on that part of it where some lighter fragments of the old boat, blown down last night, had been scattered by the wind – among the ruins of the home he had wronged – I saw him lying with his head upon his arm, as I had often seen him lie at school.

* * * * *

Margery Allingham (1904 – 65): Writer of detective stories, for which she is best remembered, featuring her most famous creation Albert Campion. In the 1930s she was part of an exclusive triad of mystery writers with Agatha Christie and Dorothy L Sayers. Her husband Phillip Carter helped with the writing of several novels – *The Mind Readers* (1965) and *Cargo of Eagles* (1968) towards the end of her life. Allingham was brought up in Essex and lived for many years at Tollshunt D'Arcy on the edge of the marshes where 'Tis Not Hereafter' and 'The Sexton's Wife' from the collection *Mr Campion's Lucky Day and Other Stories* (1973) are both set.

'Tis Not Hereafter

MARGERY ALLINGHAM

When I was sent out to the small house on the marsh to look for the ghost there, I went stolidly and uncomplainingly, as is my nature.

I was an ugly, over-energetic little beast in my late teens, and had just begun to realize that my chosen profession of journalism was not the elegant mixture of the diplomatic service and theatrical criticism which my careers mistress had led me to suppose.

The general direction in which the house lay was pointed out by the postmaster of the most forlorn village ever to have graced the Essex coast. He stood leaning over a narrow counter with a surface like cracked toffee and shook his head at me warningly.

'That's no place for a young lady,' he said. 'That's a terrible funny place down there. You don't want to go there.'

It was encouraging to hear that the house on the marsh not only existed but that there was something definitely odd about it.

Our editor was a difficult man whose pet maxim was 'If you hear something, go and tear its guts out.'

His present story sounded unhappily vague. Someone, he said, had come to him at the Thatcher's Arms in the High Street and told him of a terrorised village which was in a state of near panic because of a ghastly white face, a woman's face, which had appeared at the window of a lonely house on the marsh. It was my duty to go and bring back the ghost or its story.

'It's great,' he said. 'Most important thing that's happened down here since the municipal election. Go and thrash it out. They'll all be on it.'

By 'all' he meant our rival, the *Weekly Gazette*, with offices a little lower down the town. I rather hoped they would. Bill Ferguson, their junior, was a friend of mine and I had looked out for him on the road. However, he had not appeared and I had been depressed at the prospect of unearthing yet another mare's nest when the postmaster had raised my hopes.

'I want to see the ghost,' I said cheerfully. 'Who's seen it so far?'

'There's a lot on 'em seen it,' he confessed unexpectedly. 'That's a proper vision.'

I got out my notebook.

'Who's seen it? Who can I talk to?'

'They'll be out at work now,' he said. 'Best wait till tea-time. They'll be home just after five.'

I looked out through the cluttered window at the sky. It was getting on for four o'clock and as grey and bitter as only a February day on the marsh can be.

'I'd better see the house now and get the stories when I come back,' I said. 'What's the tale about the house? Why should it be haunted?'

He eyed me thoughtfully.

'There was a shootin' down there years ago,' he said. 'Likely that's it.'

'Very likely,' I agreed blithely. 'Who was it?'

He was vague, however. At first it looked as though he was hiding something but at last it became obvious that he actually knew very little.

'There was a young couple took it from London,' he said. 'The lady she got herself drownded and the man 'e shot hisself. Now she's come back and sets peerin' out the window. You don't want to go down there, I keep tellin' you.'

'I do,' I said. 'Who were these people? When did it happen?'

The postmaster sighed.

'That I couldn't say. Afore my time. I ain't been here above twenty years. Ah, that's a dreadful tumble-down sort of a place!'

In the end he directed me. He was not actively against my going; merely passively disapproving.

I drove down that chill, windswept little street to the point where the road suddenly ceased to be a road and became a water-logged cart-track, and where a decrepit gate barred my path. I left my car since it was impractical to take it farther, and set out over the saltings on foot.

The house came into view after about half a mile of cold and uncomfortable walking. It sat huddled up on a piece of high ground, a miserable wooden shack of a place with a brick chimney leaning crazily on one side. At the big spring tides it must have been surrounded and, having a simple gregarious nature, I felt I understood the young woman who had drowned herself rather than live in it.

It was still some considerable distance away, and I plodded on, hoping with cheerful idiocy to see something pretty grisly in the way of spectres for my trouble.

It is hard to say at what particular moment I suddenly became afraid. Alarm settled down on me like a mist, and I was aware of feeling cold and a little sick long before I realised what it was. I think I must have recognised fear at the instant that I came near enough to the house to see the details of those two upper windows which peered out at me like dreadful dead eyes under the rakish billycock hat of a roof.

I remember pulling myself together irritably and then staring round aghast at that wide, desolate world of cold grey sea and marsh and sky.

The sight of the man struggling along behind me restored my balance. The sober earth returned to me, and with it a rush of relief. I was not alone. The human race had not miraculously died out in half an hour. I stood hesitating.

It was not Bill. The newcomer was not a labourer nor a fisherman. I saw his short raincoat with satisfaction. Here, no doubt, was the rest of the Press.

I shouted at him, my voice sounding very small and shrill in the cold emptiness.

'Hullo!' I bellowed. 'You from the *Gazette*? Come to see the ghost?'

He shouted back but I did not catch the words. His voice, too, was caught up and dispersed in the void. I heard scraps of it, unrelated notes, before it was sucked upward and devoured in that hungry air.

As he came closer I saw that he was a pale, ineffectual young man, hatless and with fair hair. His coat was buttoned up to his chin and he was blue with cold.

'Well, there's the house,' I said as he came up.

He nodded and surveyed the decrepit cottage, which looked more shabby and less horrific now that I was not facing it alone.

I glanced at the sky.

'If we're going to burgle the place by daylight we'd better hurry,' I said. 'At first this whole thing sounded like a cock-and-bull story but down in the village they seem to have seen something.'

'Yes,' he said and regarded me with unhappy pale grey eyes. 'I've heard them talking. They've seen a woman in a sun-bonnet.'

'A sun-bonnet?' That was something new to me and I felt a momentary resentment against my friend the postmaster. 'I'm glad she needs it,' I said facetiously.

He did not smile.

'It's hot down here in the summer; just as hot as it's cold now. There's no shade anywhere.'

The thought seemed to depress him and we ploughed on towards the house. The nearer I came to the place the more scared I grew. It was not a blind, exciting terror; rather a cold suffocating sense of disaster and frustration and despair.

I glanced at my companion and thought he must have experienced much the same reaction, for he looked wretched, and his teeth chattered slightly. The sight of his alarm gave me courage and amused me. It was a natural feminine desire to show off. I struggled against my terror and became almost hearty.

'I'm glad it's a woman,' I said foolishly. 'She's more likely to be at home. There was a tragedy down here some years ago. You've heard all that, I suppose?'

'Oh yes,' he said. 'I know what happened. But I don't see why the woman should come back. It was the man who had hell down here.'

'Ah,' I said complacently, 'that's what you think because you're a man. It's the woman who always feels things most. She's come back to look for the boy friend, of course.'

'Do you think so?' he said and looked so soft and sentimental that I began to lose interest in him. The discovery that he was dopy made him seem less useful as an ally and the cold began to creep up and down my spine again.

We had reached the high ground by this time and we made our ascent to that horrible cottage in silence. There was no need to climb in through the windows. The door hung crazily on one hinge and when I pushed it it clattered back with a noise that sounded like an explosion in that damp, silent greyness.

My colleague hung back.

'I don't want to go in,' he said.

There was more than repugnance in his voice. It rose on to a note of pure terror and combined with my own unreasoning alarm to make me thoroughly irritable. I regarded him coldly.

'Do what you like,' I said, and added with unpardonable priggishness, 'If you want to do your job properly you'll search the house with me.'

I stood, half in, half out, of the little brick-floored hall.

There were two rooms downstairs, a kitchen and a parlour. A flight of stairs led up between them. From where I stood I could see the ground floor was deserted.

I looked at the rickety stairs, and then at the man.

'Coming?' I demanded.

He went to pieces rather horribly. His face began to work.

'I'm sorry,' he gasped. 'I can't. I can't. I don't want to see . . . anything.'

Leaving him I clattered up the stairs making as much noise as my shoes would let me.

The two little rooms under the roof were empty and I was glad of it. They were dry and airy, too, which was queer, and they had an odd lived-in feeling. Downstairs the place was like a tomb. Up here it was almost pleasant. I stood listening.

I thought I heard someone breathing. It was a beastly delusion and I was afraid again. There was a cupboard in one room, but I did not open it. I went back to the staircase.

Something on the top step caught my eye and I stooped to retrieve it. Then I fled.

He was waiting for me, his face pale and blue with cold and his hands deep in his pockets. Now that the ordeal was over I was inclined to swagger.

He stood staring at me with a forlorn weariness on his face.

'Nothing there?' he said, and he seemed disappointed. 'No beautiful girl in a sun-bonnet and leg-o'-mutton sleeves?'

'Nothing at all,' I insisted.

He did not seem to hear me. He was looking back at the cottage and his face was twisted and disappointed. He stared so fixedly that I turned myself and looked up.

Then I screamed.

The face at the upper window was surrounded by a faded lavender sun-bonnet, the crumpled streamers hanging limply beside that pale and sunken countenance. The woman looked straight at me. I saw her eyes.

'Come,' I said hoarsely. 'Come.' And I gripped the little thing I had picked up on the stairs.

It was a moment of panic, but I saw him hanging back, his face drawn and puckered like a child's, and I remember his idiotic remark, so completely foolish in the circumstances.

'She's old,' he said. 'Oh, my God, she's old!'

I left him. I dashed into the house, raced up the stairs, and jerked open the cupboard door in the second bedroom. An old woman crouched in the corner and remained quite still as if she were invisible.

I pulled her out violently.

'I knew you were real,' I spluttered. 'I knew it. I found a new hairpin on the stairs and I knew a real woman had been here. What are you doing?

What are you doing, frightening people?'

She looked up at me and began to cry, and I was ashamed of myself. She was so little and old and faded. She looked silly, too, in a rough tweed coat and skirt, with the ridiculous sun-bonnet perched on her sparse grey curls.

'I didn't mean to frighten anyone,' she said in a thin little voice. 'I'm so sorry. Oh, dear, I've been so silly, and now I shall be late for tea. Miss Fell does get so cross if we're late for tea.'

I pricked up my ears. I knew Miss Fell. She kept a guest house on the other side of the marsh and did a lot of entertaining in the summer.

'Are you staying at Fairview?' I demanded.

'I used to live here long ago,' she said. 'At least, I once came on a holiday here, and last month I suddenly made up my mind to come and see the old place again. I took rooms with Miss Fell and I've been walking up here in the afternoons. I'm so sorry if I've frightened people. I had to see the house again. I was happy here for a little while, and then – I wasn't.'

I looked down at her. She was very small and had once been pretty in a fluffy, unintelligent way. It was then that I had one of my rare flashes of insight.

'So you weren't drowned?' I said.

She gave me a single frightened glance.

'Don't tell anyone,' she whispered. 'No, I ran away. I was a silly, melodramatic girl. I left my scarf and my hat on the sea wall and I walked to Burbridge and went back to London. I was so young. We were both so very young. I never dreamed that he – poor, poor boy!'

'We came down here to live on love and pennies when I was nineteen and he was twenty-two,' she went on softly. 'We thought we'd live on the edge of the world together and be happy. He was happy, but I couldn't bear it after a while, it wasn't what I'd been used to and I dared not tell him. I didn't want to break his illusion, you see, so I did the silly thing I did do. I ran away and pretended to be drowned. My cousin took me in and hushed it up. We never told, even when it came out in the papers that he had –'

'Shot himself?' I asked brutally.

'Yes,' she whispered, and shut her eyes. 'Poor boy, he was so gentle, so romantic, so much in love.'

I went over to the window. The marsh lay wild and sad and lonely in front of me. Presently I turned to her. She was so old, so pathetic, so helpless. I felt very cross with her.

'Look here,' I said, 'you mustn't come here again.'

'Oh, no – no, I won't. I do promise that.'

I felt silly.

'You can come, I suppose,' I said. 'Anybody can; but you mustn't peer out of the window in a sun-bonnet, because you're terrifying people. You used to wear the sun-bonnet here then, did you?'

Her lips quivered.

'He liked it,' she said. 'He said it made me look so charming. Oh, dear, I have been silly. Suppose people find out? Suppose it gets in the papers?'

'You won't be able to keep it a secret,' I said. 'There's that man downstairs as well as –'

She interrupted me.

'What man is that?'

'I think he's from the *Gazette*,' I said. 'He wouldn't come into the house. He's the man I was with when you looked out of the window at me.'

She stepped back from me and I saw fear in her eyes.

'You were alone,' she said. 'I saw you talking to someone, but no one was there. That's why I stared at you. You were quite alone.'

Her stupidity infuriated me.

'Don't be silly,' I said. 'He was a boy, really. Tall and thin, with fair hair and a pale face, and a raincoat buttoned up to his chin.'

I got no further. I saw the horror grow in her eyes and in her little wizened birdlike face.

'He came,' she said, huskily. 'He came.'

There was a long pause in which the world heeled over and those dreadful poignant words came back to me: 'Why should the woman come? It was the man who had hell here.'

The little old lady plucked my sleeve. Her face was trembling.

'Did he see me?' she said. 'Did he see me?'

I looked her full in the face and lied.

'No,' I said shakily. 'No. Come along. You'll be late for tea.'

* * * * *

Toby Litt: Studied Creative Writing at UEA under Malcolm Bradbury. He has written several novels including *Beatniks* (1997), *Corpsing* (2000), *Finding Myself* (2003), *Ghost Story* (2004) and most recently *Hospital* (2007). In 2003 he was one of Granta's 20 'Best of Young British Novelists' and is author of two collections of stories, most notably *Exhibitionism* (2002) from which 'The New Puritans' is taken.

The New Puritans
TOBY LITT

Their bungalow was called Sea-View Cottage. It was located on the East Anglian coast, a few miles south of Southwold. The walls of the bungalow were whitewash white. Had it not been for the seagull shit, the slate roof would have appeared almost perfectly black. They had taken the bungalow in November. It was now almost April. A small lawn was dying slowly on either side of the crazy-paved garden path. Through the bay windows one could gaze directly out over the North Sea, towards the Netherlands. Depending on whether the tide was in or out, the garden gate was anything from twenty to eighty steps away from the water's edge. This is where Jill stood, enjoying the final ten minutes before she had to go back on shift.

Jill was wearing a navy blue coat over a woollen Breton sweater, blue jeans and Army Surplus boots. Although there had been no discussion, the three of them had adopted this as something of a uniform. At first, John had thought wearing these kind of clothes might help them blend in with the locals. Now, they realized that their uniform merely made them stick out – but only in the way that non-locals trying to fit in anywhere always stick out. And that was a good enough reason for continuing to dress this way.

Jill had become proprietorial about the beach. Apart from the Dog-Walking Man, and someone fishing once, she had always been able to be alone here. These walks Jill called her Wind-Baths, after something Jack once said. (The proper name was Air-Baths.) Every morning for the past three weeks Jill had made an enjoyable little ritual of them – walking, in as straight a line as possible, from the bungalow to the sea. On the way, she collected pebbles, driftwood, rope, plastic. Anything that she could reach without having to step off her imaginary straight line. The beach was empty, open. The beach helped her clarify herself.

This morning the breeze felt delightfully mellow. It wasn't exactly warm, but the threatening North Sea chill was for the first time this year entirely absent.

Jill turned to look back at the bungalow. The sight of it still gave her pleasure.

Sea-View Cottage was perfect for their purposes. On the outside, it looked like any other bungalow. But the man who built it, back in 1979, had been taking the Cold War very seriously. A nuclear fallout shelter of similar dimensions to the upstairs rooms was embedded six feet beneath the foundations of the cottage. It was entered through a pair of metal doors, and down a flight of concrete stairs.

Two other white and black bungalows stood to the left and right of Sea-View Cottage: Kittiwake (after a kind of seagull) and The Old Cove (after someone with a shit sense of humour).

Jill started back towards their bungalow. She hadn't gathered anything much this morning, only a piece of driftwood of a particularly exquisite grey.

She intended to nail this to the living-room wall, as part of her collection of particularly exquisite grey pieces of driftwood.

Back in London, Jill had been a website designer. She liked to think that what she once did with Shockwave 4.0, she now did with real, physical objects. Only, she did it a lot better. And it was a great deal more satisfying.

Half-way back to the bungalow, she spotted a floppy circle stuck on top of a grey rock. These rings were all the sea left of condoms, before it shredded them completely.

Jill peeled the floppy circle off the rock and stuffed it in her side pocket. She had a nailed-up collection of condom rings, too.

Just then, she heard a car engine. It was getting louder.

She hurried towards the cottage.

By the time she reached the garden gate, the car was negotiating the last couple of hedge-hidden bends in the road.

Jill knew that it couldn't be anyone they knew. When they had left London, she and Jack hadn't exactly advertised where they were going. Or what they would be doing when they got there. Steve, and Steve alone, knew their location. (Steve was their boss.)

She hid herself in the porch, listening.

The car drew up outside Kittiwake.

Jill crouched down.

A car door opened. The engine kept running. The gate squeaked. The car moved forwards. The engine was cut off. The gate squeaked shut. Another car door opened.

'Well, we're here,' said a male voice.

'Yes, we're here,' replied a female voice. They sounded young.

'This is going to be fun,' said the man. 'Fun-fun-fun,' said the woman.

Jill listened a moment more, as the young couple opened the boot and began to unload. Then she slipped inside as quickly and quietly as possible.

She now had two minutes until she was due on shift. She would tell John about the newcomers when she went down into the basement. He could then pass the information on, when Jack woke up.

Just to make double sure, she wrote a message on the white board in the kitchen. *A couple have moved into Kittiwake. Caution. Meeting tomorrow morning?*

She looked over the food on the white-painted table. Since moving out of London, she had learned to bake bread. It was something she'd always wanted to do. The loaf on the table, ready for John to toast, was one she had made yesterday. The milk, butter and eggs came from a farm down the road. Even the marmalade, bought from a church sale, was homemade. Only the teabags seemed in any way industrial. She would have to ask Steve for some loose-leaf, the next time he came.

'Jill!' John shouted up from the basement.

She knew she should always be a little early for the handover. Otherwise John got angry. It was just the light had been so beautiful outside. And then she'd been delayed by the newcomers.

The car boot slamming only twenty yards away made her jump. She was no longer used to such loud, unexpected noises.

'Jill!' John called, louder.

Jill laced her fingers together and pushed them away from her until they clicked. Then she went downstairs into the basement.

The system was this: They each worked one of three eight-hour shifts: morning (7 a.m. to 3 p.m.), evening (3 p.m. to 11 p.m.), night (11 p.m. to 7 a.m.). It was important they kept the machines going twenty-four hours a day. Steve had customers waiting. Customers it wasn't a good idea to disappoint. At the moment, Jill was on mornings, Jack on evenings and John on nights. In seven days' time, when the month came to an end, they would all have two whole days off. When they started up again, Jill would be on evenings, Jack on nights, John mornings.

The machines they worked on were AMX-3000s. It took an AMX twenty minutes to make a decent enough tape-to-tape copy of a ninety-minute master. With ten machines running in tandem, they could turn out thirty videos an hour. 720 a day. 20,160 a month.

For this, they were well paid. They all cleared several thousand a month. Avoided tax. And had hardly any outgoings. The money, paid them by Steve, in cash, just seemed to stack up. In drawers. Under mattresses. None of them dared use a bank. Three months in, and already they didn't know what to do with it all.

The film they were doing at the moment was an ultra-violent Swedish hardcore movie. It was mostly gay sex, although a woman made a brief but memorable appearance. The images weren't the kind of thing any of them were likely to get off on. Although Jill sometimes had her doubts about John. At the start, she had tended to watch each video through – just to see what it was about. They soon became very monotonous. Blood was involved. And screaming. And shit. Lots of shit. She still fast-forwarded through the new tapes – making sure there weren't children involved. That had been her only stipulation.

When they first arrived at the bungalow, John had been waiting for them. John was a complete surprise, and not a particularly pleasant one. (He had almost immediately told them about the twenty-four-hour shift system.) Jill had disliked John from the moment they met. She thought him seedy. John's past was infuriatingly – Jill thought *deliberately* – mysterious. It involved drugs, in quantities vaster (he hinted) than any they had ever come across. And prison, also. For the time being, though, John said all he wanted to do was 'mellow on back to grass roots'. If this meant smoking dope, it did anything but make him mellow.

Despite the shift system, Jill tried to avoid John as much as possible. This wasn't difficult. Because she and Jack were coupled up, they tried to maximize their shared off-time. She took a long nap during the afternoon, then stayed up late with him after his shift was over. This left them from about 11 p.m. to 1 am. to hang out.

The three of them were only ever together when a meeting had been called. Usually, only John called meetings. And then, it was usually to complain about something. (The food, usually.) But the arrival of the newcomers was something they *had* to talk about. Which is why Jill had called the meeting.

Jill got up at 6 a.m., especially. She woke Jack, who had slept most of the seven hours since his evening shift had finished. John, coming to the end of the night shift, was waiting for them when they came down the stairs into the basement. As the three of them talked, he kept working – taking tapes out of cardboard boxes, putting them in machines, copying, checking, taking tapes out of machines, putting them in cardboard boxes. The machines made a loud, slightly grindy, whirring sound.

'I think one of us should go round,' said Jill, having to raise her voice a little. 'You know, to say hello. We need to appear as normal as possible, don't we?'

'Why?' said John. 'None of us are. And I bet they're not either.'

'You know exactly what I mean,' said Jill.

'Hey,' Jack said, 'let's think about this.'

'We never let them in the house,' said John. 'We're perfectly polite and all that. But they never come inside.'

'Won't that make them suspicious?' said Jill.

'Of what?' shouted John. 'If they come in, even only into the kitchen, they'll hear that something's going on down here.'

He patted one of the machines. It continued to whirr.

'We could tell them it's the boiler,' said Jill.

Most of the time, Jack kept quiet. He knew that his attempts to peace-make only inflamed the others. John accused him of being in Jill's pocket. Jill tried to force him to agree with her. Generally, he did agree with Jill. But, because of that, he worried that John was right, and that he *was* in Jill's pocket. 'Why don't we leave it and just see what happens?' he suggested.

'No,' said Jill. 'We need a policy.'

'I agree,' said John, making one of his unexpected tactical switches. With only three of them, realignments like this were always decisive. They operated democratically, and two was an instant majority.

'Okay,' said Jack.

'I think Jill should go over and make friends with them,' said John. 'They're less likely to suspect a woman.'

'Oh, thanks,' said Jill.

'Of doing what we're doing,' John said.

They both of them looked at Jack.

'Well?' said Jill.

'Fine,' he said, still surprised they were agreeing.

'Fine,' said John. 'Then I'm going to bed.'

233

As soon as he was out of earshot, Jill said, 'Think he means it?'

That evening, a couple of hours after coming off shift, Jill went round and knocked on Kittiwake's front door.

When she'd introduced herself, the young woman invited her in for tea.

The kitchen was very warm, overheated by an Aga. A couple of cardboard boxes full of food were jammed against the far wall.

'I'm Molly,' she said. 'And this is –'

'Mark,' said the good-looking young man, getting up from the bleached-pine table.

They were both around twenty-two, twenty-three. Five or six years younger than Jill and Jack, and eight younger than John.

'We're just here for a week,' said Molly, after they'd sat down around the table. 'Getting out of London.'

'What are you doing here?' asked Mark.

'I live here,' said Jill. 'For the moment, at least.'

'But you're not *from* here,' said Molly.

'Not originally, no,' Jill replied. 'I'm living here with my boyfriend –' She decided at that moment not to mention John. He would just have to keep out of sight for a while.

'What do you do?' asked Mark.

Jill had to think about this. 'I'm an artist,' she said.

'Oh, really,' said Molly. 'What kind of thing?'

'I work on the beach, mostly. I collect things and put them together. It's not very original or anything. I just do it for myself, you see.' Jill realized she was gabbling, but she couldn't stop herself. Here, at least, was something she could be honest about. 'It's good therapy.'

'I'd love to see some of your stuff,' said Molly.

'Me, too,' said Mark.

'I don't really show anyone,' said Jill.

'Not even your boyfriend?' asked Mark.

'No, not really.'

By the time she got back to Sea-View Cottage, Jill had found out all about Molly and Mark. She knew they both worked in the theatre, but only backstage. That they both – just like Jack – wanted to break into film. That Molly was two months pregnant, and that the two of them were trying to fit in as many little holidays as they could before the baby was born.

'I just wanted some fresh air,' said Molly.

'We got the address off some friends who came last year,' added Mark.

'Isn't it lovely?' said Molly.

Jill went down into the basement, where Jack and John were awaiting her.

'Well, they *seem* harmless enough,' she said.

When the meeting was over, Jack and Jill went upstairs to their bedroom. They got in under the covers with their clothes on for a cuddle. All of a sudden, they both started giggling.

'I can't believe you forgot to tell them about John,' said Jack.

Jill giggled some more. 'Well, you know,' she said, 'I probably subconsciously wanted to punish him for being so horrible to us all the time.'

Jack said, 'So now, he'll have to stay hidden till they leave.'

'Good,' said Jill.

They rubbed noses, like they always did.

'So, you're not worried about them,' said Jack.

'As long as they don't find out what we're doing,' said Jill, 'we'll be fine.'

As Jill was Wind-Bathing and beachcombing the next morning, Molly trotted up alongside her.

'Mind if I join?' she said.

'No,' said Jill. She found it slightly disconcerting to know this young woman was pregnant, but not be able to see it.

'The beach is lovely, isn't it?' said Molly. 'So desolate.'

'I find it quite cosy,' said Jill.

'Cosy, too,' said Molly.

Jill felt all the advantages of being a twenty-seven-year-old talking to a twenty-two-year-old.

They walked to the water's edge.

'It makes me just feel so clean and refreshed,' said Molly, and stuck her arms out to either side.

As she stood there with her eyes closed, Jill took the chance to look Molly over. Molly's hair was reddish, and her skin fashionably freckled. At least, that had been the new thing in models the month Jill left London. There was an unlovely clenchedness about her face, however.

It was too hard. Vertical lines were incised on either side of her mouth. Jill knew them for what they were: speed-cuts.

'Whoo,' said Molly, when a stronger than usual gust of wind almost made her take a step backwards.

She opened her eyes before Jill had a chance to look away.

'It's not Mark's baby,' said Molly. Then she said hurriedly, 'I don't know why I told you that.'

Jill was stunned. 'Does he know?' she said.

'No,' said Molly. 'I brought him here to tell him.'

That evening, there was a knock at the door of Sea-View Cottage. As agreed, Jill answered. It was Mark. She was very aware of the whirring sound of the tape-to-tape machines.

'We were wondering if you'd like to come round to dinner,' said Mark. 'Not tonight. Tomorrow. Both of you.'

'That would be very nice,' said Jill, images of blood and shit flashing behind her eyes. This was difficult: Jack would have to switch shifts with John – that was the only way he'd be able to go out for the evening. 'I don't think we could stay very late.' Jack would have to go on nights.

'No problem,' said Mark. 'How about six?'

'Jack doesn't like to stay out too late,' said Jill. What if John refused? He couldn't. It was either this or risk getting caught.

'See you at six, then.'

Jill closed the door, keeping the whirring sound in.

The next morning, Molly again joined Jill on the beach.

'Did you tell him yet?' asked Jill.

'What?' said Molly. 'About the baby?'

'Yes,' said Jill.

Molly looked thoughtful. 'No,' she said. 'It's just too difficult. You didn't tell Jack, did you?'

'Of course not.'

'I'm *so* looking forward to meeting him. I don't want him to feel at all awkward. At dinner.'

'I didn't tell him anything.'

Molly started the conversation again.

'You and Jack eat everything, don't you? I'm going shopping today. I don't want to get anything wrong.'

'Oh, there's *nothing* we won't eat,' said Jill.

They both laughed.

Jack and Jill knocked on the door of Kittiwake at ten past six. Jack held the bottle of red wine. (They had promised John a crate of the stuff, to get him to switch shifts – and let him off washing-up for a month.)

It was Mark who answered.

'I'm afraid Molly isn't feeling very well,' he said, and mimed puking. 'Sorry I couldn't come round and tell you earlier. I didn't want to leave her alone.'

'We understand,' said Jill. 'Shall I go in and see her?'

'I think she'd prefer it if you didn't see her this way.'

'Hope she gets better soon,' said Jack.

'How about we do it tomorrow evening instead?' suggested Mark.

'Lovely,' said Jill.

Molly did not join Jill on the beach the next morning.

The air was wet with sea spray. A solitary seagull walked along behind her.

Jill's first thought was that Molly was still feeling sick. But then she realized that she might, at that very moment, be telling Mark the truth about the baby.

The morning seemed an odd time to do it, but you never knew with other people. If she did tell him, he'd almost certainly get into a real state. It wouldn't surprise her at all if he got into the car and drove off.

She looked back towards Kittiwake, but it gave little sign as to what was going on inside. Tufts of white smoke were ripped away from the chimney-stack as soon as they appeared.

That evening, they turned up on Kittiwake's doorstep again. Jack had the same bottle of wine. Jill had gathered some wild flowers for Molly. She it was who answered the door. 'Oh, come in,' she said.

'Feeling better?' asked Jill.

'Much,' said Molly. 'You must be Jack.'

The smell of butter-frying garlic suffused the hall.

They walked through into the kitchen.

'Hi,' said Mark, and wiped his hand on a dishcloth before holding it out towards Jack.

He was half-way through slicing a chopping-board full of kidneys.

'Mark,' said Jack.

'Jack,' said Mark.

'Sit down,' said Molly.

They began to talk, mostly about the film industry. The conversation was good, if a little awkward at times. Molly was charming. Mark was amusing, in a slightly sarcastic way. He seemed to like teasing Molly.

The food, when it came, was delicious. Stilton soup. Kidneys on a bed of rocket with garlic mash. Even the plastic tubs of Gooseberry Fool tasted almost homemade.

'It's terrible,' said Molly, as they were having coffee. 'We're only here another three days. The time seems to have gone so fast.'

Jill looked at her. She was obviously referring to not having told Mark.

'I want to show you something,' said Molly suddenly. She grabbed Jill by the hand, tugged her into the bedroom and slammed the door behind them.

Jack and Mark were left alone in the kitchen.

Mark wasted no time in leaning over to Jack. 'Molly isn't pregnant, you know,' he said. 'She lost the baby about five months ago. Just before Christmas. It sent her a little bit mad.'

'Really?' said Jack.

'I just play along with it, most of the time. It's better than having her constantly in hysterics.'

Jack thought this an odd comment. 'What do the doctors say?' he asked.

'She's in denial, plain and simple. She's been two months pregnant ever since November.'

'That must be difficult for you,' said Jack.

'I can cope,' said Mark. 'But please don't tell Jill. It's better if there's at least one person who can be completely natural with her.'

'I understand,' said Jack, thoroughly confused.

Just then, Jill came out of the bedroom. In her hands she held a half-knit baby sweater.

'Isn't it cute?' she said.

Jack was half an hour late in relieving John that night. He and Jill hadn't said anything much on the short walk home.

'Nice people.'

'Yes,' replied Jill.

'Strange.'

'Very strange.'

John was pretty pissed off at having to stay hidden the whole time.

'Don't tell me how nicey-nice it was,' he said, before stamping upstairs. 'Because I don't want to fucking know.'

Jack knew what John would do now - head straight for his Technics decks in the living room, put on his massive headphones, close his eyes and pretend he was DJing at some superclub in Ibiza.

During the night shift, Jack decided he'd better not tell Jill that Molly was mad. He'd wait until after Mark and Molly had gone back to London.

The next morning, the beach was aslant with rain. It was colder, too. Determined never to miss a day, Jill put on her waterproofs and went out to take her Wind-Bath. The weather being what it was, she hardly expected to see Molly outside. And so, when she heard Kittiwake's front door slam shut, Jill was a little startled. But, on turning round, she saw that it was Mark and not Molly who was walking towards her.

'Morning,' he hollered, when he'd caught up. 'What are you doing out in this?'

'I don't mind it,' yelled Jill. 'How's Molly?'

'Not too bright today, either.'

'Oh dear.'

They walked towards the sea.

'You know,' Mark shouted conversationally, 'Molly and I haven't had sex since she got pregnant. Not once.'

'Oh,' said Jill.

'She just . . . doesn't want to. Says the very thought makes her feel ill.'

'Perhaps that's understandable. A lot of women feel that way.'

'Yes, but what am I meant to do?' he asked. 'Never have sex again?'

'I'm sure she'll come back to the idea.'

'I'll have exploded with frustration by then. I need to have sex regularly. It's like breathing or something.'

Jill stopped. 'Why exactly are you telling me this?'

'Why do you think?'

'I hope it's not what I think it is.'

'What *do* you think it is?'

'I'm going back inside.'

'What do you think I meant?' Mark stood in her way. '*What* do you *think* I *meant*?'

Jill tried to wither him. 'How can you be so crass?'

Mark leaned closer, so he didn't have to shout.

'It's the touching I miss, as much as anything. She never even does that any more.'

Mark was sticking his hands down the front of his trousers.

Jill dodged to one side, then back the other way. Mark, a little off balance to begin with, was wrong-footed.

She sprinted up the beach.

As she neared Sea-View Cottage, she saw Molly standing on the porch in her dressing-gown.

Molly waved and smiled.

Jill spent most of her shift feeling furious with Mark. But, when she calmed down, she began to feel sorry for Molly.

If she told Molly about Mark, she might leave him. And if that happened, the baby would lose its father.

Who was she to risk making that happen?

She really wanted to tell Jack. But Molly had looked vulnerable, standing on the doorstep.

Jill decided she'd tell Jack all about it, after Molly and Mark had left.

In the afternoon, when they were in bed together, Jack asked Jill what she thought of Molly.

'She's very nice,' said Jill. 'Why do you ask?'

'I don't know,' said Jack. 'She's just a bit young to be pregnant, isn't she?'

'Perhaps it was an accident.'

'Perhaps.'

They were silent for a while.

'What do you think of Mark?' Jill asked.

'I'm not sure if I like him very much.'

'Why not?'

'He seems a bit creepy.'

Jill felt very relieved. 'I agree,' she said. 'There's something indefinably nasty about him.'

'Do you think they think it's odd, us not inviting them back for dinner?'

'Let them think whatever,' said Jill. 'They'll be gone in two days.'

About two in the morning, just as he'd finished changing over another twenty tapes, Jack thought he heard someone knocking on the front door, knocking hard.

But John was upstairs. If it *was* the door, then he'd get it.

The knocking came again.

John was probably DJing, wearing his big headphones.

After closing up the basement, Jack went to investigate.

Molly was there, wearing only a dressing-gown. She didn't look at all mother-to-be.

'Can I come in?' she said.

Jack didn't seem to have a choice. John was in the living room. Jack led Molly through into the kitchen. 'Noisy, isn't it?' he said, meaning the whirring sound.

'Don't worry,' said Molly. 'I won't stay long.'

'It's the boiler.'

Jack sat down, terrified that at any moment John would come through to fetch another beer from the fridge.

'Are you alright?' asked Jack.

'I'm fine. I'm fine. I just had to come and tell you.' She hesitated. 'This morning, on the beach. I think something happened between Mark and Jill.'

'Something, what?'

'Well, it's pretty obvious that they're attracted to each other, isn't it?'

Jack thought about this for a moment.

'I saw them *kissing*,' said Molly.

'No,' said Jack.

'I did,' Molly said. 'He thought I was still asleep, but I looked out the window and saw them.'

'I don't believe you,' said Jack. He felt quite convinced that this delusion was another sign of Molly's madness – along with believing herself pregnant, she had started to believe her boyfriend was serially unfaithful.

'But it's true,' said Molly, a little too loud for comfort. Even with headphones full of Euphoric Trance, John would hear.

'I think we should get you back to bed.'

'Why don't you believe me?'

'I do,' said Jack. 'I'm just sure it didn't mean anything. Come along.'

He put his arm around Molly and led her to the front door. While they'd been talking, the whirring sound of the machines had ceased.

Luckily, Molly didn't seem to have noticed. Her torch was on the doorstep, lit but pointing into the concrete.

'I'll come with you,' Jack said.

They walked down Sea-View's garden path, through the gate, along a dozen yards to the right, through Kittiwake's gate, up the path.

Before they'd even reached the door, Mark had yanked it open. 'What's all this, then?' he said.

'Molly just –' But Jack didn't know what to say.

Molly elaborated the lie for him, '– wanted to talk to Jill about something.'

'Yes,' said Jack. 'I was just walking her back. Quite innocent.'

Molly turned as she went in the door. 'Thank you, Jack,' she said. 'And say thank you so much to Jill, too.'

'I will,' said Jack.

By the time he got back to the machines, Jack reckoned he'd lost about twenty minutes.

The tapes which had been stacking up for a fortnight were due to be collected the following night. The routine was this: Steve, accompanied by either Geoff or Keith, arrived around midnight in the van. They took two and a half hours in total to unload the blank tapes and then load up the finished ones. They were usually well away before it started to get light.

Jack felt anxious about collection day all through his shift. He already knew he couldn't mention anything about Molly's midnight visit to Jill. He was sure that Molly had been lying, though she might not herself know it.

During the night, Jack had started copying a new movie. He watched it through at normal speed on their quality control machine. It was the hardest porn he had ever seen: camcordered in a concrete bunker of some sort, five ugly men raped an ugly woman, and then each other. He could see the the woman trying to fight back, even though she was obviously smacked off her tits. The violence was homicidal.

He wanted to tell Jill not to watch it, but he knew that – if he did that – she would slam it on the moment he left the room.

The shift passed very slowly.

When Jill came to relieve him, he gave her a big kiss. She looked at his box of uncompleted tapes.

'I dozed off,' he said, before she asked.

242

During her sleepless night, Jill had almost decided to tell Jack about Mark's clumsy pass the previous morning.

For the first time since they had arrived, she'd not gone out for her Wind-Bath. She hadn't wanted to risk meeting Mark alone again. In some ways, he'd ruined the beach for her.

Jack went to bed.

But he couldn't sleep. After half an hour, he went back down to see Jill. She had been watching the new movie, and was obviously quite sickened. 'I have to tell you something,' he said. 'You have to promise to keep it a secret.'

'Yes?' asked Jill, putting the tape on pause. 'What?'

'Promise.

'I did.'

'Molly isn't pregnant,' Jack said. 'She just thinks she is because she lost another baby.'

'Rubbish,' said Jill.

'Mark told me the other night, when we were round at dinner. You were in the bedroom. Looking at baby clothes. Molly's a bit mental.'

'She's not.'

'Well, you don't have to believe it. I just wanted to tell you, so you knew.'

Jill thought for a moment about returning the favour, and telling Jack about Mark not knowing the baby wasn't his. But if there wasn't a baby, or even if Jack just believed there wasn't, then that didn't really mean anything.

'You're nuts,' she said, and kissed him. 'Go back to bed.'

That evening, Molly appeared on the doorstep. Jill answered when she knocked.

'Hello,' said Molly, a little formally.

'Hi.'

'We wondered if you'd like to come round to dinner again. Tonight's our last night. I know it's a bit short notice. We'd like to see you both again before we go.'

'Oh,' said Jill. 'Lovely.'

Molly beckoned Jill to come outside. They went a few steps down the garden path. 'I told him,' said Molly.

'My God,' said Jill. 'How was he?'

'Much better than I thought it would be.'

Jill didn't know what she believed any more.

'He says we can always have one together in a few years time.'

'Does he know the father?'

Molly blushed, very convincingly. 'It's his best friend from school.'

'That's terrible,' said Jill, at that moment believing it.

'I know,' said Molly, naughtily. 'Can you come around seven?'

'We'll be there,' said Jill.

'We can't go,' said Jack when Jill told him. He was still a little worried about letting Jill and Mark spend any more time together. Even though he knew Molly was mad, he thought there had been some truth in her suggestion that two of them were attracted to each other. The fact that he himself fancied Molly seemed somehow to confirm this.

'We have to,' said Jill. 'Anyway, they'll be gone tomorrow morning. What harm can it do?'

'Steve is going to be shifting half a ton of extremely hard-core porn into the back of his van tonight,' said Jack. 'What *harm* is it going to do?'

'We'll just tell him to keep it quiet.'

'They're *bound* to notice.'

'What do you want to do? Tell me.'

'Phone him. Tell him not to come. Tell him to come tomorrow.'

'He won't do that,' said Jill.

'We'll tell him the police are sniffing around.'

'He'd just come to see for himself.'

Jack knew this was true.

'I'm going for a walk,' he said.

'You haven't got time,' said Jill.

'Do you want to get us caught?' shouted Jack. 'Do you know what will happen if they catch us with this stuff?'

He picked up a tape and hurled it towards the bedroom wall. Frustratingly, it landed flat, dropped to the floor, and didn't shatter.

'I'm *going* for a walk,' Jack said. 'Don't worry – I'll be back in time.'

Jack was half-way down the garden path when he spotted Molly. She was standing right in front of Sea-View Cottage, looking down the beach. There was no way he could get round her without her noticing. He thought for a moment about going back into the bungalow. But he was too angry with Jill for that. He needed to walk away from her for a while. He needed, perhaps, to let himself think that he might never go back.

When she heard the latch of the garden gate being lifted, Molly turned to see who it was.

'Jack,' she said, apparently relieved.

'Molly,' said Jack. He intended to walk straight past her, and on towards the shoreline. Without being rude, of course.

'I was waiting for you,' Molly said. 'I was hoping you'd look out and see me standing here.'

'Did you?' said Jack.

She took a couple of steps towards him. 'You were so kind when I came round last night.'

'It was nothing.'

'No,' said Molly. 'No, it wasn't.'

She was now close enough to touch him, which she did. She reached out with one of her hands, and gently stroked his cheek.

He flinched away. 'Get off,' he said.

'Mark's busy cooking,' said Molly. 'We could find somewhere to go.'

'But you're pregnant', Jack said.

Molly took another step forwards. 'You know that's a lie,' she said.

'Fucking hell,' said Jack, backing away. 'What the fuck is wrong with you?'

Molly followed him.

Jack tried to turn round, so that he could run. But the sandy ground gave way beneath him, and he fell on his side.

Molly jumped on top of him. 'That's more like it,' she said. With her groin, she pressed down on his hips. When he reached to try and push her off, she grabbed his wrists.

'Don't,' said Jack, warning violence.

Molly was surprisingly strong. Jack struggled, but Molly was able to ride him.

'Let *go*,' he shouted.

'Only if you kiss me.'

Without waiting for a response, Molly pushed her face down on his. Their teeth clicked sharply together.

'Fuck,' said Jack.

Molly pressed down again. He could feel her tongue licking along his lips.

He tried again to push her off, and this time he succeeded – but only because she let him.

She landed, quite hard, on her back, on the grass. As he scrambled to one side, he heard her saying, 'Beat you.'

After a second to get his breath, Jack stood up. 'You are sick,' he said.

She closed her eyes and pretended to sunbathe. 'Would you mind?' she said. 'You're standing in my light.'

For a moment, Jack thought he wasn't going to kick her - then he kicked her.

His toes caught Molly's thigh. She doubled up, and he guessed he'd dead-legged her.

He bent down. He was about to start apologizing when he heard her whisper, 'Now that's more like it.'

Jack was only a few steps away from the porch when Jill opened the door.

'I'm sorry,' she said.

'Let's go inside,' he said.

'I said I'm sorry.'

'Okay,' he said. 'Apology accepted. Inside.'

He felt himself on the point of shoving her back. She was looking dangerously out over the beach.

'We need to get ready,' he said.

She took a final deep breath, and turned back inside. Just then, Jack saw Molly standing up from behind the garden fence.

He almost leapt through the door into the bungalow.

Jack and Jill took another bottle of the same red as before round to Kittiwake at seven o'clock.

'Come *in*,' said Molly.

'How *are* you?' said Jill.

'Oh, very well,' said Molly, looking directly at Jack.

They walked through the hall and into the kitchen.

Jack felt Molly pinching his bum.

'Hi,' said Mark, who had just been prodding something in the oven.

'Smells lovely,' said Jill.

Mark kissed her on both cheeks, and she was in control enough to let him.

'Make yourselves at home,' said Molly.

They sat down in the same places as before. Jack immediately felt Molly's toes crawling up his calf. He reached down and pushed them away. They started again, at the ankle.

'It's not quite as elaborate as last time,' Mark said. 'I'm afraid we're using up the last of our food – so, it's baked bean surprise.'

'Lovely,' said Jill.

The meal was torture for Jack and for Jill. Molly kept pestering Jack beneath the table, with both feet and hands. Jack tried to ignore her pinchings, strokings and fondlings. Mark sent yearning looks in Jill's direction. Jill tried her best to avoid them. Jack, even whilst being distracted by Molly, couldn't help but notice what Mark was doing. He looked at Jill, to see if she reciprocated. Jill caught Jack looking at her a couple of times. She knew what he was thinking. To reassure him, she directed all her conversation towards Molly. This only made Jack's under-the-table situation more desperate.

The food was fairly disgusting: undercooked potatoes on top of lukewarm baked beans and half-cold spam.

After they'd finished eating, Molly took Mark's hand and said, 'We've decided that, if the baby's a boy, we're going to call it Jack, and if it's a girl, we'll call it Jill.'

'I don't know what to say,' said Jill. She avoided the eye contact Mark kept trying to make.

'That's very sweet,' said Jack, who was a little more used to treating Molly as the nutter she was.

Just then, they all heard an engine approaching.

'I wonder who that is,' said Mark, and went to the back window.

Molly joined him there. 'It's a white van,' she said. 'It's coming this way. Is it some friends of yours?'

Jack looked anxiously at Jill. 'It might be,' she said.

'Well, don't you know?' asked Mark. 'You must have arranged it.'

The van's lights raked through the candle-lit kitchen. The horn beeped three times, making everyone jump. Jack and Jill, looking at each other desperately, heard the engine swittch off.

'It's a man,' said Molly.

Jack leaned over to Jill and whispered in her ear, 'What do we do?'

'He's coming this way,' said Mark.

'He looks very tough,' said Molly. 'He's wearing a leather coat.'

Jack got up out of his chair and crossed quickly to the window. He was just in time to see Steve disappearing behind the side of Kittiwake. For a moment, everyone stood still. Then the front door opened. Steve walked into the kitchen, leaving the door open behind him.

'Molly,' he said, nodding. 'Mark.'

They nodded back at him.

'What?' said Jack.

'Oh,' said Steve. 'I see you lot have already met.'

'Do you know them?' said Jill.

Just then, John came through the open door. He walked straight into the kitchen.

'About time,' said Steve, angrily. 'You and Molly grab ahold of her. Me and Mark'll get this one here.'

* * * * *

Susan Hill: Brought up on the east coast, Susan Hill was drawn to Aldeburgh by Britten's *Sea Interludes* and each winter throughout the 1970s she rented a cottage on the sea front. The clear, vibrant air seemed charged with an intensity and the stories began to flow as she tramped along the shore. The result is a series of moving tales set on this bleak stretch of coast, notably her novella *The Albatross* and several short stories including the title story from her collection *A Bit of Singing and Dancing* (1973). Her celebrated ghost story *The Woman in Black* (1983) conjours up the atmoshpere of the Essex marshes.

A Bit Of Singing And Dancing
SUSAN HILL

There was no one else on the beach so late in the afternoon. She walked very close to the water, where there was a rim of hard, flat sand, easier on her feet than the loose shelves of shingle, which folded one on top of the other, up to the storm wall. She thought, I can stay out here just as long as I like, I can do anything I choose, anything at all, for now I am answerable only to myself.

But it was an unpromising afternoon, already half dark, an afternoon for early tea and banked-up fires and entertainment on television. And a small thrill went through her as she realized that that, too, was entirely up to her, she could watch whichever programme she chose, or not watch any at all. There had not been an evening for the past eleven years when the television had stayed off and there was silence to hear the ticking of the clock and the central heating pipes.

'It is her only pleasure,' she used to say, 'She sees things she would otherwise be quite unable to see, the television has given her a new lease of life. You're never too old to learn.' But in truth her mother had watched variety shows, Morecambe and Wise and the Black and White Minstrels, whereas she herself would have chosen BBC 2 and something cultural or educational.

'I like a bit of singing and dancing, it cheers you up, Esme, it takes you out of yourself. I like a bit of spectacular.'

But tonight there might be a play or a film about Arabia or the Archipelagoes, or a master class for cellists, tonight she would please herself, for the first time. Because it was two weeks now, since her mother's death, a decent interval.

It was February. It was a cold evening. As far as she could see, the beach and the sea and the sky were all grey, merging into one another in the distance. On the day of her mother's funeral it had been blowing a gale, with sleet, she had looked round at all their lifeless, pinched faces under the black hats and thought, this is right, this is fitting, that we should all of us seem bowed and old and disconsolate. Her mother had a right to a proper grief, a proper mourning.

She had wanted to leave the beach and walk back, her hands were stiff with cold inside the pockets of her navy-blue coat – navy, she thought, was the correct first step away from black. She wanted to go back and toast scones and eat them with too much butter, of which her mother would have strongly disapproved. 'We never had it, we were never allowed to indulge ourselves in rich foods, and besides, they've been discovering more about heart disease in relation to butter, haven't you read that in the newspapers, Esme? I'm surprised you don't pay attention to these things. I pay attention. I don't believe in butter at every meal – butter on this, butter with that.'

Every morning, her mother had read two newspapers from cover to cover – the *Daily Telegraph* and the *Daily Mirror*, and marked out with a green ball point pen news items in which she thought that her daughter ought to take an interest. She said, 'I like to see both sides of every question.' And so, whichever side her daughter or some visitor took, on some issue of the day, she was informed enough by both her newspapers to take the opposing view. An argument, she had said, sharpened the mind.

'I do not intend to become a cabbage, Esme, just because I am forced to be bedridden.'

She had reached the breakwater. A few gulls circled, bleating, in the gunmetal sky, and the waterline was strewn with fish-heads, the flesh all picked away. She thought, I am free, I may go on or go back, or else stand here for an hour, I am mistress of myself. It was a long time since she had been out for so long, she could not quite get used to it, this absence of the need to look at her watch, to scurry home. But after a while, because it was really very damp and there was so little to see, she did turn, and then the thought of tomorrow, and the outing she had promised herself to buy new clothes. It would take some months for her mother's will to be proven, the solicitor had explained to her, things were generally delayed, but there was no doubt that they would be settled to her advantage and really, Mrs Fanshaw had been very careful, very prudent, and so she would not be in want. Meanwhile, perhaps an advance for immediate expenses? Perhaps a hundred pounds?

When the will was read, her first reaction had been one of admiration, she had said, 'The cunning old woman' under her breath, and then put her hand up to her mouth, afraid of being overheard. 'The cunning old woman.' For Mildred Fanshaw had saved up £6,000, scattered about in bank and savings accounts. Yet they had always apparently depended upon Esme's salary and the old age pension, they had had to be careful, she said, about electricity and extra cream and joints of beef. 'Extravagance,' Mrs Fanshaw said, 'it is a cardinal sin. That is where all other evils stem from, Esme. Extravagance. We should all live within our means.'

And now here was £6,000. For a moment or two it had gone to her head, she had been quite giddy with plans, she would buy a car and learn to drive, buy a washing machine and a television set, she would have a holiday abroad and get properly fitting underwear and eat out in a restaurant now and again, she would . . .

But she was over fifty, she should be putting money on one side herself now, saving for her own old age, and besides, even the idea of spending made her feel guilty, as though her mother could hear, now, what was going on inside her head, just as, in life, she had known her thoughts from the expression on her face.

She had reached the steps leading up from the beach. It was almost dark.

She shivered, then, in a moment of fear and bewilderment at her new freedom, for there was nothing she had to do, she could please herself about everything, anything, and this she could not get used to. Perhaps she ought not to stay here, perhaps she could try and sell the house, which was really far too big for her, perhaps she ought to get a job and a small flat in London. London was the city of opportunity . . .

She felt flushed and a little drunk then, she felt that all things were possible, the future was in her power, and she wanted to shout and sing and dance, standing alone in the February twilight, looking at the deserted beach. All the houses along the seafront promenade had blank, black windows, for this was a summer place, in February it was only half alive.

She said, 'And that is what I have been. But I am fifty-one years old and look at the chances before me.'

Far out on the shingle bank the green warning light flashed on-on-off, on-on-off. It had been flashing the night of her mother's stroke, she had gone to the window and watched it and felt comforted at three a.m. in the aftermath of death. Now, the shock of that death came to her again like a hand slapped across her face, she thought, my mother is not here, my mother is in a box in the earth, and she began to shiver violently, her mind crawling with images of corruption, she started to walk very quickly along the promenade and up the hill towards home.

When she opened the front door she listened, and everything was quite silent, quite still. There had always been the voice from upstairs, 'Esme?' and each time she had wanted to say, 'Who else would it be?' and bitten back the words, only said, 'Hello, it's me.' Now, again, she called, 'It's me. Hello,' and her voice echoed softly up the dark stair well, when she heard it, it was a shock, for what kind of woman was it who talked to herself and was afraid of an empty house? What kind of woman?

She went quickly into the sitting-room and drew the curtains and then poured herself a small glass of sherry, the kind her mother had preferred. It was shock, of course, they had told her, all of them, her brother-in-law and her Uncle Cecil and cousin George Golightly, when they had come back for tea and ham sandwiches after the funeral.

'You will feel the real shock later. Shock is always delayed.' Because she had been so calm and self-possessed, she had made all the arrangements so neatly, they were very surprised.

'If you ever feel the need of company, Esme – and you will – of course you must come to us. Just a telephone call, that's all we need, just a little warning in advance. You are sure to feel strange.'

Strange. Yes. She sat by the electric fire. Well, the truth was she had got herself thoroughly chilled, walking on the beach like that, so late in the afternoon. It had been her own fault.

After a while, the silence of the house oppressed her, so that when she had taken a second glass of sherry and made herself a poached egg on toast, she turned on the television and watched a variety show, because it was something cheerful, and she needed taking out of herself. There would be time enough for the educational programmes when she was used to this new life. But a thought went through her head, backwards and forwards, backwards and forwards, it was as though she were reading from a tape.

'She is upstairs. She is still in her room. If you go upstairs you will see her. Your mother.' The words danced across the television screen, intermingling with the limbs of dancers, issuing like spume out of the mouths of comedians and crooners, they took on the rhythm of the drums

252

and the double basses.

'Upstairs. In her room. Upstairs. In her room.

Your mother. Your mother. Your mother.

Upstairs . . .'

She jabbed at the push button on top of the set and the picture shrank and died, there was silence, and then she heard her own heart beating and the breath coming out of her in little gasps. She scolded herself for being morbid, neurotic. Very well then, she said, go upstairs and see for yourself.

Very deliberately and calmly she went out of the room and climbed the stairs, and went into her mother's bedroom. The light from the street lamp immediately outside the window shone a pale triangle of light down onto the white runner on the dressing table, the white lining of the curtains and the smooth white cover of the bed. Everything had gone. Her mother might never have been here. Esme had been very anxious not to hoard reminders and so, the very day after the funeral, she had cleared out and packed up clothes, linen, medicine, papers, spectacles, she had ruthlessly emptied the room of her mother.

Now, standing in the doorway, smelling lavender polish and dust, she felt ashamed, as though she wanted to be rid of all memory, as though she had wanted her mother to die. She said, but that is what I did want, to be rid of the person who bound me to her for fifty years. She spoke aloud into the bedroom, 'I wanted you dead.' She felt her hands trembling and held them tightly together, she thought, I am a wicked woman. But the sherry she had drunk began to have some effect now, her heart was beating more quietly, and she was able to walk out into the room and draw the curtains, even though it was now unnecessary to scold herself for being so hysterical.

In the living room, she sat beside the fire reading a historical biography until eleven o'clock – when her mother was alive she had always been in bed by ten – and the fears had quite left her, she felt entirely calm. She thought, it is only natural, you have had a shock, you are bound to be affected. That night she slept extremely well.

When she answered the front doorbell at eleven fifteen the following morning and found Mr Amos Curry, hat in hand, upon the step, inquiring about a room, she remembered a remark her Uncle Cecil had made to her on the day of the funeral. 'You will surely not want to be here all on your own, Esme, in this great house. You should take a lodger.'

253

Mr Amos Curry rubbed his left eyebrow with a nervous finger, a gesture of his because he was habitually shy. 'A room to let,' he said, and she noticed that he wore gold cuff links and very well-polished shoes. 'I understand from the agency . . . a room to let with breakfast.'

'I know nothing of any agency. I think you have the wrong address.'

He took out a small loose-leaf notebook. 'Number 23, Park Close.'

'Oh no, I'm so sorry, we are . . .' she corrected herself, 'I am twenty-three Park *Walk*.'

A flush of embarrassment began to seep up over his face and neck like an ink stain, he loosened his collar a little until she felt quite sorry for him, quite upset.

'An easy mistake, a perfectly understandable mistake. Mr . . . Please do not feel at all . . .'

'. . . Curry. Amos Curry.'

'. . . embarrassed.'

'I am looking for a quiet room with breakfast. It seemed so hopeful. Park Close. Such a comfortable address.'

She thought, he is a very clean man, very neat and spruce, he has a gold incisor tooth and he wears gloves. Her mother had always approved of men who wore gloves. 'So few do, nowadays. Gloves and hats. It is easy to pick out a gentleman.'

Mr Curry also wore a hat.

'I do apologize, Madam, I feel so . . I would not have troubled . . .'

'No . . . no, please . . .'

'I must look for Park Close, Number 23.'

'It is just around the bend, to the left, a few hundred yards. A very secluded road.'

'Like this. This road is secluded. I thought as I approached this house, how suitable, I should . . . I feel one can tell, a house has a certain . . . But I am so sorry.'

He settled his hat upon his neat grey hair, and then raised it again politely, turning away.

She took in a quick breath. She said, 'What exactly . . . that is to say, if you are looking for a room with breakfast, I wonder if I . . .'

Mr Amos Curry turned back.

He held a small pickled onion delicately on the end of his fork. 'There is,' he said, 'the question of my equipment.'

Esme Fanshaw heard his voice as though it issued from the wireless –

there was a distortion about it, a curious echo. She shook her head. He is not real, she thought . . . But he was here, Mr Amos Curry, in a navy-blue pin stripe suit and with a small neat darn just below his shirt collar. He was sitting at her kitchen table – for she had hesitated to ask him into the dining room, which in any case was rarely used, the kitchen had seemed a proper compromise. He was here. She had made a pot of coffee, and then, after an hour, a cold snack of beef and pickles, bread and butter, her hands were a little moist with excitement. She thought again how rash she had been, she said, he is a total stranger, someone from the street, a casual caller, I know nothing at all about him. But she recognized the voice of her mother, then, and rebelled against it. Besides, it was not true, for Mr Curry had told her a great deal. She thought, this is how life should be, I should be daring, I should allow myself to be constantly surprised. Each day I should be ready for some new encounter. That is how to stay young. She was most anxious to stay young.

In his youth, Mr Curry had been abroad a great deal, had lived, he said, in Ceylon, Singapore and India. 'I always keep an open mind, Miss Fanshaw, I believe in the principle of tolerance, live and let live. Nation shall speak peace unto nation.'

'Oh, I do agree.'

'I have seen the world and its ways. I have no prejudices. The customs of others may be quite different from our own but human beings are human beings the world over. We learn from one another every day. By keeping an open mind, Miss Fanshaw.'

'Oh yes.'

'You have travelled?'

'I – I have visited Europe. Not too far afield, I'm afraid.'

'I have journeyed on foot through most of the European countries, I have earned my passage at all times.'

She did not like to ask how, but she was impressed, having only been abroad once herself, to France.

Mr Curry had been an orphan, he said, life for him had begun in a children's home. 'But it was a more than adequate start, Miss Fanshaw, we were all happy together. I do not think memory deceives me. We were one big family. Never let it be said that the Society did not do its best by me. I see how lucky I am. Well, you have only to look about you, Miss Fanshaw – how many people do you see from broken families, unhappy homes? I know nothing of that: I count myself fortunate. I like to think I have made the best of my circumstances.'

255

His education, he said, had been rather elementary, he had a good brain which had never been taxed to the full.

'Untapped resources,' he said, pointing to his forehead.

They talked so easily, she thought she had never found conversation flowing along with any other stranger, any other man. Mr Curry had exactly the right amount of formal politeness, mixed with informal ease, and she decided that he was destined to live here, he had style and he seemed so much at home.

He had an ordinary face, for which she was grateful, but there was something slightly unreal about it, as though she were seeing it on a cinema screen. All the same, it was very easy to picture him sitting in this kitchen, eating breakfast, before putting on his hat, which had a small feather in the band, each morning and going off to work.

'I do have some rather bulky equipment.'

'What exactly. . . .'

'I have two jobs, Miss Fanshaw, two strings to my bow, as it were. That surprises you? But I have always been anxious to fill up every hour of the day, I have boundless energy.'

She noticed that he had some tufts of pepper coloured hair sprouting from his ears and nostrils and wondered if, when he visited the barber for a haircut, he also had these trimmed. She knew nothing about the habits of men.

'Of course, it is to some extent seasonal work.'

'Seasonal?'

'Yes. For those odd wet and windy days which always come upon us at the English seaside, and of course during the winter, I travel in cleaning utensils.'

He looked around him quickly, as though to see where she kept her polish and dusters and brooms, to make note of any requirements.

'Perhaps you would require some extra storage space? Other than the room itself.'

Mr Curry got up from the table and began to clear away dishes, she watched him in astonishment. The man on the doorstep with a note of the wrong address had become the luncheon visitor, the friend who helped with the washing up.

'There is quite a large loft.'

'Inaccessible.'

'Oh.'

'And I do have to be a little careful. No strain on the back. Not that I

256

am a sick man, Miss Fanshaw, I hasten to reassure you, you will not have an invalid on your hands. Oh no. I am extremely healthy for my age. It is because I lead such an active life.'

She thought of him, knocking upon all the doors, walking back down so many front paths. Though this was not what he did in the summer.

'Sound in wind and limb, as you might say.'

She thought of racehorses, and tried to decide whether he had ever been married. She said, 'Or else, perhaps, the large cupboard under the stairs, where the gas meter . . .'

'Perfect.'

He poured just the right amount of washing up liquid into the bowl; his sleeves were already unbuttoned and rolled up to the elbows, his jacket hung on the hook behind the back door. She saw the hairs lying like thatch on his sinewy arms, and a dozen questions sprang up into her mind, then, for although he seemed to have told her a great deal about himself, there were many gaps.

He had visited the town previously, he told her, in the course of his work, and fell for it. 'I never forgot it, Miss Fanshaw. I should be very happy here, I told myself. It is my kind of place. Do you see?'

'And so you came back.'

'Certainly. I know when I am meant to do something. I never ignore that feeling. I was intended to return here.'

'It is rather a small town.'

'But select.'

'I was only wondering – we do have a very short season, really only July and August. . .'

'Yes?'

'Perhaps it would not be suitable for your – er – summer work?'

'Oh, I think it would, Miss Fanshaw, I think so, I size these things up rather carefully, you know, rather carefully.'

She did not question him further, only said, 'Well, it is winter now.'

'Indeed. I shall, to coin a phrase, be plying my other trade. In a town like this, full of ladies such as yourself, in nice houses with comfortable circumstances, the possibilities are endless, endless.'

'For – er – cleaning materials?'

'Quite so.'

'I do see that.'

'Now you take a pride, don't you? Anyone can see that for himself.'

He waved a hand around the small kitchen, scattering little drops of foamy water, and she saw the room through his eyes, the clean windows, the shining taps, the immaculate sinks. Yes, she took a pride, that was true. Her mother had insisted upon it. Now, she heard herself saying, 'My mother died only a fortnight ago,' forgetting that she had told him already and the shock of the fact overcame her again, she could not believe in the empty room, which she was planning to give to Mr Curry, and her eyes filled up with tears of guilt. And what would her mother have said about a strange man washing up in their kitchen, about this new, daring friendship.

'You should have consulted me, Esme, you take far too much on trust. You never think. You should have consulted me.'

Two days after her mother's funeral, Mrs Bickerdike, from The Lilacs, had met her in the pharmacy, and mentioned, in lowered voice, that she 'did work for the bereaved', which, Esme gathered, meant that she conducted seances. She implied that contact might be established with the deceased Mrs Fanshaw. Esme had been shocked, most of all by the thought of that contact, and a continuing relationship with her mother, though she had only said that she believed in letting the dead have their rest. 'I think, if you will forgive me, and with respect, that we are not meant to inquire about them, or to follow them on.'

Now, she heard her mother talking about Mr Curry. 'You should always take particular notice of the eyes, Esme, never trust anyone with eyes set too closely together.'

She tried to see his eyes, but he was turned sideways to her.

'Or else too widely apart. That indicates idleness.'

She was ashamed of what she had just said about her mother's recent death, for she did not at all wish to embarrass him, or to appear hysterical. Mr Curry had finished washing up and was resting his reddened wet hands upon the rim of the sink. When he spoke, his voice was a little changed and rather solemn. 'I do not believe in shutting away the dead, Miss Fanshaw, I believe in the sacredness of memory. I am only glad that you feel able to talk to me about the good lady.'

She felt suddenly glad to have him here in the kitchen, for his presence took the edge off the emptiness and silence which lately had seemed to fill up every corner of the house.

She said, 'It was not always easy. . . . My mother was a very . . . forthright woman.'

'Say no more. I understand only too well. The older generation believed in speaking their minds.'

She thought, he is obviously a very sensitive man, he can read between the lines: and she wanted to laugh with relief, for there was no need to go into details about how dominating her mother had been and how taxing were the last years of her illness – he knew, he understood.

Mr Curry dried his hands, smoothing the towel down one finger at a time, as though he were drawing on gloves. He rolled down his shirt-sleeves and fastened them and put on his jacket. His movements were neat and deliberate. He coughed. 'Regarding the room – there is just the question of payment, Miss Fanshaw, I believe in having these matters out at once. There is nothing to be embarrassed about in speaking of money, I hope you agree.'

'Oh no, certainly, I . . .'

'Shall we say four pounds a week?'

Her head swam. She had no idea at all how much a lodger should pay, how much his breakfasts would cost, and she was anxious to be both business-like and fair. Well, he had suggested what seemed to him a most suitable sum, he was more experienced in these matters than herself.

'For the time being I am staying at a commercial guest house in Cedars Road. I have only linoleum covering the floor of my room, there is nothing cooked at breakfast. I am not accustomed to luxury, Miss Fanshaw, you will understand that from what I have told you of my life, but I think I am entitled to comfort at the end of the working day.'

'Oh, you will be more than comfortable here, I shall see to that, I shall do my very best. I feel . . .'

'Yes?'

She was suddenly nervous of how she appeared in his eyes.

'I do feel that the mistake you made in the address was somehow . . .'

'Fortuitous.'

'Yes, oh yes.'

Mr Curry gave a little bow.

'When would you wish to move in, Mr Curry? There are one or two things . . .'

'Tomorrow evening, say?'

'Tomorrow is Friday.'

'Perhaps that is inconvenient.'

'No . . . no . . . certainly. . . our week could begin on a Friday, as it were.'

'I shall greatly look forward to having you as a landlady, Miss Fanshaw.'

Landlady. She wanted to say, 'I hope I shall be a friend, Mr Curry,' but it sounded presumptuous.

259

When he had gone she made herself a pot of tea, and sat quietly at the kitchen table, a little dazed. She thought, this is a new phase of my life. But she was still a little alarmed. She had acted out of character and against what she would normally have called her better judgement. Her mother would have warned her against inviting strangers into the house, just as, when she was a child, she had warned her about speaking to them in the street. 'You can never be sure, Esme, there are some very peculiar people about.' For she was a great reader of the crime reports in her newspapers, and of books about famous trials. The life of Doctor Crippen had particularly impressed her.

Esme shook her head. Now, all the plans she had made for selling the house and moving to London and going abroad were necessarily curtailed, and for the moment she felt depressed, as though the old life were going to continue, and she wondered, too, what neighbours and friends might say, and whether anyone had seen Mr Curry standing on her doorstep, paper in hand, whether, when he went from house to house selling cleaning utensils, they would recognize him as Miss Fanshaw's lodger and disapprove. There was no doubt that her mother would have disapproved, and not only because he was a 'stranger off the streets'.

'He is a salesman, Esme, a doorstep pedlar, and you do not *know* what his employment in the summer months may turn out to be.'

'He has impeccable manners, mother, quite old-fashioned ones, and a most genteel way of speaking.' She remembered the gloves and the raised hat, the little bow, and also the way he had quietly and confidently done the washing up, as though he were already living here.

'How do you know where things will lead, Esme?'

'I am prepared to take a risk. I have taken too few risks in my life so far.'

She saw her mother purse her lips and fold her hands together, refusing to argue further, only certain that she was in the right. Well, it was her own life now, and she was mistress of it, she would follow her instincts for once. And she went and got a sheet of paper, on which to write a list of things that were needed to make her mother's old bedroom quite comfortable for him. After that, she would buy cereal and bacon and kidneys for the week's breakfasts.

She was surprised at how little time it took for her to grow quite accustomed to having Mr Curry in the house. It helped, of course, that he was a man of very regular habits and neat, too, when she had first gone into his room to clean it, she could have believed that no one was using it at all. The bed was neatly made, clothes hung out of sight in drawers – he had locked the wardrobe, she discovered, and taken away the key. Only two pairs of shoes side by side, below the washbasin, and a shaving brush and razor on the shelf above it, gave the lodger away.

Mr Curry got up promptly at eight – she heard his alarm clock and then the pips of the radio news. At eight twenty he came down to the kitchen for his breakfast, smelling of shaving soap and shoe polish. Always, he said, 'Ah, good morning, Miss Fanshaw, good morning to you,' and then commented briefly upon the weather. It was 'a bit nippy' or 'a touch of sunshine, I see' or 'bleak'. He ate a cooked breakfast, followed by toast and two cups of strong tea.

Esme took a pride in her breakfasts, in the neat way she laid the table and the freshness of the cloth, she warmed his plate under the grill and waited until the last minute before doing the toast so that it should still be crisp and hot. She thought, it is a very bad thing for a woman such as myself to live alone and become entirely selfish. I am the sort of person who needs to give service.

At ten minutes to nine, Mr Curry got his suitcase from the downstairs cupboard, wished her good morning again, and left the house. After that she was free for the rest of the day, to live as she had always lived, or else to make changes – though much of her time was taken up with cleaning the house and especially Mr Curry's room, and shopping for something unusual for Mr Curry's breakfasts.

She had hoped to enrol for lampshade-making classes at the evening institute but it was too late for that year, they had told her she must apply again after the summer, so she borrowed a book upon the subject from the public library and bought frames and card and fringing, and taught herself. She went to one or two bring-and-buy sales and planned to hold a coffee morning and do a little voluntary work for old people. Her life was full. She enjoyed having Mr Curry in the house. Easter came, and she began to wonder when he would change to his summer work, and what that work might be. He never spoke of it.

To begin with he had come in between five thirty and six every evening, and gone straight to his room. Sometimes he went out again for an hour, she presumed to buy a meal somewhere and perhaps drink a glass of beer, but more often he stayed in, and Esme did not see him again until the following morning. Once or twice she heard music coming from his room – presumably from the radio, and she thought how nice it was to hear that the house was alive, a home for someone else.

261

One Friday evening, Mr Curry came down into the kitchen to give her the four pounds rent, just as she was serving up lamb casserole, and when she invited him to stay and share it with her, he accepted so quickly that she felt guilty, for perhaps, he went without an evening meal altogether. She decided to offer him the use of the kitchen, when a moment should arise which seemed suitable.

But a moment did not arise. Instead, Mr Curry came down two or three evenings a week and shared her meal, she got used to shopping for two, and when he offered her an extra pound a week, she accepted, it was so nice to have company, though she felt a little daring, a little carefree. She heard her mother telling her that the meals cost more than a pound a week. 'Well, I do not mind, they give me pleasure, it is worth it for that.'

One evening, Mr Curry asked her if she were good at figures, and when she told him that she had studied book-keeping, asked her help with the accounts for the kitchen utensil customers. After that, two or three times a month, she helped him regularly, they set up a temporary office on the dining-room table, and she remembered how good she had been at this kind of work, she began to feel useful, to enjoy herself.

He said, 'Well, it will not be for much longer, Miss Fanshaw, the summer is almost upon us, and in the summer, of course, I am self-employed.'

But when she opened her mouth to question him more closely, he changed the subject. Nor did she like to inquire whether the firm who supplied him with the cleaning utensils to sell, objected to the dearth of summer orders.

Mr Curry was an avid reader, 'in the winter', he said, when he had the time. He read not novels or biographies or war memoirs, but his encyclopedia, of which he had a handsome set, bound in cream mock-leather and paid for by monthly instalments. In the evenings, he took to bringing a volume down to the sitting-room, at her invitation, and keeping her company, she grew used to the sight of him in the opposite armchair. From time to time he would read out to her some curious or entertaining piece of information. His mind soaked up everything, but particularly of a zoological, geographical or anthropological nature, he said that he never forgot a fact, and that you never knew when something might prove of use. And Esme Fanshaw listened, her hands deftly fringing a lampshade – it was a skill she had acquired easily – and continued her education.

'One is never too old to learn, Mr Curry.'

'How splendid that we are of like mind! How nice!'

She thought, yes, it is nice, as she was washing up the dishes the next morning, and she flushed a little with pleasure and a curious kind of excitement. She wished that she had some woman friend whom she could telephone and invite round for coffee, in order to say, 'How nice it is to have a man about the house, really, I had no idea what a difference it could make.' But she had no close friends, she and her mother had always kept themselves to themselves. She would have said, 'I feel younger, and it is all thanks to Mr Curry. I see now that I was only half-alive.'

Then, it was summer. Mr Curry was out until half past nine or ten o'clock at night, the suitcase full of brooms and brushes and polish was put away under the stairs and he had changed his clothing. He wore a cream linen jacket and a straw hat with a black band, a rose or carnation in his button hole. He looked very dapper, very smart, and she had no idea at all what work he was doing. Each morning he left the house carrying a black case, quite large and square. She thought, I shall follow him. But she did not do so. Then, one evening in July, she decided to explore, to discover what she could from other people in the town, for someone must know Mr Curry, he was a distinctive sight, now, in the fresh summer clothes. She had, at the back of her mind, some idea that he might be a beach photographer.

She herself put on a quite different outfit – a white piqué dress she had bought fifteen years ago, but which still not only fitted, but suited her, and a straw boater, edged with ribbon, not unlike Mr Curry's own hat. When she went smartly down the front path, she hardly dared to look about her, certain that she was observed and spoken about by the neighbours. For it was well known now that Miss Fanshaw had a lodger.

She almost never went on to the promenade in the summer. She had told Mr Curry so. 'I keep to the residential streets, to the shops near home, I do so dislike the summer crowds.' And besides, her mother had impressed on her that the summer visitors were 'quite common'. But tonight walking along in the warm evening air, smelling the sea, she felt ashamed of that opinion, she would not like anyone to think that she had been brought up a snob – live and let live, as Mr Curry would tell her. And the people sitting in the deckchairs and walking in couples along the seafront looked perfectly nice, perfectly respectable, there were a number of older women and families with well-behaved children, this was a small, select resort, and charabancs were discouraged.

But Mr Curry was not to be seen. There were no beach photographers. She walked quite slowly along the promenade, looking all about her. There was a pool, in which children could sail boats, beside the War Memorial, and a putting green alongside the gardens of the Raincliffe Hotel. Really, she thought, I should come out more often, really it is very pleasant here in the summer, I have been missing a good deal.

When she reached the putting green she paused, not wanting to go back, for her sitting-room was rather dark, and she had no real inclination to make lampshades in the middle of July. She was going to sit down, next to an elderly couple on one of the green benches, she was going to enjoy the balm of the evening. Then, she heard music. After a moment, she recognized it. The tune had come quite often through the closed door of Mr Curry's bedroom.

And there, on a corner opposite the hotel, and the putting green, she saw Mr Curry. The black case contained a portable gramophone, the old-fashioned kind, with a horn, and this was set on the pavement. Beside it was Mr Curry, straw hat tipped a little to one side, cane beneath his arm, buttonhole in place. He was singing, in a tuneful, but rather cracked voice, and doing an elaborate little tap dance on the spot, his rather small feet moving swiftly and daintily in time with the music.

Esme Fanshaw put her hand to her face, feeling herself flush, and wishing to conceal herself from him: she turned her head away and looked out to sea, her ears full of the sentimental music. But Mr Curry was paying attention only to the small crowd which had gathered about him. One or two passers by, on the opposite side of the road, crossed over to watch, as Mr Curry danced, a fixed smile on his elderly face. At his feet was an upturned bowler hat, into which people dropped coins, and when the record ended, he bent down, turned it over neatly, and began to dance again. At the end of the second tune, he packed the gramophone up and moved on, farther down the promenade, to begin his performance all over again.

She sat on the green bench feeling a little faint and giddy, her heart pounding. She thought of her mother, and what she would have said, she thought of how foolish she had been made to look, for surely someone knew, surely half the town had seen Mr Curry? The strains of his music drifted up the promenade on the evening air. It was almost dark now, the sea was creeping back up the shingle.

She thought of going home, of turning the contents of Mr Curry's room out onto the pavement and locking the front door, she thought of calling the police, or her Uncle Cecil, of going to a neighbour. She had been humiliated, taken in, disgraced, and almost wept for the shame of it.

And then, presently, she wondered what it was she had meant by 'shame'. Mr Curry was not dishonest. He had not told her what he did in the summer months, he had not lied. Perhaps he had simply kept it from her because she might disapprove. It was his own business. And certainly there was no doubt at all that in the winter months he sold cleaning utensils from door to door. He paid his rent. He was neat and tidy and a pleasant companion. What was there to fear?

All at once, then, she felt sorry for him, and at the same time, he became a romantic figure in her eyes, for he had danced well and his singing had not been without a certain style, perhaps he had a fascinating past as a music hall performer, and who was she, Esme Fanshaw, to despise him, what talent had she? Did she earn her living by giving entertainment to others?

'I told you so, Esme. What did I tell you?'

'Told me what, mother? What is it you have to say to me? Why do you not leave me alone?'

Her mother was silent.

Quietly then, she picked up her handbag and left the green bench and the promenade and walked up through the dark residential streets, past the gardens sweet with stocks and roses, past open windows, towards Park Walk, and when she reached her own house, she put away the straw hat, though she kept on the dress of white piqué, because it was such a warm night. She went down into the kitchen and made coffee and set it, with a plate of sandwiches and a plate of biscuits, on a tray, and presently Mr Curry came in, and she called out to him, she said, 'Do come and have a little snack with me, I am quite sure you can do with it, I'm quite sure you are tired.'

And she saw from his face that he knew that she knew.

But nothing was said that evening, or until some weeks later, when Mr Curry was sitting opposite her, on a cold, windy August night, reading from the volume COW to DIN. Esme Fanshaw said, looking at him, 'My mother used to say, Mr Curry, 'I always like a bit of singing and dancing, some variety. It takes you out of yourself, singing and dancing.'

Mr Curry gave a little bow.

* * * * *

The Sexton's Wife

MARGERY ALLINGHAM

'They say it's unlucky to marry for love,' said the old woman, peering across the rag hearthrug to where I sat in the shadow. 'But I don't know. I often wonder how it would have been.'

'If you hadn't married for love?' I said.

Old Mrs Hartlebury shook her head and the firelight played over the wrinkles on her brown face.

'No,' she said. 'If I had.'

We were sitting in the downstairs room of her cottage, which stands midway between the church and the turning which leads through the Street to the Hard and the sea.

It was pouring, and I had dropped in to see her as I went back to the house after an expedition to the landing stage to get some fresh fish off the boats.

We had sat talking for some time while the room grew gradually darker. Now it was so dark that I could only catch a glimpse of the gold-spotted spaniels on the mantelshelf high above my head when an extra big flame spurted from the wood fire and lit up the small warm room for a second.

But it was still raining and I did not want to move. There was plenty of time to get back when it stopped, and I was drowsy and comfortable sitting there in the warm.

Mrs Hartlebury did not mind. She went on talking and sighing, hardly noticing me as I sat on the far side of the hearth, on a hassock borrowed from the church and with my back against the log heap which filled that corner of the room.

There was a long pause after her last remark. I did not speak. If she wanted to talk I was ready to listen; if she did not want to her business was not of any account to me. Like herself I had been bred on the Essex coast and we understood one another.

After a while I heard her stirring in her chair and I saw her eyes for a moment as they reflected the glow of the fire when she turned her head.

'Have you heard about Hartlebury, the way he died, or anything?' she asked suddenly.

'No,' I said not very truthfully.

I had heard something, of course, but then you hear something about the way everyone dies and I did not know if the gossip were true.

'He died the way he deserved to die,' she remarked, and although I could not see her face I knew it was unforgiving.

I made some non-committal sound and drowsed again.

'When I was a girl I was wonderful pretty,' she went on after a bit.

I could believe that, for she is a very fine looking old woman now and she is eighty-two years old.

'I had black hair,' she said proudly, 'and a skin you'll never see these days when girls get as many victuals as their fathers and brothers. That time there weren't much food about and men can't go fishin' hungry, so the women weren't overfed and I count that done 'un good. I had a sweetheart long before I was sixteen,' she added, and she spoke comfortably as though she was glad to think of it even after all this time.

'A fine boy he was,' she went on quickly. 'Seventeen or eighteen, with yellow hair and a soft sort of smile when he saw me coming down to the Hard to meet 'um.'

She paused and I saw her as she bent down to lift a stick on to the fire. For a moment she startled me. The shadows had crept into the hollows of her face and filled them, so that I suppose I saw her as she must have been when she stood on the Hard waiting for her sweetheart all that time ago.

When the flame died down she went on talking.

'We went about together, Will and me. Did I tell you his name? Will Linde. His father, Joe, had a smack, and they two went out together almost every day. We couldn't get married. Neither on us had enough to live on. So we went on sweethearting, years it was, until I was turned nineteen.

'He was true to me,' she said. 'All that time he was wasn't very old and I crossed him time and again, and I'd say things to hurt, the way girls do. Yet he'd never walk out with another girl, but would look at me puzzled and sort of wondering why I'd hurt him, so that I'd be ready to tear my tongue out rather than speak so again.'

She paused and I suppose I sighed, for she laughed and I could feel her grinning at me in the darkness.

'Ah, you're young,' she said. 'I'm old, and, though I ain't forgot, I'm

267

different.'

I did not say anything and presently she went on in a sing-song which was addressed more to herself than to me:

'I reckon I loved Will just as he loved me, and when it's like that you can't be much less than happy. We counted we should get married some day and we were content.'

She paused a moment and when she spoke again her voice was sharper.

'But when I was nineteen Hartlebury stepped across to see my father one day and told him and my mother that he was after me.'

She broke off and mumbled rather irritatingly, as very old people do, and I was sorry that I could not see her clearly as she sat huddled up in her chair.

Presently, when I had almost forgotten what she had been talking about, she went on with the story again.

'James Hartlebury was the carrier at that time, and he was sexton too, so he lived right over against the church where the Reading Room is now. Pretty little house he had, with a long path up to the door which had rosemary bushes all down the sides of it. I can't bear the smell of rosemary even now,' she put in suddenly, 'though many's the time I've washed my hair with it when I was a girl. It's a wonderful fine thing for black hair, is rosemary.'

She stopped talking and I kicked the fire to make it blaze.

Outside the rain was lashing against the house and I was glad to be indoors.

There was another long silence and I thought that perhaps she had gone to sleep, so I did not move lest I should wake her. But she was just thinking, for suddenly she went on again as though there had been no lull.

'No one knew much about James,' she said. 'There were one or two who called him Jim, but not many. I never did, not even after I married him. It wouldn't have been right somehow.

'He was a queer man. No one knew much about him. He kept himself alone among them all, yet he wasn't surly or proud. He'd take his drink at The Starlings with anyone. He went to church twice a Sunday, and people said he was rich. Yet he wasn't liked. He might almost have been one of the gentry, the way that no one spoke or stopped him when he came down the Street.

'My father was pleased right through when he came to our house that day. He didn't like him much, but he thought like everyone else did what

268

a fine thing it was for me to get a husband who was carrier and sexton too.'

Once again she stopped, and then talked on much more briskly, as though she were coming to a part of the story which she did not enjoy remembering.

'Well, I married 'um,' she said. 'I don't know why, save that I counted it was time that I got married and I couldn't see that Will would ever be able to keep us both. And besides – ' she hesitated, '– besides, I was taken by James at that time.'

She hurried on; she felt no doubt she ought to excuse herself.

'He hadn't never been after a girl before. There was a kind of mystery about him. It wasn't his money – for all anybody said, it wasn't his money. It was the honour of it. I was the only girl he ever went for. He was nearing forty, too, mind you. He wasn't a lad, and that pleased me.

'Besides,' she added, half laughing, as though she were remembering something after a long time, 'he had a sad, quiet way with him, as though he had some secret. I was sorry for him, all alone in the little house.'

It was eerie sitting there in the dark, listening to her droning voice talking of things that had happened so long ago. I made myself more comfortable against the logs.

'Life seems as though it's going on for ever when you're young, and almost any change looks good,' she remarked. 'I had a fine wedding. James being the sexton and to do with the church knew how a wedding should be.

'I had a fine wedding.' She repeated it softly. 'There were as many people outside the church as if it had been a gentry wedding. You see, everyone knew James and nobody liked him; and, too, they guessed the boy'd be there and they came to watch us.'

I nodded. People did not seem to have changed very much.

'James was always kind to me,' she remarked suddenly. 'That day in the church and before I couldn't have wished him better. But I was scared of him.

'No,' she corrected herself abruptly, 'I wasn't scared of him then. That came later. At the wedding I was shy of him, shy and a bit proud.'

'You would be,' I said feeling that it was about time I made some remark.

She sniffed. 'Ah,' she agreed. 'It was natural. Will did come to the church,' she continued, 'and at first I was afraid to look at him. But when we came out, and everyone was shouting and laughing and cheering us, I

269

heard him louder than the others and I looked round and saw him staring straight at me and waving and shouting with the rest. I knew he meant to be laughing at me, so I looked at his eyes and he laughed louder and cheered louder. But I'd seen, and he knew I'd seen.'

She paused.

'I reckon I loved him,' she said and sighed, but she laughed afterwards and I remembered how terribly old she was.

'James took me down between the rosemary bushes to his house,' she went on, 'and I lived there after that. I didn't see Will, for I was never a bad girl, but I thought on him. I had plenty o' time for thinking,' she added dryly. 'James wouldn't let me out of the house, and I didn't see my mother more than five or six times all that winter.'

Her voice died away, and when she spoke again there was something about her tone which gave me my first feeling of uneasiness. She was certainly not trying to frighten me, but some of her remembered terror crept into her voice and I could hardly help but recognise it.

'It was then,' she said, 'that I began to notice James. He was so quiet. He'd sit whole evenings puzzling over figures and writing letters and never saying a word. And sometimes he'd get up in the night and go out, leaving me asleep. Just the same as he was to everyone in the village, so he was to me his wife; quiet and telling nothing. I was young,' she said, nodding at me, 'and I was used to being with people, but he wouldn't let me out of his sight a minute if he could help it. And when on Tuesdays and Saturday he went off in his cart, carrying, he'd give me so much to do that I couldn't leave the house. And when he came back he'd make me go through everything I'd done, if I'd seen anyone I had to tell him everything they'd said to me and everything I'd said back to them.

'And when I'd told him he'd put his hands on my shoulders and look at me with those dull eyes of his and say "Is that true?" And I'd say "Of course. Why should I lie to you?"

'Then he'd kiss me again and again, but he'd never tell me anything.'

A great squall of wind rattled the shutters and one or two raindrops fell down the chimney and the fire hissed.

'I soon found out I didn't love him,' she went on, glancing at me. 'But I made up my mind to that. I wasn't no fool. But, by and by, as the winter went on and I worked about the house, not seeing anyone but him from Sunday to Sunday, I began to watch him, and the more I watched him the more frightened I grew.

'He was queer,' she said, 'especially just after there'd been a burying. It was terrible cold that winter and there wasn't much food for them. There was several died.'

She lowered her voice and I, who am not very imaginative, began to feel uncomfortable.

'While James was at work on a grave he'd be more talkative and not so sad,' she went on, 'and then, after it was all done, he'd take to his going out at nights again. I'd lie awake wondering what had taken him out, and guessing and guessing aright, and yet not believing it.'

I moved closer to the old woman and I felt her small hard brown hand on my shoulder.

'At those times he wouldn't let me load the cart for him, as I usually did,' she whispered, 'but would keep me indoors while he did it himself. I grew more and more frightened, for I wasn't very old.'

I shivered. There was something gruesome in her suggestion and I was glad of the roaring fire.

'Soon after that,' she said, 'my mother came round to see me, and all the time she was with me he never left us alone. She was a cheerful body and she talked and told me what they were saying in the village: how the Playles – a wild lot, they were, who lived down by the Hard – had begun their smuggling tricks again, though one of 'em had got shot for it less than two years before.

'Then she told me that an old woman called Mrs Finch, who lived round the back of the church, was putting it about that she'd seen a ghost-light in the graveyard the night after young Nell Wooton was buried.

'I knew James had been out that night and as my mother was speaking I looked across at him, and I'll never forget his face.'

Mrs Hartlebury stopped and I realised suddenly that she was looking behind her. I stirred up the fire and moved closer to it, and she went on.

'When my mother had gone James sat indoors doing nothing, looking out of the window, and for a month after that he never went out at night.

'Then I began to think of Will again. I knew it wasn't right, but as the spring came round again and I could get out into the garden I used to find myself standing at the gate looking down the road and hoping maybe that I'd see him.

'I didn't want to talk to him. I only wanted just to see him again. I reckon James knew that, for he used to call me into the house and keep me busy there. Sometimes he used to make love to me, in his own way, and he'd bring me presents from the town. But I knew how he got his money, though I wouldn't think of it. I knew what he was and I was frightened out of my life.'

I had guessed what he was too, and I mentioned the ugly word to the old woman.

'Yes,' she said, 'that's what he was. Resurrection men they called them then. An awful thing for a young wife to find. He'd sell the bodies in the town to men who'd sell them to the doctors. But mind you, I didn't know that then as clear as I do now. If I had, I'd have run home and let the village say what it would. As it was, I was frightened enough although I'd only half guessed what he was. But I stayed with 'un.' She nodded her head. 'Yes, I stayed with 'un.

'And then one day,' she said in an entirely new voice, 'when I was cutting rosemary to put with the little linen I had, I heard someone going by in the road. I looked up and saw Will, as I had always known I should see him, swinging past with an eel fork and splashers on his shoulder. He didn't look at me and I couldn't help it, I called to him, and he turned and smiled at me and said "What cheer, Sis?" – they called me that then.

'I went down to the gate and we stood there talking. He stared in my face and of course I didn't look what I had been. How could I after a whole winter shut up in a little house?

'Presently he said "Are you all right, Sis?"

'I don't know what I said. Maybe I didn't speak. But anyway, he leaned over the gate and said, "Why, girl, I don't blame ye, I don't blame ye," kindly, just like that.

'When he had gone, and he didn't stay long, I turned round and saw James watching me through the window, and when I went in he stared at me angrily. He didn't say anything, but from that day he never left me alone if he could possibly help it, and Will didn't come again.'

The rain had stopped outside and the fire was dying, so I made it up. I moved quietly, though, and I did not disturb her thoughts and presently she went on with the story.

'Then for a long time no one died, so there were no buryings, and James used to come home from the town sullen, and drunk too sometimes. Then he began to talk in his sleep, saying terrible things, and I used to lie there trembling, staring up at the thatch, trying not to listen and wondering what I would do.

'Then one night –' her voice sank so low that I had to strain to hear her '– he came in quite different. He kissed me and started talking about the town and the folk he had seen, and making me laugh until I could hardly breathe.

'And the next morning this new way of his was still there. He seemed pleased about something, for I saw him smiling to himself when he thought I wasn't near.

'I thought perhaps I had been mistaken about him, but a week after that I woke in the night and I heard horses galloping past the house down the road to the Hard.

'I called to James, but he was awake already.

'"What would that be?'" I said.

'"Nothing," said he. "You go to sleep, girl." But I lay still, thinking for a while, and then I knew what it was.

'"God Almighty, the Excise Men!" I said. "Was there anything doing tonight at the Hard?"

'James didn't speak at first and then he said "How would I know?", but I heard him laughing to himself in the dark and I lay shivering beside him, wondering what he knew. I was more frightened of him than ever after that.'

Her voice died away again and I resettled myself against the log pile, after edging my way across the hearth.

'I heard all about it the next morning,' she said. 'My sister came up and told me soon after daylight. A fine morning it was, I remember; clear and hard, the sea a dull green and not very rough. Everywhere smelt fresh and clean. I'll never forget the rosemary. The whole house was sick and faint with it. It was quiet, too, like a Sunday.

'Cuddy came up the path as I was giving James his breakfast. She sat down with us, but she never ate, so busy was she telling us.

'I knew before she told us just how it had been: the Excise Men coming on the Playles and holding them up, and they – a wild lot they were – telling them to shoot and be damned to them, and the riders not shooting at first, but, when the boys took to their horses in the dark, letting loose and chasing after them all along the Winstree Road.

'Cuddy told it well and James listened to her every word, for she was talking more to him than to me. Women liked James for his very quietness and the way he never cared for them.

'Long before she had told all he said so carelessly that I knew he was play-acting, "Was there anyone killed?"

'"One," she said, and I caught her looking at me as though she was watching for something.

'"Did the others get away?" said James.

'"They did," she said. "But they think they've been seen, and they've

273

gone out fishing for a bit till we see if anything more happens."

"'Did the Excise Men get the contraband?" said James.

"'Yes," she said.

"'Then you'll not hear any more of them," said he, and he laughed.

'She smiled at him and then she said "It'll teach they Playles a lesson, but it's bad for 'un who's killed." And she peeked at me again.

"'Who's he?" said James, and he looked at me and not at her as an ordinary man would have been sure to do.

"'Haven't I told you?" said Cuddy, though she knew as well as anyone that she hadn't spoken his name "It was Will Lintle. He was out with the Playles and they got him first shot."

'She didn't say any more and they two just sat and peeked at me under their eyelashes, making believe they weren't looking. But I knew they were watching and so I didn't say anything, or look anything, for I was getting used to play-acting by that time, having lived with James so long.

'By and by Cuddy got up and said she was going back home, and I thought she looked at me angrily, as though I'd cheated her of something. I had cheated her, I expect.

'When she had gone I peeked at James the same as they two had peeked at me, and I saw he was laughing to himself.'

She leant forward as she spoke and I saw that even now she was angry with him for that.

'I could have killed 'um,' she said. 'I could have killed 'um, but I didn't say a word. I cleared away the breakfast and I washed the dishes, while he sat there laughing quietly to himself in the doorway. He just sat there mending a bit of harness and laughing to himself.

'For a time I thought about Will and I couldn't believe him dead. Several times I wondered if I would run down home to find out if it were true, but every time I turned to the door, there was James in the way, still laughing to himself.

'And then I went upstairs to make the bed and I began to think clearly for the first time in my life.'

Old Mrs Hartlebury's voice grew harder and her chair creaked as she leant forward.

'I knew he'd informed,' she said. 'I stood by the window thinking, and all in one minute it came to me that Will was dead and that James was downstairs laughing. I hated him, but I daren't do anything.

'By and by I saw Joe Lintle coming up the path, and I heard him speaking to James through the window. I didn't listen, but I knew what he was asking, and I knew then that it was true. That was a long time ago and I was only a girl,' she said slowly. 'So when I came from the window I lay on my face on the bed and I cried as if Will had still been my sweetheart and I had not been married to James.'

She paused and I wondered if she really remembered how she felt, or if it was like a ghost of an emotion after all that time.

'He came up and found me, James did,' she said suddenly. 'I didn't move. I lay there on the old bed sobbing and crying like a child would. He didn't say anything. He just stood there in the doorway looking at me, and laughed, and I hated him.

'By and by he grew tired of standing and staring, so he went off, stamping downstairs and out of the house, still laughing to himself. I heard him all the way.

'I didn't go to the burying,' she went on. 'I sat upstairs by the window. Hidden behind the curtain, I watched the people go by. They all looked up at the house and nudged each other as they passed. I knew they were wondering would I go to the church or not.'

She laughed.

'I hated them. I could have leant from the window and shouted to them that I loved Will and that I didn't care who knew it, but I didn't do anything. I only stood there watching the church gate.

'I could see it from the window, just the gate and no more. I waited till they brought the coffin up the Street and took it into the church, four of them carrying it and the others following.

'I remember it seemed an awful thing to me at that time that he should be dead.'

She sank lower in her chair and the firelight shone on her twisted, capable hands where they lay crossed and quiet in her lap.

'I don't want to die, even now,' she said. 'But the thought of it doesn't make me sick, as it did then. It's horrible when you're young.

'When I saw that they'd all gone into the church and the Street was empty I came away from the window and went down the stairs to get some victuals ready for James, for he was always wonderful hungry after a burying. And as I set the table and drew the ale for him, I hated him worse than ever, I did.

'By and by he came in, and that was the second and last time I saw him really happy and content with himself. He sat down at the table and I waited on him. He was smiling all the time he ate, and when he had done he pushed his chair back and pulled me down on to his knee, and he held me there whilst he told me every bit about the burying. And he watched me all the time he told me.

'I couldn't bear to listen to him,' she said, 'but I was too frightened to break away. So there he held me, laughing in my face and searching for something in it that would show the way I felt.

'I didn't show anything for a while, but he went on so long. It was a deep grave, he said, and a well-dug one. There were plenty worms in it.

'I felt right faint as I thought about it and I nearly fell off his lap. He saw I was beginning to give way and he held me tight to him.

'"He'll rot soon," he said, "and good riddance. He was a thief and he died like a thief".'

Old Mrs Hartlebury stirred.

'Then I could stand no more,' she said. 'I was sick and wild with his tale of the burying. "You're an evil devil," I said, "and as a devil, so you'll die." I don't know why I said it, but I knew it was true as soon as I heard my own words. James wouldn't die in any usual way.

'I pulled away from him and began to clear away the dirty crocks. All the time I daren't look at him. I knew he was staring at me, but I was frightened to look behind.

'Then suddenly he banged his shut hand down upon the table, so that the ale jug toppled over and spilt. I stood where I was, holding a plate just off the table, looking down at it, too frightened to move.

'I heard him get up slowly and come round towards me. I knew he was angry, but still I didn't stir. He put his hand on me and it was shaking and so strong that it bruised my shoulder.

'Then he jerked me round before him and I had to look up at his face. He was terrible. His great dull eyes were dead, like a fish's. His lip was drawn up and I saw his gums, red above his yellow teeth. Then he shook me and called me terrible things, and spoke of Will in a way that made me sure of all I thought.'

Mrs Hartlebury laughed a little bitterly and I felt uncomfortable. She was a strange old woman.

'I did nothing,' she said. 'I was so frightened of him I couldn't even speak. Presently he beat me. I'd not been thrashed before, so I wasn't used to it. He half killed me.

'When he had done he went out and left me on the floor. I couldn't move for a while. I just lay there crying and I called out to Will like a mad woman. But that wasn't much good with him lying dead in the churchyard.

276

'At last it grew dark and cold, and the smell of rosemary hung about the place, making me sick with it. I got up and cooked the supper as well as I could. Then I set it, and sat down shivering, waiting for James to come in. I hated him as I sat there, but when he came in I did what he told me and served him his food.

'He saw I was frightened and that pleased him, but he was still angry and we said nothing all that evening.

'After supper I cleared off the things and sat down sewing, and he sat in his chair looking up at the clock.

'When it was ten o'clock he spoke to me for the first time since he came in.

'"Go up to bed and sleep sound, Sis," he said.

'I stared at him, for it was that he always said before he went out at night, and I knew what that meant. I opened my mouth to speak to him, but I saw that dull look in his face and I daren't say anything, so I went upstairs without speaking a word and got into bed, but I did not sleep.

'Outside the window I could see everything, quiet and cold in the moonlight, and over by the churchyard the trees were black like lace against the sky. I thought of Will lying in there and I could have screamed with terror. I was young, and half mad with pain from James' beating, you see,' she put in apologetically, as though I might not understand.

'And when I thought of that man below stairs, creeping out at night to steal the boy's body and take it up out of its shroud to sell to a lot of doctors to cut about all sense went from me, and I lay panting and crying on the bed, praying to God one minute and screaming silently into my pillow the next.

'It was all so dark and so quiet, and even then the smell of rosemary seemed to be choking the breath out of me.

'After a while I grew quieter and I listened, holding my breath as I lay up there all alone under the thatch. There was no sound downstairs and I began to hope that James wasn't going out after all. I was always trying to fool myself that he wasn't what he was, you see.

'It grew later and later, and by and by the moon came full up over the garden and shone in upon my bed. It was quiet and I was tired and full of pain. James had beaten me well.

'I lay quite still and shut my eyes, hardly thinking at all. And then,' she said suddenly, leaning forward towards me, 'I heard the latch go. It sounded so loud that I thought it would have wakened half the village. I was sitting up in a moment, straining to hear everything.

'I heard him go out of the door, take his pick and shovel from the corner in the porch where they were always kept, and go out down the path.

'I crept out of bed and hid behind the window curtain to peek out. I'd never dared do that before, but tonight, as it was Will he was going for, it was different somehow.

'I saw him going softly down the road and I stood there by the window, praying and hoping he wasn't going for that. I could just see the church gate, as I told you, and I saw him getting nearer and nearer to it. I knew that he was going in.'

Mrs Hartlebury shuddered as though she still saw him.

'He went in,' she said quietly. 'He went in, and I watched him from the window. Then everything was lonely again. I wondered what I should do. One moment I was half a mind to rush out and wake the village and let them find him at his work, but we were some way from another house and to get to the Street I should have to go by the church gate, and I daren't do that.

'I was so frightened,' she whispered. 'Oh, I was so frightened. Presently I went downstairs and found the old horse-pistol James took against footpads. It hung on a nail by the chimney and I took it down and charged it, and then I went upstairs and got into bed again, and I lay there waiting with one arm out on the quilt and the pistol in that hand.

'I didn't think. I was past thinking. I knew when he came in I should kill him and I lay there waiting for him to come.'

The old voice died away and there was no sound in the little room. It seemed to have grown colder, but I did not move. I was trying to make out her face in the darkness.

Still she did not speak.

'But I thought . . .' I began at last.

'Ah,' she said quickly, 'there's been many tales, but this is the truth. That night I waited close on two hours with the pistol in my hand.

'And then at last,' she said, her voice dropping, 'at last, after hours and hours it seemed, I heard footsteps coming down the path. An awful fear of him came over me. I held the pistol as though it was the only hope I had.

'I heard him put the pick and shovel back in its place in the porch and I lay waiting for the latch to click.

'But I didn't hear it. Everything was still, quite still, like an empty church.

'Then I heard the steps going off again down the path. I jumped from the bed and ran to the window and pushed up the sash. I didn't care if he saw me or not that time. The moon was very bright and I could see almost as clear as if it was day.

'There was someone going down the path and when I leant out I saw it was not James. He had his back to me, but I saw it wasn't James. It was too tall and he wore a jersey like a fisherman and had no hat.

'I stood staring. I knew who it was. The pistol fell on to the floor, but I didn't notice it. I only thought about him who was going down the path. I thought I must be mad. He went slowly, as though he was loth to go, and when he reached the gate, which was swinging open, he turned and looked right up at me. I saw his face quite clearly in the moonlight. Then I was sure.

'It was Will.'

On the last words Mrs Hartlebury's tone had sunk to a whisper. Now it died completely. Outside the rain had stopped and the moon was coming up over the trees. I stirred up the fire and made it blaze, so I could see about me.

The old woman was sitting hunched up in her chair, her chin on her breast, her hands still folded in her lap. The thick chenille hairnet she wore looked like bands of iron on her white hair, and her thin wrinkled face glowed like old yellow ivory.

'Then?' I said.

She looked down at me.

'He stood there a long time and if I could have found breath to speak to him he might have answered me. But I couldn't. I couldn't speak.

'I don't remember any more of that night. I reckon I must have fainted.

'In the morning they brought James in dead, with an awful story of how they had found him lying by Will's grave with the lad's body half out on top of him and the lad's arms round his neck.'

Once again she paused.

'That's all,' she said.

'But,' I said, 'wasn't there some sort of inquiry? I mean, even in those days . . .'

Mrs Hartlebury interrupted me. She was smiling contemptuously, her wide toothless mouth twisted at the corners.

'Ah, they had an inquest,' she said. 'I was there. But I didn't say any more than I was asked to. After a lot of talk they said James had been set on by Resurrection Men and had died defending the lad's grave. They proved it wasn't James himself who was body-snatching because his pick and shovel were back at home and never in the churchyard at all.'

'You didn't say anything?' I asked in surprise.

Old Mrs Hartlebury looked at me queerly.

'No,' she said. 'Who would have believed me?'

That was true and I had no answer.

'Still, I think I should have said something,' I said, rising to my feet.

The old woman shook her head.

'Say nothing or say all,' she said. 'Besides, what sort of a life should I have led afterwards, as a body-snatcher's wife? No, that was Will's way. He wanted it all left quiet. That's why he brought the pick and shovel back, I reckon.'

I looked at her sitting there by the fireside, quiet and smiling a little.

'Is . . . is it true?' I said suddenly.

Mrs Hartlebury shrugged.

'You needn't believe it if you don't want to,' she said in her placid Essex way. 'I know I saw him, and I know that's how James died. Anyone'll tell you James died by an open grave while his pick and shovel were at home, and they'll tell you too that he died of suffocation.'

I nodded. I knew that.

'But they'll not tell you one thing that I will,' she said. 'And that is that the pick and shovel were clogged with earth in the morning, that were clean and bright the night before.'

There was silence for a while. Then I said good-night and I thanked her for the story.

'Good-night,' she said. 'Don't believe it if you don't want to. But there's an old hurricane lamp in the corner if you like. You're going past the churchyard, aren't you?'

I hesitated.

'Good-night,' she said again. 'A good walk home to you.'

There was silence, save for the crackling of the fire. Then she looked round.

'What are you after now?' she demanded.

'I shan't be a minute,' said I. 'I'm just lighting the hurricane.'

* * * * *